"Fast, smart, and rooted in deeply likable characters, Born In Syn is a feast of rivalries, timelines, power struggles, memories, and checked and unchecked ambition."

–Juan Martinez, author of *Best Worst American*

"*Original Syn* is a heart-pounding book that will keep readers on their toes and turning the page."

–Mia Siegert, author of *Jerkbait*

"The novel's disparate worlds are revealed slowly, and the story is sophisticated enough to engage both adults and teens. The book maintains a taut pace to the end, concluding with a plot twist that turns the tables and stimulates interest in a second volume, soon to come."

–*Foreword Review*

"*Original Syn* is the kind of book that stays with you long after you've read its final pages; an unforgettable story that pulls you in and takes you along for the ride."

–Francesca G. Varela, author of *Seas of Distant Stars*

"An unforgettable story... compelling characters... a tension-filled tale."

–*Lora L. Hyler, author of*
The Stupendous Adventures of Mighty Marty Hayes

SYN & SALVATION

SYN & SALVATION

BETH KANDER

OWL HOUSE BOOKS

AN IMPRINT OF HOMEBOUND PUBLICATIONS

Published in 2020 by Owl House Books
Cover Design by Daniel Dauphin
Interior Design by Leslie M. Browning
ISBN 9781947003811
First Edition Trade Paperback

Owl House Books is *an Imprint of Homebound Publications*
WWW.HOMEBOUNDPUBLICATIONS.COM

10 9 8 7 6 5 4 3 2 1

Owl House Books, like all imprints of Homebound Publications, is committed
to ecological stewardship. We greatly value the natural environment and invest
in environmental conservation. For each book purchased in our online store we
plant one tree. Visit us at: www.homeboundpublications.com

The outsider inside will end the beginning.

–Prophecy from the Heaven algorithm, 2063

CHAPTER 1: CAL

CAL WAKES WITH A START. He is restrained at his neck, wrists, and ankles, held against a flat surface like a fish for gutting. He struggles against the restraints for a moment, testing them without exhausting himself. They're solid. He doesn't cry out, anticipating no allies, but goes still, conserving energy.

He hears a sound behind him. His hands curl into fists and his whole body tightens, ready to fight.

Someone approaches the bed.

A man.

A Syn.

The man is slight, narrow of shoulder and chin, the sort of man Cal could easily dominate in a fair fight. He wears the same dark, sleek garb all Syns wear; his face is thin, his nose beaklike. When he sees Cal staring at him, his small green eyes go wide.

"You're awake," the Syn says, voice shrill.

"Where am I?"

"The Synt," the man says, then winces, as if expecting to be slapped for giving away this information. "What's your name?"

Cal considers lying, but he's not sure what good it would do. Might be better to tell the truth now, in answer to this very basic inquiry, and save the real resistance for down the road.

"Cal."

"Cal what?"

"Cal... Harper," Cal says, unaccustomed to referencing his surname.

"Cal Harper," repeats the Syn, his gaze sliding oddly off to one side. "Well, there's no record of any Original with that name who would be anywhere near your age. No close variant. It does not appear that you exist, Cal Harper."

"Guess I'm a ghost then. What's your name, Syn?"

"Kennedy," says the thin Syn, then grimaces again, *stupid stupid stupid*. He tries to regain conversational control. "Why are you here, Mr. Harper?"

"I don't know," Cal says.

"That's a lie—"

"I don't know," Cal barks, and the Syn flinches.

An easy scare.

"Fine, if you won't tell me—" Kennedy stops abruptly, eyes going funny again. He mutters something; Cal can't quite make it out, but he's pretty sure he catches the word *prick* somewhere in there. Then the Syn turns on his heel and exits the room.

"Hey! Where the hell are you—"

Swish.

"Cal Harper."

Cal freezes. Someone else is in the room. Someone new. Someone Cal can already tell is far more dangerous; a true predator, not an easily startled little scavenger like Kennedy.

"Let's make you a little more comfortable, what say?"

Cal tenses, preparing for the words of comfort to be a sly prede-
cessor to some sort of assault or injection. Instead, the restraints
at his neck, arms, and ankles snap back, releasing him. Rubbing
his wrists, Cal sits bolt upright and turns to see his captor.

The man is shorter than Cal would have predicted, but not
as slight as Kennedy. He exudes a quiet power, his movements
conveying lean muscle and a sharp brain. Cal knows not to under-
estimate a man like this. Releasing Cal, so casually and with such
little fanfare, was a warning: *I am in control, and unafraid of losing
my grip.*

Cal takes a swift inventory of his captor's face: sharp eyes;
sallow olive skin; hair graying at the temples, indicating an older
age than the average Syn without revealing any meaningful hint as
to his actual number of years on earth.

"Allow me to introduce myself," the man says at last. "My name
is Felix Hess, and I am the Director here. But I believe you're less
familiar with my work, and more familiar with my daughter Ever.
Not too familiar, I hope."

Heaven and hell.

This man was Ever's father?

"Exactly how do you know my daughter, Mr. Harper?"

No one had ever called Cal "Mr. Harper" before. He was
always simply *Cal,* or *cousin,* or *nephew.* Hearing this formal,
detached moniker makes Cal's mouth go dry. He tries to swallow
before croaking a hoarse reply: "I don't… I don't really know her."

"And yet you were in her room. All the way up in the penthouse.
One doesn't accidentally scale several stories of any building, Mr.
Harper, let alone this one. Who are you working with?"

"I came alone," Cal says honestly.

"We've gotten off on the wrong foot," Hess says, pivoting. "You,
breaking into my building; me, locking you in a holding room.
Hard start, all around. Let's begin again."

"Let's—what?" Cal asks, confused, trying to keep up.

"I am, first and foremost, a scientist," declares Felix Hess—which strikes Cal as an odd thing for a father to say. "We have fewer and fewer Originals in the incorporated sectors. You are much younger than the average Original. That intrigues me. I'd like to invite you to stay here at the Synthetic Neuroscience Institute of Technology for a time. As my guest. What do you say?"

"Guest."

Cal repeats the word flatly. He knows that no matter what, despite fake smiles and offers of hospitality, he is not a guest. He is this man's prisoner.

"Yes," Hess says. "Of course, I'd run a few tests while you're enjoying our accommodations. I can assure you, nothing too invasive—blood work here, bone scan there. Contribute to our working knowledge and some ongoing projects."

"And if I refuse?"

"Well, Mr. Harper," says Hess. "That would be unfortunate. I'm offering you two options: Be my guest, or stay in this room, where Kennedy will check on you every few days. I highly recommend the route of invited guest rather than neglected animal."

Cal's mind races. The odds of him escaping from this room are low; security is tight and he has no idea how many more guards, alarms, or barriers stand between him and the outside world. And even if he escaped, what then? His aunt is dead, his traitor cousin fled, and all that remains of his once-proud tribe is a handful of elders shuffling toward their graves.

He came here to find Ever. Ever is still here; still the goal.

"Guest," Cal growls.

"Excellent choice," Hess says, smiling a broad and empty grin. "I'll have one of my assistants take you to your new room. And just so we're clear—you will have many rules to abide by here, but one above all: Stay away from my daughter."

CHAPTER 2: EVER

TO SAY THAT EVER'S WEEK HAS BEEN STRANGE would be as vast an understatement as saying that the Beatles had a little bit of impact on old world music. There had been the man at her bedroom window, for one thing; swiftly dragged away by her father's minions, possibly some sort of Original spy or something. He was mysterious, intriguing, obviously athletic if he'd managed to scale the walls of the Synt, and he was also handsome as hell.

But who *was* he?

Normally, that guy alone would have been enough to occupy Ever's mind. But he was just the latest in a long series of unusual events. There was also her trip to Costa Rica, which she could no longer recollect, thanks to her freak stroke and subsequent memory loss. And on top of all that, there were the nightmares.

The nightmares were baffling to her medical team, since Syns don't dream. When plugged in nightly to recharge and share data, their sleeping minds were supposed to simply power down. Dreams disappeared decades ago. Ever's sole recollection of a nightmare was one her Original mind generated a lifetime ago, a primordial vision of alligators and blackness and a great sucking swamp. She used to replay it for herself, for its spine-tingling impact. But lately, it was returning on its own, unbidden.

Her old alligator nightmare wasn't her only terrifying dream these days. She has a new nightmare: sitting in a dark room, reaching for something important, something she *needs*, something she will wither and die without—and when she puts out her hands to clutch for it, her fingers are snapped off one by one by an unseen enemy. With the loss of each digit she screams in pain, shrieks for mercy, and somehow knows that this attack is something she orchestrated.

The enemy is me, she thinks, as her last finger is ripped from her. Then world explodes in agony, and she sits up in a cold sweat, weak and shaking, wringing her hands, counting her fingers, barely certain of her own name.

She doesn't know what she did to deserve the nightmare. But her unreliability, her medical fragility, and whatever crime she committed in Costa Rica have earned her plenty of punishment from her parents. Her sentence is house arrest. She can roam the Synt freely, but cannot go out into the world unsupervised. Her days follow an unvarying pattern—breakfast with her mother, followed by a yoga, kickboxing, or aikido simulation, then a shower, then lunch with a side of all the pills she's been prescribed to prevent migraines and reduce nightmares, and then there's plenty of time to read or watch a film or something before trying not to spontaneously combust from the boredom as dinner approaches.

Most days she feels like a rerun airing on some channel no one's watching, looping without purpose or ending. She wants a reboot, a new season. She wants to scream and break things. And there's one thing that might represent just that.

Cal.

Rumor had it that the Original man had come to Central City to kidnap her. That was apparently making the Council freak out, and was probably why her father came down so hard and fast on the intruder. But for her part, Ever can imagine fates worse than being carried off in the night by Cal.

He reminds her of the paperback romances her mother used to stockpile, back in the old days. When Ever was an early reader, no more than five or six, she had secreted away one of the books. On the cover was a man with long blonde hair, donning an open-to-the-pectorals white, pirate-style shirt. The hair and the shirt were both billowing, caught in an obviously sexy gust of wind. In his arms was a swooning woman in a corset, bound tightly at the waist but loosely at the bosom, exposing a swell of cleavage and opportunity.

She edits the image in her mind, altering the blonde man into the darker-skinned, curly-headed Cal, and replacing the face above the heaving bosom with her own. She likes the look of this scene. She closes her eyes, recalling the scent of him, pine and earth and *man*. She'd seen enough of him to want to see more of him. She pictures running her fingers through the thicket of hair on his chest, exploring his muscular body…

I have to find him.

"Ever! Dinner!"

Ever twitches at the sound of her mother's voice but makes her way to the dining room. There are three places set, but only her mother is seated at the table.

"He should be here any minute," says Marilyn Hess before Ever can ask where her father is. Ever and her mother have always had a strained relationship, but the lack of trust between them now is palpable. Ever cannot recall exactly what eroded the last of her faith in her mother, but it must have been something.

Another familiar rerun of The Dinner Episode commences.

Pick up fork. Scoop up some couscous. Deliver to mouth. Chew. Swallow.

Ever repeats each action an acceptable number of times, then announces: "I'm done."

"You ate three bites."

"I ate eleven," says Ever, who counted. "And I'm full."

Angela walks in, carrying a beautiful plate of bright fruit, cut into stars and hearts and spirals. She sets it down in front of Marilyn, who gestures accusingly toward the plate, as if Ever has insulted the kiwis and strawberries.

"Look at this beautiful fruit. The meal isn't over."

"I'm done," Ever repeats, rising.

"Ever—" Marilyn begins, when to everyone's surprise, Angela speaks up.

"I'll join you for the fruit course, Marilyn," the older woman says. "Ever needs a little excursion. She's well enough now to roam out a little more—on the Synt grounds, of course. Let her step out for a bit, get some fresh air."

Air.

Ere?

The tiny syllable catches Ever like a fish on a hook; she twitches, pulled toward Angela.

"What did you say?"

"Fresh air," Angela repeats gently.

"Oh," Ever says, head buzzing, trying to net a memory fluttering like a butterfly, already out of reach. She is woozy and flushed, and feels on the verge of swooning. She recalls again the corseted damsel on the cover of her mother's old romance novel. She steels herself. Steadies her wobbling knees.

Then she practically runs down the hallway, out of her family's quarters and into the main building of the Synt. But instead of continuing down to the first floor and out into the sunlight, she slips into a research library. Pressing her finger into the nearest port, creating a faster connection, she begins her search.

FIND CAL + ORIGINAL.

The search runs for less than a second before a red

ALERT

flashes before her eyes.
Heaven and hell.
And then a second message appears, documenting the identity of the Syn searching for this classified information. She sees her name and image, and receives a message from her father.

NICE TRY, EVER.

CHAPTER 3: ASAVARI

DESPITE HAVING CROSSED a continent to find him, Asavari is struggling not to strangle the pouting, pitiful Ere Fell. He hasn't spoken a word to her since they left the Synt, and it is beginning to grate on her.

To be fair, he was rightfully furious to learn that she had known about his grandfather and kept his family's dark secrets from him. He was enraged that their initial "mission" together was all conducted under false pretenses. Asavari had assured herself that upon their arrival in Original Delhi, things would change. Surely when he saw the underground city, met her tribe, learned of the resistance's momentum, he would understand how much was at stake. He would forgive her and get on board with the bigger picture.

But no. Here they are, halfway across the world, and still—not a damn word.

To be fair, she had inadvertently misled Ere by telling him they could rest for a bit once they reached India. Upon arrival in Delhi they were greeted by the news of a security breach, which overturned any plans of respite. No one knew how the Syns had pinpointed their location, but Shadower had alerted them that there was suddenly chatter about Originals overseas. Which meant the tribe was immediately on the move, much to Ere's dismay.

He spoke to the others; not much, but if someone asked him a question or offered him some water, he would toss them a meager word or two in response. Asavari's tribe adored him despite his churlishness, whispering his praises like he was worthy of reverence.

Ruth Fell's son, a boy who grew up in the sun, ever-chased by the shadow of the Syns. Ere, heir to the Fell throne, a breath of fresh air, Ere, Ere, Ere!

It makes Asavari clench her teeth.

He's not a god, she wants to snap at them. *He's not even a warrior. He's a boy. A stupid, scrawny, irritating boy.*

"Ere," she says, swallowing her frustration, trying to engage with him. He walks more quickly, ignoring her. His quickened pace is the only indication he heard her at all. He ignores her with the stoic commitment of a dull rock.

"Ere," she says again, and this time she raises her fist as well as her voice. She jabs him swiftly in the shoulder, causing him to lose his footing. He stumbles, snapping at her.

"What?"

His eyes are as tired as they are defiant. She can see now that his fury is a performance. Up close, the mask is evident, and slipping. His jutting chin is also a trembling one. His anger is a thin outer layer, a fine and melting ice coating a swirling sea of grief and fear beneath the surface. Asavari's heart cracks, seeing the reality of the boy's emotions.

His mother just died. He has no idea who I am, who we are. He is terrified.

Asavari, you insensitive jackass.

She wishes she were better equipped for things like apologies. Openness. Sharing one's feelings. But those are not skills Asavari was ever given the opportunity to cultivate. Shedding light on the emotional realm does not always come easily to one whose life has played out almost entirely in the dark.

*   *   *   *

Asavari was born underground, the third and final daughter her aging parents welcomed below the earth. The birth was attended by all members of their small tribe, as all births in Original Delhi were. The better for renewing faith, as well as having more potential aid on hand if something went amiss during delivery.

But there were no complications with Asavari's birth. She arrived with a thick thatch of black hair and strong lungs she put to immediate use. When her sharp voice pierced the dull air, everyone clapped and cheered and wept. Her mother kissed the new baby's slick-damp head. It was a moment of triumphant joy, one of the few their life allowed.

"Asavari," cooed her mother. "Spirit of the heavens."

The baby squalled again, and her father laughed.

"Our little Vari may come from heaven, but sounds like she's here to raise some hell."

"I hope so," her mother smiled. "Let's call her Asavari Ruth."

Almost as if approving her full name, the infant squawked— not a scream, but a sound all her own.

As a little girl, Vari remained loud. As the baby of the family, she fought to be noticed. Her older sisters' braids were pulled and ribs were jabbed when the little hellion did not get her way. For the first four years of her life, Vari was permitted to get away with too much. Vari and her sisters weren't allowed aboveground, because it was too dangerous. So the girls were never allowed sunshine, which meant the adults indulged them on almost every other front, feeling guilty for their limited exposure to the fullness of the world.

Going aboveground was an eventuality of adulthood. Resources were still taken from the world above, so most members of the tribe eventually had to take on the responsibility of venturing up. They went at night, but sometimes stayed out until dawn just to experience the sunrise.

When Vari's sisters were allowed to go to the surface, she swooned with envy and clung to every detail they shared of their adventures.

"It smells different up there," Vari's sister Padma declared. "I like it."

"I hate it," Sruti disagreed, wrinkling her nose. "Smells like metal and death."

"I WANT TO GO UP," Vari would scream full-volume, mad with jealousy and hating that her sisters were allowed to do an activity denied to her. Who cared if they were older? She was the bravest and the smartest! Her sisters would laugh and roll their eyes and tell her someday when she was bigger, it would be her turn.

Vari resented her sisters' stupid privilege purchased with the unearned luck of their birth order. But she also knew they had no real power, and she could not bully them into taking her up with them. It was her parents she had to convince. This was harder to achieve. Their mother was the leader of the tribe, and she was always in council meetings or on "assignments" or doing Something Else Important.

Vari's father was almost as busy. In the old world, he had been a contractor, and in the world Vari knew, he was the one overseeing all of the new tunnels and infrastructure projects. Her father was from the land once called the States; "the world's nicest wasp," Vari heard her mother call him once. Vari knew it was a joke, but did not understand what her father had in common with a stinging insect.

When the upheaval in the old world began, Preeti and John fled to her homeland. From India, they rode out the seismic shifts in society, moving underground years before the Syns had claimed full power. Already in their fifties before the Singularity came to pass, her parents lived an entire lifetime in the light before retreating to the darkened tunnels where their children would be born into a world of half-light and hidden chambers.

Vari was hungry for more than the underground world she had inherited. She wanted to go up above, to smell the death and metal for herself, to see the sunrise. She begged, day after day, to be allowed to go up.

Then something happened.

Something bad.

Vari was playing with Padma, inventing a new game, creating a small series of tunnels, slides, and pathways from hard-packed dirt, then rolling smooth pebbles through the obstacles. One roll per turn, first person to get their pebble through the entire system won. Vari was ahead and Padma was getting irritated when suddenly their laboriously-constructed game set went flat.

"What hap—"

But Vari could not complete her question before the entire world began violently trembling, knocking the girls to their feet. Vari was gripped with fear as she pictured their entire world flattening just as the game had. As the world kept shaking, the dim lights constructed by their father to illuminate each corridor and room of their tribal dwelling all went out, plunging them into darkness.

"Vari!" Padma screamed.

Nearby, others cried out as well, calling loved ones' names, yelling warnings, giving sharp startled exclamations of pain and fear.

"I'm here!" Vari screamed back. "I'm here!"

But she worried that maybe she *wasn't* there. Maybe nothing was. The entire world was gone. It was so black she could see
nothing, not her sister, not her pebbles, not her own hand before
her face.

"QUIET! EVERYONE QUIET!"

Someone shouted this command, which rang out and echoed
and then disappeared as the world plunged and lurched and shattered a small girl's belief that the ground beneath her feet was
something she could trust to always be there.

And then, for a moment, all was still.

The screams ceased.

The world stopped moving.

"Padma," Vari whispered, afraid to be the only sound in the
void.

"...Vari..." came a faint whisper back.

Vari crawled on her belly toward the small sound. Her fingers
dragged across stone and rubble, then grasped something soft,
eliciting a quiet gasp and then a firm grip. The girls held hands in
the dark, pressing against one another, huddled together in fear.

"What was it?" Vari whispered.

"I don't know," Padma was barely audible, breathing more than
speaking.

"How long will it be like this?"

Padma said nothing.

The world said the same.

The two young sisters lay there, clutching each other in
silence, for an eternity. Hours passed. Vari did not know how
long they had been there. Time seemed to have loosened itself,
shaken free; minutes slipped away into the welcoming dark pool
of nothingness.

Little Vari pressed her small body into the ground as hard as she could, to feel and smell the packed earth below. She felt a trickle on her cheek which traveled to her mouth; she tasted her sister's hot tears and felt her shaking, silent sobs. She wondered where the rest of her family was; were they somewhere in the inky blackness, or buried beneath the earth? Did she still have sisters? Parents? A tribe? Or had the darkness taken everything?

Panic rose within her, a cold lump in her stomach that folded in on itself, expanding and warming until it was fiery and thick, a fever of fear heating her, blurring her—erasing her.

Nothing, she thought. *There is nothing.*

I am nothing.

Nothing.

Then there was a buzz, and a click, and then a rumbling hum as the dim underground lighting system woke back up.

Vari and Padma slowly untangled themselves, blinking and disoriented, distrusting the sturdiness of their watery knees and the world around them. They stood like toddlers learning to walk: tentative, touching the walls and each other, seeking support everywhere. They were in the midst of shambles—ceiling half-collapsed, lights still flickering and haphazard, the sparse bits of furniture in the room all at odd angles, everything amiss.

Their father rushed into the room, scooping them up and pressing them against his chest, which heaved with his panicked breaths. He was already holding Sruti; everyone was together, except for their mother.

"Girls! Thank God."

"Mama?" Vari asked, her voice muffled, her face pressed against her father, breathing him in dust and all, finally able to believe that perhaps the world had not ended.

"Your mother is fine, we'll see her soon, she's fine," her father said.

He was right; their mother's arm was broken, but she too had survived, and they were swiftly reunited. In the days after the darkness, Vari was told that it was an earthquake. She was told that sometimes this happened, that her father would work with his team to better prepare their city for future quakes. She and her sisters were bumped and bruised, marked for life. For years after the incident, everyone would talk about how unsettled they were by the sensation of the earth moving beneath their feet, stealing their very foundation. Everyone but Asavari. For her, the shaking of the earth was something she could accept.

It was the utter darkness that haunted her.

She would never feel safe again until she could live her life in the light. The lurching world shook the innocence from her, and the plunging darkness shocked her into adulthood. In the years ahead, she was trained to go aboveground. She learned that there was more power in quiet than in noise. She was told the story of the Syns; learned that across the world, other Originals were in hiding; was assured that someday the world would be theirs again but only if they were strategic, and careful, and dutifully prepared to seize back everything stolen from them.

Each of Vari's sisters found their way within their world. Sruti became a builder, like her father; Padma taught reading to the young children in their communal school. But destiny had something else in mind for the quiet, clever youngest girl.

Vari was invited to join the Clandestine Network.

The Clandestine Network was the subset of people working most directly on the long-term plans for revolt and recovery. She did not seek admission into the network, made no loud petition to be included. In the end, she was not recruited for her ability to raise hell but rather because she had learned to control her sharp, fiery temper. She was a fighter, but a strategic one. She was not fearless, but she moved through her fears. At fourteen, she was the network's youngest-ever inductee.

Her trips aboveground were not to gather supplies, but to gather information. She shadowed her mother, their leader. She learned basic coding, so she could manipulate old technology now overlooked by the Syns. She learned how to decrypt messages. She was sent on longer and longer missions—preparing her to become a human satellite, relaying information from one enclave to another. By sixteen, she made her first overseas journey. And when word reached their tribe that Ruth Fell still lived, she was the eager volunteer who offered to make the treacherous trek to the Incorporated Sectors to find the great warrior and bring her into their fold.

That assignment came the morning after Vari's father died.

His death was nothing dramatic. A heart attack in the middle of the night. A common way for a man of seventy to die. But the entire tribe was changed by John Kansal's quiet death. It was a reminder that time was ticking on. The discovery of his breathless body immediately aged Preeti Kansal, shattered their daughters' hearts, and eroded the tribe's shaky faith that they would all live to see their world restored.

They needed hope.

They needed help.

They needed Ruth Fell.

Vari set out immediately, crossing land and sea, evading Syn detection, parsing intelligence to pinpoint the location of Ruth Fell's tribe—arriving right on time for the great warrior's funeral. The news of Ruth's death had shaken Vari almost as much as the loss of her father weeks earlier. His death, which she had not yet truly mourned, compounded the bereft feeling unfurling within her. She had ventured out seeking hope, and hope had gone into hiding, leaving only pain and despair to greet her.

But then she learned of Ere's existence.

Another Fell. Another generation, out in the wilderness, breathing air against all odds. Further proof that Originals would not easily be erased. She had convinced him to come with her, so she would not return empty-handed from her epic mission.

*   *   *   *

And now he wasn't speaking to her.

So she stares at him, this boy who has lived his life in the sun, who faced trials but exhibited little empathy. This selfish, stupid child, her age but so much younger. She should tell him that he needed to grow up, to learn when to mourn and when to move on. He wasn't the only one who had ever felt loss. Had he ever even asked her about *her* father? He knew by now of the man's recent death. Everyone mentioned it.

The lessons she had learned in the dark had not been taught to this sunlit stranger. But it wasn't her job to teach him everything. It was only her job to do what was best for her people, which—for now—included having him around. So instead of opening her mouth to offer a sharp word of advice or a gentle word of encouragement, she decided to reward his silence with her own.

CHAPTER 4: ERE

ERE KEEPS HIS EYES ON HIS FEET, becoming intimately familiar with the cracks and crevices of the Syn shoes Asavari gave him when they left his tribe. It feels like a lifetime ago. His shoes have split and torn, exposing him to the elements. His feet are as ragged as the shoes, caked in dust, raw with calluses and blood blisters.

But Ere's heart is more battered than his feet. He prefers to look down at the corporeal damage rather than let his mind linger on his emotional injuries. Unfortunately for Ere, his cruel mind will not stop counting each painful episode, loss by loss. The death of his mother, Cal spurning him, the shocking revelation of his grandfather's role in the creation of the entire Syn world, the heart-shredding decision Ever made, erasing him from her memories... each blow chipped away at his heart, his soul, his sense of self, splintering him into sharp and uncertain shards that did not quite add up to an identity. It was a lot to take in, and too much to let out.

It was better to just keep looking at his feet.

Another good reason to keep his eyes down is to avoid looking at anyone else. He particularly hopes to continue avoiding Asavari, who has lied to him at every turn. But he doesn't want to interact with anyone else, either. It's a knife in his side every time one of them asks him about his mother; a twisting of the knife when they tell him how much he favors her.

He might look like his mother. But he does not take after her. She was brave, and strong, and loyal. He is scared and weak, which is the final reason to avoid interactions: Ere knows his next betrayal is around the corner and does not want any of them to catch his eye and guess at his plans to break away from them as soon as possible.

I have to get back to Ever.

He doesn't know how the hell he'll do it. But it's his only actual goal, along with perhaps securing a better pair of shoes.

"You're a quiet one," says a voice beside him.

Ere does not look up, but he shifts his gaze from his feet to the ones deftly padding beside him. They are small, brown, leather-tough, and tucked into well-worn sandals.

"Quiet can be invaluable," says the woman with the sturdy sandaled feet, her tone as steady and even as her pace. "But silence can sometimes cost us."

Ere looks up, dully wondering if this is a piece of advice, a warning, or some sort of veiled threat. He finds himself looking into the wise, dark eyes of Dr. Preeti Kansal. Her expression is not menacing, but probing. She is examining him, as a healer examines a sick or injured member of the tribe, trying to figure out what is causing the cough or where the break in the bone has occurred. He does not appreciate such scrutiny.

"Nothing to say," Ere says, hating the whine in his voice. He hears how he sounds. Churlish. Childish.

"That, I doubt," says Asavari's mother, her mouth twitching slightly. "But I understand your hesitation to trust us. When you first arrived, Ere, I told you that I had met your mother. I met her because she was living with your great-uncle; I was there in the early days of the resistance. But in your family, the very first person I met was your grandfather."

She does not deliver this news with any more intensity than anything else she has said, and yet Ere feels as if she has placed a grenade within his chest and might, at any moment, pull out the pin. Her next words might detonate the device and demolish him. Breathing is momentarily a struggle. Finally, he manages to suck in some of the dry desert air and exhale a question.

"How did you know my—how did you know Nathan Fell?"

"My cousin worked for him," she says. "We all have… family members whose choices we question. When they were readying for the first procedure—Nathan's augmentation—they needed a neurologist on call. I was that neurologist. Do you know that word, *neurologist*? It means a doctor of the brain, spinal cord, nerves… I did not know, at the time, what the experiment was that they were undertaking. I just knew I would be on call during the procedure, and if there were a sudden hemorrhage, seizure, or other issues during the process, I would be taken immediately to treat the patient. I got the call, that something had gone wrong…"

"With my grandfather," Ere says flatly, finally looking at her, eyes hard and cold.

The gaze she returns is calm, warm.

"Yes. When I arrived in the laboratory—that's when I realized just how wrong this whole situation was. That's when I connected with your uncle Howard. I wanted to be on the other side of the equation."

"What was he like?" Ere asks, wishing away the tremor in his voice.

"Your uncle?"

"My grandfather."

"Brilliant," Preeti says. "And dangerous."

The two words confirm what Ere already pieced together about his mother's father. He wants to know more but doesn't know what to ask about. He is embarrassed. Ashamed. Everyone else knew who his grandfather was, what his grandfather did. Everyone but Ere.

"Were people scared of him?"

"No. Your grandfather was very calm, measured. Calculating. Harsh, certainly. His students, his team working with him—they admired him greatly. He was respected."

"Respected."

Ere suppresses a shudder, picturing the ravaged, still-breathing carcass of his grandfather floating in Hess's box, his brain connected to a sea of wires, powering the Syn entity called Heaven. A hollow, rotting corpse, kept alive to serve as a human battery. Nothing about that seemed respectful.

"Your uncle Howard loved him very much," Preeti adds. "He always thought your grandfather was worth saving. That he could be redeemed."

"Too late now," Ere mutters.

"Maybe," says the doctor.

Ere stares at her. Nathan Fell, the Original Syn, is the last of Ere's family. (Other than Cal, who Ere imagines is probably off somewhere growing more chest hair, flexing his muscles, and throwing sharpened knives at an effigy of Ere.) And this woman is insinuating that he might still be redeemable—or at least he could be released, or his work undone, or something. It sounds like the noblest of missions for Ere to take on; which, if nothing else, makes it the perfect ploy.

"I have to go back," Ere says.

"Yes," Preeti agrees. "Eventually."

"Eventually," Ere mumbles, wishing he had a ready argument to protest *no, right now*. He returns his gaze downward. There is a new blister on the back of his left heel. It hurts the most, being the newest and rawest, but soon it will be absorbed into the larger misery of his entire foot. "Why wait? We're not getting anything done here. All we're doing is walking in circles."

"So you've noticed?"

"Noticed what?"

"That we're walking in circles. Very astute, Ere."

Ere looks up again, staring at the infuriatingly placid face of Dr. Preeti Kansal. She was as bad as her daughter, this woman, talking in riddles and making things sound obvious when he had no idea what the hell she was talking about.

"This was the plan, if we thought we were discovered by the Syns. Walk in larger and larger circles, leaving electronic footprints and small clues that will lead back to the center of the circle. But really, we are moving outward, and when we reach the largest edge of the circle we will move downward again, to the beta site of our city-structure."

"The... beta site?"

She nods.

"My husband worked in city planning in the old world, including in cities where natural disasters were expected. He always believed in having a backup plan, and I always believed in having at least three. We had to leave a lot behind in our primary location, a lot which might soon be discovered by the Syns—but nothing that will point them in the correct direction of our new location. When we reach that destination, we will renew our planning and you will be brought... into the circle, so to speak."

She quickens her pace, and in an instant is far ahead of him. Ere lifts his eyes from his ruined feet and looks in front of him, at the hundreds—thousands?—of Originals walking with him, teeming forward, striding with purpose, circling toward the future.

CHAPTER 5: KENNEDY

THIS DATE IS NOT GOING WELL.

Considering how many other archaic practices had swiftly been sloughed off after the Singularity, it blows Kennedy's melded mind that the skittering cockroach called courtship somehow survived. Yet here he is, sitting across from a stranger, sipping bland old oaky Chardonnay. On a date.

These awkward tête-à-têtes seem even more pointless now than they did fifty years ago. In contemporary Syn society, all artifice is stripped away. Biological clocks had stopped ticking. Marriage was passé. Leisure activities were best enjoyed with friends, not awkwardly attempted with beddable strangers. Yet for some reason, dating persisted.

Kennedy would have preferred if all pretense was dissolved. Why not just show up, glance at someone, let each one say "yes" or "no," and then leave together or separately, depending? No muss, no fuss.

Apparently, people thought that was crass. Kennedy had little patience for crass-shaming. Why stigmatize crudeness? Getting straight to the point was the sort of thing this world was supposed to value, not disdain.

"I grew up in Louisiana," the oddly beautiful Syn seated across from him says, without any discernible dialect.

"Oh?" Kennedy says, since he's supposed to say something.

"On the bayou," his date confirms. "I won't say exactly what year I was born, because why bother with ugly little details like that! I started lying about my age years before it became irrelevant. So. What about you? Where did you spend your wayward pre-tech youth?"

"Connecticut," Kennedy says automatically.

He tries to remember his date's name. Chaz? No—he does a quick scan, pulls up the name from their earlier exchanges: *Chase.* That's it. Kennedy is curious as to whether Chase identifies as male, female, non-binary, or in some other way. He has no internal record of it coming up before, and interestingly, it's not available in their public record. Kennedy's interest in his date would not necessarily be swayed one way or the other by learning how his date identifies. But the scientist in Kennedy always wonders about origins and diversions, choice and chance. He shouldn't think about his dates this way, he knows. Reducing them to an opportunity for study and analysis. But he can't help it. He blames Hess for that.

Chase has had so much work done that Kennedy cannot decide what features were given by nature and which by scalpel, laser, or pill. A wide swath of Syns of all identities were overdoing it with the alterations these days. Upgrade, upgrade, upgrade.

In fact, finding someone still clinging to their old-world-self—now, *that* would be even more interesting. He wonders exactly when Chase's Southern dialect had gone missing; hearing a good old-fashioned drawl might be a turn-on. Slower, softer syllables might tantalize Kennedy's uptight Connecticut-country-club-cultivated mind. Kennedy also wishes that the mouth delivering the Southern speech could be a little too thin, or crooked. He might want to kiss an imperfect, unpredictable mouth. The plum, perfect pair before him is as unappealing as a bowl of overripe, swiftly-rotting cherries.

"Connecticut," Chase says. "So. You had money before."

"You must have, too. To get in on the Syn action, as early as you did."

"Money isn't everything. I had connections."

"As did I," Kennedy said unnecessarily.

"I had—information. Some gritty old Southern dirt, let's say," Chase says, with an unreadable smirk of rotting-cherry lips.

"Whatever works," Kennedy shrugs.

Kennedy wonders if Jorge ever goes on dates. If he does, he's probably as efficient and effective over dinner as he is in the lab. No more talking than necessary, but everything that needs to be said is said and everything that needs to be done is done. Dinner, sex, shower, depart. Everyone's needs are met, and then it's on to the next task.

Bastard.

As ever, Kennedy is irrationally irritated by his co-worker, even when the guy's not there to drive him up the wall in-person. That Vost has been even weirder lately, quiet and lurking and walled off. Seems like Jorge is suspicious of something. Maybe he found accounts of some of the missions Kennedy was sent on in recent months—the ones he subsequently erased from his memory logs. Maybe Jorge thinks Kennedy is the actual creep.

That judging bastard!

"You work with Dr. Hess, right?"

Kennedy is startled back into the conversation by the intensity with which this question is asked. His romantic prospect is leaning across the table, voice lowered, eyes wide, expression suddenly crackling with energy.

"I, uh—yes."

"What's he like?"

Discussing one's sociopath of a boss is a terrible aphrodisiac, but Kennedy has already given up on this date so decides to answer as honestly as he can without risking a firing squad.

"Intense. He's a very—driven person."

"Still?"

"What do you mean, still?"

"I mean, his career peaked at the Singularity, didn't it? Scaled the big mountain, hauled all of us up over to the other side? Quashed the rebellions, dealt with the Originals. Now I'd think it's all downhill. No more mountains, just… minutia. Good for him, for remaining driven, but really, what's the point?"

What's the point?

The simple question lands heavily on Kennedy, stunning him with its simplicity. How has he not been asking himself this, every day? At some level he has, of course. But to distill it so crisply, and apply it to the ongoing work of the Synt, an organization that was groundbreaking around the Singularity but now seems so automated—what in Heaven and Hell *was* the point anymore? Yes, there are projects and deadlines and updates to upload and a never-ending series of assignments… but what was the point of any of it? Would anyone miss a day of system upgrades? How much more collective knowledge needed to be amassed?

"Just… continual progress, I suppose."

"Progress toward what, exactly?"

"I don't know," Kennedy says, exhaling and feeling a bit light-headed. Maybe he shouldn't have had that second glass of wine. He's always been such a lightweight.

"Doesn't it get to you? The monotony of it all… the weight of waiting for nothing? I suppose I should give Hess credit, not only for his own commitment but also for continuing to inspire y'all…"

The *y'all* catches Kennedy by surprise. There it is: a southern sound. Something distinctive. Something real.

"Chase," he says, without knowing what he might ask or say next, but realizing that he does want this conversation to continue.

"Kennedy," Chase says, almost teasing. "Would you like to take this… conversation… back to my place?"

"Okay," Kennedy says a little too eagerly. He feels real heat flushing his cheeks for the first time in a long time, blood sparking wildly in his veins, more electric than any synthetic charge.

CHAPTER 6: JORGE

IT'S RARE FOR JORGE to get direct communication from Shadower. Too risky. Only in true emergencies, such as the arrival of the Fell boy, has Jorge gotten an alert like this one. And Shadower has *never* requested an in-person meeting—not since the life-changing meal in the basement cafeteria. Jorge should be unnerved by this request for a meeting. It undoubtedly means something dangerous. He should feel fear.

But when he gets it, he grins like a kid at Christmas.

Urgent.
Meet me at midnight.
One Eyed Alice.

He allows himself a single second of the massive grin. Then he erases the missive, and just as smoothly erases his expression. Pace steady and breath normal, Jorge walks stone-faced into the sterile Synt laboratory.

"You're early," Kennedy whines when Jorge strides in, a complaint as ludicrous as it is unnecessary. Jorge is always early. His timeliness is not the oddity; it's Kennedy who generally ambles in, doing what he can to get there as late as possible while avoiding reprimand from their superior. So Jorge coolly turns the question on his fidgety colleague.

"I'm here at my usual time, which you would know if you were ever here this early. So. What brings you into the lab before six?"

Kennedy rubs his eyes. "Do you really want to know?"

No, not really, thinks Jorge. But aloud he says: "I asked."

"I was on a date last night."

"Ah," Jorge says, hoping they can stop talking now.

"It went well," Kennedy says, rising, taking a step—*Jesus, was he trying to swagger?* This was embarrassing. "Came here straight from their place, actually, and truth is I'm exhausted—"

"Coffee," Jorge says, and turns on his heel, leaving Kennedy alone in the early morning quiet of the laboratory. He has no interest in hearing about Kennedy's romantic exploits. And Jorge is still so excited about his upcoming adventure, he was almost afraid if he didn't walk out of the laboratory right then, he might have inadvertently smiled at Kennedy.

D R. FELIX HESS STARES AT THE LARGE, glowing image of his own brain. This scan, like the last hundred, reveals nothing of interest. No sign of stroke or Parkinson's, no erosion—nothing. But still, something could be hidden. Undetectable. Alzheimer's disease can be definitively diagnosed only after death, by linking clinical measures with an examination of brain tissue in an autopsy.

We think we beat it, with our upgrades and enhancements. But what if we didn't? What if the invisible variable is still waiting, waiting, patient in the dark, to suck my mind down into the shadows with it? What if there's something we still can't see?

Hess snaps shut his own paranoid thoughts as swiftly as he snaps the image of his glowing brain off the monitor. He begins his daily series of tests, measuring his reflexes, his coordination, muscle tone, eye movement, speech, sense of touch. He records all of his data, sealing it in his own private medical record files. He is fine. But he cannot trust that he will remain fine.

Though he has not celebrated his birthday in years, he always marks its passage on the calendar. Today marks his eighty-third—the same age his grandmother was when she ceased to remember him. Despite all his safeguards, Hess fears that something in his mind might begin to deteriorate. He is far from the oldest Syn, in terms of natural years, since plenty of wealthy early adopters had synched in their fifties. But he has been a Syn longer than most. If a synthetic aging issue arises, he doesn't want to be the harbinger.

See you in ten minutes, Felix.
Don't be late.

He flinches at the message from Lorraine. The unreasonable bitch is still insisting on thrice-weekly meetings of the Syn Council, and she took it upon herself to remind Hess every Monday, Wednesday, and Friday that he was expected in the board room.

Her initial impetus for instituting the insane new level of bureaucracy was her alarm over the self-terminations. When her husband's body was discovered she went white as a sheet. In Hess's view, she remained blanched in both appearance and intellect ever since. She took the whole thing too personally. And then there had been the episode with the Fell boy, showing up and subsequently escaping. Apparently his brief visit to Central City had lit a match and tossed it into a pile of old kindling Hess had thought long swept away: the threat of Original uprisings.

If a pack of flea-bitten old Original skeletons want to come rattling at our door, I think we can handle that, Hess had snapped at Lorraine when she mentioned the possibility.

That Fell boy looked pretty damn good for a flea-bitten old skeleton, she fired back. *And what about the other one you're holding captive here, Felix?*

And so the endless meetings began.

The Council meetings were furtive, not publicly logged, and full of heated debate. The two topics addressed at each meeting were the self-terminations within their population, and reviewing the rumors of a new Original rebellion. This irritated Hess because the Original rumors were just that—rumors—and if anything, the Syn self-terminations were a self-correction. Clearly, Hess deduced, there was a flaw in those who chose to terminate themselves. They were taking care of the problem for him, saving his team hours of tests and analysis. Why look a gift horse in the mouth?

But as long as his Generation Next project wasn't added to the Council's agenda, he mostly kept his mouth shut so as not to draw attention to the issues he actually cared about and wanted to continue solely controlling. If he had his way, oversight would be eliminated entirely.

Have you forgotten who I am? Hess was always on the verge of snapping. They somehow did not recall that *he* was the genius, the one who moved synthetic synchronization from dream to reality. He did what even Nathan Fell could not. Hess knows the reason he succeeded where everyone else failed was due to a powerful alchemy of intellect, determination, and flat-out destiny. Like Arthur pulling Excalibur from the stone, this monarchy gave itself over to Hess because he was meant for the mantle. Everyone else struggled. Hess came, gave a gentle tug, and there it was: the chosen king of this technological Camelot.

He likes the feel of this hilt in his hand. He has no interest in allowing anyone to pry it from his cold fingers, and woe to any who might try. Past lords had only men and horses. He has cyborgs and mules, Nathan Fell's brain, and the full power of Heaven. Felix Hess's gleaming Camelot will not crumble. Anyone who attempts to take him down will be met with the full force of his augmented armory.

CHAPTER 8: MARILYN

'M FINE, MARILYN HESS THINKS.

She's been lying to herself a lot lately.

She sends a command to the screen on her dining room wall, and it instantly becomes reflective. She stares at her reflection, smooth face framed by soft fawn locks, loose at her shoulders instead of in her perennial chignon. She can't put her finger on it, but something looks wrong to her.

Is it my eyes? A little puffy? Or maybe it's my brows, they look uneven—no, no, it's my mouth—drooping, maybe?

No. Nothing. It's all in your head. You look terrific.

"You're going to be a star," she says, fluttering her eyelashes at the mirror.

It was something she used to do every morning when she was a little girl. She wanted to be an actress, a million years ago. So she would stand in front of the mirror, lock eyes with herself, and begin making a series of faces. She challenged herself to cry convincingly, or make the most confused face of all time, or be so sultry that no one could possibly have resisted her advances.

If you can't cry on cue, you'll never be a star, she would tell herself. *If you can't be the best, you won't be anything at all.*

Her father could have bought her a Hollywood career. Few directors would have turned down a request from an oil baron who could finance their next film. He sure as hell would have bought her a condo in Los Angeles, given her whatever she wanted—and he would have done all that and more, if only she had agreed to ditch Felix Hess.

But Marilyn didn't ditch Felix.

She also never extended any effort toward pursuing the stage or screen. She was never in a play, never took an acting class or went to auditions. Not in high school, not in college, not ever. Marilyn didn't necessarily want to be an *actress.*

She just wanted to be a star.

It was probably the first lie she ever told herself—that she deserved to be famous. If asked, she could not have articulated why this mattered so much to her. She read every celebrity magazine she could get her hands on, devouring the glossy pages and wanting to see her name printed there. She heard a quote once: *A hero is well known for doing something great. A celebrity is well known for being well known.* She knew she was supposed to infer from the quote that this meant being a hero was good and being a celebrity was shallow. But it only reinforced her desire to be famous simply for being who she was, without putting in the effort necessary to cure cancer or slay a dragon.

In an ironic twist of fate, instead of becoming famous herself, she was married to the world's most famous man. A man who was bored with her long before he skyrocketed to stardom. She was not famous. She was the forgotten wife of someone who would forever outshine her.

There were a few brief and shining moments when the paparazzi descended on Marilyn. The biggest one came when she herself underwent the augmentation process. As the needles plunged into her body, she had reminded herself that this was the price she paid for fame.

Now. Now, you're going to be a star.

She knew it would be *Time* and *Newsweek* and not the shiny *People* and *Hello!* magazines she adored, but she didn't care. As long as people looked at the pictures, read the captions and wondered what it would be like to be the beautiful Marilyn Kensington Hess, that would be enough.

When Felix paraded her out in front of the cameras, the first woman synched, she preened. She purred. She eagerly picked up the next morning's paper.

FELIX HESS SUCCESSFULLY SYNCHS HIS WIFE the headline read.

His wife.

Even when the cameras finally, briefly turned toward her, she was not really the focus. It was always about *him*, *his* science, *his* story. All Marilyn was in the eyes of the press was *his* wife. Worse: *his* successful experiment.

For a while, Marilyn's consolation was her daughter. Little Ever, too young to understand what was going on and why she could no longer see her friends, went through a brief period wherein she clung to her mother. When she aimed her adoring eyes at Marilyn, it was almost as powerful as the imagined envy of the masses. Almost.

Marilyn would doll them both up, spend hours applying makeup to her face and her small daughter's already-perfect complexion, then they would photograph one another, and pick their best pictures and paste them into mocked-up magazine spreads. After dozens of these sessions, each knew their best angle, when to smile and when to smirk, what colors made their eyes stand out and which styles were most flattering on them. It was an activity as flat and glossy as Marilyn's old magazines had been, but they both enjoyed it.

In the days immediately following Ever's recent hospitalization, Marilyn was inappropriately giddy. Between Hess's tasking her with making Ever comply, and Ever's illness, Marilyn was buoyed by the sudden, fierce sensation that she was necessary. To Felix, when he needed her to subdue their daughter and turn her over to him; and to Ever, who would need someone at her side as she recovered.

She'll need me now, Marilyn thought as her daughter convalesced. *It will be a fresh start. Something good for both of us. A blessing in disguise! We can rebuild, we can become close...*

But after the strange series of events earlier this year, Ever's resentment toward Marilyn only intensified, and Felix went back to ignoring her. The flash of usefulness, of connection, of excitement, was a match that quickly burned out, singeing Marilyn's overeager fingertips.

Marilyn can no longer look at herself. She sends the wall back to its flat gray state and sips her cloyingly sweet coffee. Marilyn has finally varied her morning routine; she now skips the creamer and instead adds what she refers to as "a splash of Irish cream" to her coffee. More accurately, she fills her mug with the sugary alcohol, then tops it off with a thin veneer of coffee. She's not even worried about the calories. Her "special coffee" is all she consumes most days lately.

Exhaling, she decides to send a message to Angela. Not about the dinner menu, but about something else. Like in the old days. She just wants to pour out her heart to a friend, which is something Angela used to be. Maybe she can be Marilyn's friend again.

Maybe there's still hope.

Or maybe hope is just another lie.

CAL WRINKLES HIS NOSE. He'll never get used to the sour smell of metal and chemicals in this unnatural air. Exhaling with a huff, he drops to the ground to begin his first set of push-ups.

He's grateful to his great-uncle Howard, who taught Cal and Ere at an early age a whole series of exercises popular back in Howard's youth. Ere had never liked push-ups and crunches, pointing out that he got plenty of exercise hauling water and climbing trees and hiking for days on end. Cal knew Ere was right, but he enjoyed the additional workouts. He would move through the series his uncle taught him, relishing the feel of his muscles flexing and going taut. In his present circumstance, his gratitude has deepened. If he didn't have a go-to routine that required only his weight and a solid surface beneath him, he would have been reduced to running in circles around this small room. Which would have made him lose his damn mind.

As Hess's "guest," Cal is permitted to walk around the Synt. But no matter which direction he goes, after a few minutes' walk he reaches a locked door requiring access codes he doesn't have. He also has to endure the stares of the Syns who roam the hallways. Some of them walk with purpose, toward some job or appointment or task; others meander, as if they began their sojourn before deciding on any particular destination. No matter their pace or preoccupation, all of them take the time to let their eyes slide over him in a way that makes Cal feel violated.

Allowing those stupid Syns to stare and gape at him, the snared prey on display, is something he cannot stand. And so this morning, when he completes his workout, Cal sits back down on his bed. He does not want to go out and be subjected to the stares. He looks over at the blank wall a few feet past his bed, the wall opposite the door. Dr. Felix Hess had shown him how to activate this wall, which is in fact a screen, capable of displaying selected bits of information about the world.

"It's restricted-access, of course," Hess sneered when orienting Cal to the strange technology. "Can't have you poking around all of Heaven, Mr. Harper. But if you need some entertainment, it's there. If you need basic information, it's there. I'm sure a little education wouldn't hurt, either."

It was the first time a wall had made Cal feel stupid.

To access it, he simply has to align his eyes with a small scanner on the western corner of the wall. He was nervous to do so the first time, afraid of injury or having something taken from him in the interaction with the little piece of tech. But eventually his curiosity got the better of him, and now he does not think twice before placing his eyes before the little black box and waiting for its small screen to shift from flat red to glowing green in recognition of his eyes.

Heavily kerned black letters appear in the middle of the flat white wall.

Harper, Cal.
Restricted Access.

Then the words disappear, and the white wall dulls, fading to an expectant gray. A tiny, bright blue dot appears in the center of the wall, and widens and enlarges until it is the size of Cal's fist. The blue circle in the center of the screen sits level at his face, waiting. Cal knows that for the Syns, no words need be spoken for these screens and machines to fetch information, convey messages, respond to the whims of the citizens. For Cal, with no mechanic components embedded in his flesh, the computers must await a verbal command.

Talking to a wall makes Cal feel like he's losing his mind, but he knows it's the only way to get the information he needs. So he sighs and steels himself, glowering at the room.

"History," he mumbles.

The blue circle expands, contracts, then disappears. Instantly the screen begins to fill with long strings of words and images, some still, some moving. Soon the entire wall is covered, a collage of images and articles and information layering thickly on top of one another until the wall is a black and teeming mass too heavily stacked to reveal a damned thing. Some of the clips have sound and there is a cacophony that nearly shatters Cal's eardrums as the wall keeps pouring out information, populating itself with even more—

"STOP. CLEAR." Cal says loudly, and the wall erases itself. Almost lazily, the blue circle reappears, pulsing faintly as it awaits its next directive. Cal could swear that wall and its piece of shit blue ball is mocking him.

"History of the Synt," Cal growls carefully at the screen, hunching his shoulders.

The blue circle expands, contracts, disappears. This time one large moving image fills the screen. A woman's face. She does not look real. Cal cannot tell if it is her Syn modifications or some other trick of technology, but there is something unnatural about the countenance before him. Her gleaming white picket fence teeth, her smooth skin, wide round eyes and heavy midnight-black lashes. Cal cannot even find her beautiful; she is like a painting brought to life.

"The Synthetic Neuroscience Institute of Technology: A History," says the too-perfect woman with a blinding smile. "The central educational and administrative body of the Syn Center. Commonly referred to as The Synt. This institution always has and always will be committed to one primary purpose: Progress."

"Progress," Cal mutters.

Immediately the scene freezes; the woman's face is shrunk and pulled into a corner as a new clip fills the screen, calling up other results for the word *progress*. Cal huffs, irritated. He has made this mistake so many times before. At least now he knows how to correct it.

"Cancel," he says. "Back—resume."

And the big face of the pretty woman is back onscreen, smiling blithely.

"The Synthetic Neuroscience Institute of Technology was informally established as a modest research outfit in Cambridge, Massachusetts. A small team, led by Dr. Nathan Fell and Dr. Felix Hess, began the earliest phases of the bio-mechanical synthesis process."

Nathan Fell?

Each phrase the screen-woman utters triggers an image or symbol to pop up on the screen beside her. Cal had figured out that these things were all little jumping-off-points, live portals where you could change course or get more information. He is still taken aback by the sensory overload of the experience, but he does know how it works now, a bit. If he touched the image of the Synt building, the screen would shift and display a series of related images, each of which would yield more detailed information if subsequently selected. If he touched the words "Cambridge, Massachusetts," he would be presented with moving images and articles and information on the history of the now-demolished city adjacent to what was once Boston.

Cal touches the words, *Dr. Nathan Fell*, wondering why this choice was represented in words only, with no accompanying photograph of the man.

Cal catches on to patterns quickly; in all other articles, when an individual was named, their likeness appears, usually providing a portal to more information—stroke their cheek, learn more about their life. Dr. Felix Hess's smug face hovered beside his name. Why was this name, Nathan Fell, presented without images or related articles?

No sooner does he touch the words than the screen snaps to black, then returns to its neutral wall self. The heavily kerned black letters reappear:

Harper, Cal.
Restricted access.

"Dammit," Cal snarls.

Why was further information about this Nathan Fell restricted? Cal's seething converts quickly to conspiracy theorizing. This mystery man, Nathan Fell, was obviously important in the Syn world. He was part of the establishment of the Synt itself. If he was also related to Cal's family—would this make Syns more or less trusting of Cal? Maybe this was something he could use to gain some traction. Unless the information was restricted because this Fell had betrayed the Syn world, and claiming a connection to him would be suicide? Cal could not use this information until he knew more. And the wall had snapped off, forbidding him from further inquiry.

Hating the wall, he faces it again. He needs to give it another try. Maybe it was a fluke, it shutting down when it did. And so, grudgingly, Cal returns to it, speaking slowly and clearly so the cursed flat screen can understand his command words:

"Back. Resume."

But the wall does not respond.

"Back," Cal says, louder. "*Resume.*"

Nothing.

Cal rises, and is seriously considering punching the wall when the door behind him hisses open and Hess strides into the room.

"Might as well give those commands a rest, I terminated this screen so we could have a little chat," Hess says casually, mouth twitching as if he might be about to smile.

"Chat?"

"Yes," Hess says, looking almost amused. He licks his lips, slowly moistening them and dragging out the moment before delivering an entirely unexpected question: "Cal Harper— how would you feel about getting a job?"

MOMENTS BEFORE MIDNIGHT, Jorge reaches One Eyed Alice. He has not visited this particular landmark before, though he has passed her many times. She resides near the Synt, but a world away, tucked into a manicured but otherwise largely ignored corner of the Syn Central Greens, once known as Central Park.

One Eyed Alice is a stone relic that managed to survive the chaos all around it and come out relatively unscathed. A piece of shrapnel had landed in the statue's eye, gouging it out of the bronze statue along with a small bit of her cheek. In another era, she represented innocence and inquisition. She was called Alice then. Now, One Eyed Alice has lost her wide-eyed wonder; she looms, wary and war-torn, a battered homage to innocence lost.

Jorge never saw Alice before she was scarred. Strolling through parks was something he'd had little time for in the old world. Too many other little distractions—working three jobs to keep his family fed, serving time for a crime he didn't commit. Jorge's life was never one of parks and privilege. Back when Alice still had her innocence, Jorge was already jaded.

Jorge never read Lewis Carroll's book, but he had seen the Disney version of *Alice in Wonderland*. Even in the bright Technicolor interpretation aimed at children, the story felt dark. Going down the rabbit hole, falling into a world where everything was topsy-turvy, old rules were scrapped and new ones called the shots. Mad hatters and angry queens, games rigged against most of the players. A little too familiar. And then of course the crazy rabbit running around, frantic, always behind schedule, a neurotic New Yorker with a cotton tail.

I'm late, I'm late, for a very important date, no time to say hello! Goodbye! I'm late, I'm late, I'm late…

"You're punctual."

The voice is a whisper, barely above a breath. He recognizes the tone, the timbre, though the voice is not quite as robust as the last time he heard it. Much as he wants to turn around and see from whence it comes, Jorge forces his muscles still. He holds his ground, keeping his gaze on One Eyed Alice.

"Yes."

"And already in private mode."

"Of course."

"I need you to assure me that you have not yet been compromised."

"I have not."

"You are certain."

"Yes," Jorge says. "I once trusted the wrong people. Now the wrong people trust me."

"Well said."

Jorge feels a soft hand against his. The hand presses something into his palm. Thin, scratchy, crumpled; a piece of paper, like a note passed between children in old-world classrooms.

"Is this—"

"Too dangerous for discussion or electronic transmission. Stay in private mode, read the note carefully, destroy the physical paper and protect the memory to the fullest extent. Follow the instructions. You will?"

"I will."

"Be safe, Jorge. Long live the resistance."

The midnight wind picks up a bit. The note in Jorge's hand flutters and he clutches it tightly. He's alone. Shadower's departure was as silent and immediate as their arrival.

Jorge brings the note in front of his face. He reads it quickly. Twice to be sure. Then he triple-encrypts the memory and marks it SEXUAL ENCOUNTER, so that anyone daring to unlock the encryption could be flagged for privacy violations. His pulse is racing, heart pounding. He cannot recall the last time he has been this excited.

All he has to do is justify a trip to India without raising any suspicion, and fast.

No time to say hello! Goodbye!

I'm late, I'm late, I'm late…

CHAPTER 11: EVER

E VER STALKS THE HALLWAYS of the Synt like a cat,
ludicrously arrogant for a creature with nothing on its
agenda but naps and preening.

She heard rumors that Cal, the Original who once crawled
through her window, is sometimes seen walking these same
passageways. Ever has found more covert ways to search Heaven
for breadcrumbs that might lead her to him. Scanning public
records of others' daily memories, looking for when they logged
observations like *Original* or *stranger*.

But she has yet to see him, and today is no exception.

Frustrated, Ever returns to her family's penthouse residence,
scowling. She heads directly for her bathroom, and grabs a sleek
vial of hair color. Ever touches Dandelion #1,007 with the tip

of her finger, wondering if shifting the hue of her tresses will purchase her even five minutes' worth of distraction.

Then she gets a better idea.

Angela is in the kitchen, standing at the stainless-steel island in the center of the room, slicing vegetables. A patient potato rests beneath her firm knuckles, awaiting its inevitable dicing; bright piles of tomato, green herbs, red onions and orange carrots all crowd near the chopping block. Angela looks up when Ever enters, cocking her head at the girl. Ever does not so much as glance at her, instead simply bee-lining for the long shallow drawers at the rear of the room.

"You looking for something, Ever?"

"Yes," Ever says, without further explanation. She hunches over the drawers, back to Angela, blocking her view. Pulling each out quickly, almost violently drawing each drawer to her stomach, Ever slides open one, then another, and in the third finds what she wants. She slides the kitchen shears up her sleeve, then selects a second random object—maybe it's a melon baller?—and holds it aloft as she lets the drawer slide shut and twirls around to face Angela.

"Got it."

"Girl, what do you need a strawberry huller for—"

Security-locking the bathroom door behind her, Ever slips the shears from her sleeve. This time, she does look at herself in the mirror, eyes ablaze. With her left hand, she twists a large section of her long, dark hair, and pulls it taut. With her right hand, she opens the gaping jaw of the kitchen shears.

CHAPTER 12: PREETI

D R. PREETI KANSAL IS OLDER THAN SHE LOOKS. She has both of her parents to thank for her good genes. They went to their graves in their nineties, both of them, still lean and sharp and able to pass for seventy. She was the last of their children, the youngest of eleven. They were old already when she was born, almost as old as she had been when her children were born. Having children in your fifties isn't for everyone, her mother joked, years before Preeti lived out that very punchline.

Preeti is grateful that her parents passed away before the world began to burn. She does not know how she would answer the questions they might ask, especially if they knew of her prox-imity to the Synthetic match that kindled the blaze—*how did you allow this to happen, if you knew it was coming…?*

When she left her parents and went to America to study as an undergraduate, she knew it pained them. She promised to return home to India. But then she got in to medical school, and then there was a fellowship, a residency, opportunity after opportunity, and somehow more than a decade after she left her aging parents, she was still in America. Funny how she used to think that the guilt she felt over that was monumental—and that guilt is only a base layer now, the cracked foundation upon which an entire empire of guilt has been constructed.

She was still so young, so new to being an expert in her field, so stupid and so flattered when she got the call from her cousin Felix Hess. When she unknowingly opened a door into a new realm of guilt, a guilt so deep and all-consuming that it overpowered any previous concept of shame she had experienced.

I could have stopped them.

She believes this with all the intensity made possible by acute hindsight. If she had paid more attention, asked more questions, pulled a plug, called someone. If she had not been an idiotic, NDA-signing bystander to this crucial moment in history.

This is a feeling Preeti cannot simply live with; it is one she must accommodate. She began addressing her guilt by fulfilling the long-abandoned promise to her parents. She returned to India. She was grateful that her parents were still alive for her return—and just as grateful that they died a few years after she made her way there, never witnessing the wicked world that their very own daughter might have prevented.

"Mother," Asavari says. "What next?"

Preeti stares at her improbable daughter, somehow so sturdy despite a life spent in dirt and desperation. Vari is unlike Preeti. This girl is a warrior. Preeti has never been a fighter. She's a healer.

That's how she contributes. Heal and tend, find the damage and mend. But now, before she can heal, she has to expose this old wound.

Though she has been a conduit of information for years, she has guarded as best she could her role in those pivotal days. She has withheld details, particularly from the ones whose condemnation she fears the most: her children. But her secret-keeping days are running out. She must face her fears of judgment and reprise, or risk endangering everything she holds dear.

She swallows hard.

"As I told Ere this morning, I was... nearby, when the Singularity occurred. I have some... insights, into how the Synthetic Heaven might be controlled."

Her daughter's eyes reveal little, but seem to shine more with interest than indictment.

For now.

"Tell us everything," Asavari says.

CHAPTER 13: ASAVARI

"WE COULDN'T HAVE KNOWN," Preeti whispers as she continues her confession of being adjacent to the room where the Singularity began.

Using *we* instead of *I* to downplay her prominence as she shares this history is something Asavari finds particularly grating. But the whole thing is difficult to hear. It is the account of a bystander, when it could have been a hero's tale. A story wherein a young Preeti could have pulled the plug on Nathan Fell and made sure he was dead, and his work along with him; could have notified authorities, or at least informed his precious funders that he'd gone rogue. Or she could have led early rebels into the heart of

the Synt and burned it into a carcass. It could have been a story of
Preeti saving the world.

Instead it was a story of Asavari's very own mother mutely
letting the Syns rise to power. A story that her mother had largely
withheld from her until now, but apparently recently shared pieces
of with Ere. Ere, before her own daughter! Asavari clenches her
fists.

"We do not need every damn detail," Asavari growls as her
patience wears thin. "Just tell us what we need to know."

"I am telling you what you need to know," Preeti says, voice
quivering. Asavari hates the weakness of that tremor. "Sometimes
you do not simply need facts. You need context, you need an image
to embody the story—"

"No imagery!" Asavari yells. "No bullshit! We do not have
time for some poetic metaphor, we just need the truth—"

"This is not bullshit," Preeti snaps, hard, startling Asavari.
She draws herself up to her full not-five-feet height and juts her
chin, in a move that neither mother nor daughter realizes marks
them as family. "Metaphor is a lie that serves to tell a clearer truth,
Asavari. Details are not a waste of time. It is not bullshit. It is how
I help you see. If I say that 'her eyes are stormy seas'—her eyes
are not literally stormy seas, but when I say that, do you not get a
clearer picture than if I say 'her eyes are gray?'"

"I do not see—"

"Correct," her mother says, cutting her off again. "You do not
see, when you do not listen. Felix Hess, Nathan Fell—the whole
Singularity didn't happen because of one simple decision. It wasn't
an isolated incident, it was a culminating moment. It was made
possible by greed yelling louder than compassion; it was driven
by division, fueled by fear. So much fear. Fear of other people, of
aging, of women's bodies, of those in power losing their power, of
disease, of planetary famine… Felix Hess emerged with a clear
vision of a new world at a time when people thought the old one

was dying. It is never just what we say. It is always how we say it. Sometimes it takes a goddamn poem."

Asavari backs down, surprised by her mother's unexpected defense of poetry.

"Ere," Asavari's mother says, turning from her daughter to face the Fell boy. "When you were in the Synt, you saw… you saw Nathan Fell."

"Yes," Ere swallows, his small Adam's apple bobbing.

"So he is still part of the equation," Preeti says, nodding. "And I have some theories as to how he functions within their Heaven, and I believe our friend Shadower can help us connect the remaining dots. Still, there is so much we still must determine—"

From out of nowhere, a silent silver hovercraft zooms down from the flat gray sky above—and in one impossibly fast movement, a Syn man leaps from the vehicle. He is wielding a glinting knife, which he plunges into Ere.

CHAPTER 14: JORGE

STABBING ERE FELL WASN'T JORGE'S FIRST CHOICE, but it was his only option. And truth be told, it was kind of a rush.

Immediately post-stabbing, he flings his hood from his head. Looking around wildly, he finds the girl called Karma and locks eyes with her. He has one arm wrapped around Ere's neck, hand over his mouth to stifle the boy's screams; his other hand holds the hilt of the blade now buried in the flesh of the boy's arm.

The girl takes a step toward him, prompting an older woman beside her to cry out: "Stay back, Asavari!"

Dammit.

He wishes he hadn't heard her real name. He still has to think of her as Karma. But first and foremost he has to convince her that he's still on her side. Holding Ere roughly and tightly, he addresses the girl.

"You know who I am," he says.

"Yes," she says, glancing at the older woman beside her, then back at him. She has a knife of her own drawn, and is crouching, ready to protect and defend, to rescue the boy. But she is waiting; giving him a moment.

"Trust me," he says. "There's something we gotta remove from this kid's arm. Will you help me hold him? This will hurt like hell. I'll explain when it is over but we have to move fast. I swear this is necessary."

"I will assist you," says the girl, and Jorge feels the Fell boy thrash harder against him.

"Let's get him on the ground," says Jorge.

The boy protests, but between Jorge and the girl, he is swiftly flipped face-down on the earth. He continues writhing, but Jorge can now sit on the boy's back, pinning him, so the flailing does little. Jorge holds the boy's left arm out straight, pressing it too into the ground.

"Keep his arm steady," Jorge instructs Karma.

Ere screams in protest, the sound muffled by the dirt against which his face is pressed. The girl's jaw tightens, but she holds the boy's arm still. *Karma really is one tough bitch*, Jorge thinks. Then he grasps firmly the hilt of his knife, and slices deeper into the boy's bicep, earning a muted shriek. Jorge then gives a sharp twist, eliciting a much higher-pitched yelp from the boy.

"I need him to be quiet," Jorge growls. "I have to listen for it—"

Wordlessly, and while still firmly keeping hold of his arm, the girl slides her elbow to the base of the boy's neck and drives his face all the way into the ground. His screams are entirely silenced, and Jorge sincerely hopes Karma doesn't wind up suffocating the kid.

He twists the knife again, but hears nothing; he twists it the other way, hears a metallic click and feels the knife catch, like a screwdriver slipping in to the head of an awaiting screw. *Yes, there it is!* Jorge pulls upward, slowly, knowing how agonizing this must feel but also aware that he must do this thing, and do it right.

When he finally pulls the knife from the boy, speared on the blade's tip, coated in blood, is the device Jorge came to extract.

"A tracker," he explains. "Implanted to monitor his movements. This is how the Syns found you. I'll explain more later, but first I need your help. We need to manufacture a memory, for me to share with Felix Hess."

"What memory?" Karma asks.

"The memory of me killing Ere Fell," Jorge says.

CHAPTER 15: HESS

BOUT DAMNED TIME!

Hess was initially delighted when Jorge told him that the tracker had finally picked up the Fell boy. The tracker had been in Ere's arm for months, implanted during the little show Hess had put on for him. While Ere had wandered through the simulation of his ancestors' past, staring dumbly at the images of his grandfather and great-uncle in their younger years, Hess had generated the image of a bee. Ere experienced only a small sting, followed by a large and revelatory memory that overshadowed the momentary prick of pain. The boy had no idea that a tracking device was implanted, infiltrating his future while he was distracted by his family's history.

But for all these intervening months, the tracker had been unreliable. A blip here, a blip there, nothing lasting long enough to pinpoint an exact location—and for the past two weeks, radio silence. The tracker was beginning to look like a failure, but Hess still had Jorge monitor the signal, periodically rebooting the grounded connection within the Synt—and finally it was working. Now Hess just had to wait for whatever might happen when the Vost reached the boy.

Because once that happened, things would really get interesting.

Hess still didn't understand how the boy wound up in India. When Jorge had given that location to Hess, he might as well have said he was just a little bit north of the moon. *India?* How could an Original kid with no access to planes, or even boats, make it halfway across the planet?

Jorge had volunteered to personally retrieve the boy. Although Hess was always hesitant to allow the strong-willed Vost to venture out of Central City, he didn't trust anyone else to get the job done, discreetly and efficiently. The Council didn't have the stamina. Hess didn't have the time. Kennedy didn't have the balls.

"Take a team," Hess told Jorge.

"I think I should go alone," Jorge said. "Sir."

This request had unsettled Hess.

"Why do you want to go alone, Jorge?"

"With all due respect, this situation has gotten out of hand more than once. He was in the Synt, talked his way into your residence; he slipped past me there. He's cunning. Fast. High-profile. Too many people here know that we had him, and we lost him. We can't risk another screw-up… I screwed this up. Let me fix it."

Hess watched his old-fashioned wooden office door click shut behind his employee. He stared at it a moment, his eyes traveling the length of the shining polished wood. It was a good door. Sturdy. It would last another hundred years, at least.

Then Hess sent a message.

Kennedy.
My office.
Ten minutes.

Precisely ten minutes later, Hess's more diminutive assistant was knocking on that same wooden door.

"Come in."

Kennedy entered, looking nervous, as was his way. "Yes, sir?"

"I have an assignment for you."

CHAPTER 16: EVER

L EVEL ONE APPLICATION RESEARCH ASSISTANT.

It sounds so formal. So corporate. The wordy and forgettable job title is imprinted in dark-silver engraved letters on the surface of a lighter-silver micro-chipped identification card, directly beneath the stubbornly engraved words HESS, EVER.

"So, does it feel weird? First day on the new job?" Red Shirt asks cheerfully.

Red Shirt is one of Ever's new supervisors. Red Shirt has a name, but Ever has already decided never to use it. Despite the name being monogrammed on the front of the man's crisp bright red shirt and printed on his micro-chipped card, hanging from a clip on his stupid old-world belt.

Probably written on the inside of his underwear, too, like we had to do at that stupid camp my mom sent me to a million years ago…

Ever looks around the room where she will be spending eight hours a day until she can figure out how to quit or get fired without her father overruling the action. She has to admit it's kind of a nice space—huge floor to ceiling windows, lots of natural light flooding the stainless-steel filled room. There are tables, monitors, but also some oddly charming if somewhat bland touches here and there, such as the large framed photograph of the old New York skyline.

Her new supervisor is still looking at her expectantly, waiting for Ever to say something.

"Application Development," she says, since it's something to say.

"Yeah, well, we just call it App-Dev most of the time. More fun."

Ever has nothing to say in response to that stupid statement.

She runs her fingers through her hair, still surprised by the shortness of it. She chopped off nearly eleven inches with the kitchen shears, and lost another two when her mother saw her and screamed and immediately dragged her to a stylist to get the hack job touched up. Ever actually likes the look of it, a short bob hanging just below her chin, emphasizing her lean neck and slim shoulders. Even easier to color, too.

"So! Have you ever—oh! Ha! That's funny, how I was asking if you'd 'ever,' but also your name is Ever…" Red Shirt grins like an idiot, as if this is the funniest thing he's ever heard. "I mean, man-o-man. Does that get confusing, now and then? Does it ever, Ever?"

"No," she says without a smile.

"Right, sure, probably used to it," Red Shirt nods. "Context clues, sure, easy enough to… Anyhoo! What got you interested in App-Dev?"

"My father told me I had to start showing up here for work. So here I am."

"Here you are," Red Shirt says, his stupid grin becoming fixed and false.

Ever knows that he was given as little choice about hiring her as she was about joining his team. He was just more polite, or maybe more genuinely nice, trying to make her feel welcome even though neither of them wanted her to be there. She almost feels sorry for him, but is too busy feeling sorry for herself.

"What exactly is my job as a…Level One Application Research Assistant?"

"Well, that'll depend a little bit. On your skillset."

"My skillset."

"Yep. As a research assistant, you'll be doing all the support work for a Level Two or Level Three Researcher. You'll support them in developing apps and products to enhance synthetic life. Better living through technology, every single day, that's our goal!"

"But what will I be *doing*, exactly?"

"Whelp! That's where we get to your aforementioned 'skill-set.' Do you have any technical training—working with hardware, circuitry, that sort of thing?"

"Nope."

"Okey-doke. How about software development? Coding, information architecture, or—"

"Nope. I mean I can download the basics, obviously, if that's what I have to do—"

"You can't just download working knowledge, we're really looking for team members who bring a curiosity to the baseline and then…" Red Shirt pauses, and for some reason it looks as if *he* feels sorry for *her*. "I mean… what would you say your skills are, Ever?"

"My French is pretty good," she says, deadpan.

"I was told you had plenty of aptitude," Red Shirt says, and Ever can see he wants to make an *app*-titude joke, but thankfully he doesn't. "So! Here's what we're going to have you do. I'm going to turn you over in a minute here to your manager, Marti—you'll

love her, she's great. Been keeping me on my toes since she transferred over here from Yale last year."

Red Shirt closes his eyes to send the message, an unnecessary
old maneuver, but Ever suspects the guy's tired of looking at her.
She wonders how neutral the message he's sending right now
really is—just *Marti, come to the main office*, or something more
desperately honest, like *Dammit Marti get your ass in here I need
you to take the little Hess bitch off my hands right the hell now!*

Within moments, Marti appears. She's small and fit, wearing
a neutral dark top and well-tailored pants. Nothing red, nothing
monogrammed. She gives Ever a nod instead of a smile.

"Ever. I'm Marti."

Marti extends a hand, which Ever awkwardly takes and shakes.

Marti's grip is firm. She gives Red Shirt a small, tight smile.

"You can go check in with the other teams. We'll get settled
in here."

With a look of relief akin to a death-row inmate freshly
pardoned, Red Shirt gives two thumbs up and scampers from the
room.

"How many 'other teams' are there?" Ever asks, only mildly
curious.

"About five hundred," Marti says.

"Five *hundred?*" Ever was expecting something closer to a
dozen. "All just developing new apps?"

"Researching them, developing them, testing them, rejecting
or recalibrating them, then disseminating them. Yes."

"How long have you been working here?"

"I've worked for one department or another in the Synt for..."
Marti runs the calculation, barely pausing for a breath: "...twenty
years, three months, two weeks, five days and—thirteen minutes.
Here in App-Dev less than a year, though."

"Do you like it?"

Marti shrugs.

"It fills the time. And App-Dev is a reasonably interesting place to be. Every once in a while we do put out something pretty cool."

"What did you do—before?"

"Before transferring to this department?"

"Before the Singularity."

"Oh. Advertising," Marti says, almost wistfully. "I hated it, back then. Coming up with ways to convince people to buy something. Manipulate them into thinking that what my client was selling was something they should be buying. Brainstorms, assignments, campaigns that got awards and campaigns that totally bombed. But God, I miss it."

"Huh," Ever says.

"And you? Did you have a job, before the Singularity?"

"No," Ever admits. "I was just a kid, when my dad.. you know. I never got to be a grown-up in the old world."

"Are you a grown-up in this one?"

"What's a grown-up?" Ever asks, and for some reason the question stings.

Marti looks at Ever.

"Your hair's different."

"I just... cut it. But how did you know what it was like before—?"

"Ever Hess, famously under-scrutinized," Marti cracks, and Ever finds herself grinning. Of course Marti knew what Ever looked like. Everyone knew what Ever looked like. But Marti softened the celebrity dig, adding: "Anyway, all new hires get a thorough profile review. Photos included. Lots of different colors, but your hair was always long."

"I decided to change it up."

"Change is good," Marti says. "So. Let's get you started on the research."

"Research? But I'm only a level one—"

"Yes, sorry, let me clarify. You won't be researching the tech, you'll be researching the market. We have a request pipeline, and we get plenty of requests every single day. You'll review requests, do some analysis of that data, and write up some recommendations for new and improved apps. Some suggestions are solid, some are stupid, some are... well, let's just say there are more disturbing sex-app requests than you'd guess."

"So I review the requests people send in?" Ever asks, somewhat confused. "One-by-one? I don't mean to be a jerk, but isn't there, like... an app for that?"

"There's an app that compiles, sorts, and categorizes the requests. But we do still need real people to review them, decide which ones go into the scrap pile and which go into the pending further review pile. Can't turn everything over to the machines, now, can we?"

"We're part machine."

"True. But we're still human enough to send in weird sex requests."

Ever can't help but smile, again.

"Guess so."

"Come on," Marti says. "Let's get you oriented, Ever. Welcome to the working world."

CHAPTER 17: ERE

RE BITES HIS LIP ALMOST hard enough to make it bleed. He needs a small pinch of pain to distract from the larger discomfort he is experiencing. His torn flesh has already been hastily but tightly wrapped and bound, but the recent knifing still hurt like hell.

Everyone around him seemed to accept pretty damn quickly that the golden-eyed Syn maniac who attacked Ere was somehow on their side, but Ere had his doubts. After all, he was the only one who had just been a little bit *pinned down and stabbed* by the guy.

"We met before," the man says, as Ere's arm is bound by Preeti. "At the Hess's. The garbage chute?"

"Oh, so the first time we meet you shoved me into the trash, and this time you brought a knife to the party," snaps Ere.

But he has to grudgingly admit that the guy saved his ass, getting him out of Felix Hess's home while he was too distraught by Ever's erasure to know what to do. So maybe he is, in fact, be on their side—even if he was also a stab-happy lunatic.

The man quickly explains that Hess implanted the tracker in Ere by means of a bee sting during that simulation-thing. This, too, had the ring of truth. As soon as he says it, something in Ere vibrates with a forgotten memory. A brief pain in the middle of his strange trip down someone else's memory lane.

"What's your name?" Ere asks.

"He won't tell you," Asavari says sharply. "And he shouldn't. It's not safe."

"It's Jorge," says Jorge, and Asavari stares at him. "Your friend is right—it's not safe for me to share my name with you. But none of us are safe, and we have to move quickly. So my name is Jorge, and now I'm exposed too. Can you please just trust me so we can move the hell forward?"

"I… yes," Ere says, his stomach coiling.

"Good," Jorge says. "Because if my memory doesn't have a timestamp showing your death in the next ten minutes, I'm going to have a hell of a lot of explaining to do, and that won't be good for any of us."

"I thought Hess wanted me alive," Ere says, confused.

"He does," Jorge says. "Which is why I have to make it look like you're dead."

Asavari nods, as if this insane statement is entirely reasonable.

"If he believes that you are dead, Hess will stop pursuing you," Asavari says.

"Oh," Ere says, feeling as dumb as they all thought he was.

"So let's do this," Jorge says, and despite the urgency in his tone, the way his mouth twitches and his golden eyes gleam makes Ere think the guy might be enjoying this. "When I say 'now,' I want you to lunge toward me. Like you really want to hurt me."

"I can do that," Ere says a little too quickly.

"When you lunge for me, I'll grab you, but will let you get one arm free. With that arm, you'll take this—" Jorge hands Ere a knife, not the one with which he'd been stabbed, but a dull-er-looking blade—"and say 'You'll never take me alive!' and then stab yourself in the heart."

"Uh," Ere says. "That sounds like it might actually make me dead."

"No, watch this, this is great," grins the golden-eyed man. He presses the blade of the knife into his hand. Ere winces, but watches as the blade retracts into the handle, without leaving a scratch on Jorge's upturned palm. "It's a trick knife. Like for the stage? Harder to come by than you'd think, but I know a guy—anyway the point is you'll stab yourself, and it'll look real, especially if I'm in panic mode. And you'll have this—" Jorge pulls a small pouch from his pocket, a little bag bound with a length of rope. "It's full of blood. Fake blood. When you stab yourself, the knife will collapse, but be sure to hit yourself hard enough to make this bag leak so we get a nice little bloodstain under your shirt."

He slips the rope over Ere's head, tucking it beneath his shirt to hide the length of cord, and carefully positioning the pouch in front of Ere's left nipple.

"Ready?"

"Wait," Asavari says. "After Ere is killed—"

"*Fake* killed—" Ere interjects, and is ignored—

"—what then?" Asavari continues. "Wouldn't Hess want you to return with the body?"

"Yes," Jorge says. "He would. So after Ere stabs himself I want you to scream and come running forward wearing this." He tosses his dark cloak with the large hood her way. "Keep the hood over your face. In the pocket of the cloak, you'll find a firestick. Are you familiar with firesticks?"

"Yes," Asavari says.

"Is it a stick that makes fire?" Ere asks, aiming for world-weary wit and landing somewhere closer to what his mother or Helena might have referred to as bratty sarcasm.

"You'll rush forward with the firestick and light Ere's body on fire."

"You mean *pretend to* light my body on fire," Ere says loudly.

"No, she'll have to really start the fire. Aim for his feet," Jorge says, matter-of-fact. "The soles of those shitty old shoes will cause a lot of smoke. That will help blur my vision. Might actually sting my eyes."

"Poor you," mutters Ere, to no one who cares.

Jorge is still talking: "…then I'll retreat, get back on my Chariot and head for my ship to survey and assess how many of you there are. It will turn out to be only you, and so then I'll pretend to shoot you from my ship—when you hear the shots, just fall down. I promise not to actually shoot you. Go ahead and aim to fall on Ere, that way you can hopefully put out the fire quick enough to minimize the damage."

"MINIMIZE THE—" Ere starts to protest.

"This seems like an awful lot to get right," Asavari says, talking right over Ere's indignance. "Should we not practice before we attempt to—"

"No time for a rehearsal," Jorge says. "This has gotta be a one-take scene. But it'll work. I played the whole thing out over and over when I took private mode breaks during my flight here."

This somehow does not reassure Ere.

"All right," Asavari says.

"Great. Now go wait for your cue."

Asavari does as she is told, which is almost the most bizarre part of this entire surreal experience for Ere.

"This is crazy," Ere says to Jorge, loud and direct.

"Yes," Jorge says. "But it'll be a little fun, if you let it—but take it seriously, you hear me? Or you really could wind up dead."

"Is that supposed to be encouraging?"

"It is what it is, man," Jorge says. "NOW."

Something shifts in Jorge's golden eyes, and he stares directly at Ere.

Ere hesitates for a moment before realizing that the eye-shift thing was his cue that their little drama had begun. He lunges forward, flailing his arms and giving an improvised battle cry (some variation of "*you jaaaaaaaackassssssss!*") and even manages to land one semi-solid punch to Jorge's jaw before the larger man catches him, restrains him, and then deftly allows Ere to wriggle his right arm free.

"Hold still, you little bastard," snarls Jorge.

Ere almost obeys, before realizing that this is all part of the charade. Then he drops his hand into his pocket and pulls out the trick blade. He swings it once at Jorge, just for effect. Then he screams, full volume:

"YOU'LL NEVER TAKE ME ALIVE, YOU SYN PIECE OF SHIT!"

And he stabs himself with the knife.

And nothing happens. The small sack of fake blood remains intact.

Oh, hell…curse of the world… shit!

Ere knows he cannot pull the knife from him—it could reveal the collapsible nature, and would show no resistance or blood, which a real knife would certainly display. Thinking fast, he recalls the most painful part of his very recent actual stabbing, and twists the knife, appearing to grind it into his heart, pushing it against the bag as hard as he can.

There is a soft plopping sounds as the bag bursts.

Blood begins seeping through the fabric of Ere's shirt. Fake blood, he has to remind himself, because it's pretty convincing. Dark and sticky and spreading quickly, dampening his shirt and almost making him faint at the sight of it

"Heaven and hell!" Jorge swears.

Ere has to admit the guy's not a bad actor.

Then, like a crash of thunder and lightning made flesh, a dark and hooded figure comes barreling toward them from the wood, holding aloft a large, thick and flaming baton. Bellowing a battle cry fit to wake the dead, low and loud and animalistic, the figure is upon them almost at once. Waving the firestick, smacking it against Ere's feet. Heat is everywhere, and Ere closes his eyes against the smoke (and also because, he realizes, he should probably appear to have bled out soon, and keeping his eyes closed will be easier than keeping them unblinking and open).

He hears Jorge swear again, leap onto his Chariot, and sail away.

His smoldering shoes are beginning to hurt and he whispers fiercely, eyes still closed:

"Put out the damn fire on my feet!"

"Wait," Asavari whispers from beneath her hood. "We have to wait until he shoots—"

"NOW," Ere whisper-yells, his feet literally on fire.

To Ere's dismay, Asavari still isn't responding to him the way she responds to Jorge. And now Ere can smell the burning soles of his shoes. He begins picturing his flesh reddening, burning and cracking and starting a fire that will travel up from there and consume him and—

Rat-a-tat-a-tat-a-tatatatatatatat.

A loud round of ammunition sends shrapnel uncomfortably near them. It takes all of Ere's willpower not to open his eyes. He swears he can feel the breeze of the bullets, small missiles landing within inches of him. With a sharp cry, Asavari falls on top of him, the hood she wears smothering the flames, the smoke beginning to dissipate.

Even after the flames have died down, she does not move from him, just lies stretched out over him. For several long moments, she says nothing, and Ere begins to fear that Jorge's aim was not as good as he claimed. That maybe one of the bullets really did get her.

No, please. She's such a huge pain in the ass but she might be the closest thing I have to a friend in this whole stupid world—

"Asavari?" Ere says, barely above a whisper.

"Shhh," she says. "Keep playing dead."

Ere does, just relieved for the moment that she's alive. And that he himself is no longer slowly burning from the bottom up.

"How long do you think—"

And then they hear a triumphant whoop. Jorge swings down from the sky, still on his Chariot, hovering several yards above them, grinning from ear to ear. He raises a hand, as if to wave, and instead curls it into a fist and pounds at the air.

"HA!" He yells. "YES! *That's* how you do it! Just like in the movies!"

And then his grin disappears. His expression moves in nanoseconds from confusion to surprise to contorted in pain. Jorge lets out a guttural grunt, clutches his head, and plunges from his chariot, landing with a sickening crunch on the indifferent earth.

THE FIRST PULSE

CHAPTER 18: KENNEDY

KENNEDY AND HIS TEAM STAYED a half-hour behind Jorge the entire way to the Asian continent. He was terrified of the idea of the Vost figuring out that he was being tailed. Whether or not Jorge was up to anything, he'd be pissed to find Kennedy sneaking after him. And if he knew Hess had sent him with explicit orders to take him down if he appeared to do anything traitorous, well. Kennedy didn't like the idea of facing off against a fighting-for-his-life Jorge.

So Kennedy told the pilot to hang just a little farther back—they could easily track Jorge's movement, thanks to the

Synt-owned aircraft that he was using. If he disembarked on his Chariot, that would show up on their monitors. They weren't at risk of losing him, and it was better to hold off giving themselves away until they knew they needed to take action. Hess had been very clear about that when he deployed Kennedy.

The pilot was a woman called Shai, who had been irritated with the restrained and anxious Kennedy ever since takeoff.

"Just go easy," Kennedy told her, about three thousand times. "We don't want him to know we're following him."

"Right," Shai said through gritted teeth. "Just like we didn't want him to know it five minutes ago. And we won't want him to know in ten minutes, either, I'm guessing."

"We won't, we definitely won't," Kennedy said, not listening. If Jorge turned out to be helping the boy, going against Hess, or getting into some other sort of unauthorized mess—was Kennedy really supposed to assassinate him?

"He's out of his rig," Shai informed Kennedy. "Taking a Chariot down. We're going to have to kick it up a notch to catch up with him, we're well behind now. Hold tight."

Before Kennedy could protest, the ship barreled forward, trying to make up the nearly hourlong lead Jorge had on them thanks to Kennedy's anxiety. So they are still not caught up to Jorge when Kennedy hears a strange, low whine that seems to be emanating from within his own skull. The sound gets louder, buzzing his ears, becoming painful. Kennedy opens his mouth to ask if anyone else hears the strange sound, but that's when he starts hearing screams.

Everyone around him is screaming.

Clutching their heads and screaming.

The world around them seems to blink, pressing and crushing itself and all of its inhabitants out of existence and into darkness, then widening and stretching and re-making the world into something unrecognizable as everyone's mind is ripped open from one end to the other, like a jacket violently unzipped.

With no one commanding the large aircraft, or even able to shift it over to autopilot, the plane lurches, dives, begins plummeting.

CHAPTER 19: EVER

E VER IS READING THE FIRST ROUND of new app requests. Predictably, she chose the category called *Strange [Sexual & Other]*. If she has to have a job, she's sure as hell going to seize every opportunity to make it interesting.

But she hasn't even made it through the first request when a brief high-pitched sound makes her shake her head in irritation, as if having received an electric shock. Then she looks up, disoriented, vision blurring. The sound triggers something—a memory—something she was looking for—she can see it but not reach it before the sound is followed by a massive explosion in her brain.

With a gasp, Ever stands and reels and falls, connecting hard with the sharp edge of a steel table before hitting the floor and going still.

CHAPTER 20: MARILYN

MARILYN IS LOOKING IN THE MIRROR, and therefore she sees up-close the mangled expression of shock followed by the twisted pain contorting her face when the small whining beep is immediately followed by a searing attack, something ferociously tearing the fabric of her mind like an old rag being ripped for scrap.

CHAPTER 21: HESS

E VEN DR. FELIX HESS DIDN'T SEE IT COMING.
He is about to check in with Kennedy and the team when
a small sound causes him to turn his head, and then a
massive wave of pain sends him collapsing to the floor.

CHAPTER 22: SHADOWER

A WHISPER BEFORE THE BEEP.
A beep.
A scream.
The time for one thought:
No—

CHAPTER 23: HESS

A S SOON AS HE IS ABLE to get to his feet, re-orient himself to the room, steel himself against the receding but still sharp pain and take action, Hess runs a quick systems scan. The command is slow to load, as if Heaven itself is still reeling from whatever-it-was.

Before reporting on individual Syns, the cloud generates a self-report. It is incomplete and incoherent, like nothing ever before issued from Heaven:

Electric.
Overload.
System halt.
Unknown error.
Re-start.
Re-start.
Re-calibrating…

Hess shakes his aching head, frustrated, feeling weak and powerless and propelled solely by rage. Was it an electric surge? Some sort of pulse of energy, overloading the system? Where would that even happen—no.

Diagnostics later.

Assessment now.

Hess shifts from the self-report to the still-loading analysis of this event's total impact.

Event level: Catastrophic.
Event category: Unknown.
Fatalities: None yet reported.
Citizens impacted: All.

An uncategorized catastrophic event that somehow impacted all citizens?

There were many categories of events which Heaven could catalog and analyze, from wide-ranging natural disasters to limited-impact events like vehicle collisions. But a reading like this was bizarre. Not just the lack of event description, but the fact that it impacted everyone is flat-out impossible. Other than an asteroid hitting the planet (which, incidentally, was an existing event category) and sending them into oblivion... almost nothing could impact *everyone*, just like that. The idea was ludicrous.

Hess closes his eyes for a moment, trying simultaneously to stem the still-swelling waves of pain crashing and breaking through his head, and to make some sense of this senseless information. He barely registers the one bit of good news—no one actually died.

A message from Lorraine flashes before Hess's eyes, broken and barely decipherable.

F l x

W a t e he l h p n d?
Re rt / s t s

Getting most of it, he tries to send a reply to Lorraine, and finds that his own messaging system is shorting out. He can think of what he wants to compose, but the actual text is incomplete, just as her message had been. He grits his teeth, reloads his message system, and tries again, this time getting nearly all of the content of his message to load and send:

Running reports n w.

Having sent his mangled but passable reply, he begins composing a message demanding Jorge and Kennedy get their asses in here and start helping him run a deep diagnostic—when he remembers that neither of his assistants are in the vicinity. They were both en route to India: Jorge in pursuit of the Fell boy, Kennedy tailing Jorge.

The initial report said all citizens were impacted. Even the ones in Asia? Or did it just mean in the incorporated sectors? Perhaps Jorge and Kennedy were unaffected. Or maybe they too were reeling, thousands of miles away, where Originals were somehow congregating in southeast Asia.

Could this have been an Original attack?

No. There's no way. Impossible.

But for the first time in years, a cold fear creeps in, settling under Hess's skin and cooling the blood in his veins. He doesn't know what just happened, and he doesn't like not knowing. He has to figure out what happened. How it happened. Who made it happen. How to make sure it never happens again.

And who will need to be punished.

CAL WAS ON THE JOB WHEN IT HAPPENED, whatever the hell *it* was.

One minute, he and his co-worker Trent were reporting to a private Syn residence to install a new charging station for their freaky finger-or-neck-port thingamabobs. The next minute, everyone but Cal was writhing on the floor.

Trent made a guttural grunt and flapped his arms once before falling straight backward. The Syn man and woman—the clients whose names Cal had yet to learn—went down at the same time. The man clutched his head while exhaling a sharp curse word; he then slumped against the wall and slid down it while his words became louder and louder and less and less coherent. The woman screamed once, an ear-splitting shriek, and then she passed out entirely, and lay on the floor, still and eerily silent.

Everyone was impacted, all at once.

Everyone but Cal.

For a brief moment, he thought they were all dying. Some horrible plague had hit, wiping out the Syns—maybe it was God exacting vengeance, or maybe their unnatural systems finally failed them—and they were being wiped out. Order would be restored. Cal would be free.

But then he realized: *Ever*.

If all Syns were dead, that included her.

No no no no.

He dropped to his knees, concern coursing through him. These Syns weren't Ever, but he still felt a sudden need to do something, to make sure they were alive. Remembering Ever made him remember that these Syns, too, were people—not his people, but people nonetheless.

He went to the woman first, since she seemed the closest to death. But when he placed his cheek near her open mouth, he could feel that she was breathing; when he placed his fingers to her neck, he felt the quiver of her pulse.

And then something shifted. Even Cal felt it.

The woman opened her eyes and blinked, though she still said nothing. Her husband managed a decipherable "the… hell." Trent slowly pushed himself up into a seated position, shoulders shuddering, jaw working mechanically, making him look like a cow chewing rotten cud against its will.

"Is everyone… all right?" Cal asks.

"No," Trent wheezes. "Yes. I don't know."

"What the hell was that—?"

"I don't know," Trent says again, then vomits violently all over himself.

"Heaven and hell, man," Cal says, scooting away from him.

The other Syn man, whose name Cal still doesn't know, crawls slowly over to the woman.

"June," he says. "Junebug. You okay?"

June blinks, and holds completely still.

"If I move it might hurt."

"It won't," the man tells her. "Whatever it was, it's over."

"How do you know?" she says, and a tear slips down her cheek, and she does not move.

He doesn't know. So he sits there, and in a tender move which Cal finds surprising, the man simply takes the woman's hand and they both hold still in silence. They wince when, to the left of them, Trent vomits again.

CHAPTER 25: EVER

A S EVER MOVES FROM LYING on the ground to an upright-seated position, she feels lightheaded. Reaching up to hold her head, her finger lands wetly into something warm and sticky, running down the side of her face. Blood.

Something moves beneath the blood, slipping and hanging, blood rushing around it like a stream flowing around a fallen log. But this is not something hard like a log, it is pliable and soft and when she pushes at it with her finger she screams and nearly passes out.

It is a strip of her own flesh, hanging from her torn face.

Willing herself not to faint, Ever looks up. Directly above her is the sharp corner of the table where she had been sitting when— when what? What even happened? There had been the sound, the stabbing pain, and then—

And then a memory, oh God oh hell oh dammit, there was a memory, some flash of something from before, from everything dark in my brain now, from before the stroke... what was it I remembered?

For a moment, because this is more important than pain, Ever's mind goes chasing after the almost-memory, the lost and found item that suddenly surfaced. Then she blinks, and even this small movement jostles her face, and she screams and kicks the floor and hates herself and the world and everyone in it.

Behind her, a door hisses open, oddly slow and loud, as if it is a great effort for the door; as if it, too, is still in some sort of shock.

"Ever?"

Ever tries to turn and can't, not without cascading more blood down her face. She opens her mouth to speak, tasting salt and acid.

"Mmmm... here."

Marti comes in to view. She is dazed, walking haphazardly, her hair mussed and her eyes bleary, but she seems otherwise uninjured. Seeing Ever, her eyes widen.

"Your face..."

The fear and revulsion reflected in Marti's eyes tells Ever more than she wanted to know.

"I... fell..."

"Yes—shit—these   stupid   tables—Jesus," Marti says, shuddering.

"What... was..."

"I don't know," Marti says. "But whatever it was—it was powerful. I was with two other people, and they all—we all—it hit every single one of us. But it wasn't an earthquake or anything, it felt like it was... oh, my God, Ever. We have to get you to a doctor."

"I can't—get up."

Ever knows if she tries to rise she will fail and fall. If she stops holding on to her face, that too might fail and fall. She will sit here even if it means dying here. She can't get up.

"I'll help you," Marti says.

Ever instinctively shakes her head, then cries out at the bursting fireworks of agony set off by that small movement.

"NO!"

"It's okay," Marti soothes, dropping her voice as if Ever were a small child or a wounded bird. "I'm going to gently, gently help you up—"

"No no no—"

"Shhh, it's all right, we have to get you some help—"

"Please," Ever whispers, tears intermingling with the sticky red rivers running down her cheeks. "Please, no."

Marti bends down, and Ever can smell her sweat. Though she is not bruised or bleeding, Marti is still weak and shaking.

She can't hold me. She's not strong enough. We'll both fall—

But before Ever can offer further protest, Marti wraps her arms around Ever's waist. Pulling her toward her, almost as if in an embrace. Her mouth beside Ever's ear, she whispers, soft but firm: "We're going to get up now. You can scream if you need to. But don't fight me. We have to do this, now. Now—"

Marti pulls them both to their feet, and Ever screams and screams until fireworks become blackness, and she slumps against Marti, and then there is nothing.

CHAPTER 26: MARILYN

MARILYN DRAGS HERSELF UP FROM THE BATHROOM FLOOR. Clutching the sink, she is relieved to see that she has no scrapes or contusions.

Heaven and hell, did I have a stroke?

At first this thought is terrifying, but then it shifts, and something slips into place. When Ever had a stroke, it was not without its costs. But it also purchased her something priceless, however briefly: Felix's attention.

If Marilyn had indeed suffered a similar traumatic episode, perhaps Felix would express similar concern. Marilyn chews her

lip thoughtfully. It was oddly pleasant to picture herself conva-
lescing in bed, attended to, worried and fussed over as she was in
her childhood.

And if she wound up dying, even better. They would wail at
her funeral, sing her praises. It would be a story to truly rock the
daily uploads—the malady and death of the first lady of the Syn
world.

She knows this is a juvenile game. The funeral fantasy was not
something a woman who had lived for nearly a century should
still be entertaining. So cliché: *if I died and they all came with their
black umbrellas and regrets, oh, they'd miss me then!*

But it's still appealing.

She embraces the notion that something is amiss within her.
She will be patient and quiet, wait it out, until it's something to be
announced and addressed. Until attention must be paid to her, by
everyone, including her very own husband.

When she smiles at herself in the mirror, there is blood on her
teeth.

Marilyn stares at it for a moment, red on white, more proof
that something happened to her. She opens her mouth wide,
trying to locate a cut on her gums or some other source of the
bleeding. She finds nothing. She rubs the blood from her teeth
with her finger, enjoying the squeaking sound it makes.

Something is broken in me, she thinks, *and soon, they'll all see it.*

With that, Marilyn opens the bathroom door and sees Angela
on the floor in the hallway, eyes open and staring, still convulsing
with the aftershocks of whatever had happened.

Whatever had happened to *both* of them.

Not just to Marilyn.

Dammit.

"IS HE ALL RIGHT?"

"I don't know."

"He's moving a little—"

"Don't touch him!"

"Do you think he can hear us?"

I can hear you, Jorge tries to say.

But the words remain in his head, never reaching his lips. He can't talk. Can't move. He is only just beginning to realize that he is in the dark, and that it's because his eyes are closed. So he focuses on that small task first, dragging his lids up with effort. The faces peering down at him are young, one paler, one darker, barely familiar. He cannot immediately place them.

"He's awake!"

"Thank God."

"Jorge. How do you feel? Can you talk?"

"Rrrmfn," Jorge mumbles. He clenches and unclenches his jaw, stills his mind and steels his nerve. He is at war with his own body, his arms and legs and tongue all rebelling, all resisting. Each word is a battle he must win. Conquering syllables one by one, exhaling hard, he wrestles them into submission: "What… happ…"

"We did as you said," says the girl. "Faking Ere's death, all if it. And then—"

"Then you were on your Chariot," the boy jumps in.

"You said everything was great, just like in the moving."

"Movies," Jorge corrects weakly. "Just like… in the *movies*."

His mind is beginning to creep closer to normalcy, as he remembers the names of these young Originals. Karma, also called Asavari. Ere, the last of the Fells. Jorge begins to remember where he is, the reason for his sojourn, the urgency. He tries to stand up, finding, oddly, that the movement begins in his shoulders, and also stops there.

"Don't try to get up," says another voice, an older voice, from behind him. Rolling his eyes up to try to see her, he squints against the harsh sun. But he recognizes the older woman. She presses a small, firm hand to his neck, checking his pulse. "It was a very bad fall. I'm a doctor. Let me do at least a quick assessment before you attempt further movement."

"No… time," Jorge pants, beginning to panic.

Still flat on his back, he realizes he has not been in private mode for any of this. He is exposing them all, he should have checked in by now, Hess would almost certainly attempt to find and retrieve him. Or retrieve his memory log, at the very least. An uninvited remote access attempt from this far would be difficult, but not impossible. He attempts to shift into private mode now, and finds he cannot, which only agitates him further.

Sweat pours down his face and he tries to make them understand: "Too... dangerous..."

"You doing anything other than holding still until I've examined you is too dangerous," snaps the woman claiming to be a doctor. "We need to rule out a spinal cord injury, check for signs of brain trauma—Asavari, bring me my bag."

Jorge wants to protest but feels so tired. Against his will, his lids drop like a curtain over his eyes, darkening the world again. And then the darkness lights up behind his eyelids, bright electric flares displaying a rare system-wide alert.

System-wide alerts were almost unheard of; few situations warranted sending an unscheduled message to the entire Syn population. Everyone already got daily updates whenever they plugged in to Heaven. A system-wide alert meant that this was something everyone had to know, *now*.

> **Source of electric pulse as yet undetermined.**
> **Teams working around the clock to identify and prevent.**
> **No fatalities and minimal core system damage sustained.**
> **No aftershocks anticipated. Plug in to Heaven tonight as usual.**
> **Loss of up to 24 hours of synthetic memories and files appears to be a common occurrence. Do not send additional individual support requests. Updates and patches will be shared as they become available.**
> **[End Council Alert]**

"Holy hell," Jorge says aloud, the shock propelling his speech back into an almost normal pace. "Someone's attacking the Syns."

CHAPTER 28: KENNEDY

*S*OMETHING'S BURNING.

Kennedy exhales sharply, pushing the acrid smell from his nostrils. He opens his eyes, trying to place where the hell he is right now. The room he's in is familiar but unrecognizable, like a child's drawing of a scene, brashly simple but somehow obscured. Comprehension starts to come in here and there, in bruised and broken pieces, bits of information wafting in on the fumes of whatever is burning.

Metal. Screens. Air masks. Seats. There—a window; through it, a wing.

I'm on an aircraft. Oh shit. Shit! Did we crash?

The engine is silent, and the plane is tilted at a slight angle. Balancing on something? Kennedy tries to stand, and gets an intense sense of vertigo, falling down before he is even inches from the floor. He thinks at first it might be just his lightheadedness, possibly from a head injury or just from general disorientation— but as he looks around and takes in the surrounding scene, he realizes the angular position of the plane is more intense than he initially comprehended. The aircraft is almost completely sideways, and he is laying not on the ground but against a windowed wall of the plane.

Instead of standing straight up, he gingerly pushes himself sideways, away from the wall, tipping out, stumbling, finding footing, and at last carefully standing upright, the side-and-ceiling of the aircraft now serving as the floor.

He tries to remember who all was on board with him. There was probably Shai, captaining this thing—a pain the ass, but a tough woman and a good pilot. She wouldn't have just crashed for no reason. There had to have been a mechanical failure.

Or some sort of attack?

Heaven and hell…

"Shai?" He whispers, not sure why he's keeping his voice down. He is afraid to move too much or too fast, to make too much noise. He might tip the balance of the already off-kilter aircraft. He might alert an enemy, if this had indeed been an attack.

"Here."

He turns at the sound and sees Shai, dazed, still seated and strapped into her pilot's chair, which now juts out at an odd horizontal angle, suspending her instead of cradling her. She looks at Kennedy, her eyes question marks.

"What the hell happened?" Kennedy asks.

"There was… some sort of sound," she says.

"Yes—like a beep, then a scream…" Kennedy says. "And then?"

"Then it felt like my head got chopped with a meat cleaver."

"Yes," Kennedy agrees.

"I mean, really. *With a meat cleaver.* Is my head split open?"

"Yeah," Kennedy says, and then: "I mean, no. No, your head's still—closed." And then, after a sharp inhale: "Hey. Do you smell something burning?"

She breathes in. "Yeah, but I don't think it's us. Something nearby, though…"

"Ungggh," grunts one of the heavies.

That's right—we brought muscle along for this trip. Why? Something to do with Jorge?

Kennedy's recent memories feel patchy and partial. He didn't know these bodyguards well before this trip; he thinks this guy's name is Marco, or maybe Beau. They've both worked security for the Synt for over a decade, but Kennedy never could keep their names straight.

"You okay there…?" Kennedy asks, not wanting to be a complete jackass.

"Crap in a barrel," comes a rough-voiced reply from the other guy. Beau, or Marco.

Both of them are stirring now, rubbing their beefy heads, blinking watery eyes. Kennedy is uncertain as to whether the crap-in-a-barrel expletive was a description of how the guy felt or an imperative *go-screw-yourself* command in response to Kennedy's inquiry. Either way, proof of life. So at least Kennedy won't catch hell for letting one of the crew members die on his watch.

About then, the system-wide alert comes through. As they each process it, their confusion increases, and they begin muttering more to themselves than one another as they try to make sense of this update.

"Electrical pulse? The hell does that mean…?"

"Stop sending requests? Who's already sent any in? How long were we out?"

"I'm going to message Hess," Kennedy finally says, a little louder than all the other mumbling. "See what I can find out." Then he stops, considers. "Hey—Shai. Before I do that. Do you think you can assess… I mean, can I get some sort of status report on, uh, us? Our aircraft? Are we stuck here, or do you think maybe—"

"Jesus," Shai says, unsnapping her safety belt and half-tumbling, half jumping from the seat. "Yeah. Give me a minute."

She steadies herself. Then, sending her shoulders back, she squats down and looks up, trying to get the right angle on her controls so she can see what… well, whatever pilots are supposed to see. Hell if Kennedy knows.

"So, how long will it take you to—"

"Dude," grunts Marco or Beau, from behind Kennedy. "If you don't shut up, she's gonna kick your ass."

"We're not too bad off," Shai finally says, wiping her brow. "We definitely crashed, I guess because of that pulse-whatever. Looks like it hit us and our tech. The nav system crashed, so we crashed, but looks like we're not too damaged. We were flying low, and I've got the exterior cameras back up, so I can safely say we landed in some trees. Don't all walk east side at once, or we're gonna fall another several yards down."

Kennedy is relieved that his augmented system can always show him east without him having to ask. There are some advantages to being a Syn. Relief floods him as he takes one small step west within the plane.

"Good! That's good."

"Yeah. But also, y'know the burning smell?"

"Yeah?"

"It's the trees."

This takes a moment to sink in.

"So, we're in a tree—trees—that are on fire."

"Yes."

"So whether or not we walk east—"

"We're going to fall again pretty soon, unless we take off before too many of the branches holding us up get, you know, burned away. We're on a giant pile of tinder."

"Can we… take off, then?"

Shai's hands fly up to her eyes, massaging them in their sockets, as if she is trying to push them back in a little. Like they were about to pop right out.

"Soon as my head stops with the pounding, I think I can get us out of here. It'll be hell on the paint job, but we'll be all right."

"What about the Vost?" Beau or Marco asks.

"Yeah," echoes Marco or Beau.

They're both big guys, both swarthy. Both still a little uneasy on their feet, but feeling with-it enough to remember their mission, which Kennedy had almost forgotten. They were here to do a job, dammit.

"Right—crap," Kennedy says. "Let me see if I can find him."

He tries to do a scan of the area, just a basic sweep using his own internal system and the tracking information Hess had provided. Nothing. His command seems to short out right after starting. Some lingering impact from the whatever-the-hell-pulse-thing.

"You getting anything?"

"Not from the general scan, no," Kennedy says, irritated. "Call up the log, let's get the coordinates for the last place we saw him, see how far we are from that. This thing must've gotten him, too, so he can't be too far away. Shai, can you—"

"System's back online, yeah," Shai says from her askew-but-functioning position at the helm. "But bad news."

"New bad news?"

"New bad news," she confirms. "Our log is gone. I mean, gone-gone. There's nothing from this trip. Whole past day is just—gone."

"We'll upload from our memories, then. Between the four of us, we should be able to—"

"I've got nothing," Shai says, shaking her head. "I mean, fragments here and there of the incident, and I can remember the past day, but I think it's just my organic memories. When I go to my synthetic files—nada."

"Me too," says Beau or Marco.

"Same here," says Marco of Beau.

Kennedy checks his own files and swears. "Damn. That's weird."

"Can't upload organic memories, so… that's one day gone," Shai says. "I don't think we're finding your Vost buddy."

"Let's just head back for the Synt," Kennedy says. "We don't know how much deep system damage this ship—or we—might have sustained in the pulse thing. Let's go back to HQ, re-group, pinpoint Jorge's location and then we'll just… take it from there."

"You're sure?"

No, Kennedy thinks.

"Yep," he says unconvincingly.

CHAPTER 29: ASAVARI

ASAVARI DOESN'T WANT JORGE TO LEAVE. An
hour ago he was catatonic. How could he now be ready
for cross-continental travel? But even as she tells herself
she's worried for his sake, her larger concern is for the movement.
When he leaves, the old guard will get scared, and tell Asavari to
wait, be patient, make sure everything is quiet and safe before they
take action. The very thought of lost momentum makes Asavari
want to retch.

After Preeti finished examining Jorge and found nothing
wrong with his organic systems, Jorge asked for some privacy.
He didn't want everyone staring as he pushed his way through

the pain. The crowd respectfully dispersed, but Asavari refused. She insisted that he needed someone nearby just in case anything happened. She watched as he dragged himself from a flat-back position to a seated one, and then to his knees, and finally to his feet. She did not look away when he vomited after his first attempt to stand. She simply gave him a rag for his face, which he accepted, and a hand to assist him, which he did not.

"You can let me help you," she says softly.

"You can help me take down the Syns," he replies, each word slow and staccato, obviously painful. "But I can get my own... ass... up."

He stands, swaying but stubborn. All on his own.

If Asavari were interested in men, she would find this one very attractive.

"Now," Jorge says. "Whatever this was—the pulse-thing that slammed into every synthetic citizen... well, the whole missing-memory thing is a definite silver lining, as far as covering my tracks. But I probably lost the footage of Ere's little death scene. I'll have to come up with some other story to—"

He stops suddenly, eyes widening as a thought occurs to him.

"What?" Asavari asks.

"Yes yes yes," he says, to himself. "That could work. That could work."

"What could work?"

"Go get Ere."

Huffing a little, Asavari runs to find the stupid Fell boy.

"Ere. Jorge needs to see you."

"I thought he was puking and didn't want me to watch."

"Something else is going on now."

"What? Diarrhea? I don't want to watch that either—"

"Get. Up."

Stuffing the last of a piece of naan into his mouth, Ere rubs his hands together to disperse any wayward crumbs, then rises, unhurried, and ambles behind Asavari as she stalks back to Jorge.

"Ere, I have a plan," Jorge says.

"Does it involve stabbing me?"

"No."

"Faking my death?"

"Yes, but not as… actively."

"Just *tell* us," Asavari says, patience gone.

"You're going to lay down and play dead," Jorge says to Ere. "And I'm going to tell Hess that he killed you."

"That he… killed me?"

"Yes. That by putting that tracker in your arm… he connected you into our system, and when the pulse happened, since it got us and our tech—it impacted you. And you had no augmented system to absorb the shock. So it stopped your heart. And you died."

"That is… brilliant," Asavari says, genuinely impressed with this idea.

"Wait," Ere says, looking somewhat less thrilled. "Are you saying… if that tracker thing had still been in my arm, I might have died…?"

"It's entirely possible," Jorge says. "Good thing I stabbed you."

Asavari expects Ere to glare, but instead, he rolls his eyes and smiles. Actually *smiles*. It is as if these two have somehow made it to the other side of a bridge that Asavari was never able to cross with Ere, and now they are compatriots. Bonded by blood and their respective infuriating near-death (or fake-death) experiences. It makes her want to strangle the both of them, these men, so pleased with themselves. But she has to admit that the plan is solid. And she will do anything for the resistance. Even put up with these self-congratulatory bastards.

Ere sits down on the ground, then eases himself onto his back. His shirt is streaked with the fake blood that soaked through the fabric earlier, so Jorge suggests he lay more to his side, to hide the bloody first-fake-death evidence. Ere twists and shifts, trying to hide his shirt and also his bandaged arm. He's not very good at figuring out the best way to do this, so when she can stand it no longer Asavari walks over, shoves his arm under his torso (he winces, but says nothing), rolls his body over his arm, turns his head so his neck is at an almost-broken angle, stretches out his legs, then steps back to admire her handiwork.

"That looks good," Jorge says to her approvingly.

She simply nods.

For several long moments, Ere lays silently, looking very much like a cadaver. Finally, he says in a half-whisper: "Um… how much longer do I have to—"

"Oh, you can get up anytime you need to," Jorge says casually. "I got the image I needed as soon as she stepped out of the frame. I was just wondering how long you could hold that strange twisted-position before you started cramping up."

"Jackass," mutters Ere, and begins untwisting himself.

Jorge winks at Asavari, and in spite of herself, she laughs. He's brought her in on the joke. It doesn't just have to be the boys' club. And if the serious Vost can take a moment to tease, to give Ere a hard time and to invite Asavari to laugh with him, he must be optimistic about their prospects. Asavari knows the danger of too much hope, but it is ballooning within her now.

This is going to happen.

We are going to rise again.

The resistance will be—

"Vari Vari Vari VARI!"

Asavari, Jorge, and Ere all turn at the sound. Laghun, one of Asavari's young cousins, is running toward them at breakneck speed. The small boy's brow is frothy with sweat, and he is panting so hard that he can barely speak.

"What is it, Laghun?"

"In… in the… in the trees…" He points in the direction from which he came. The trees to which he is referring are so far off that they seem almost an optical illusion, a desert hallucination shimmering at them across the largely barren horizon. "Something…. Big. Ship or something. Syns…"

"Get down," Jorge says, sharp and commanding. "All of you, on the ground, NOW."

Ere, Asavari and little Laghun flatten themselves against the earth. Jorge leaps onto his Chariot and kicks it into high gear, soaring almost straight up. He smacks at the console. Asavari cranes her neck and tries to see him as best she can, wishing she knew what he was able to see from that vantage point.

Jorge swoops down, hovering in his craft just above them. When he speaks, it is low—just loud enough for them to hear him above the soft hum of his vehicle.

"The kid's right," Jorge says, speaking quickly and with no room for interruption. "It's a Synt ship. Which means Hess sent a team out. Which means he was suspicious of me. I can no longer be your primary point of contact. I have to go—now. And so do you. Go underground. Lay low until you get word. It won't be from me, but I'll make sure that whoever contacts you is someone you can trust. Be careful. This isn't good."

"But you're not recovered enough to go, you could die—" Asavari protests, but Jorge cuts her off.

"You'll all die if I stay," he says. "Listen: I'll fly back on this Chariot. I came in on another ship—large enough to transport several people when the time comes. It's in stealth mode, so it should not lead anyone to you, and on my way out of here I'll disconnect it from the Synt fleet. But it'll fly. It's three miles due west of here. When you board, set the navigation system to home and it will take you straight into the Synt. But do not go to the ship until you get word from my contact."

"Who is your contact?" Asavari asks.

"I'll have to figure that out," Jorge says, and zips away on his Chariot.

CHAPTER 30: ERE

ERE SHOULD HAVE BEEN FURIOUS to learn that Syn tech had been living under his skin for weeks without him knowing. But more than anything, he's intrigued. He was always told that any concession to synthetic augmentations would fundamentally change him, would erode him, would erase the real Original human he had been before the technological invasion. But he had this tech buried within him, and it had changed nothing.

He was still just Ere, frustrated by the same things, feeling the same feelings, still himself. It was only a tiny piece of tech, not a full augmentation—but still. Maybe Syn tech wasn't as evil as his elders always told him it was. That very interesting revelation makes him all the more eager to get back to Ever, and see what their future might hold. So to everyone's astonishment, Ere asks Preeti to assemble the tribe.

Ere Fell, son of Ruth, has a proposal for the next step in the Original revolution.

No word had yet come from Jorge's contact, but after three days, Ere can wait no longer. All he has to do is convince everyone else that waiting is unacceptable. Should be easy enough; Asavari is itching for action, for one. So when the crowd assembles, Ere is ready to make his case with confidence.

"Something is attacking the Syns," Ere says, casting his eyes from face to face. "That means that they're vulnerable, maybe for the first time in my lifetime. If ever there was a chink in their armor, this is it. We need to make our move. The time is now."

Everyone is nodding along, agreeing, fearful but hungry for his words, hungry for a vision, a mission, an immediate plan.

Everyone but Asavari.

"No," she says flatly, stepping forward from the crowd, facing off with Ere. "I agree with you—mostly—but our informant was very clear with us before he departed. He will send word when it is safe for us to advance. If we move now, we will give away our position. Put him in jeopardy. We risk everything, when we might be so close to everything aligning for us to win. Going now would be foolish."

The crowd murmurs, some in agreement, others whispering irritation at her pessimism.

"And what if something has already happened to Jorge?" Ere cries, loud. "He tried to go back all that way on the small Chariot, leaving us the ship. He was still not fully recovered. He could have had trouble getting back, or been apprehended upon arrival. A thousand things could have happened to prevent him from reaching some other contact who will send word our way. Are we supposed to sit around and wait forever on a message that might never come? Or should we go with what we know, and strike while the iron is hot?"

"Ere Fell is right!" shouts a voice from the back of the crowd.

"We can't wait forever!" another agrees.

The winds have shifted back to Ere, and he smiles at the assembly before him, feeling powerful and righteous. He has almost forgotten that his motives are not rebellion, but Ever Hess. He is riding the wave of adoration, feeling noble, if only for a moment. He is a man of the people. A leader.

"Ere—" Asavari protests, but Ere raises a hand again, simultaneously silencing her and inviting her, like a practice politician. Stretching his fingers toward her, he offers her words he knows will resonate.

"Asavari, this is your mission. Don't you want to take back what's ours?"

The crowd quiets, waiting for the girl they know so well to respond to the boy they never expected. Asavari's face is a strong and sweeping plane, with clouds rolling in and out, her expression unreadable.

Ere's confidence slips slightly. If she turns him down, he might be screwed. He probably can't get back to Central City without her. And the others may abandon him if she really does walk away. He needs her.

"All right," she says, though her eyes are hard and dark. "I am with you, Ere Fell."

She takes his hand, clasping it with a violent strength. He winces.

The crowd cheers. There is a sudden rush forward, people hugging Asavari, clapping Ere on the back, hurrying to share their strategic suggestions and their offers to go or stay or help however they can. They are ready. They are eager. They are with him.

With each face-to-face exuberant encounter, Ere's self-righteousness melts away a little, as he recalls that he is not actually going to follow through on what he is promising them. A guilt begins to gnaw at his conscience, chewing its way in and becoming something irremovable. He feels guilty for misleading them.

Guilty for being so good at it, and guiltier still for using his mother's name in this cause. For using his family's legacy. A Fell asking Original people to take up the cause is a powerful thing. He can see it shining in their eyes. They are eager to follow him. They believe that he is a harbinger and hero who will see them through to victory.

But shame be damned. Regret be damned. Rebellion be damned. He slips his hand into his pocket and feels the cold certainty of the little silver gun hidden there. He's finally on his way back to the girl who gave him the weapon.

CHAPTER 31: EVER

S HE CAN FEEL THE SCAR ON HER FACE. She is aware of it every moment, all the time. But she hasn't been able to make herself look at it yet.

The electrical event, which everyone has taken to simply calling "the Pulse," brought all Synthetic citizens to their knees. Emergency responders were all delayed, even for Hess's own daughter. Medical procedures and synthetic repairs post-Pulse were scheduled in order of urgency. Elective surgeries would not be available for weeks yet.

And so her scar has healed and hardened, altering the once-smooth landscape of her famously flawless face. Ever knows that even with surgery, she will never be the same. There will either be a jagged scar or its faint white shadow; without a complete re-contouring of her entire face, there will always be evidence of the trauma. Damage so severe cannot be easily erased.

She can feel it without touching it. The scar is a living thing, slithering into Ever's pulse and claiming it as its own throbbing heartbeat. Though she has never seen her scar, she knows the shape and weight and volume of it.

But today, Ever needs to know more. She needs to see it.

At Ever's request, Angela had draped a dark cloth across the mirror, pinning it to the wall above the long reflective glass. The cloth has been Ever's guardian, allowing her to brush her teeth and relieve herself without risking a glimpse of her injury. Hands shaking, Ever reaches up, rising to her toes, and pulls at the top right corner of the makeshift curtain. The fabric folds, but slips only slightly. She pulls out the next pin and the weight of the freed fabric pulls itself down, and there she is, caught in the glass.

She is captivated at the visage. The scar screams for all attention, leaving every other detail of her face diminutive by contrast. Her eyes seem smaller, her chin recessed. All of her features kowtow to the almighty scar.

It runs almost the entirety of the right side of her face, beginning just below her right eye and snaking cruelly from there all the way down her cheek, curving and finishing itself at the edge of her lip. Its red and angry origins are melting now, purpling and giving way to sharp white tightened edges. There is no minimizing it, no looking away from it. Her countenance is now the scar's sovereign land.

I'm ugly.

Ever has never thought this before. Not as a child, not as an adolescent, certainly not as an augmented almost-eighteen-year-old kept perpetually fresh and appealing. She tries to remember how the world treats ugly people. How *she* had once treated them. Her stomach turns.

I never want anyone to see me, ever again.

Slowly, Ever crawls up onto the countertop of the bathroom, beside the sink. She is so close to the mirror now that her nose very nearly touches the glass. Her real scar and the reflection of it are almost overlapping. Keeping her eyes locked on her eyes, forbidding them to drift toward the interloper on her face, Ever reaches for the fabric, and covers the mirror again. The soft black fabric is all she sees now, lowering her head with relief after replacing the final pin.

Now she knows.

"Ever? You okay in there, honey?"

"No," Ever whispers, and then says louder, for Angela to hear: "Yeah. I'm fine."

"You got a visitor."

"I don't want to see anyone."

"It's Marti."

At this, Ever reconsiders. She still doesn't want to see anyone ever again, but Marti is the one who found her. She saw Ever's face when it was even more frightening than it is now. She might have an even uglier memory of Ever, a bloody mess of half-gone face— and that's not how Ever wants to be seen, either. So she relents, and feels a drop of relief land in her swirling sea of self-pity. A life spent conversing only with her mother and the housekeeper would be torture.

"…all right. Give me a minute."

Ever considers taking the cloth down again, fixing her hair and trying to make herself somewhat presentable. But she knows if the cloth is down, the scar will cajole her into looking at it, and once she does, it will cast its Medusa spell. She will become stone, fixed and frozen. So she leaves the mirror covered, runs a tooth-brush across her teeth, and steps out of the bathroom.

Ever prepares herself for Marti's look of horror when she sees Ever's face. Even Angela had been unable to hide the alarm in her eyes when she saw Ever post-surgery, and little fazed that woman.

When Ever enters the living room, Marti is sitting on the couch, sipping a hot tea provided by Angela. She is wearing a blazer and slim dark pants. She looks professional and casual, if a little out of place sitting in the Hess's elaborately decorated Southern-gauche living room—a room decorated by Marilyn and abhorred by Felix. At Ever's arrival, Marti looks up—and smiles. Her expression is not one of disgust, but of genuine relief.

"Ever," Marti says, setting down her tea on the coffee table. "It's so good to see you up and about. How are you feeling? You look great. Seriously."

"I don't."

"Last time I saw you, it looked like half your face was gone. This is nothing."

"It's not nothing."

"Fine, it's not nothing," Marti says, giving Ever one of her trademark curt nods. "But it's not the worst thing I've ever seen. And the scar will keep fading. And you can get it removed later, or at least reduced to—"

"What if I can't?"

Marti shrugs. She starts to offer more words, then decides to show rather than tell, and rolls up the soft dark pant leg of her slacks. Ever gasps at what she sees—Marti's leg is a patchwork of quilted flesh, varying shades, a range of textures creating an uneven topography of flesh, taut and haphazard.

"Burn," Marti says simply. "When I was thirteen. On a camping trip. I was stomping out a fire and wasn't paying attention and was wearing apparently highly-flammable polyester pants, and the next thing I knew—no more shorts for the rest of my life. But turns out the rest of our life is a really long time. A really, really long time. So now I wear shorts, because screw it."

"I've never seen you in shorts."

"It's cold at the Synt. And it's seriously cold in here—I mean Jesus, this place is like a polar bear's butthole. Is your mother menopausal or something? I thought we got rid of that condition."

Ever giggles, then swiftly swallows the insultingly carefree sound. She is not yet prepared to stop wallowing. It's only been a week. She only just looked at the scar. She wants to dig in her heels and mope. She wants to reject the world. She can't let go of her misery, just like that.

"At least you can hide the burn scars. This is right out there on my face."

Marti gives her a look that is unsympathetic without being cruel.

"It's not as bad as you think it is."

"Yes. It is. I just saw it."

"You were just looking at your scar. You weren't looking at your face."

"Same thing."

"No, it's not."

Marti rolls down her pant leg, covering her scarred leg. She stands up, and takes off her jacket, then rolls up the sleeve of her shirt. Her arm, too, is patchy with scars, though not nearly so bad as her leg.

"Heaven and hell," Ever says, exhaling sharply.

Marti nods.

"I tried to take the pants off, when they caught fire. Earned myself a little memento here, too. I used to look at my arm and leg and just see the burns. Now, the burns are there—but I see an arm. And a leg. And mostly I try not to just stare at myself. It's not useful."

"Did you come to show me your scars?"

"I came to check on you. But it seemed like this might be useful."

"There are lots of cosmetic options available for… burns like those. Why didn't you get any work done after you augmented?"

"By the time I augmented, I'd lived with these scars for the majority of my life. Keeping them meant keeping a part of me. For me… becoming a Syn didn't mean that I would stop being myself. So the scars stayed."

Ever nods, appreciating the authenticity of this logic—although not quite understanding why Marti would want to hold on to these scars, and the memory that caused them. Why not lessen the trauma by getting rid of its evidence?

"When you got the burns… did it hurt?" Ever asks.

"Hurt like hell. What a stupid question."

"I thought there were no stupid questions."

"Seriously?" Marti raises an eyebrow. "I hate to break it to you, but 'did it hurt when a campfire roasted you like a marshmallow?' is actually a pretty stupid question."

At this, Ever bursts out laughing. Wildly inappropriate funeral laughter—and Marti joins in. As her giggles subside, Ever aims a teasing question at Marti.

"So you voluntarily wore *polyester pants?*"

"What can I say. It was the nineties, pants thought it was the seventies," Marti cracks. Then she turns serious. "I want you to come back to work."

Ever's stomach clenches, and she feels the scar throb, scolding her for almost forgetting that everything is not all right. With each pulse the scar reminds her: *you're ugly, you're ugly, you-are-ug-lee.*

"I can't."

"Of course you can. And I'm short-staffed because some of our team has been pulled to work on Pulse stuff. I want you back on Monday."

"It's Sunday."

"That's right. I expect to see you tomorrow."

"I don't want anyone to see me."

"It'll just be us in there, at least this week. We won't do anything with other teams, to ease you back in. But Ever… you'll change your mind. And maybe you'll have another surgery, and maybe not. Either way, that scar will fade. Trust me."

Angela walks in, carrying a silver tray with more of Marilyn's porcelain on proud display. A teapot, several more cups, rose-adorned little homes for sugar and cream and sliced lemons.

"Marti, can I refresh your tea? Ever, you thirsty, honey?"

"Thanks—Angela, was it?—but I've got to get going," Marti says, rising quickly. "I'm actually late for a quick meeting. But Ever, I'm glad you're recovering well, and I look forward to seeing you tomorrow."

"Let me walk you to the—" Angela begins, but Marti waves her away.

"You've got your hands full. I can see myself out."

With a final little nod to Ever, Marti leaves. Angela carries the platter of tea accoutrements to the coffee table and sets it down, then eases herself onto the couch and pours herself a cup of chamomile.

"You want to have some tea with me?" Angela asks, squeezing a lemon into the teacup.

"No, I'm good."

"You really going back to work tomorrow?"

"We'll see."

Angela sits on the couch, and notices something to her left. She lifts it up, looking at it.

"What's this…? Did your friend leave her jacket?"

Ever looks over at Marti's blazer. Something at the edge of the fabric glints. Marti's identification card. With her Heaven credentials.

"I'll take it," Ever says quickly, lunging forward and grabbing for the blazer, very nearly knocking over the tea tray.

"Careful," Angela chides, leaning out of her way, letting go of the garment. "You gonna run, go try to grab her now?"

"No, she—said she had a meeting, so—I'll send her a message," Ever says quickly. "See if she wants me to meet her somewhere, or if I can just bring it to her at work tomorrow."

"So you *are* going to go to work tomorrow," Angela says, smiling maternally at Ever.

"Well anyway," Ever says, backing out of the room, clutching the blazer to her chest. "Thanks, for letting Marti in and making the tea and—everything. I'm going to send her a message and then go lie down... I'm tired."

"Sure, baby," Angela says, stirring her tea.

Ever practically runs down the hallway, securing the door behind her when she reaches her bedroom. Holding the blazer at arm's length, she carefully pulls the gleaming identification card from the lapel, holding it in her arms and staring at Marti's name and title.

MARTHA MANUEL
Level Four Application Developer

Especially with their solidified connection today, Marti is the last person Ever should betray. But even while wallowing and moping about her scar, Ever hasn't forgotten about the Original man. Cal. And having level four credentials might actually allow her to find out where her father is keeping him.

Nervous and unsure if it would even work, or if this card might require a secondary mode of identification, Ever calls up a screen on one of her bedroom walls. Signing out of her own account, she goes to a public records site and calls up the command to sign in a new guest to this location. Then she holds the card up to the wall, and waits for it to scan.

Welcome Martha Manuel

CHAPTER 32: HESS

H ESS WAS WARY OF JORGE when the Vost returned to the Synt.

"Tell me everything," he said, staring into those unsettling golden eyes.

Jorge provided a thorough accounting. An easy flight to India. The tracker had maintained intermittent communication, so Jorge was able to confidently set his course toward the Fell boy. He was apprehending him when the Pulse hit, knocking both of them out.

"It must have been the tracker," Jorge said, shaking his head. "Enough tech to make him susceptible to the Pulse, same as us. And with fewer backup systems. Weak Original structure."

Jorge presented Hess with images of the dead Fell boy, captured through those golden eyes, downloaded directly from Jorge's own memory files, once all systems were back online. But there was no record of the boy's moment of death, since it occurred during the Pulse and was swallowed up in the black hole that ate that day's data.

"Why didn't you bring the body back with you?"

"The ship I took was still offline. I only had the Chariot. Carrying him with me the whole way might have eaten up my fuel too quickly—that's already a helluva long ride over water. But I did bring the tracker with me for verification."

He handed Hess the tracker, cut from the dead kid's flesh. It did appear charred and short-circuited, and when Hess had it tested, the lab confirmed that it was indeed the tracker that had been implanted in Ere Fell. It was verified not only through the tracker's own code, but also via the genetic material still present on the battered piece of tech. Blood. Skin. Sinew. There was no doubt that the gadget had been extracted from Ere's body.

Still. Hess couldn't shake the feeling that the Vost was withholding something.

"Did you know I sent Kennedy after you?"

"At the time, no. But I saw the ship when I was departing. And I put two and two together. So. Didn't trust me to handle the job?"

"I don't trust anyone," Hess said. "You know that."

"Right," was all Jorge said, without protest or apparent insult.

"You've seen Kennedy since getting back?"

"No. I came straight to you."

"Don't confront him about going after you. He was following orders. I can't have any dissent in the ranks. If I bring you back into the lab, you two will work together like nothing happened."

"If? Are you considering not bringing me back?"

Hess gritted his teeth. Jorge was capable, and the Synt was working everyone to the bone. At the very least, having Jorge oversee daily operations would help. And he had no proof of any betrayal. No reason to cut his best player from the team. But Hess didn't get to where he was by ignoring his gut.

"You're on probation the rest of this week," Hess said, no further explanation. "Have you had any internal aftershocks or post-Pulse side effects?"

Jorge shook his head.

"I'm fine. I—I heard Ever was injured in the Pulse. Is she all right?"

"She hit something when she fell," Hess said, irrationally irritated at his employee's polite inquiry as to his daughter's well-being. "Cut up her face. Looks like hell. But she's alive."

After that, with nothing further to review and no desire to discuss the injuries of others, Hess dismissed Jorge.

Since that conversation, he has scanned Jorge's archives over and over. He has double-checked all data available from his ship (which is still offline and unaccounted for), his Chariot, Kennedy's team and their records. His debrief with Kennedy was even less insightful than the one with Jorge. The idiot stammered and sweated, apologized for the lack of information, practically pissed himself.

So things went back to normal, relatively speaking. Jorge returned to work. Kennedy continued cowering. Hess's patience was extinct. Everything was as it had been, except for the Damocles sword dangling over their head. The Pulse. Worse: the chance of another pulse. They still knew little about what the Pulse even was. A surge of electric energy; that's all they had determined so far. Hess believes the only solution is to trace the event back to its source. If they can pinpoint ground zero, determine where it all started, maybe then they can figure out the entire genesis.

Much as Dr. Felix Hess dreads another Pulse, if he ever wants to solve the mystery behind it, that's exactly what he needs. A chance to be more prepared, and document the bastard. So that's what he's planning on, waiting for, anticipating and dreading: A second incident.

They were unprepared for the first, which was a mistake that will not be repeated. Hess has added tertiary backups for all tech, all generators, and all Heaven storage. He is also working furiously on a program that will be triggered by another Pulse, whose only function is to identify the source of the surge. Like a fuse lit at the end of a cartoon bomb, the program will ignite and race back to its initiator. But it will only work if there is another Pulse.

The Council is assembling today, and Hess is on deck to update them on every step he's taken to ensure their future safety. He has received three reminders that he is due with his report at nine. It's 8:58.

"I have a Council meeting," he tells his assistants, blinking off his screen. "Jorge. I want you to go down by the Triboro. Do a manual check of the cameras there. Make sure there's no sign of activity."

"You're worried about a perimeter breach?"

"I don't want to be."

"Yes, sir," Jorge says, and shuts down the screen in front of him. "I'll go now."

As soon as Jorge is out of the room, Kennedy pipes up from behind Hess with a nervous question, very nearly squeaking.

"Do you want me to follow him…?"

"No," Hess says, without further explanation.

CHAPTER 33: CAL

Cal traces his finger along the letters emblazoned on his little silver identification card. While he doesn't like being labeled, this is his first piece of tech and he's somewhat glad to have it. He knows that slim as the card is, it has information imprinted. Swiping it can now get him through doors once closed to him. He knows that his identity is also keyed to this card, that it tags him as the one opening the door. That idea unsettles him.

But it's still a new tool in his arsenal. At some point, he will figure out how to alter this tool and use it for his own purposes. It will take time, but this thin silver tag is already moving him closer to Ever. He's out of the little holding cell. He's walking the halls of the Synt, working with the maintenance team—a team he grudgingly has to admit is full of some pretty nice people.

The maintenance team consists mostly of Vosts. After a few weeks with them, Cal has learned a lot about these sort-of-Syns. He's learned it less from asking questions and more from simply paying attention and picking up on context clues, then researching as much as was allowed on his screen at night.

Before joining this work team, he hadn't realized that there was a second-class citizenry among the Syns. At first, learning about the volunteer synthetic testing program, he couldn't imagine why anyone decided to sign up. Knowing they'd be experimented on. Knowing it might work, might not, and that either way, it would be other people—weak, rich *cowards*—who would be the ones to benefit from the risks taken by the Vosts.

Who would choose to do that?

The more time he spends with the maintenance guys, though, the more he's able to put it together. Very few of them did it out of a sense of adventure, though that had apparently been the marketing approach. They mostly did it to help out their families, or to get out of a desperate situation.

Like Trent, the guy he was out with when the Pulse hit. Trent talked more than the other guys, and the morning of the Pulse, he'd told Cal why he augmented. His aging parents were losing their home, and he wanted to help them but he'd been unemployed for three years—the economy had tanked, everyone was struggling—and the Vost program allowed him to pay off his parents' home, give them a little something for retirement.

Not that it mattered. The rug got pulled out from under them pretty quickly when the Original War began. Their home was burned to the ground. They probably died penniless, around the time money stopped mattering—but Trent had no idea what was to come when he desperately signed up for the "medical testing" his buddy had told him about.

"Oh," said Cal, realizing that as familiar as he was with desperation, he was not the only one. Still, he felt certain he would not have done what they did. Voluntarily selling your soul to synthetic culture was a bridge too far.

Cal begrudgingly began admiring Trent and the rest of the guys he worked with each day. They were decent people. But they were all *guys*; Cal found it strange that the maintenance crew was all men. Certainly women were just as capable of wielding tools and installing charging docks. He asked about it a week into the job, and the team exchanged glances. One of them cleared his throat, and then they all blinked. Something strange happened to their eyes, and a pale guy named Pete stepped forward.

"We all just went into privacy mode, so I'm gonna say this real quick and not worry 'bout sugar-coating it," he said. "All the teams Vosts work on, they're either male or female. It was something they put in place to try to cut down on—you know. Relationships. Not that that was a hundred percent effective." At this, Pete reached out and briefly interlaced fingers with another guy, Brian. "But it was one more way to keep the Vost population from—you know. Repopulating. Kickin' out more Originals. So as a preventative measure, they kept us apart. Until they went ahead and sterilized us all."

"You're... all...?"

The entire maintenance crew nodded. The sharpest sting of embarrassment had faded years before, although it still echoed in their expression.

"Yep," Pete said. "But by the time they got around to that, we all had our, you know—training. So we stayed in our jobs. Which meant we stayed gender-segregated. All right. Now ya know."

They all blinked, went back to their regular settings, went on with their days.

*   *   *   *

"Cal, we're being sent over to the hospital wing," Isaiah says.

Isaiah was assigned to work with Cal while Trent was laid up. The poor bastard still hasn't recovered from the Pulse. Cal wonders how much one person can vomit before they just turn inside out like an emptied pocket.

"What's the call?"

"Toilet issue," Isaiah says with a wry grin. "All backed up."

"Great," mutters Cal.

Cal does not relish the idea of dealing with clogged toilets for the day, but at least he'll be out with Isaiah. He likes Isaiah. The tall, dark-skinned man was kind to Cal from day one, even before they were paired up for making repair calls. He was patient when teaching him basic maintenance tasks, and seemed respectful of his Original status. And although Cal would never say this aloud, Isaiah kind of reminded him of his dad.

Cal had been so small when his father died. Having a guy like Isaiah teach him how to wield an electric screwdriver, how to open up a control panel and check for common wiring issues—there was something paternal about it. And despite the fact that Isaiah looked only a few years older than Cal, he was born sixty-some years earlier. More like a grandfather than a father, actual age-wise.

"Grab the plumbing toolkit. Couple pairs of gloves, each. And the big buckets."

Cal suppresses a groan, already knowing that if he needs gloves that means he's about to be up to his elbows in crap, literally. He wants to ask why, with all their other upgrades and add-ons and whatnots, these people haven't figured out how to avoid having to take a dump—or at least could've found a way to eliminate the odor. *That* would be smart science.

As Cal and Isaiah walk to the awaiting toilets, it's Isaiah's card they use to gain access to the main hall, the elevator, the hospital wing. Cal's card is mostly useless, other than for accessing public halls during business hours, or his own quarters.

It's a long walk to the hospital—all the way on the other side of the campus. The other maintenance guys are always looking for shortcuts, taking elevators and levitators, wanting to get each assignment hammered out as quickly as possible so they can go back and hang out at their office with its well-stocked pantry and endless onscreen entertainment. But Isaiah doesn't rush anything. He goes the long way, enjoys the walk, does his job thoroughly, strolls back. His demeanor seems an acknowledgment of his extra-lifelong sentence.

It's one of the many reasons Cal prefers being paired with Isaiah. Although he wishes they'd been tasked with a landscaping job today, or a carpentry task, or even pest extermination. Anything but the damned toilets. The maintenance crew never knew what they were going to get, though. As Isaiah had explained it to Cal, in the old world there were maintenance specialties—plumbing was one job, landscaping quite another, electrician a vocation all unto itself. But thanks to the quickly downloadable skill-building programs from Heaven, the maintenance team was expected to be able to fix whatever was broken.

Cal didn't have that capability, of course. He couldn't download a program to his internal whatever-it-was and know how to wire a residence within an hour. So he was always the backup guy, handing over tools, learning on the fly.

"Isaiah?"

"Yep."

"If you don't mind my asking… how'd you wind up here?"

"In maintenance?"

"In Central City."

The Vost rubs his stubbled jaw as they turn a corner, walk down another hallway, swiping through another door. "Well, that's a long story."

"Well, I've got time. And you've got even more time."

"That's true, I suppose," Isaiah says. "All right, well. The short version."

"You can tell me the long version."

"Not sure I can," Isaiah says, and Cal gets the feeling that there is a surging underground sea of meaning churning beneath the surface of that statement. "I had a girlfriend. Rosie. She was from the other side of the avenue, you know what I mean? High class. You ever hear the old Billy Joel song, 'Uptown Girl'?"

Cal shakes his head.

"Well. She was my uptown girl, livin' in her white bread world… I was the downtown guy. Working class. Little older'n her, but she'd already finished college and I'd barely made it through high school and sure as hell didn't go back for any more studying after that."

Isaiah stops and swipes his card against a flat black box. A panel drops down, revealing a door. Isaiah strides down the sleek hospital hallway. Cal nearly stumbles, not paying attention to his surroundings, wanting to hear Isaiah's story.

"When the whole transhuman movement was catching fire, her family was all about that whole thing. Bought in early. Figured augmenting'd kill two birds with one stone— they'd get to live forever, and make sure Rosie would have that nice long life without me in it. Her parents hated me. Real Romeo and Juliet type shit."

Cal stares at him blankly.

Isaiah looks at him with full-force pity when he pinpoints Cal's confusion.

"Man, you don't know Romeo and Juliet?"

"No."

"Well, there's your assignment for tonight, Harper. Download it on Heaven. Do a little reading. Listen to some Billy Joel while you're at it. Anyhow. Rosie was a real piece of work when she needed to be. Put her foot down with her parents. Said she wouldn't synch with 'em. If I couldn't synch too, she'd stay in the old world, join the resistance, we'd go down fighting together."

"Damn," Cal says with admiration.

"Damn right," Isaiah agrees. "Kinda wish that's what happened. But instead, her parents said they'd pay for me, too. We'd all augment, and la-di-da. 'We don't like him, but we love you, so we'll do it,' they told her. So she agreed. Went through with her augmentation. Only her parents hadn't been straight with her. They never intended to pay for my procedure. Never made me an appointment. They played her good. She was a wreck when she figured it out. Kicked herself, said she'd been so stupid, should've insisted that I go first, that sort of thing. I told her we'd figure something out."

"I can't believe her parents did that."

"You'll believe it if you ever meet them. Which you might, if their toilets get clogged."

"If—oh. They're still here," Cal feels dumb, forgetting that people in stories from decades ago are still youthful and walking around in this world. "And Rosie—?"

"Well, funny how things work out." The way Isaiah says it, it's clear that there's nothing funny about how things worked out. "Rosie's family synched so early, there was one final call for Vosts—volunteer synthetic test subjects, you know? So they could perfect the next-round, second-generation Syn tech stuff. I signed up."

"So you could be with Rosie."

Isaiah nods.

"It all happened real fast at first, the announcement and all; I tried to get word to her, but by then her parents were pretty good at preventing communication. I couldn't get to her, couldn't get word to her. So I decided I'd just do it, get into their world and then go find her, give her the good news. Figured it might take a couple weeks, but what's a couple weeks when you're gonna live forever? I went in, applied, found out I was in—but then I was quarantined, pre-procedure. Couldn't be in touch with anyone during the whole process. So there I was, making sure I could be with her... but she didn't know."

"How long were you... quarantined?"

"Long time," Isaiah says. He runs his tongue across his teeth, like the next words are going to taste bad. "By the time I got out, it'd been a real long time. First thing I did was try to get a message to Rosie, using all my fresh tech, but I couldn't find her in the system. I figured there was some sorta glitch, or her parents found out first and managed to block me or something. But no. I finally got hold of one of her friends, who I knew had also synched but also had a soft spot for me. She told me the straight truth: Rosie was dead."

"No," Cal says, heart twisting for his coworker and almost-friend.

"Yeah. Apparently when she didn't hear from me for all that time, she figured I was killed in one of the uprisings or something. She was always pretty fragile, and that just—well. They don't like us to talk about self-terminating Syns, but it happened early on. People like Rosie, forced into it. Missing someone on the other side. Desperate."

"I'm sorry," Cal says, feeling sick and useless.

"Me too," Isaiah says. "But that was a long time ago."

"I don't mean to... you don't have to answer this, but..." Cal looks at Isaiah's strong profile. "Why did you... stay...?"

"Stay here? Stay alive?" Isaiah shrugs. "I don't know. Felt like I had to. Felt like maybe someday I'd get the chance to do somethin' good. Who knows."

"You could've joined the resistance—"

"They were real hesitant about Vosts. Anyone who wasn't Original."

Cal had never heard of Vosts before he came into this world, knew nothing of them being barred from resistance fighting—but it made sense. He couldn't see his Aunt Ruth trusting anyone with Syn parts. A few months ago, he couldn't have seen himself trusting any of them, either.

"Yep. So I stayed. Stayed here. Stayed alive. Stayed up late learning a bunch of nonsense. Rosie always used to say I was so smart, should've gone to college, coulda got a scholarship. Well. I could teach just about any subject at any old-world college by now. 'Stead I'm the world's greatest goddamn janitor. Anyhow. That's it. That's all."

Cal understands that the conversation is over. The men walk in silence for a moment, one remembering old regrets, the other wrestling with new knowledge. They turn right down a final hallway.

"Here we are," Isaiah says with a swipe of his card.

The smell hits them as soon as they step into the hospital lavatory.

"Curse of the world," Cal chokes, his hand flying to his mouth.

"You said it," Isaiah agrees grimly.

The warm stench of the room makes Cal's stomach roil. Isaiah wordlessly reaches into his pocket and pulls out two face masks, handing one to Cal. They slip the masks over their nose and mouth, then Isaiah presses a small black button on the wall. A sleek silver door slides down on the first stall, revealing a gleaming metal commode full to the brim with excrement. Cal very nearly retches at the sight.

"Shit," is all he can say.

"And plenty of it," Isaiah nods. "'Least we can be grateful it's not overflowing yet."

They are all but silent for the next hour or so, the Vost and the Original, cleaning up the putrescent Syn mess. When Isaiah instructs Cal to take the buckets outside, Cal feels a rush of gratitude that the kind man is allowing him to be the one to go outside, into the fresh air. He hauls up the two massive buckets, careful not to let any of the vile contents slop over the side. Isaiah uses his identification card to swipe the lavatory door open, and leads Cal into the hall, where he opens an exterior service door for him.

"Nearest sewage site's just west of here. Dump and pump site fifty-three, remember? It was in the work order they messaged us—" Isaiah stops himself, shaking his head. Remembering that Cal doesn't receive the direct-to-brain messages that his synthetic counterparts do. "Sorry—forgot—right, well. It's around that corner, green building. I'll send a request to management, so your card'll work when you get in there. You know how the dump and pump works?"

Cal nods; unfortunately, this is not his first clogged toilet assignment.

He steps outside, and a cool breeze greets him. Even with his mask still on, even with the full fecal pails still in-hand, his entire body sighs with relief. He looks around, blinking in the brightness, his enthusiasm dimming a bit as he registers the cement stretching endlessly ahead of him, dotted here and there by highly manicured parks.

On his first trip out on a plumbing call, Cal learned that the dump-and-pump process was exactly what it sounded like. When the plumbing is working, all the waste is funneled to a sewage site, where it's then pumped through a series of mechanized chemical treatments, and ultimately converted into fertilizer for all those pretty parks. When the plumbing is backed up, there's an underground dump site at each facility, where waste can be manually dumped—either by large trucks and machinery when needed, or bucket by bucket—and then pumped and chemically treated as usual.

Reaching the sewage treatment site, Cal sets down the buckets. He swipes his card on the small security pad beside the door to the underground dump site. It flashes green, and the door slides down in front of him. A levitator lights up on the floor in front of him. Cal hates levitators. He feels too big for them, and holding the disgusting shit-buckets makes him feel even more off-balance. Gritting his teeth, he steps onto the levitator, tightening his stomach to stay upright as the thing lowers him to the basement level.

The deodorizing chemicals crinkle Cal's nose, but do their job. While the unnatural vanilla scent is not one he cares for, it does provide effective odor neutralization. Saccharine sweet vanilla is preferable to post-Pulse poop.

Once in the basement, Cal sets down the buckets. Before him, a massive flat metal panel stretches out across the next section of floor, so long and wide he cannot see the ends of it. Cal scans his card on a second small black security pad on the wall, which rests above the point where the flooring and metal meet. With a flash of green and an accepting beep, the metal sheeting slides smoothly apart, revealing the murky hell-bog of sewage awaiting treatment.

Cal empties his buckets, holding his breath the whole time. There's not enough fake vanilla in the world to cover the smell. Turning his face away as the contents glop from the pail, he recalls hauling buckets of water for his tribe. Sloshing water and exchanging small stories and jokes with Jonah, with Ere—it feels a lifetime ago. He wonders if Helena is still alive, if any of the elders have taken ill or run into trouble. He feels guilt at leaving them, especially since all he has to show for it is toilet duty and isolation.

But it's Ere's fault as much as mine...

He finds, however, that he cannot blame Ere as easily as he once could. Cal understands the intense feelings inspired by Ever. Cal assumes his cousin is in some sort of trouble, but cannot allow himself to think that he is dead. As much anger as he harbors, he cannot imagine what it would feel like to know that Ere was truly gone.

As soon as he's finished with the buckets, Cal swiftly swipes at the waste-cover pad again, heaving a sigh of relief when the metal slides together, locking into place and sealing off the worst of the smell. He heads to the sanitization station.

The sanitization station is an impressive little piece of tech, and one that would have come in handy back when Cal and his tribe had to try to keep their small belongings clean. The buckets are set onto the machine, travel along an internal conveyor belt, are power-washed with bleach and something stronger, rinsed, and high-heat dried. They come out on the other side of the machine, gleaming. The whole thing takes twenty seconds.

Isaiah claims you could eat your supper out of the buckets when they come out the other side—an idea that makes Cal want to vomit like a Pulse victim.

But they do come out clean.

Blinking again in the brightness as he exits the dump site, he sets down the buckets and stretches his arms toward the sky. He breathes in, and the face mask pulls taut against his skin. He slides it off, freeing his nose and mouth and eagerly sucking in a rushing breath of unscented air.

"It *is* you."

Cal turns around, mask dangling from his fingers, buckets beside him, and very nearly cries out. For there, standing beside the sewage treatment building as though it is the most natural place for her to be, her face hidden by a hood but her identity unmistakable, is Ever.

THE SCAB FORMING ON ERE'S ARM IS crumbling and crimson-black, almost regal in its ugliness. He's kind of proud of it, and oddly glad to know that it will forever mark him. Before now, Ere has earned no scars.

He used to get injured a lot, but those old and long-healed scrapes were only minor battle wounds from play-warring with his cousin. When the boys went after one another, you could always tell who was getting hit by the sounds of the strikes. The *thwap-thwap* of stick-like arms landing on a solid trunk: Ere hitting Cal. The solid *whump-whoosh* of thick muscle connecting with skin-and-bones, resulting in the breath knocked out of a small frame: Cal hitting Ere.

I wonder what Cal's doing now. Is he still mad at me?

"Ere," Asavari says, appearing as if from nowhere. He hates how she always does that. "Stop staring at your little scratch. You are slowing us down."

He opens his mouth to snipe at her, but she's already loped ahead of him again.

Earlier, Asavari convinced her mother that the best course of action would be for Ere and Asavari—no one else—to fly back to the Syn center. Especially since they had not yet received word from Jorge or the new contact, and thus could not be certain of the risk until they got there. Sending just the two of them, who had been there before, would mitigate the danger.

Ere frankly thought sending two teenagers alone into the mouth of the wolf was stupid. But since he was mostly just looking for a free ride back to Ever, he went along with it.

"There it is," Asavari says, and even before she points he sees it, too.

Jorge's ship.

Ready and waiting to carry them back to the Syn world.

The vessel dwarfing the two Originals as they approach. It gleams sleek and silver, stark against the muted browns of dirt, tree, and rocks upon which it is perched. It seems expectant, a giant bird with its wings bound, awaiting the arrival of a master who will set it free and bring it soaring back into the sky.

"You're sure you're gonna be able to fly this?" Ere asks, throat dry.

"Yes," Asavari says. "As soon we figure out how to get into it."

Entrance does seem a mystery. The ship's pristine gleam comes from the fact that its metal is so smooth. There is no evident point of entry. There is one long, wide glass section that Ere decides must be the front of the ship—you have to look out somewhere to see where you're going, he knows that much about flying. But there are few other structural clues as to the feature or functions of the massive cylindrical ship.

Wordlessly, Asavari walks up to the massive machine and begins running her small hands across it, testing, searching. Ere has no idea what she's even looking for, but he follows her lead and begins touching the ship. Ere's mind begins to numb as his hand travels the homogenous plane of the ship, smooth and same and same and same and *wait—indented!*

His fingers slip into a recessed plate on the ship. Before he can even call out to Asavari, Ere feels a weird sensation as the metal re-shapes itself beneath his fingers, curving around beneath them until he is gripping a handle. He gives a slight tug, and with a hiss and a quiet *ping*, the small panel lifts. Ere startles and drops his grip on the handle as a larger swath of metal around it shifts, and drops, revealing a door, wide enough for two people to walk through—but positioned several feet above the ground.

"Curse of the world," Asavari says.

She takes a few steps back, then sprints forward, running past Ere and leaping in through the opening as if it might suddenly disappear. Ere scrambles to follow her, awkwardly jumping up, grabbing the bottom of the door with his elbows and hoisting his skinny ass into the ship. As he does so, his foot hits a small button at the base of the door. Ere scrambles away as the door slides out of its recessed holder then angles downward, smoothly connecting with the earth and creating a ramp.

Neither Ere nor Asavari says a word.

Turning from the ramp to the interior of the ship, Ere draws in a sharp breath. Based on Hess's lab, he would have thought the ship would be crammed with tech, screens and machines and buttons and all manner of objects foreign and frightening to figure out. Instead, this interior seems totally empty.

Asavari is contemplating this as well, standing in the middle of the wide and vacant space, a rounded room with gleaming walls, one large curved window, and no evident control panels of any sort. There are small slatted vents across the ceiling, and Ere notes with relief the welcome cool air emitting from the vents.

Behind them, the hidden door lifts itself from its ramp position, emphatically returning to its place in the wall. With another hiss it presses in and becomes part of the seamless ship wall; Ere's eyes blur, and he's not even certain he could find the door again if he tried.

"Jorge said that the navigation system was already set to return to the Center," Asavari says, still looking up. "All we have to do is find the navigation system, and get it to start, and then it will auto-pilot its way back to the Synt."

"Right, that's all," Ere says.

Asavari gives him a withering look.

"Fine, if you prefer, you may head home—"

"HOME," repeats a detached, feminine voice, making Ere and Asavari jump.

The walls glow faintly, then fade again as a screen appears directly below the long, curved window. On the screen, a map suddenly flashes into being. In front of the screen, four panels on the floor of the ship shift aside, and sleek padded silver seats emerge.

"Heaven and hell," Ere says.

CHAPTER 35: SHADOWER

WHY ARE THEY FLYING HERE?
Shadower has yet to make contact with Ere and Asavari. It's been too risky since the Pulse. They were supposed to await contact before coming to Central City, that's what Jorge's hasty, highly-encrypted message had said. They needed to be on the same page. Needed to plan.

This isn't how uprisings succeed.

This is how rebels die.

E VER KEEPS HER HEAD LOW as Cal approaches.
Eager as she was to find him, she is nonetheless nervous.
No—not nervous—terrified. She dreads revealing her new
face, and seeing his desire for her diminish before her very eyes.

*I shouldn't have done this—why did I go looking for him? I could
have lived on, perfect and preserved in his memories, until the day he
died. Now he'll know. He'll see the new me. The scarred me. The ugly
me. He'll probably even hate my hair.*

Heaven and hell...

Ever curses herself for not thinking this through more thoroughly. She had just been so excited to be able to do it. With the
help of Marti's stolen (not stolen; *borrowed*) credentials, and no
doubt aided by the post-Pulse system slowdowns, Ever was able

to circumvent her father's barriers and get to the Original who had once scaled a wall into her bedroom.

It was exhilarating, finding him in the system. Quickly learning about his jobs, finding the day's work orders for his maintenance crew, tracking him down to this less-than-savory location. It had been exciting. Fun. So fun, in fact, that she had forgotten the reality of her very own face.

Pulling her hood down lower, she takes a step backward as Cal steps toward her.

"Wait," she says.

"Why?" Cal asks, and his low but gentle voice tugs at Ever.

Despite asking him to hold back, Ever's own imagination cannot. She has waited so long to see him, has had so many delicious fantasies about this handsome Original. Taking him in with her eyes, she imagines the feel of him, the weight of him, the smell—then she notices what he's carrying.

The sight of the empty shit buckets helps jolt her out of this momentary fantasy.

The smell of him might not actually be appealing right this very second.

"Are you out here with anyone?"

"Isaiah," he says. "From my maintenance crew. He's up in the hospital bathroom we're working on."

"So he'll be expecting you—"

"I'll tell him I'm not feeling well and—"

"And you think he'll believe you?"

"Yes," Cal says, taking another step toward her. "And if he doesn't, I'll tell him the truth. Part of it, anyway."

"What part?"

"The part about the beautiful girl I need to see."

At the sting of the word *beautiful*, she drops her hooded head even farther, chin nearly to her chest, sinking further into the shadow of her hooded cloak.

"I'm not beautiful."

"You are the most beautiful thing I've ever seen."

"You haven't seen me recently."

"I see you every time I close my eyes."

"Keep them closed, then," she says.

Then a shock runs through her as she feels his rough but gentle fingers against her face, beneath her chin. She was so intent on looking down, warning him away and preventing her own hot tears, that she missed him advancing on her.

"Look at me," he says.

"I can't," she says, pressing her chin against his fingers, at once glad to be touching him and terrified that he is so close to seeing her new face. "I don't want you to see me like this."

"I want to see you," he says. "All of you. Always."

Trembling, she allows him to lift her face toward his, and as she tilts her head up, the hood slides down her shorter and recently re-colored hair (Autumn Envy #87). Cal's fingers travel from her chin, up her cheek and to her scar. She shudders as he traces the length of it; watches he takes in the imperfection, then meets her gaze.

"The Pulse?"

She nods, unable to speak. He leans down and kisses her scar, near her eye, then on her cheek. He pulls back a little, looking at her entire face.

"Beautiful."

"Don't lie," she says. "I'm ugly."

"Because of a scar?" He takes a step back, and begins to unbutton his maintenance uniform shirt. The very motion of his hands moving from button to button stirs something powerful in Ever. He pulls the shirt open, revealing his brawny brown chest, covered in a thicket of dark hair. "Look."

She sees only the coarse curly hair and the hard muscles beneath.

"Look closely," he says. "Feel, if it helps."

Tentatively, she extends her hand, resting it on his chest and then letting it explore. Her tentative fingers find a harder, raised and jagged segment of skin, and she looks first at it, then up at Cal.

"From an accident, as a child," he says. "I fell from a tree, impaled myself with a branch on the way down. And here."

He pushes back some of the curls on his forehead; his hair is longer than it was when last Ever saw him. A jagged scar lines the front edge of his scalp.

"Run in with a Syn drone," he says. "I was trying to take it down, it sliced into me. Ever… I have other scars. Life has given me many. Do you think I'm ugly?"

"No," she says. She recalls Marti's scars, as well, and briefly wonders how many others in her life carry hidden damages on their flesh and in their hearts. But the fact that they are hidden makes those secret scars different from hers. Cal's scars, and Marti's scars, are shown only at their discretion. Ever's wounds are on display for the world to see, upstaging her face. "But your scars aren't where anyone can see them. Mine are right here—"

"So what?"

"Yours are out of sight. And hidden in hair."

"Well, I'm glad there's not hair covering your face."

She smiles, then quickly erases the expression, shaking her head and giving him a doleful look, clinging to all of the bitterness and self-pity she has stored up these past few weeks.

"Don't try to make me laugh. I know I'm ugly now. I know it. I have mirrors."

"Your mirrors are stupid."

"Cal, come on—"

"You're strong," he says. "And beautiful. Someone without stories, without scars—they can be pretty, but they cannot be as strong or beautiful as someone with stories and scars."

With her hand still resting on the scar decorating his chest, he leans down swiftly but gently, and kisses her full on the mouth.

She kisses him back, fierce and grateful. She believes him, if only for a moment. Melting into his embrace, she confirms that she is still in private mode, then wonders if it even matters. With everything that's going on, is her father even paying attention to her these days? She decides it is likely that she is all but unmonitored, forgotten, no longer important to her father.

And then, for a few moments, she stops thinking at all.

It is Cal who stops the kissing, returning his hand to her face, cradling it and demonstrating again that he will not be put off by her scar.

"I should go check in with Isaiah. He'll be wondering what kept me. Or he'll come after me himself. He's not going to deal with that sh—mess on his own."

"You… you weren't hurt in the Pulse, were you?"

He shakes his head.

"From what I understand, only Syns were impacted. Syns and Vosts. Those of us without tech were undamaged."

"I received that update, but I only know Syns, so I didn't know if that was true or propaganda."

"Propaganda?"

"Something they—something my father wants us to believe, whether or not it's true."

"Oh," he says.

"You're the only Original I've seen in years, you know."

He gives her a strange look, but says nothing.

"Cal? Cal!"

Ever quickly slides the hood back onto her head, pulling it low to hide her face. Cal turns to see the person calling him.

"Isaiah—I'm here."

"Where have you—is that a girl you got with you?"

"…yes."

The older Syn chuckles and shakes his head.

"Willing to meet you on your shit bucket run, she must really like you."

Cal grins, and looks down at the hooded Ever.

"Do you really like me?"

From beneath her hood, Ever nods.

She really does.

CHAPTER 37: LORRAINE

AGENDAS WRITTEN OUT IN NEAT and neurotic script on crisp white paper are absolutely unnecessary. Everything is electronic, instantly shareable and viewable and editable, forever saved and accessible. But for Lorraine Murray, there is something deeply satisfying about writing out an agenda. Before every meeting she has, she puts pen to paper. It soothes her.

But she doesn't like what's on the agenda these days.

For the Syn Council, the items include:

I. The Pulse
  What the hell was it?
  When the hell might it happen again?
  How the hell can we stop it, and how much will it cost?

II. Self-terminating Syns (a group that, shamefully, includes her very own husband, the late Joshua Murray, whose name has been all but erased)
  Any additional bodies?

III. The Prophecy
  Progress on deciphering
  Any new prophecies?

For her second and more secret meeting of the day, her agenda is even briefer:

I. Felix Damned Hess

That man has been a festering thorn in her side for years. Unfortunately he was a thorn plugging a gaping wound, and if she just pulled it out thoughtlessly she would bleed to death. After all, so much of Lorraine's life came down to Felix Hess. Without him, she would have been dead decades ago.

Felix's brilliant scientific advancements and relentless drive, funded by her deep pockets, had created the world they now ruled. Trouble was, ruling the world with someone you despised was exhausting.

Lorraine wants to rip the thorn from her side, but she's too smart for that. So she is developing an extraction plan. Slow, but effective; something that could ultimately separate her from Hess without costing her everything. She began a half-dozen years ago to assemble a team: like-minded individuals who collectively had brainpower to rival Hess's own. None of them were members of the Syn Council. Too many of her colleagues who helped build this world still felt they owed it all to Hess, and that without him their Camelot would crumble. Hess fed this belief, of course, by offering new issues and ideas while deftly concealing information (like his somehow ready-to-go breeding program, obviously developed in secrecy over many years) and encouraging everyone to continue subscribing to the notion that only he could steer this ship.

Which is bullshit.

Hess is just a man. An augmented man, a brilliant man, but a man nonetheless. Lorraine knows better than anyone, with the possible exception of that pitiful wife of his, that Felix is fallible. Temperamental, egotistical, and perhaps his greatest Achilles' heel is his antisocial nature. He is a man with many admirers but few true allies.

Lorraine used to be his ally. But she went on the fence about him way back when he augmented his seventeen-year-old daughter, breaking his own rules to serve his own needs and demonstrating what she saw as a shocking overreach of patriarchal rule. And there have been many episodes since then that kept Lorraine wary, finally leading her six years ago to begin recruiting others for her secret campaign to keep Hess in check.

The final straw was when her husband died, and Hess's lack of sympathy proved that he saw Lorraine as nothing but a funder. Worse; now that money mattered less, she was nothing but one of the faceless figureheads placed on the Syn council to give the appearance of checks and balances in a world that Hess felt confident was his to command.

Assembling a team to plot Hess's eventual takedown was no easy task. But she's relished the challenge. Back in the old world, when she oversaw friendly mergers and hostile takeovers alike, Lorraine Murray felt almost majestic. Her precise suits, clicking heels, and unforgiving smile during unexpected announcements were a rush.

It feels good to be back on the throne.

*   *   *   *

Lorraine's was a rags-to-riches story, not like Hess who married into money, or his wife who inherited it. She was born working-class in Pittsburgh to a stay-at-home-mom and a father who worked the line at an automotive assembly plant. She should have admired how hardworking they both were, but from an early age Lorraine felt little for her parents other than pity. They lacked imagination, and she could not forgive them that.

Lorraine wasn't a star student, but she was more motivated than most. She struggled with algebra. Equations and powers tied to numbers took time to learn, but she was incredibly savvy when it came to figuring out equations and power in social settings. She didn't graduate at the top of her class, but she was class president. Then sorority president. Then the intern who elbowed out all the others to become the executive intern, reporting directly to the CEO (a disgusting old man who enjoyed leering at her and occasionally grabbing her ass—years later, she had him fired). She parlayed her internship into a job, her job into a management position, her management position into a vice presidency, her vice presidency into a head-hunter's safari as she was recruited to larger and larger acquisitions firms until she established her own.

Lorraine didn't get to the top by being the best player.

She got there by being the most strategic one.

Delaying marriage was an important strategy for Lorraine. Whatever society said, she knew that if she allowed herself to be slowed down by a relationship—or worse yet, children—she would lose momentum. So she waited until menopause hit her in her mid-forties, mercifully early. That's when she decided that with the chance of children off the table, she might as well find a companion with whom she might enjoy sharing her homes, jets, and bottomless resources.

She met Joshua Murray when he came to interview her for an article he was writing, some stupid fluff piece about female CEOs.

We prefer just being called CEOs, she told him, and he smiled at that.

Joshua was quiet and reserved, attractive and divorced. He was younger than Lorraine, which she found appealing; but he was old enough to be somewhat world-weary, which was essential. He was on amicable terms with his ex, lived alone, kept himself in decent shape. She quickly ascertained his one liability—a daughter from his first marriage—and decided it was not a dealbreaker. When she showed him out of her office at the end of the interview, she grabbed his ass and told him to call her. They were married a year later.

Joshua was a good husband, useful in many ways. He was a sharp reporter; not all of his assignments were fluffy nonsense about bosses who happened to have vaginas. Sometimes his sources spilled information that might tip a savvy strategist off as to weaknesses or innovations ahead. Good as he was at tracking down details, Joshua wasn't good about password-protecting the fruits of his investigative research. Lorraine plucked what she needed, pruning here and there and reaping huge fiscal rewards.

It was from a small round-up article on innovation that Joshua was working on that Lorraine first learned about Hess. He was one of five "rising stars of R&D" catching the attention of the business world, and Lorraine skimmed the bullet points on him with a moderate amount of interest. He was working with Dr. Nathan Fell, a bullish but brilliant man whose work had been on her radar for some time. Hess had some potential, by association alone.

But the person in the rising stars article who truly caught her eye was Claudia Lee.

That woman and her robots were starting to make some serious noise. And right there in the interview, she said something the other scientists all seemed to be skirting: she wanted to be profitable. She was ready to connect with investors who saw the commercial opportunity in her work. She was, in other words, for sale.

Lorraine was not an impulse buyer. She did her due diligence, then established a nonprofit foundation—separate from her other endeavors, not exposing her to any unwarranted risk—before reaching out to Lee.

When they met, they clicked. Lorraine found Claudia not only intelligent but also socially astute, an attribute most high-level scientists seemed to lack. Claudia was quick-witted and unapologetic, but deferred to Lorraine just enough to satisfy the born boss bitch. Lorraine was ready to roll with this woman and her robots, until Hess and Fell unexpectedly reached out to her.

Forget robots; they're child's play. You're a businesswoman. If you want to make a long-term investment, and see it through to its payoff, invest in something that keeps you alive long enough to watch the world evolve. Invest in something that lets you evolve along with it. Invest in your own infinite future.

She switched sides, dropping poor Lee, although she did send her a very generous severance package. She felt vaguely bad about putting her money behind yet another team of men, but she couldn't let latent feminist guilt sway her away from the surer bet.

It was a sound business decision. Even when Fell foolishly stepped into his own as-yet unproven machine and rendered himself a vegetable, Hess pressed on. He promised Lorraine he would deliver on their promises, and he did. When Lorraine augmented, not as young as most but still vital, she experienced something she had never really felt before: satisfaction.

It was a fleeting experience.

As her foundation became the Synt, and her board of directors stayed in their same seats but became the Syn Council, everything changed. The Singularity was a messy process. Lorraine's team had of course theorized the inevitable dissent this evolutionary leap would bring. But as the Singularity loomed, it became clear that those who were protesting the process had not only ethical concerns, but also pragmatic ones. Synthetic citizenship became a question of privilege.

Lorraine hated the word *privilege*, especially when it was applied to her. She felt it was a particularly undeserved label, since she didn't have anything that she didn't earn. *Don't they know I pulled myself up by my bootstraps? If they want in on things like this, they should have done better for themselves.* She rejected the premise of any ounce of her privilege being unearned.

So what if she stepped on others, slept with supervisors, stole information from everyone including her husband? That was how the game worked. She always was a strategic player. She didn't believe that made her privileged. It just made her a winner.

Right?

The uprisings were far lengthier, bloodier and more brutal than anyone anticipated. That was why Lorraine had championed the idea of infiltrating the water systems, cutting off Original fertility and putting in place a solid plan for ultimately eradicating this nuisance. Stopping the war from stretching on endlessly by eliminating future generations of opponents.

Long-term strategy was always her strength.

Hess listened to her. The plan worked. But in the ensuing decades, that egomaniac had steadily built wall after wall, separating the Syn Council from his laboratory work. He still showed up for most meetings and gave lip service for Council approval of projects and enhancements. But Lorraine could tell that he saw them all as a joke, and saw himself as an untouchable genius.

But Lorraine knew he wasn't irreplaceable. She'd been in the genius-recruiting business for a long, long time.

* * * *

So Lorraine had assembled her new brain trust, keeping the members' identities secret even to one another. The long-game mistress knew that her time was as unlimited as her resources, and she felt no need to rush.

Until her husband killed himself.

Lorraine held Hess personally responsible for Joshua's death. The soft-hearted man had wanted Hess to augment his ailing Original daughter. Yes, it was an impractical and unreasonable request. But Joshua made so few requests; in fact, despite all of Lorraine's wealth and power, this was the only thing he had ever really asked of her. So she called in a favor with Hess. And that bastard had clearly forgotten just how much he owed her, so he said no to her husband—who subsequently took his own Synthetic life, alongside his daughter.

Lorraine took Joshua for granted; she realized that as soon as he was gone. She missed his quiet, comforting aura. His solid presence at their dinner table, in their many living rooms, in her now-vast bed each night. He had put up with her eccentricities, and provided her the sort of stability that was hard to find in a constantly-climbing life.

And then he was gone.

All because Hess wouldn't do one simple favor for Lorraine.

Lorraine's new team of geniuses was solid. In a perfect world, she would have stacked the group with even more ringers. A few years earlier, Derek Abelson would have been a natural choice—he was a lazy jackass, but as smart as Hess and far more persuadable. But that moronic genius died in the damned uprisings. Claudia Lee, too, would have been an ideal candidate, but the stubborn thing had refused to augment and died of natural causes decades ago. Their absence around the table was felt, but also underscored the lesson for Lorraine that genius is always, always replaceable. True visionaries like her, who could pull the strings and make the geniuses bend to her will—those were far harder to come by.

Hess's days as the self-styled lord of the entire Syn empire were numbered. Lorraine will make sure of that. It's all part of protecting her investment, diversifying the assets and ensuring that with or without Hess, this world will go on.

"**Y**OU'VE BEEN TALKING IN YOUR SLEEP," says Marilyn.

"What?" Hess says, his eyes fixed to the left of her, obviously scanning some report.

They're sitting at their breakfast table, together for the first time this week. Ever is still in her bedroom, where she spends most of her time these days, and Angela knows better than to bother them when Hess is at the table. For once, Marilyn has her husband all to herself.

"You've been talking in your sleep," she says, louder.

"We don't sleep," he reminds her warily.

"You know what I mean. Overnight. When we're plugged in. You've been talking."

"Whatever you think you're hearing—"

"Don't write me off," she snaps. She hates that he's still not looking at her. "You've been saying some really interesting things. Like about... a prophecy?"

His eyes snap, shift, and for once, focus in on his wife.

"What did you say?"

"It's what *you* said,'" Marilyn says, looking at him coquettishly over the top of her mug.

His flat expression does not change.

"What did you hear me say. About the prophecy."

"You didn't say anything *about* it," Marilyn says, setting down her cup. She dabs delicately at her mouth with an embroidered white linen napkin. She just had a lip enhancement yesterday, since optional work is being allowed again, *finally*. "You just kept repeating it."

"What do you mean?"

"I mean—you sound like an old record-skip sort of thing, just repeating and repeating: *Prophecy. The outsider inside will end the beginning. Prophecy. The outsider inside will end the beginning. Prophecy. The—*"

"STOP SAYING THAT," her husband thunders, rising and slamming his hand down on the table, rattling their good china.

"Jesus, Felix, calm down," Marilyn says, swallowing hard enough to force her heart out of her throat and back down into her chest.

"That is confidential information."

"Everyone knows there's some prophecy that—"

"All prophecies are confidential until deciphered."

"Well, you're the one who was—"

"Just keep your damn mouth shut," he glowers, condemning her mouth without ever noticing its new fullness. "I'll figure out whatever stupid glitch is making me talk in my sleep, and until I get it worked out I'll stay at the lab."

"Felix, don't be ridiculous—"

But he is already out the door, his coffee and his wife equally easy for him to abandon.

Marilyn sits there, southern-belle smile frozen on her face, wondering when the hell even speaking to her husband had become a crime. She isn't stupid; she knew that whatever the prophecy was, it was sensitive information. But she was asking about him in their own home, over breakfast. She was his damn wife, and it's not as if she was bringing it up out in the open where someone might overhear them. As usual, his reaction was selfish and over-the-top.

She's glad she didn't mention the other thing she heard him mumbling about, while he was plugged in to Heaven and allegedly offline. It was something entirely separate from the prophecy nonsense. Something about Syns terminating themselves.

She remembers the periodic surges of self-terminations, especially around the time when many Syns' family members— those who remained Original—began to die off. Some citizens suddenly decided they didn't want to live forever without "those who made life worth living." Sweet, but stupid, she had thought at the time. Her husband and his team had dealt with the issue, added a suppressant patch, and the rash of self-directed deaths went away like weeds well-pulled.

Self-termination was rarely mentioned now, and the Council wanted everyone to believe the problem had been permanently solved. But evidently, it had not. And this time around, Marilyn is not quite so hasty to judge the self-terminators.

Any act of autonomy has some understandable appeal. Deciding to die pretty, preserved, finally free of responsibility? Not such a bad notion. Especially if these crazy Pulse things continue.

Maybe the real crazies are the ones not considering something like that.

Marilyn has always been scared of aging, but much less so of death. She's always imagined that at whatever point she dies—surely, she'll die someday, won't she?—she'll see her father. The Heavenly one and the earthly one. On some level, Marilyn still believes in Jesus and the real heaven, not just the one her husband built. She pictures her beloved Daddy, Four, welcoming her with his big ruddy smile and open arms on the other side. She'll finally be reunited with the man who cut her off when she chose Hess over him.

You were right, Daddy. Like always.

I should have chosen you.

Angela steps in to refill Marilyn's coffee cup. Marilyn catches her by the wrist, sudden and cat-like, and looks up at her former friend with pleading eyes. She can't be alone with her thoughts for one more moment; she can't.

"Sit down and have a cup with me, won't you, Angela?"

Angela sets down the carafe of coffee and takes a seat. It is only after Angela sits that they both notice that there is no cup for her. She deftly rises, and for a moment Marilyn has an irrational fear that this woman, too, will walk out as her husband had.

"Be right back," Angela says, as if reading her mind. "Need anything while I'm up?"

"No," Marilyn says, and then: "Tylenol."

Angela nods and slips into the kitchen.

Alone once more, Marilyn's mind begins racing again. The stillness grows somehow loud. The bright light pouring in from their wide skylight over the dining table is harsh and seems to have a clanging sound to it. The sounds stalk her and make her sweat—the hiss of the kitchen door sliding shut behind Angela, the hum of the electricity powering the place, the horrible scrape of Marilyn's own manicured fingertips as she picks up her porcelain coffee cup. She could swear she even hears the sound of her heart beating, maybe also her internal augmented mechanisms, which she pictures sometimes as little cartoon gears turning and churning within her. Her skin feels as if it doesn't quite fit. She wants to shed it. She wants to shed everything.

I need to schedule something.

Breasts, maybe.

Over the years, Marilyn's enhancements steadily ticked upwards. Cosmetic stuff, nothing medically necessary. The enhancements felt increasingly important to Marilyn's well-being. It was the lips, this week, still bee-stung and swollen today. The week before the Pulse, it had been her forehead. The cool needle slipping into her already-taut skin and smoothing imagined wrinkles into oblivion brought a sigh of relief.

Before the lips and forehead, it had been her stomach, nipping and tucking and flattening her slim frame. Reducing herself, taking up a little less space after the procedure than she had before it; she was almost recovered from that one, ready for another big one. Breasts, yes, they were about due. She doesn't want bigger ones, she wants shapelier, perkier, smaller ones. The downsizing trend is hot right now. Be less, but better. This idea calms Marilyn.

Be less, but better. Yes.

Yes, definitely the breasts.

She breathes in, and out, and manages to still the invasive sounds of the oversaturated world around her, just a little. Another hiss, and Angela crosses from the kitchen back into the dining room. She hands two small white pills to Marilyn, pours herself a mug of coffee, and sits again beside the woman who brought her in to Syn society.

"So," Angela says, sipping her coffee. "What's on your mind?"

KENNEDY HADN'T NECESSARILY PLANNED on seeing Chase again. They had gone on a second date, shortly before the Pulse—and it had been interesting. Very interesting. But then the Pulse happened. And then more time passed. And he heard nothing from Chase, until today, when a message came through requesting they meet up.

And now, here they were. Strolling through the park in another classic old-world date scenario. Chase had even brought some stale bread crumbs, to toss into the pond for the placid ducks sometimes stationed there. It was oddly charming.

Chase ambles beside Kennedy easily, matching his pace, not getting ahead or behind. They have not talked much since meeting up fifteen minutes ago. Each seems to be waiting for the other to spread out the conversational map and choose a destination, or at least a starting point. But so far, today— nothing.

*   *   *   *

On their first date, Chase had taken Kennedy home—but not much had happened, despite what Kennedy tried to boast to Jorge. A chaste kiss at the door, then they both seemed to lose their nerve. After their second date, a quick dessert at some snooty French place, Chase had invited Kennedy back to their place again. This time was more eventful.

Chase's place was distinctive—lots of white walls, white plush carpeting, bright-red furniture, an oversized Warhol (Kennedy never understood the appeal of that artist; what was so great about a giant soup ad?) and several other less-famous pop art pieces adorning every wall. Chase had played Kennedy a vintage Billie Holiday album which was soothing and also darkly foreboding. Chase stopped talking entirely to listen to *Strange Fruit* in silence, with something like reverence, which left Kennedy feeling guilty and ill at ease.

"I want to show you something," Chase said.

Chase grabbed Kennedy's hand, leading him down a hall. Into a bedroom. Kennedy's armpits immediately went damp; whatever expectations Chase had of him, Kennedy felt instantly certain he would be a disappointment.

The bedroom was like a work of pop art itself—white shag carpet, black and white photos on the wall, and a massive round bed with a bright red comforter taking up most of the space, asserting its dominance. Chase, still holding Kennedy's hand, pointed with their other hand at the bed.

"Look."

"Uh, it's…very…" Kennedy realized Chase was pointing not at the bed, but at the wall behind it, the one covered in neat rows of framed black and white photographs. "Oh. Wow."

Kennedy walked over to examine the photographs. The topmost pictures each featured a child; the same child, growing year after year, into lanky middle schooler and sullen-eyed teen. By the second row of framed moments, the subject had matured into a reedy young androgynous adult wearing a suit. Another row down, the same young person, but now in a ball gown. In the next row the now middle-aged subject wore nothing, instead holding a few strategically placed placards which read STOP ASKING, START BELIEVING, and at some point Kennedy realized.

"This is… these are… you."

Chase nodded, eyes on the images.

"Yes. This has been my… project."

"What sort of project, exactly?"

"Documenting my journey. Chasing after some… greater sense of self. Greater understanding. I call the photo series The Chase."

"'The Chase.'"

"Yes," Chase said, and their gaze drifted to one photo in particular.

Kennedy followed Chase's gaze to the only picture which had two subjects within its frame. It took Kennedy a moment to place what was odd about the photograph. There was Chase, in a dark tunic and leggings, gazing at the camera. And there beside Chase was a second Chase, in a white tunic and leggings.

Each was seated on a plain stool, hands folded in laps, gazing calmly at the camera. As if this sudden doubling was the most natural thing in the world.

"Did—do you have a twin?"

"Sort of," Chase said, which only confused Kennedy more. "We can talk about this more another time, but for now… let's go have some wine. Do you like wine?"

Kennedy's heart was hammering in his chest. This was what he had been waiting for; something out of the ordinary. *Someone* out of the ordinary. How could he have almost written Chase off as augmented to the point of being uninteresting? This self-changing challenge obviously predated the Singularity and revealed something essential about this person. What did Kennedy have to show that could match this intimate revelation? Nothing. Absolutely nothing.

Hell yes, he needed some wine if he wanted to keep their interest.

They drank wine, debated whether or not anyone had made any good music since the Singularity, and then Kennedy passed out on the red vinyl couch.

*   *   *   *

Proving beyond the shadow of a doubt that I'm the one who's uninteresting.

But Chase had been the one to call and invite Kennedy on this third date, to feed the ducks. So Kennedy must not have completely killed his chances with them.

"Are you happy?" Chase asks suddenly.

"What?" Kennedy says, taken aback.

"Are you happy?"

"Oh, uh," Kennedy says. "Sure?"

"You don't sound sure."

"I'm not sure," Kennedy says.

A heavy moment of honesty hangs between them like humidity, and sweat prickles along Kennedy's spine.

"Look," Chase says, pointing. "Ducks!"

Kennedy follows their finger toward the pond before them, where a half-dozen ducks are floating in lazy and meaningless circles, not going anywhere at all. Chase digs out the half-loaf from their bag and unwraps it. At the sound of the cellophane, one of the ducks turns her head to look at them. Chase smiles and pulls off a few small hunks, tossing the oversized crumbs into the water. All of the ducks are immediately alert, their swimming becoming purposeful as they paddle toward the offering and shove their bills toward the unexpected food.

"Guess they're hungry," Kennedy says.

"They'll always eat," Chase tells him, tossing more crumbs to the greedy waterfowl. "Here, you throw some."

"Okay," Kennedy says, digging his fingers into the bread, feeling stupidly powerful at how easily it crumbles.

"What's the worst thing you ever did?"

Kennedy stares at Chase, who is looking at him with eyes as calmly expectant as if they had just asked him if he wanted to grab a drink after feeding the ducks.

"I... don't remember," Kennedy says.

This is true, and not true. Kennedy has erased from his internal records all of the worst things he has done, but that doesn't mean he doesn't know. Some of the activities were top-secret, but others were matters of public record. He knows he has a lot to regret, and is selfishly grateful for the ability to obscure the details of these transgressions.

"Because you erased memories," Chase says.

"...yes," Kennedy says, baffled and suddenly frightened. "How did you—"

"But you know you've done terrible things."

"Look, I don't know who you think you are, but I'm not comfortable with—"

"I can give you a chance to do some good things," Chase says, tossing some crumbs to the never-satisfied ducks. "Good, important things. Redemptive things."

Kennedy stares open-mouthed as behind him, the ever-ravenous ducks gorge themselves on carbs. Chase has information they shouldn't have. They're clearly not who they said they were.

Who did they say they were?

Chase has run out of bread. The ducks' thrusting bills snatch the last of the food floating on the surface of the water, and then they plunge their heads below the surface, looking for whatever they might have missed. Finding nothing, they resume paddling and circling, going nowhere, treading water.

"What sort of 'opportunity'?" Kennedy asks.

Chase grins, and Kennedy notices there's no lipstick on their mouth today. It makes Chase look more like all of the iterations displayed in the black and white photographs in their bedroom. Someone truly singular. Kennedy suddenly wants to kiss those smiling naked lips.

"There's someone I want you to meet," says Chase. "Come on—we'll pick up some wine on the way."

THE JOURNEY between India and the Incorporated Sectors is far swifter by air. Ere and Asavari are awestruck as the scenery flies by, the world a swirl of greens and browns and blues. As the strange, self-guided ship approaches Syn territory, the navigation panel beneath the window illuminates,

"Greetings, Karma and Ere," says a voice.

It's not the ship's navigation system.

"This is Shadower. I'll be sure you land safely. Do not deplane until I send someone for you. Do you understand?"

They look at each other, and Ere wonders if Shadower can see them exchange this glance. If Shadower, or others, have been watching them the whole time, as they gazed out the window, slept, used the lavatory.

"We understand," says Asavari.

"Buckle up," says Shadower. "You land in four minutes."

Ere's empty stomach churns as he feels the ship drop, veer left, tilt on its side. Then it seems to pick up speed—*this is wrong, shouldn't we slow before approaching, not go faster?*—and with a sudden *sh-sh-sh-sh-whirrrrrrr-THUD*, they slam into the earth with a teeth-rattling impact.

"Open your eyes," Asavari says.

Ere hadn't realized he closed them. Blinking, he looks around.

In the distance, the skyline of Central City is visible, with the massive Synt building towering above every other structure and disappearing into the clouds. A dusty pink sunset backlights the scene. There is no sign of activity anywhere near them.

The ship glows softly again, and Shadower addresses them again:

"In case you didn't find the food onboard… MEAL."

A panel on a side wall opposite the window slides out and forms a sturdy steel table. Then from the opening left by the converted panel, a plate full of hot food slides forward.

"MEAL," says Shadower again, loud and clear, and a second serving slides out beside the first plate. "Eat and lay low. I'll dim the lights and keep you in stealth. All nearby monitors have old footage replaying; you'll be safe here. I'll be in touch by morning."

"Morning?" Asavari asks, sharp, clearly not wanting to be trapped onboard this ship with Ere for several more hours. But there is no reply from Shadower.

The eating is over quickly.

Then there is more silence.

Finally, Ere says: "I wonder what other commands this thing recognizes."

Asavari looks at him, head tilted slightly in confusion. "What do you mean?"

"You know, like 'home'—"

"HOME," repeats the ship, rumbling to life.

"No—STOP," Asavari yells in a panic.

"STOP," the ship agrees, engines quieting again.

Ere can't help it, and bursts out laughing. And then, to his surprise, so does Asavari.

"You could get us in real trouble, Ere Fell."

"Why do you say my whole name so much? You can just say 'Ere.'"

"There is more power in your whole name."

"Why?"

"It is true for most people, but most of all for you, Ere Fell. *Ere Fell.* You have the honor of carrying the most noble of Original names. It should be a reminder, each time you hear it. You are a Fell."

"That's pretty hard to forget, whether or not you say it," Ere says, feeling the full weight of his full name. "And turns out Fell is a pretty powerful name in the Syn world, too."

"Everything powerful can be good or bad," Asavari said. "Like the legend of the wolves. You've heard this story?"

He shakes his head.

"An old woman tells her granddaughter that we all have two wolves within us—a good wolf, and a bad wolf. The good wolf represents every wonderful thing we might do with our strengths; the bad wolf howls for us to break and burn things with whatever power we have. The grandmother asks: *Do you know which one gets stronger, child?* The girl does not know. Her grandmother pulls her into her lap, hugs her, and whispers in her ear: *The one you feed.*"

Ere does not know what to say to this, fearing the call of the wild has already ruined him.

After a moment, he simply says: "I have one more idea for a voice command to try."

"Careful—"

"Music," Ere says.

"MUSIC," the ship replies, and a full orchestral number burst into vibrant life around them, filling the space with an unfamiliar golden and glorious melody.

"Beautiful," Asavari breathes.

"Wait, hold on," Ere says, racking his brain, then finding what he sought and speaking it aloud, hoping it will work: "Play Schubert's Symphony Number 9 in C major—the Great Symphony!"

There is a momentary silence.

And then the achingly beautiful piece begins. First a single instrument, pleading and simple and slow, calling as if in hope of an answer. And then come replies, new instruments joining in, layering and uniting, building an ever more powerful and heartbreaking and hopeful sound until Ere feels his soul might lift out of his body and carry him straight to the sky.

He turns instead to Asavari.

"Do you want to dance?"

"I do not dance. And I do not think this is music for dancing."

"I don't really know how to dance either," Ere says.

He offers a hand. She takes it.

They dance, the orphan boy and the warrior girl.

They dance with eyes closed, holding one another but feeling no desire. They dance with no one watching, or perhaps with Shadower or other spies witnessing their slow movement to the music that transports them somewhere far beyond the life of struggle each has known. When the piece ends, they step back from one another, separate and strange once more. It was only a dance.

"My parents used to dance together," Asavari whispers, looking at the floor as if she is searching it for the smallest of cracks.

"That's nice," Ere says. "I don't know if mine ever did."

"You don't know who your father is, do you?"

Ere shifts uncomfortably. His mind snaps back to his exchange with Dr. Felix Hess, in the core of Heaven, standing feet away from the floating shell of his grandfather while hearing the madman's damning words about Ere's father—a man who had worked with Hess, and with Ere's own grandfather; a man named Derek Abelson. A man who, according to Hess, was assassinated by Ere's mother.

Ere does not want to let Hess's claim— a claim that might well be false, or exaggerated—tear down his image of his mother. But the accusation haunts him, and he fears he will always wonder. Did his mother kill his father?

He slips his hand into his pocket, wrapping his fingers around Ever's gun. He allows the silver steel to center him, comfort him, remind him that he had a purpose. The past was the past, whatever the truth of it might be. He had to focus on the future.

"No," he says, too loudly. "I don't know who my father is."

"Well," says Asavari, "your mother was more than enough."

C AL HAS NEVER BEEN HAPPIER. Since finding him, Ever has been reluctant to let him out of her sight for more than a few hours. Since they both have jobs, the society is heavily monitored, and Ever's father specifically forbad them coming into contact, daily visits were no small task. But they were swiftly becoming experts in romantic espionage.

Ever, the experienced manipulator of Syn monitoring, was more successful in finding her way to him. She would be there when Cal broke for lunch, when he wrapped his final repair job of the day, somehow sometimes even on bathroom breaks. Her arrival always jump-started his heart into enthusiastic overdrive, since seeing her meant within moments he would be kissing her, touching her, pressing up against her in a hidden hall closet or darkened supply room.

Cal wants to simply enjoy their encounters. But after a lifetime of conditioning, he cannot ever quite turn off his watchfulness. Even as Cal lost himself in Ever's kisses, he would stop their embrace, freezing, asking again if they might be detected.

"No," she would assure him, breathing hard. "I'm in private mode. We disabled the cameras in here. And anyway, I used to be valuable, but I'm not anymore. No one gives a shit where I am."

"I do," Cal breathed. "I want you here."

"I want you everywhere."

And the kissing would resume.

"HELLO," SAYS A VOICE.
A new voice.
Not Shadower.
Not the ship.

Asavari elbows Ere, still sleeping on the floor beside her.

"Hello," the voice says again, light and feminine. "I'm your new contact. Chameleon."

"Chameleon," Asavari repeats.

"Yes," confirms Chameleon. "Now listen carefully: All recording systems in this ship are disabled, so our communication here is secure but I will not have easy access to you when you leave this ship. We have reason to believe another Pulse is on the horizon. When you exit this ship, it will be taken completely offline to minimize the damage its tech may sustain in a surge. You are currently a day's walk from the Synt. CARGO ONE."

At these loudly and clearly spoken words, a panel in the floor of the ship slides aside and a large metallic box rises from the revealed space.

"In this box you will find Syn garments, and the emergency bundles all ships are supplied with in case of landing in an under-resourced area—food, water, analog compass, flashlights, matches. Follow the compass north, then shift west at the waterfront. Karma, you will cross the bridge by night; the checkpoints there are automated and I will tamper with the systems so you will pass undetected. When you reach the Synt, you will wait in the park where you met your last informant. Ere, you cannot be seen. You are believed dead, and we need you to stay that way. You will wait at the bridge."

"But—"

"You cannot enter the Syn Center, Ere Fell. It will put the entire rebellion in danger."

"We understand," Asavari says, hoping to give no opportunity for Ere to speak up again.

"Good," says Chameleon. "See you soon."

E VER HAS BEEN HAVING DREAMS. Not nightmares, which had plagued her ever since her stroke and continued to baffle her doctors. But *dreams.*

She thought the Pulse-driven blips might be impacting Heaven upload processes, crossing wires and feeding snatches of others' memories into her subconscious feed. But the more she tuned in to the episodes, and the more she recalled and reflected on them the next morning, she knew that they were not someone else's thoughts, they were her own. And they felt rooted in something real. Something she had experienced, and somehow forgotten.

Someone she had experienced, and somehow forgotten.

A boy.

Ever had heard once, back in the old world, that one could not dream about strangers. Original dreams were populated by people whose features you had seen in real life, at least once, if only in passing. Since the return of dreams, she had tried to verify this information, and found conflicting articles on the phenomena in Heaven's archives. None of the articles were very recent—when dreams disappeared from the population, eventually so too did the ongoing study of them. But this article was one that resonated with her:

Dreams often seem full of strangers, playing prominent roles. However, scientists believe that the slumbering mind is not invent-ing those unrecognized faces. All such appearances, even if apparently unknown to the dreamer, are faces of real people the dreamer has seen before in their waking life. They may not remember them—they might be someone seated across from them on a train, a face they glimpsed across a restaurant, or a parent's friend who showed up at a holiday party once—but they have met them before. The evil killer or hand-some prince who seems new is in fact a recalled countenance. Every person has seen hundreds of thousands of faces throughout a lifetime, giving the brain an endless supply of seemingly "new" faces used to create characters in dreamscapes. [Update Post-Singularity: Dreams do not occur during data transfer. The information contained in this article is still assumed to be correct for Originals.]

Ever is convinced that this boy, the one who keeps appearing in her dreams, is someone she has indeed met before. He is slight and often in shadow, but his luminous brown eyes find her by the end of each dream. He says little but infers much. He makes her feel… something. Something strong and strange. She doesn't know his name, but feels a change in the air whenever he makes his appearance.

She is always aware that she is not awake, that the time they spend together is not real. But something about it feels more real than her daily Syn life. Original and authentic. She hadn't realized how much she craved that sensation. When she sees him, she is overwhelmed by an odd emotion. It's not excitement, or even passion.

It's relief.

It's as if she has been unable to really breathe in between their encounters, and when she finally sees him she can exhale, and inhale, and feel like things really will be all right. She only feels this way around him. And he's not even real.

She has to remind herself of this, over and over.

He's not real.

It's just a dream.

But she can't write it off as "just a dream" when dreams are, in and of themselves, something unheard of and incredible.

Ever keeps her mouth shut about the dreams. She doesn't want to be studied or tested. When her nightmares were reported as a side effect of her stroke, the doctors worked to regulate her medications, to eradicate the night terrors. If she told anyone about these new visions coming to her as she slept, the dreams might be taken away, just like her nightmares were. But this time that would mean that the boy would be taken away. And that's not something Ever could stand. She can't lose that boy, even if he lives only in her imagination.

She forces herself to remember that Cal is the real, tangible, flesh-and-blood man who should be holding her attention. *He's real he's real he's real,* she reminds herself as he runs his hands across her body. She tries to focus on the details of him, honing in on one each time—his warm brown eyes, his sturdy muscular chest, the raised skin of his scars. His ass.

But today, even when she tries to keep herself in the room with Cal, her mind is wandering. And he notices it.

"What's on your mind?" Cal asks between kisses. "You seem very far away."

They are in a utility room, lights dimmed, surrounded by switches controlling wiring for an entire wing of the Synt. Their arms are around each other's waists, their fingers tangled and noses touching but he is right: Her mind is somewhere else.

"I'm here," she insists, somewhat truthfully. "With you."

He's real he's real he's real.

Cal drags a gentle thumb down her cheek, lingering gently, as always, on her scar.

"And I am glad you are. But you seem distracted."

"Oh, it's just—work," she says, because it seems like the sort of thing people say.

"What about work?" Cal asks, with genuine interest.

"Nothing interesting."

"Everything about you is interesting to me."

Sweet words like this help drive the dream-boy a little further from her mind. Cal is so attentive, so protective, and so swiftly invested in her—how can she take that for granted? Especially once her beauty was lost, she never assumed anyone would find her worthy of a pedestal ever again. But here was this handsome, strong Original man, breaking dangerous rules to be with her and constructing a pedestal taller and sturdier than any she could have imagined.

"Yeah, right," she can't help saying, but her tone is light and teasing. He nuzzles her in response rather than taking offense.

"I mean it."

"All right, well. I should get back to work... but if anything interesting happens there, I promise to tell you the next time I see you."

"And when will that be?"

"Soon."

"Good," Cal says, leaning in for a final kiss before they part ways.

Walking back to her office, Ever replays both of her secret encounters—the heated make-out with Cal, and last night's forest-encounter with the other Original boy. The two sides of her brain seem to juxtapose the scenes and the suitors, running each alongside each other, captivated by each but also wanting to draw a curtain between them, to keep them from ever crossing paths.

Which is stupid, since the dream boy doesn't exist.

A more realistic fear is her father finding out about Cal. Contemplating this risk makes Cal all the more terrifying and all the more appealing. In addition to being real and kind and hot as hell, Cal is the greatest coup she has ever managed. A giant middle finger given to her parents. She willfully pulls the curtain all the way across the dream-boy's corner of her mind. She focuses instead on Cal, deciding she'll get out of work early and surprise him at the—

She nearly runs into Marti as the door slides down to the workspace they share.

"Ever! There you are," Ever's supervisor smiles. "I was wondering if I'd run into you before I headed out."

"Yeah, hey," Ever says, giving an apologetic sidestep to avoid collision but not really looking at the other woman. "Where are you off to, Martha?"

"Oh, just a meeting. And when have you ever called me Martha?"

Ever freezes. She had been so lost in her own thoughts, she blurted out the name on Marti's credentials, which Ever still guiltily uses daily to track down her Original boyfriend. The credentials were long since returned, casually clipped exactly where they had rested before, on the breast of the blazer Marti had left at the Hess household. Ever had returned the garment and ID badge to Marti the very next day, that Monday when she had returned to work—but not before creating a copy for herself. But there was no reason for Marti to ever suspect that her identity had been stolen by her employee. No reason unless Ever made stupid slips like this.

"Sorry—I don't know why—"

Marti waves Ever's stuttering away, obviously not really interested in an answer.

"Yeah, no, definitely just always call me Marti. I hate Martha, always have. Sounds like with that name, I should know how to fold napkin swans, and that's a skill I absolutely don't have. I should be back within the hour, if you can get started on the day's requests...?"

"Sure thing," Ever says, relived.

"Feeling okay? Any aftershocks?"

"Nope," Ever says.

"It's not just nausea, you know. Folks have reported other weird blips—epilepsy, seizures, spotty vision. The theory is it's all Pulse-related. Little errors in our brains, showing up differently in everyone. Like, everything from headaches to hallucinations."

Or dreams, Ever thinks.

"No, I'm fine," she says aloud.

"Good, well. You know you can talk to me about anything that comes up, right?"

Ever looks at Marti, and realizes that she should feel more grateful for this woman. Not only because she saved her, dragging the bloodied Ever to help and safety in the wake of the Pulse, but also because she seems to actually care for her. Ever was so resentful when her father assigned her a job, but it has brought her much more than a reason to get out of their residence. It has brought her something she hasn't had in years. A friend.

She feels another pang of guilt about using Marti's credentials and not telling her about Cal, or her dreams, or anything, really. It would be too risky. But maybe on other topics, she can be a little more conversational with Marti. Share what she can, even if it's just a complaint about her mother here or a rave review of

Angela's cooking there. Maybe they will have a drink together after work sometime. That would be nice.

She smiles at her supervisor.

"Thanks, Marti."

"Sure thing. I'm going to be late, so. See you in a bit."

Ever calls up her task list for the day, noting with mild interest that her app request reviews for the day include a few interesting items and not just Pulse patches, which have dominated recent inquiries. Ever has only been back at work for a week, and this might prove the first interesting day in a while.

Work keeping her out of her home all day, then another rendezvous with Cal in the evening, then a night of dreams to look forward to, all while living in fear of her father one day remembering to check in on her...for the first time in a long, long time, Ever Hess is not bored.

CHAPTER 44: KENNEDY

KENNEDY WAKES UP FEELING ODD. But he runs a system check, and gets a report that everything is fine. He can't quite remember the previous evening, though.

He rolls over in his bed, and finds himself eye to eye with the mysterious Louisianan.

"Good morning," Chase says. "Sleep well?"

"Yes," Kennedy says.

He must have. He doesn't feel tired.

"No headache? We had a lot of wine last night."

That must be it. He must have had too much to drink, forgot whatever happened, and that's why he's feeling a little odd. Not bad, though; not hungover.

"No headache," he confirms.

"You might have one later," Chase says. "Don't worry if you do. I won't judge."

"Right," Kennedy says. Then he notices the time. Nearly six in the morning. "I'm going to be late to work."

"Better get up, then. I don't want to get you in trouble."

Kennedy gets out of the bed, naked but unselfconscious about this fact. He dresses himself methodically, fingers a little wooden, but functional. He tries again to call up some memories from the previous evening. Chase, yes, and not much else. But his memory is a little patchy in general, he reminds himself. Too many erasures. Plus, the Pulse. And wine. Nothing to worry about.

"I'll see you later?"

"You will," Chase confirms.

By the time Kennedy makes it to work, he does have a small headache—but nothing like the ones he used to get post-augmentation. Nothing like the pain of the Pulse. He decides he doesn't even need to take anything. It'll pass.

He arrives only a few minutes late. Jorge is already compiling the highlights of last night's Heaven uploads, flagging anything that might be relevant to the Pulse, or anything else on Hess's running list of potential threats and opportunities.

"You're late," Jorge says.

"Lay off," Kennedy says agreeably, shaking his head at the always-robotic Jorge. "How do last night's uploads look? Anything interesting?"

"Just got started," Jorge says, seeming slightly surprised at Kennedy's jump straight into legitimate work details.

Kennedy stands next to his coworker and begins perusing the data. He points at something flagged for multiple occurrences, noticing it before Jorge does. He grabs the data point with his finger, pulling it to the center of the screen and expanding it for examination.

"See that?"

"Yeah," Jorge says, eyes narrowing as he analyzes the implications.

"In their sleep, hearing a small sound—"

"Like the beep before the Pulse," Jorge says, wincing a little at its memory.

"But there was no Pulse last night."

"And it wasn't enough to wake anyone up."

"You think it's a pre-Pulse signature?" Kennedy posits, processing the small bits of information and swiftly constructing them into a fairly sturdy theory. Early warning sign some Syns are picking up on—subconsciously, anyhow— that others are missing?"

"Could be," Jorge says, openly staring at him.

He's not used to Kennedy arriving at conclusions first.

Chase is a good influence, Kennedy thinks.

CHAPTER 45: EVER

S HE IS IN A SMALL ROOM, dark with a bed, and he's there, in the bed. So is she, she realizes. Beside him, gazing into his eyes. Waiting for him to speak. Knowing that this time, he will. There's something he wants to tell her. Something he's been trying to tell her for a long time. She wants to tell him that it's all right, whatever it is, he can tell her and she'll listen. She opens her mouth and finds that now it is she who cannot speak. She tries to reach out a hand to touch him but she cannot move, either. All she can do is be there, and wait, and know that he is within reach and yet a world away from her, untouchable and unknowable.

His mouth moves in slow motion, and she wants to scream, to speed up time, to get to the part where she will hear what he is saying. As the word forms, it too is excruciatingly sluggish, dragged out and unnaturally unhurried. But the word finally takes shape:

"Wait," says the boy.

*   *   *   *

"Ever?"

"What? Yes. Sorry."

Marti smiles.

"Daydreaming?"

Sometimes, her supervisor's guesses are a little too on-the-nose. Ever has indeed spent a lot of her day thinking about her dreams. Luckily she's gotten good enough at app request processing that even when distracted she can sail through her tasks quickly.

"Something like that," Ever says, with an awkward hopping little laugh. "Hey, if I can get wrapped up in the next few minutes—is it all right if I take off a little early today?"

"Why?" Marti teases. "Got a hot date?"

Seriously.

On the freaking nose.

Ever is prepared to lie, but something stops her. She looks at Marti, whose expression is open and genuinely interested. It's so different from the competitive boredom she sees in her mother's face. Maybe it's time to attempt the friendship-thing she's been contemplating.

"Well. Sort of."

Marti's interest is obviously piqued.

"Really? Anyone I know?"

"Yeah. Red Shirt."

Marti laughs.

"All right, don't tell me, then."

Ever shifts into private mode automatically, as she has conditioned herself to do before experiencing or even thinking too long about anything that has to do with Cal. She gives a coy look to Marti, and lowers her voice.

"Go into private."

"What? Why?"

"You know my dad. I'm sure he runs the occasional scan on my public conversations."

"This is a private conversation."

"Not unless it's in private mode, it's not. Nothing's really ours, not even our conversations. You know that, right?"

Marti gives Ever an odd look, and Ever knows how paranoid the woman must be thinking she is; but Ever knows her father well, and knows she can never be too cautious. Marti's eyes shift and re-focus.

"I'm in private. So who's the guy?"

"I… can't say."

"Even in private mode?"

"Yeah. For now. It's—complicated. But… it's good."

"You look happy."

"I think I kind of am," Ever says, and she actually is.

"Well. Go get it, girl. Have fun with…?"

"Let's just call him 'big guy,'" Ever says.

"Big guy, huh?" Marti teases.

The giggle. It feels so weird and so wonderful. Confiding in a girlfriend. Joking about boys. It's something Ever saw in movies as a little kid, back in the old world. Not something she ever experienced before augmenting. Or after.

They shift out of private mode, after one final wink from Marti. Wrapping up quickly, Ever hurries down the hallway, checking in on the publicly available work orders maintenance crews are out on. She doesn't even need Marti's credentials for this anymore; it's easy to figure out which call Cal is on. Since her dad doesn't want her to find him, his name is left off of all work orders. So whichever one lists only one name, or none—that's where he'll be. Real, solid, and waiting for her.

Wait.

In a rush the moment from last night's dream comes back, for the hundredth time that day. A single infuriating moment. The boy, finally saying something, but all it was… was a request that she remain in this purgatory dreamscape with him. Every other time she re-lived this moment today, she felt intrigued. But now, buoyed by the brief but delicious moment of girl-talk with Marti, propelled by the upcoming encounter with Cal, she feels resentful of the dream-boy. Why should she wait on an ephemeral evening companion, who never really said anything or did anything? Who never showed up?

She'd convinced herself that there was something real about him, about those moments while she slept. But that was ridiculous. What was real was someone you could touch and hold and taste. What was real was something solid, something definite and defined. What was real was Cal.

She reaches his worksite, a dangerously nearby location this time—Cal is rewiring the lights in a library just two floors down from her father's lab. Slipping into private mode, she waits outside the library until she sees the first uniformed maintenance worker step out. Then she enters the library, where Cal is packing up the tools, closing up shop… and, as his twinkling eyes suggest when he turns around to greet her, expecting her arrival.

"There you are."

"Am I getting predictable?"

"Anything but."

"How many cameras in here?"

"I thought you were the one who always knew the lay of the land," he teases.

"I was busy today."

"Working hard?"

"Yessir. And I think I'm making friends."

"Look at you," he smiles. Then he nods toward the corner. "Just one camera. And wouldn't you know, it's not working. Gonna have to get a crew down here on that, first thing in the morning."

He steps toward her, shutting the door behind her and pressing her against it, kissing her and leaning his full weight against her.

He's real he's real he's real.

CHAPTER 46: SHADOWER

S HADOWER IS UNEASY. This morning, siphoning information from the hidden underbelly of Heaven's uploads, there were some interesting little morsels. No new bodies—in fact, no bodies or even implications of self-terminating Syns whatsoever, post Pulse—and no new prophesies. But there was something new; a shivering little electric current, whispering clandestine secrets. Something foreign, not part of the normal Syn systems.

Scanning the hidden archives for similar patterns, Shadower found a match. Just one other instance of a little electric signature like this, barely discernible but distinct to one committed to noticing small details.

It appeared about twenty-four hours before the Pulse.

And it appeared again last night.

Shadower can't be sure, but trusting hunches has paid off before, and this one can't be ignored. Another Pulse is going to strike, probably sometime this evening, probably harder than the first time because everyone and everything is still reeling. It will be the perfect time for the Originals to leave the ship, slip undetected into the Center, witness the Pulse, see how long it lasts and how much damage it does—possibly even check in with Jorge or Shadower directly, since if this Pulse is like the last it will temporarily disable their synthetic components from witnessing or retaining their interactions.

Assuming Jorge and Shadower are not both killed in the Pulse.

But before dealing with that potentiality, Shadower first had to retrieve the Originals from the ship where they had been huddled all night. Ideally, someone else would fetch them, but it might have to be Shadower—not outed overtly as Shadower, of course; but with Syn eyes everywhere and an imminent Pulse, sending anyone else was too risky.

Shadower's eyes close in concentration. Logging in to the ship's communication system should be easy, but maintaining an extreme level of cover will be the challenging part, so it's best to be sure that—

What the hell?

When Shadower attempts contact with the ship, there's nothing. The ship is completely powered down and offline. Not just off the grid from everyone else, but entirely off. Inaccessible, even to Shadower.

Shadower goes deeper, overriding the entire system and powering the ship back up. Shadower can almost feel it even from all these miles away, the lights warming and glowing as they twinkle back on, the vessel's embedded computer system clicking into active mode. The cameras turn back on, and Shadower accesses the live feed.

The ship is empty.

Shadower furiously shifts from live feed to recorded images, before recalling that the recording had been disabled as an added measure of protection. There's no way to know exactly when the Originals left the ship, or why, or where the hell they thought they were going.

What in Heaven and hell is going on here?

Did they just leave, on their own, once again?

Or—curse of the world!—did someone else find them?

No… surely there would be rumblings, whispers, something I could tap into if the Syns found Ere and Karma… unless I really have lost my touch?

Shit. Shit shit shit shit.

CHAPTER 47: JORGE

JORGE WAS NOT EXPECTING communication from Shadower—or anyone in the clandestine network, possibly ever again. But now there's a message, barely encrypted and so straightforward that Jorge would have to wonder if it were some sort of forgery, save the very last detail:

> Our friends are in danger. They came, then left the vessel.
> Their whereabouts are unknown. It is just the two.
> Options are limited. Time running out.
> Cannot transmit further.
> We will meet where first we met. Noon. Fried chicken.

Every sentence in the brief missive speeds up Jorge's heart rate. He is standing in the middle of the laboratory as he reviews the message, private mode offering a small measure of protection in the mouth of the wolf.

Time is running out.

Had Shadower picked up on an upcoming Pulse?

This, too, curdles Jorge's stomach. Despite having a high threshold for pain, nothing had prepared Jorge for that attack on his system. Not prison fights, not augmentation experiments, not any of the abuses to which his body had been subject over the last century. The idea that another such experience might be around the corner makes him flinch.

"You all right?"

Kennedy's question startles Jorge. Quickly erasing the message, keeping his expression neutral, Jorge gives his coworker a nod. He calls up a report onscreen.

"Fine, thanks," Jorge says, his mind still stuck on the now-deleted communiqué from the clandestine contact. "Just wondering if we picked anything else up, markers that might indicate when there might be another Pulse. Have you looked at last night's data?"

"Just started in on it," Kennedy says.

"Well. Flag anything interesting. Hess wants to meet up in an hour."

"Yeah, I saw that. You think the meeting'll go long?"

"I don't think so. He's busy. And I have—lunch plans," Jorge says.

"Really?" Kennedy smirks.

Jorge pushes his irritating coworker from his mind and takes quick stock of the situation. He still doesn't know where he stands with Hess. He has become an obsessive self-scanner, making sure no tracking devices or additional observation apps were somehow ferreted into his system. It has killed him, not knowing at all what was going on with the rebels, with the clandestine network; but he couldn't put their lives at risk, so he has gone cold turkey. No checking in on any of the network channels. No visiting any of the physical checkpoints where the occasional package or transmitter was left. No messages sent. Nothing.

Being this disconnected from the only element of his life that made him feel useful has nearly killed him. Furthering Hess's initiatives without feeding his insider information to people who could ultimately dismantle it makes Jorge feel like, every day, he is selling off more and more of his soul, with no outlet to redemption available any longer.

So there is a bright spot simply in receiving a message from Shadower. Whatever happens next might kill him, but Jorge feels pretty sure that death is preferable to daily damnation.

CHAPTER 48: "MARTI"

GINA FINALLY HAS SOMETHING interesting to report at her weekly meeting. Ever since taking on this assignment, there has been a lot to keep track of, but so much of it was mind-numbing minutiae. What makes it worse is having to also keep up with the day-to-day requirements of the regular App-Dev job, to keep up appearances. It wasn't that hard, she mostly just had to make sure other people were doing their jobs, which was a lot like her last management position. But juggling what really amounted to two new gigs was still kind of a lot.

It's been almost a year since she took on the new role—*roles*, more accurately. The first half of that year had all been training and preparation. Then the slog of getting going, slowly. So she dreads these weekly meetings, because she usually has nothing meaningful to say. This time, she has something to share. As luck would have it, she just doesn't want to share it. But she has to; it's her job, and her boss made clear from the beginning that zero slack would be cut.

Just get through it, Gina.

Then she corrects herself, sharply, pinching the sensitive inside of her wrist to remind herself.

No. I'm not Gina.

I'm Marti.

*   *   *   *

Eleven months earlier, Gina Torres was a mid-level manager. She had an important role, though she worked way over in the New Haven satellite site, in one of the austere buildings on the campus of what was once Yale University. She was part of a large team housed out there, reviewing personal histories uploaded to Heaven and creating more palatable digests of the information for easy archival access. It was interesting enough to keep her from going numb, which was enough. Most days.

She would have liked living in the more modern Syn sector, but at least the cleaned-up synthetic New Haven, now just called "Yale," in honor of the regal old campus that somehow survived siege after siege, had some real old-world character. She lived in a nice three-level home, a much bigger place in a much nicer neighborhood than she could ever have afforded back in the old world, when she was a struggling actress sharing a three-bedroom apartment with four other people in Queens.

She was even seeing someone, although that was a pretty recent development. She was hesitant to use the word 'boyfriend,' but she and Max had a pretty good thing going. He didn't work at the Synt. He was a personal trainer, helping fitness-minded Syns maintain and maximize the potential of their long stays in once-aging bodies. Gina wasn't quite sure how he made it into the new world, but she assumed it had something to do with how hot he was. He wasn't a very good personal trainer—she'd noticed no improvements since he began working with her—but he was very good at keeping himself in shape. He had a huge client roster, all of whom were fairly obviously in love with him. Or at least wanted to screw him.

At first, Gina thought Max knew that he only got hired by people who wanted to sleep with him. But he was apparently oblivious. He was maybe a little dumb, she realized. Still, as the one who got to sleep with him (and *that*, he was very good at), she didn't get too hung up on that. Not at first.

"An actress dating a personal trainer," she joked to Max once. "Glad to know clichés survived the Singularity."

"What?" Max said.

"Clichés," said Gina.

"It's cute when you talk Spanish," said Max.

Max was actually *very* dumb.

Then one morning, she received an odd summons, directly from the Director of the Synt.

> **Ms. Torres**
> **You are up for a promotion.**
> **We'll discuss the particulars in my office.**
> **Six this evening—sharp.**
> **FH**

FH: Felix Hess.

Gina was in awe of that man, and couldn't believe he knew who she was. Max was an anomaly—brains had always been a real turn-on for Gina, and you didn't get much brainier than Hess.

Well, Nathan Fell, maybe. He was the real architect of the Syn world, and had those smoking gray eyes and strong Fell chin and all that fiery visionary heat—but he'd died young, so that fantasy was never happening.

Meanwhile Hess was the savvy contractor who took Nathan Fell's blueprints and constructed an even bigger, better building. He had intense eyes, and that full silver-fox head of hair, and that compact and in-constant-motion figure of his was also pretty exciting.

Good Lord, Gina. Don't go all fan-girl before you're even in the room.

She could barely contain herself for the rest of the day. She wrapped up work at four, giving herself plenty of time to catch the light rail and hit the Synt well in advance of her appointment. She sat in the lobby for more than an hour, just waiting, wanting to be sure Hess didn't have to wait on her.

At five fifty-nine, the savage-eyed receptionist who manned the front desk at the Synt sent Gina up to Dr. Felix Hess's office. At exactly six o'clock, Gina knocked on his old-fashioned, heavy wooden door.

"Come in," Hess called, and Gina pushed open the intimidating door and began her interaction with the intimidating man.

"Hi, I'm—"

"Miss Torres, yes. Have a seat."

Gina sat in one of Hess's maroon vintage-leather chairs, which squeaked softly beneath her as she adjusted her ass in its slick-soft cushion.

"You were an actress, in the old world."

"Yes," she said, surprised.

"Were you any good?"

Gina remembered something she'd read once, about how powerful men are drawn to confident-but-vulnerable partners. Lead with confidence, then let a little of your vulnerability slip down your shoulder like a silken bra strap, the probably-bullshit article had advised. Gina had nothing else coming to mind at the moment, advice-wise, so she decided to follow this motif.

"I was very good," she said, surprising herself with the sultry confidence in her voice.

"You didn't get many big roles," Hess said, unimpressed, expression unchanged.

His casual indictment of her entire acting career caught her off-guard. In a rush, every cold read that went nowhere and every callback that culminated in a thanks-but-no-thanks email flooded through her, washing away her brazen front.

Time to let the bra strap slip already? No, not yet.

"I was young," Gina said, still aiming for some measure of bravado.

"Your scarring didn't keep you from leading lady opportunities?"

"Oh," she wavered, ravaged arm and leg humming, remembering the violent crescendo of the flames that nearly consumed them. "From film work, yes."

"Why didn't you have your scars smoothed over?"

"Couldn't afford it back then."

"But you were able to augment."

"Yes."

Gina was always good at getting other people to pay for things. The one thing she was always too proud to ask someone else to pay for was cosmetic surgery. She felt no need to explain herself to Hess, despite his stare crawling under her skin.

"Well," said Hess, as if he already knew more about her than she did. "Let me tell you why you're here, Miss Torres."

"The message said a promotion—"

"Yes and no," Hess said. "Or yes and yes, depending on how we want to look at it. I have a rather unique assignment, and you fit the specialized profile required. You were under thirty when you augmented, you like your life in synthetic society but are not particularly invested in your current job or apartment or lover, you have a performance background, you're smart, you can charm your way into anyone's good graces, and you have a willingness to make moral compromises when they'll clearly further your ambition. Have I said anything that sounds unlike you?"

She wished she could refute any of his claims, but he had her pretty pegged.

"Good," Hess said. "We'll be moving you from Yale over here to the Synt. Effective immediately. I'm sending a request now for movers to pack you up. Your new apartment is here, in the Synt. You'll be managing a team in the application request division, and—"

"But I've never worked in app—"

"Don't interrupt me," Hess said, not raising his voice. "You can learn what you need to know about the work of the department in an hour, particularly because, if you were paying attention, I told you that you'll be managing a team. Your management responsibilities here will essentially mirror your managing responsibilities at Yale. You don't have to know how someone does what they do in order to make them do it. Understood?"

Gina nodded, throat dry.

"The management position is a cover. Your real assignment is something extremely sensitive and confidential."

Gina's stomach fluttered. She wanted to ask what he meant by that, but was afraid that she might be accused of interrupting him again. She waited an eternity, making certain he was not just taking a deep breath or long, thoughtful pause.

"What's... the assignment?"

He grinned at her, and her heart stuttered, fear and attraction interrupting its regular beat.

"It's the role of a lifetime."

"You want me to...act?"

"Yes," Hess said. "An immersive and ongoing performance-based assignment. Think of it as experimental theater at its very finest."

"What's the part?"

"You're going to play my daughter's best friend."

"I don't understand. Is your daughter in a show—?"

"My daughter will never know that you are anything other than a female who she comes to regard as a close personal confidante. This is an acting assignment, Miss Torres, but a subtle and strategic one. Thespian espionage—that's catchy, now, isn't it? You will report directly to me on the activities and mental and emotional states of my daughter Ever."

"But... why?"

"My daughter is vital to an extremely important research project."

"What's the project?"

"That's above your pay grade, to use the old vernacular. But it's very much for the good of society."

"Oh. Well. I assume, then, that she's already—"

"She is already quite tightly monitored. But she's a skilled manipulator, exercises her privacy mode allowances to the fullest extent of the law—and no matter what I pick up on camera, there's no telling what's going on in that head of hers. I need someone in her head."

She should have stood up then, shaken her head and asked to be sent back to Yale. *Thanks but no thanks*, she should have said. *I lied when I said I was a good actor. I'll fail. I don't want to do another woman like that.*

But then Hess stood up, walked over to the front of the desk, and leaned easily against it, inches from her.

"I've had my eye on you for some time," he said, low, conspiratorial. "We had to find just the right person for this role. I think you'll be brilliant, Miss Torres."

She swallowed hard.

"Call me Gina. Please."

"Actually," he said, "we'll call you Marti."

*   *   *   *

And so, faster than she could have imagined, Gina became Martha Manuel, better known as Marti. She got a new haircut, a new wardrobe, and some rudimentary training in App-Dev. Hess escorted her himself to her new residence in the Synt, a spacious high-ceilinged flat with jaw-dropping views of the gleaming city and the ocean beyond its borders.

Gina got into the spirit of things, developing a mild Midwestern twang for Marti, parting her hair on the left side instead of the right each morning, deciding that she had worked in advertising back in the old world and looking up as much as she could on that industry. While she prepared for her initial introduction to Ever, she imagined every possible question the girl might ask of her and made sure that she had an answer at the ready, solid and convincing.

It was by turn exhilarating and boring. Managing in App-Dev was a breeze; the team was so well-established they were practically automated. Deciding ahead of time what "Marti" might possibly task the skill-less Ever Hess with doing once her father sent her to work was a challenge. There was really no gap within the team. They had to invent a need for her to be there.

No one else in App-Dev knew about Marti's assignment, or that back in Yale she had gone by another name. Hess had altered all of the records, and anyhow no one on that team really cared enough to go digging up the likely boring background of a new mid-level manager. No one from her old job really missed her, and it was a good three weeks after Gina had started her new life that she remembered to shoot Max a message to let him know he probably wouldn't be seeing her anymore. (His reply: "No worries, girl. It's cool.")

The anticipation was building, and Marti was actually excited to finally meet the infamous Ever. She had to do a lot of deep breathing and several old MFA-class warm-ups in her residence that morning to set her intention, get into character and make sure that despite *Gina's* giddiness, *Marti* would appear calm, no-nonsense, and none-too-desperate to push a personal connection agenda with Ever.

Hess's instructions were clear. *Ever can't know you're trying to cozy up to her. Let her approach you. Let her believe it's all on her terms. Think of it like this: she's a stray cat. If you try to pet her too soon, she'll run away. Leave out the milk. Let her find it.*

Marti felt good about her first interaction with Ever. There was some banter, a good rapport by the end of the conversation. Very promising. But then things just got boring. Ever seemed like any other uninteresting pissed-off-ageless rich girl. She was warm enough to Marti, but didn't open up to her about anything personal.

But then there was the Pulse. The unexpected opportunity for Marti to save Ever and solidify their connection. The doubly shocking chance to use her scars to cement a sense of understanding between them.

I really was born to play this part, Marti thought as she pulled up her pants leg in the middle of the Hess residence.

She had to keep her face hidden for a minute there, afraid she might grin like an idiot, willing all of her actor training to keep her neutral, authentic and in-the-moment as possible for someone completely manipulating their audience of one.

Hess had instructed Marti to leave her jacket behind that day, making certain that her unprotected credentials were left with it. Marti still didn't know why Hess wanted Ever to have access to her ID (which she returned the very next day), but knew the director must have his reasons. Marti delivered the lines, followed the blocking, left the prop onstage.

It was a great meeting with Hess, when she was able to replay that exchange for him. The reveal of her scars, the casual forgetting of the jacket, everything. It all played out perfectly. Even in the wake of the Pulse, with the world around them still reeling, it was a bright spot. After watching it for a second time, he put a hand on her shoulder, and squeezed it.

"Brilliant," he said, and she soared.

*   *   *   *

Since that post-Pulse meeting, their weekly appointments have gone back into the disappointing routine of Marti having little to share and Hess sighing through his teeth at her lack of insight, dismissing her swiftly since she had nothing of value for him. Fortified with something new to report, she hopes for a better reaction today. Maybe he'll give her a hug, or at least an appreciative pat. Maybe he'll comment again on her brilliance, on how well she's playing this part, day after day. Taking a deep breath, she knocks on the door.

"Come in," Hess says.

Marti opens the door, walks confidently into the room and stands before his desk, beaming. "She's seeing someone."

"I know that."

Marti's face falls.

"But—"

"There are cameras on her all the time, even when she thinks there aren't," Hess snaps, impatient. "I'm well aware of her cavorting with the Original. Were you unaware of that before today?"

"Of course not," Marti lies, hoping she really is the halfway decent performer Hess's research team had deemed her to be.

It's hard to keep up the pretense when she's also trying to

guess his next statement or question, figure out his state of mind, and why the hell he even needs her if he's already got such ample coverage on the girl. If he knew she was hooking up with the Original, and he doesn't approve, why was he letting that happen? He could stop her at any time.

"Then what's the 'exciting development' you were so eager to share with me today?"

Marti's mind races, and thankfully returns to their very first meeting and the phrase Hess had used back then: *I am to report on her mental and emotional state, not just her activities. Where her mind is at—he can't get that from his cameras.*

"She's serious about him," Marti says.

At this, Hess lifts an eyebrow.

"You're sure."

"Yes," Marti breathes, flooded with relief at her successful improvisation. "She's—in love."

"Good," Hess says, surprising her. "And does she think I know about the two of them?"

"No," Marti says confidently. "Absolutely not. She swore me to secrecy."

Hess rewards her with a grin. "Good thing I got to you first."

She smiles back at him, almost shy. His praise eases her guilt. If she lets herself think too long about what she's doing to the girl, she gets a little queasy. Marti does genuinely like Ever. Which means constantly lying to her and reporting on her to her father feels increasingly crappy.

But it's for the good of society, Marti reminds herself. *Hess knows what he's doing.*

"Do you want me to… steer her away from this guy?" she asks.

Hess gives her a sharp look.

"Of course not," he says. "I'm the one who got them together in the first place."

MARILYN'S BOOBS HURT. The procedure earlier in the day had gone just fine. No complications, no issues. A little tucking, a little tightening, and Marilyn had the small, shapely bosom she requested. Currently tightly wrapped under snug medical binding, she couldn't really see what the results had precisely yielded. She's sure they're great. But the initial painkillers she was given wore off too quickly, and now she's sore.

She shifts on the bed, which makes it worse. The doctor had told her she could be up and about, it was a minor surgery these days, blah blah blah. Marilyn feels sluggish, uncomfortable, and frankly disagrees with the doctor. Had he ever had *his* breasts augmented? Doubtful.

She sends a message to Angela, who is in the kitchen prepping lunch.

Bring me my pills.

It's been awhile since she's summoned Angela into the bedroom. Angela isn't a maid. They have a company who sends various Vosts to do the housekeeping, which Marilyn prefers because that way she doesn't have to make nice to the same person over and over, she can just ignore the string of faceless toilet-scrubbers.

Angela appears, pills and a glass of water in hand.

"Didn't even know you were awake."

"Of course I'm awake. It's hard to sleep when you're in so much pain."

Angela hands Marilyn two pills and the glass of water.

"Here."

Marilyn tosses the pills against the back of her throat, flushing them down with a swift gulp of water. She wipes her mouth with the back of her hand, not caring about the gracelessness of it because she just went through surgery and it's only Angela, after all.

"Wait."

"You want something else?" Angela asks.

"Yes, I—I mean, no, just… sit a minute," Marilyn says, not even sure why she's asking her one-time friend to stay. She just suddenly very much doesn't want to be alone, and as is often the case, Angela is her only option.

Angela hesitates, looking around; there's no place to sit. The Hess bedroom is sparse, a room reflecting Felix's aesthetic. A large maple bed, slate gray sheets and comforter, very minimal furnishings—all old-world, heavy, made-of-real-trees. The only indication that Marilyn inhabits the space is the long, low bureau with a large vanity mirror. The surface of the bureau is covered entirely in bottles and tubes and pots of various creams and cosmetics, flanked here and there by glittering scattered orphan earrings and dainty necklaces.

Marilyn pats the bed, then adds sharply: "Sit gently. Don't jostle me."

Holding herself stiff and barely denting the comforter, Angela sits on the edge of the bed.

"What are you—working on? In the kitchen," Marilyn says, praying for the painkillers to kick in soon.

"I was just fixing you some supper. Comfort food seemed like a good idea today. Been awhile since I made matzoh ball soup," Angela says. "Figured that'd be good for you while you're recovering."

Marilyn notes the absurdity of her situation— a synthetic African American woman fixing a bedridden synthetic southern WASP some old-world Jewish comfort food. Marilyn pictures the fat matzoh balls floating in the temperature-controlled water, preserved and waiting to be served and devoured by this unlikely duo. She imagines their puffed-up confusion, and she bursts out laughing.

"Matzoh ball soup," she says, giggling.

"What's so funny about matzoh ball soup?"

"Everything," Marilyn says, snickering, and then adds: "Matzoh boobs."

"Those meds kick in fast, huh?" Angela says.

"Guess so," Marilyn says, feeling mercifully blurred. "How're you, Angela?"

"I'm fine," Angela says. "Just wanna get that soup finished up 'fore you pass out."

"I don't need to eat anything."

"You do."

"Nah," Marilyn says, waving away the idea of needing nourishment.

"I'll bring it in on a tray, and you can have it when you get hungry."

"Felix has been talking in his sleep. Still."

Angela raises an eyebrow. This makes her look younger to Marilyn.

I should tell her to always raise an eyebrow, so she looks younger. Or to just go get a damn lift already. Why doesn't she ever get any nips or tucks? Does she think she looks so great? Does she think she's so perfect? Everyone needs a little help. Even you, Angela...

"Still, huh? What's he been saying?"

Marilyn's mind shifts again, rolling from harsher to more pleasant thoughts with the ease of an anchored boat shifting which way it rocks in response to any variance in wind. She likes that Angela is interested, she likes talking to her, she wants to keep this conversation going.

"All kinds of... stuff."

"Stuff like?"

"Stuff about... meetings."

"Meetings with who?"

"With all sorts of... folks. Lorraine, he says, sometimes. But I don't get jealous because she's an old bitch."

Marilyn giggles again when she says this, feeling like a naughty schoolgirl who just called the principal an old bitch. Another name floats to mind.

"Nathan. Nathan friggin' Fell. That's who else he says he sees. That old ghosty-ghost. He says he's meeting with Nathan, and they have tea. Tea time with Nathan Fell, that's a hoot, huh? Little dollies and teddies at a table and a fancy tea set, you think? I used to have tea parties with my dollies and teddies in Texas, long-long time ago with my Daddy..."

Marilyn's eyes drift. She stares at the cosmetics and jewelry on the vanity bureau, the mirror doubling all of the containers and baubles, the medicine doubling everything again, into a seemingly endless collection. Some of the earrings and necklaces once belonged to her mother, that beautiful angel who died giving birth to her. Died before aging or doing anything to make her daughter see her as anything other than perfect and shining and gone.

Marilyn is not even seeing the vanity anymore, she's seeing her angel mother and her handsome father, both dead now but they're having a tea party, sitting at a table with her dollies and teddies and Marilyn wants to be there with them.

I want to be with them.

Mama and Daddy.

I want to be with them…

"Let me help you lay down, now," Angela says, after a long moment or maybe after no time at all.

Obediently, like a small child, Marilyn lets the other woman ease her down onto the bed. Marilyn's eyes stay open, fixed and imagining something not there, half-aware enough to know that when she closes her eyes and goes to sleep, there will be no dreaming. There will just be her husband's hungry Heaven, pulling her thoughts and giving her new information. Though still gazing wide-eyed ahead, Marilyn does not see when Angela slips from the room, and by the time Angela returns with the matzoh ball soup, Marilyn's eyes are closed.

"ALL RIGHT," ASAVARI SAYS. "Here's where we part ways. If I'm not back by tomorrow night, don't come after me. Fly the ship back to my tribe. Tell them to remain there until—"

"I know," Ere says, irritated. The girl still thinks she knows more than he does, is privy to information of which he is not yet aware. But they were on the ship together. He heard the same stupid instructions. And he's already pissed off that she's the one who gets to go to the Synt, right to where Ever is, while he's supposed to hang back here at the bridge and kill time for a day.

All right," Asavari says again, and Ere realizes the brazen girl is nervous.

Why wouldn't she be? She should be. She's about to go into the unknown, into the middle of a world where she is unwelcome and possibly even wanted for criminal activity. Ere knows he should offer her some sort of support or encouragement, but damned if he knows what to say or do, and so he remains silent and allows the girl to talk herself into forward movement.

"All right," she says for the third time. And then she's on her way.

Ere watches her in the darkness as she moves swiftly down the bridge, farther and farther away from him. In the intermittent moonlight, for the first several moments he can see her form and figure fairly clearly. Then she becomes more abstract, a slightly lighter shade of dark melting and moving into the blackness. Then she disappears entirely, and he is alone.

Finally.

From the moment Chameleon had commanded the plan—*Asavari, go; Ere, stay*—Ere knew that as soon as he was alone, he would head for Ever. Patience was never one of his virtues. Under any circumstance, huddling and trying to remain unnoticed on a boring bridge for an entire day would be a tough sell. But knowing that he is within mere miles of the girl he came here for, the one who awakened in him a desire and a tenderness that continue to propel him—well, waiting be damned. He'll wait just long enough for Asavari to be well ahead of him. Then he'll take off. He's wearing the Syn garb provided by the well-equipped ship; his outfit includes a conveniently large, face-hiding hood. He'll pass as a Syn, get into the Synt, and then—

And then what, shit-for-brains?

Hess thinks you're dead. If he sees you, you really might be dead.

And so will Jorge.

And Asavari. He can't go into the Synt. He can't. But he can't just sit here, either. And surely if he's in the city, he'll find a way to reach Ever. She must leave the building sometimes. She's independent. He's resourceful. They found each other before, against all odds, and he knows they can find each other again. Even though she won't remember him.

And then he thinks of his mother.

He recalls her face when she walked into the cottage where he had spent the night with Ever. That mix of shock, rage, and worst of all—the utter betrayal. He had lied to her, chosen a Syn girl's affection over his mother's trust.

And soon after that, he lost his mother forever.

But he also thinks of her final words to him,

Love, Ere—that is your heritage…

Love. Wasn't that what was propelling him toward Ever? Who else in the world could he ever love? His mother was dead, his other relatives all dead save Cal, who hates him. The only other Originals his age are strange rebel warriors like Asavari, not interested in love but focused instead on justice.

Love, Ere.

That is your heritage.

He takes off for the bridge.

His legs pump furiously beneath him, ignoring all recent blisters and cracks, pulled muscles and aching limbs. The bridge is longer than he thought it would be, and he is soon winded, but he keeps going. Once he reaches the end of the bridge, he'll be at the inner edge of the sprawling metropolis. Though Chameleon had assured them the checkpoint would be unmanned, that didn't mean there would be no Syns in proximity. As he finally nears the end of the bridge, he slows his stride, in response to the overhead lights flooding the bridge's exit and to the relief of his howling calves and rasping lungs. He walks cautiously, keeping his head low and peering out from beneath his hood, making certain he is alone.

He forces himself to move quickly, dashing through the wild exposure of the floodlight and keeping up the pace as he puts distance between himself and the bridge. He half-jogs, as best he can with his ragged lungs screaming at him, toward the darkened stretch of manicured nature that stretches from the bridge several more miles before giving way to the industrial boxes and impossibly tall skyscrapers of the city surrounding the Synt.

After the first hour of making his way through the darkness, he finally realizes that one advantage to manicured nature is that it has very clearly laid paths, and so long as no one else is there he really ought to stick to them. The tidy, swept-dirt footpath made for much easier travel than forcing himself to go through the woods, where the trees were all quite evenly spaced but nonetheless stubbornly prone to poking him with branches and tripping him with roots.

After several hours of walking the clearer path, having seen no signs of life or threat whatsoever, his vigilance dims. His mind begins to wander. He wonders how far ahead Asavari is, and whether or not she's met up with Chameleon. He wonders what the tribe back in India is thinking, as they wait and hope and pray. He is so distracted by his guilty wondering that he almost runs right into a Syn couple, pressed up against a tree, furiously kissing and clutching at one another.

He is only a few yards away when he sees them, and fortunately they are so distracted by one another that Ere manages to notice them first. He swiftly scales the nearest tree, hugging the trunk and avoiding the limbs with their dangerous rustling leaves. Dragging himself up as quietly as possible, he gets high enough to find a wide branch that will support his weight and clings to it, heart beating with a deafening thud.

The footlights of the bridge are too far away to illuminate this swath of land—there's nothing but a half-moon and sprinkling of stars, fighting to peek through the hazy curtain draped across the sky. Ere squints in the darkness at the couple, hoping to determine if they will be moving on anytime soon or if he will have to head back into the thicker, pathless portion of the forest to get around these obnoxious synthetic lovers.

"Cal."

The word is as distinct as the voice uttering it, and the combination of the two nearly causes Ere to topple from the tree. Surely it was just a similar voice, and another Cal. The world is small, but not that small.

It can't be.

"Cal, slow down."

"Aren't you enjoying yourself?"

"I always do."

They laugh, and the sound rips through Ere.

Ever and Cal.

How the hell can this be happening?

"What's on your mind, my love?" Cal asks Ever, and Ere very nearly vomits.

"I'm not sure how long we can keep getting away with this," she sighs, nestling herself into him. "At some point someone is bound to find us."

"I've thought of that, too," Cal says, his hands on her ass. "And I've made a decision. Please—listen to me before you say anything. All right?"

"All right," says the most beautiful girl in the world.

"I want to augment."

Ere nearly yelps.

"Cal, no—" Ever gasps, but Cal shakes his head and places a finger to her lips.

"Listen first," he reminds her. "Your father sees me as a threat, but he won't if I demonstrate my loyalty. My desire—my commitment—to be with you, to be a part of your world. I want to be with you, Ever. My world, the people and customs that I grew up with... it's dying. It's dead. For better or worse, your father is right. And maybe that's how it's meant to be, I don't know. But I know that *we* are meant to be."

On the verge of exploding, Ere shifts his weight, and a small chunk of tree bark crumbles beneath him and tumbles to the ground, falling with a soft thud. It is a small sound, but enough noise to alert Cal, now that his face is no longer melded with the Syn girl's.

"What is it—" Ever begins, sensing Cal's reaction to some unseen threat.

"I heard something," Cal mutters, so low Ere can scarcely hear him. Ere fears that his pounding pulse is louder than Cal's whispered words. Any minute now, Cal will spot him, snatch him from the tree, and then—

"We should go," Ever whispers, fear in her voice.

"I should see who or what is out there—"

"No," Ever insists. "Come on."

Reluctantly, still on guard, Cal allows Ever to take his hand, and they flee.

Ere finally releases the breath he has been holding for far too long. In releasing his breath, he also loosens his grip, and nearly slides right down the tree trunk. Steadying himself, he holds on for another few long moments, then shimmies down a few feet before letting go and dropping to the forest floor.

He has heard too much to understand any of it, felt too much to feel anything any longer. He knew Ever had erased him—how could he have thought she would not have replaced him? But even if he had allowed himself to be caught in the net of that fear, never would he have imagined that it would be his own cousin who would slip into the space vacated by Ere.

And he's willing to augment for her. To become a Syn, and leave behind the Original ways... all for a girl who could, in the blink of an eye, erase him from her memory. What an idiot—oh curse of the world—!

Evidently, Cal was exactly as idiotic as Ere, who had extended the same offer to Ever mere months earlier. Hearing his cousin make that offer sounded so different to Ere than when he was the one considering it. It sounded so much less noble. So much more traitorous. Suddenly the guilt Ere has been suppressing overwhelms him.

Would I really have become a Syn? Just like that? After all my family has been through?

If he became a Syn, the shame inherent in that act would be a corrosive ever-present in his life, rusting through him like the browned and rotted bodies of the old metal cars and boats littering long-abandoned Original cities.

The Syns took everything from his people, and he was so blinded by one girl—one *Syn* girl—that he had forsaken all that he had once held dear. He was on the cusp of abandoning an entire nation of Originals who stood ready to follow him—all for a girl who didn't even remember him, and was now in love with his bastard of a cousin.

And just like that, Ere knows what he has to do. He turns his back, straightening his spine and walking east, back to the bridge, to wait for Asavari. He will not tell her what he saw. There is no way to reveal that without revealing his near-betrayal. And as far as he's concerned, Asavari never has to know about his near-abandonment of her or her people. Their people.

Our people, he reminds himself.

He might be dull and dead inside as he does it, but he'll be damned if he's not going to be loyal now to the ones who have shown him loyalty, and punish the rest. He will lead the charge against the Syns. Including Cal, if it comes to that.

"Ere Fell?"

Startled, Ere grabs for the small silver gun, clandestinely transferred to the pocket of his Syn garb.

A small, slim figure slips out from behind another tree. In the almost starless night, determining any detail about this person is impossible. Ere tenses for whatever this person might do or say next.

"What an honor to meet you," says the shadowy form. "Sorry about the tranquilizer, but it's just a precaution. You understand."

"What tranq—" Ere begins, then feels a small sting in his thigh, and collapses.

MUCH AS HESS HATES MEETINGS, he has several regular ones now. He finds them to be of varying importance, though unfortunately none are entirely expendable at this particular moment in time.

First, there are those damned weekly Council meetings. If he could let any of the meetings go, this would be the first one to get cut—or it would have been, before the Pulse. Though he still rankles at their attempts to oversee him, Hess has to admit that having multiple minds debate how to prepare for the next Pulse is useful, because for the first time in a long time, Hess himself has no idea what to do.

Then there are his bi-weekly appointments with Martha Manuel, aka Gina Torres, the washed-up actress he'd plucked from obscurity and tasked with befriending his daughter. Those appointments had been feeling a little useless until recently, when the long game of getting Ever to open up to someone was finally starting to pay off. Getting her to open up to Marti was an important step in the longer con of connecting her with the Original.

The paths that Cal and Ever had followed to find one another were all breadcrumbs baked, broken, and scattered by Hess himself. He knew his daughter well enough to know that the absolute surest way to interest her in something was to forbid her from it. He could have stopped her from getting to Cal—and even easier, could have stopped Cal from getting his hands on her—at any moment.

But Hess needed them to find one another.

To fall for one another.

Others may well have overlooked the obvious, since he doesn't bear the same famous surname as Ere, but Cal Harper is just as direct a descendent of Nathan Fell. Both boys were from the same stock, held the same potential. The same line, the same inheritance of intellect and drive. Nathan begat both Ruth and Rachel. Ruth begat Ere. Rachel begat Cal.

Imagine what Cal and Ever might beget.

Ever has no notion that her father has pushed her toward this Original suitor. The whole thing would have fallen apart had she any inkling of his approval. Both she and the boy had to think it was of their own free will, and not some sort of set-up. But in fact, it was manipulated, manufactured, urged on by someone who had something to gain from this union.

Dr. Felix Hess, matchmaker.

There was no longer any bandwidth to run the full mule program, but he could still experiment with the cream of the crop. He has confided in no one about this plan—no one except the one confidante who would never betray him. It is that confidante he is going to meet with now, to fill him in on the latest developments. These candid confessions used to take place monthly, but ever since the Pulse, visiting his confidante has been incorporated into Hess's daily routine.

The ritual does not vary. Hess's tea is delivered by dumbwaiter, from his private residence—English breakfast, hot and black, perfuming the air with its fragrant steam. He steps onto a levitator, and glides smoothly to the core of Heaven, never spilling a drop.

To enter the core of Heaven, Hess first presses all five fingers onto the little flat-black security box, which glows green, then blue, once his prints are recognized. Next he enters a code on the adjacent keypad, before finally looking directly into the retinal scanner and allowing the swirl of a precision laser to complete the scan that confirms the third security check. Then the door slides down, dropping open so he can walk calmly into the inner sanctum of Heaven.

By the time he reaches his seat, his tea has cooled enough for him to place his lips to the mug's rim and take his first satisfying sip. He imbibes as he sits beside the most complicated entity in the entire world—his old friend and mentor, Dr. Nathan Fell.

He regards Fell, suspended and wizened, unblinking and unresponsive as ever. He wonders what would have happened if Nathan had not been a casualty of the war for progress—if he had survived the augmentation process, stepped out victorious, claimed his throne, the true lord of this world.

If he, and not Hess, had taken the crown—what would be different? Would he have built the same world? A poorer one? A better one?

Having to play second fiddle for endless years would not have sat well with Hess. At least in the old world, when someone died, a place was vacated at the head of the table. Put in enough time and you would advance. But if Fell had lived, he would have ruled forever. Just as Hess intends to.

He looks up at his mentor, suspended in his tank, powerless to weigh in with whatever he might be thinking. If he had any thoughts at all.

"Oh, Nathan," Hess sighs, sipping the last of his tea. "We never know how our stories will end, do we?"

CHAPTER 53: LORRAINE

LORRAINE LOOKS AROUND THE TABLE. Before now, her brain trust has been known only to her. She has met them individually or in small groups, two or three at a time. In a world dominated by technology, the only way to avoid electronic eyes is to do things the old-fashioned way. In person. Discreetly.

"So," she says, lifting her hand and indicating each of the people around the table, uniting them all as her subjects in one sweeping gesture. "Here we are. I'd say let's go around the room and introduce ourselves, but I think you all know each other. Any surprises?"

257

There are nervous titters. Lorraine's secret committee is comprised of almost everyone who mattered most in the old world yet were somehow excluded from the Council. Most had lobbied hard for a leadership position, but for various reasons had been denied a coveted spot. Which meant they all carried nicely marinated resentment toward Felix Hess, the man who hand-picked his advisors. Few of them realized how little Hess actually respected the people selected for the board; how he wanted yes-men, not thinkers.

The only one in the room other than Lorraine to serve on the Council was Vinnie Irby. Vinnie was old school. He didn't look like the average Syn. Though he had augmented, he did so in his mid-fifties and not in the best of health, and it showed. His skin is more weathered than the synthetic norm, his gut more sagging, his brows bushy enough to look like slow-moving caterpillars. He mistakenly believed his hair plugs, obtained in the old world, looked natural.

He had made his fortune in the scrap metal business, an overlooked opportunity for empire that had kept him in good Cadillacs and Cubans for years. He was shrewd. He was unapologetic. He liked making sure people knew what he was or wasn't, whether that meant reminding them of his wealth, or informing him that despite being named Vinnie, he was absolutely not Italian.

"I'm not eye-talian, hell no," he liked to tell people. "My ma, she was real cultured-like, and she was a huge fan of Vincent van Gogh. Y'know, crazy redheaded artist, Dutch guy, cut off his own ear? Cool as shit."

Vinnie liked puffing up about being named for an artist, liked pointing out that the world-famous artist was another non-Italian Vincent, just like him. All of this was a lie, albeit one he's been telling so long that even he believes it. Truth was, his mom had a massive girlhood crush on a kid named Vincent and never stopped loving that name. But being named after your mother's first boyfriend wasn't a great story. Vinnie was always willing to spin what needed spinning.

Lorraine likes Vinnie, warts and all. He's loyal. But today he's shifting, slumping in his seat, head low and shoulders high, channeling his inner turtle and trying to go unnoticed. He's a big guy, spilling over the sides of his chair, so it's hard to hide.

"Vinnie," Lorraine says sharply. "You look nervous."

"Well," he says, puffing then deflating. "Shouldn't we all be a little nervous here?"

There are murmurs around the room from the others at the table.

"He's right," pipes up Midge Ford. "It feels risky… just to be here."

"Having dinner is risky?" Lorraine asks smoothly, sipping her Sauvignon Blanc.

Everyone's eyes find somewhere to look other than Lorraine. They are, seated at her formal dining table. Everyone is dressed to the nines (which, for Vinnie, means a knee-length black leather jacket hanging open over jeans and a wrinkly too-tight silk button down shirt), chilled white wine in their gleaming crystal glasses. A decadent three-course dinner is about to be served. It appears to be an upscale dinner party, not a mutiny.

After much debate, Lorraine determined that this was the safest way to meet. Out in the relative open, but discreetly concealed at her home. Dinner clubs were a common practice, and attendees often stayed in private mode so that idle gossip would not later indict them.

"I think we are all just… cautious," Mimi Toshiba says, twisting her napkin in her small, well-manicured fingers.

"As we should be," Lorraine nods. "Caution will serve as well. Cowardice will not."

"None of us are cowards," Vinnie says, puffing up again a bit, and a few others nod.

Lorraine's servant, a plain-faced Vost called Bo, enters with another bottle of wine.

"Ah, Bo," Lorraine says. "Is the first course ready to be served?"

"Yes ma'am. Goat cheese crostini with blueberry and peach thyme salsa."

"And what does the herb *thyme* symbolize, Bo?"

"Courage," says the Vost, ready for his cue.

"Courage," Lorraine repeats. "It's thyme for courage, if you'll pardon the pun."

(No one did. It was unforgivable.)

"Jesus, Lorraine," Vinnie grumbled.

"Look, everyone," Lorraine said, dropping her sallow smile and her humor, shifting into all-business mode. "Let's get down to brass tacks, shall we? Vinnie here is on the Syn Council with me. That means the two of us are privy to all of the allegedly-top-level information shared with that group, which we can share with this one. In addition, I believe we all have personal insights, abilities and connections that can prove valuable in finding out whatever Felix Hess is keeping to himself. Things about the Pulse. And self-terminating Syns, which as you know is an issue that has impacted me quite personally."

At the mention of her husband's demise, everyone sinks a little lower in their seats. There is nothing to say in response to that. And most of them had been fond of Joshua Murray.

"Lorraine," Vinnie says at last, evidently the only one ballsy enough to respond. "You know I agree with you, Hess needs more regulation. But the prick is smart. We all start meeting behind his back, he's gonna find out."

"He won't," says Lorraine, then hesitates.

Is it too early to tell them?

Lorraine has been debating whether or not to share with the group that she was recently contacted by someone claiming to have information Hess lacked. Someone who claimed to have inside knowledge of the Original resistance—something Lorraine had not given serious credence to until getting that message. The anonymous source also mentioned the self-terminations, a hot button issue for Lorraine, and raised an interesting point about that phenomenon; namely, why the increasing number of self-terminating Syns had suddenly fallen to zero.

No one had offed themselves post-Pulse.

Isn't that odd? teased the source. *Wouldn't you think such a painful experience would, if anything, ramp up people's desire to get out of this world? What does Hess have to say about that?*

The very fact that this source knew about the self-terminating Syns was telling. It wasn't common knowledge. Lorraine briefly wondered if these messages were coming from someone on the Council, someone disgruntled like her. But she dismissed that idea quickly. Everyone on the Council was gutless. Everyone but Vinnie. And despite his falsely-claimed-namesake, Vinnie was artless. He couldn't compose secret messages like that.

Lorraine also has no way of responding to these messages. They are sent in odd encryptions, over channels that seem to disappear as soon as the message is delivered. It's all been a one-sided conversation so far.

She decides she's not yet ready to share this precious but mysterious contact with her handpicked secret committee. Not until she has a way to initiate contact instead of just receive missives from the stranger calling himself Chameleon.

"I have a lead on another source," she says at last. "I'll do some more vetting before I know if the source is reliable. But we are not the only ones frustrated with the Hess regime."

"You mentioned self-termination," says Midge, slowly.

"Yes," Lorraine says, her stomach curling and uncurling. She had mentioned it. But only because of the sympathy it would win her.

"I haven't heard a lot about that, not since—Joshua," she continues, apologetically dropping her voice when she names Lorraine's husband. "Is it still… happening?"

"It was," Vinnie says. "Least according to what we're currently being told on the Council subcommittee, it was—but we don't have any on record post-Pulse."

"Odd," Midge says. "No incidents, post-Pulse. Could it be, somehow, that they're just not being recorded?"

"That's a good thought," Lorraine says. "Especially since there was a big cover-up, back before—before Joshua. But because of that, I've been running periodic system-wide checks on the population, and no one has disappeared."

"Yeah, but back before, whole records were erased," Vinnie points out. "So there wouldn't be a record of disappearance. That was our goal back when—"

"It was the *goal*," Lorraine agrees. "But it never really happened. Even if we erased a person, got rid of the body, cleaned up their footprint in Heaven… we could rarely get rid of them entirely—there would be relatives' archived memories, things we couldn't erase from Heaven. So I'm confident that everyone post-Pulse is present and accounted for, thus far."

Bo wheels out a silver cart, lined with crostini adorned with ham-handed symbolism. He silently begins placing the beautiful appetizers on the table. Bo, too, is in private mode. In addition to running the house for Lorraine, he is also sleeping with her. There is little danger of him revealing whatever he overhears. He has too much to lose.

Bo slips a plate in front of her, and Lorraine bites into the crisp crostini slathered with buttery-thick goat cheese. The strong thyme matched with the creamy cheese and vibrant, fruit-forward salsa compote is so delicious she closes her eyes in ecstasy.

Thyme for a little courage.

THE FRIED CHICKEN HAS BEEN SITTING on his plate for several minutes now, slowly cooling under Jorge's stare. He was there at noon on the dot, and it's not like Shadower to be late. It's especially not like Shadower to be late without sending word.

Where is she?

He wonders if he should send a message, but decides against it. Too risky, and anyhow, if something did come up Shadower might be unable to respond. He just has to be patient.

Eyes on his tray, Jorge thinks back to his days in prison. He hates cafeteria dining because it reminds him of every miserable meal he ate while incarcerated. Though the food today is far superior to the slop he was served back then, it still smacks of his days on the inside. Jorge is on guard. His shoulders are hunched, his muscles taut, all of his senses tuned in and alert for any threat or sign that things are about to get ugly. He takes in the handful of early-lunchers in the room. Almost no one is down here. But it only takes one guy with a shank to kill you.

So Jorge does not discount anyone in the room. He begins taking an inventory, hiding his face as best he can while trying to take in the countenance of every other cafeteria-goer. He is concentrating so hard that when a message abruptly arrives, it feels like a clanging alarm bell in his skull.

Eat the chicken.
It's good for you.
And it looks better for the cameras.

The missive is barely even encoded. Jorge freezes, then robotically reaches for a drumstick and tears flesh from bone, swallowing crispy breading and tender meat that might as well have been sandpaper. But Shadower said eat, so he'll eat.

As he takes a second, larger bite, he is surprised by the woman approaching his table with a purposeful stride. She is holding a lunch tray, piled high with fried chicken, cooked greens and mashed potatoes. He recognizes her. She is the Hess's housekeeper. He has to search his archives for her name.

"Angela?"

"That's right," she says, and her voice is familiar.

No. No way.

"Haven't seen you at the place in a while, things good in the lab?"

"Yes," he says, nearly choking.

"You eating alone today?"

"Uh. Yes," he says.

"Mind if I join you?"

"Please."

She sets down her tray and slides into the booth across from him.

"Such pretty golden eyes," she says. Then she looks him right in those eyes, and he watches her shift into private mode. He does the same.

"Angela," he says again.

"Yes," she says.

"And…"

Shadower, he thinks but does not say.

"Yes," she says, as if hearing his thoughts.

"This is too risky—"

"Everything's risky," Angela says, forking some greens, shoving them into her mouth, chewing, swallowing. "But we're about to get slammed with another Pulse. You, me, the cameras—we're all about to be as fried as this chicken. We'll remember this, assuming our organic brains aren't completely destroyed in the next electrocution. But our synthetic files are about to get zapped. So you best be taking this in with your organic mind."

Jorge nearly chokes.

"Another Pulse. You think it's gonna—"

"I think it's gonna. Now listen. The Fell boy and our friend Karma are here. But they left the ship and straight-up disappeared. I'd explicitly told them to stay there until I reached them again. But the next time I checked in on the ship, it was offline and the Originals were gone."

"Why did they leave?"

"I think someone else got to them."

"Who else would even know they were here?"

"I don't know."

"Shit."

"Yes," she agrees around a mouthful of mashed potatoes. "And there's been no camera sightings, no chatter, no nothing. Which means someone is helping them stay hidden."

"So what do we do?"

"Use those pretty golden eyes," she says. "Find them the old-fashioned way. Look for them. Take another bite of chicken there, Mr. Marquez, 'fore it goes cold."

Jorge takes an obedient bite, his privacy-protected mind reeling.

"If they do show up on a monitor or someone else sees them... Hess thinks the boy is dead. I'm the one who told him so. If he sees the boy at all—"

"I know," Angela/Shadower says.

"Has it always been you?" he asks, still as shocked by the removal of Shadower's mask as by anything else. There is something deeply unsettling about talking face to face with the infamous informant. Like a harbinger of the impending apocalypse. If it no longer matters that her identity be secret, how much can anything else matter? How long do any of them have?

"Yes."

"How do you... do what you do?"

"Hell if I know," she smiles at him, and a small tuft of collard greens in her tooth renders this legendary renegade heartbreakingly human. "But I have some sorta gift, and so I set out to start using it. I... had a son who stayed Original. Leroy. Light of my life."

"He's in the clandestine network?"

"Was. Died a long time ago, but he's the one who connected me to the network."

"Oh," says Jorge. "I'm sorry."

"Well. Swore I'd keep doing everything I could even after he was gone. This isn't how the world's supposed to be, Jorge. You might be the only other person who sees as much of Felix up close and personal as I do. That man isn't God—"

"—but try telling him that," Jorge finishes.

"Oh, I intend to," Angela says.

"So what should I do next—"

"Head down. Eyes open. Eat the rest of your chicken," she says, with a stern maternal nod. "And if the Pulse hits soon, and hits as hard as I think it's about to, well. Try not to die, kiddo."

THE SECOND PULSE

CHAPTER 55: MARILYN

MARILYN IS READY TO SEE HER NEW BREASTS. She lifts her shirt, arches her back and spends one lingering moment admiring them in the mirror, giving a satisfied nod. She is snapping her bra shut and wondering *what's next?* when she hears the small sound. She barely has the time to wish she'd stolen more painkillers from the hospital before she reels, retches, and hits the floor.

CHAPTER 56: HESS

D R. FELIX HESS IS IN THE COUNCIL MEETING,
listening to Lorraine go on about them not losing focus on
solving the mystery of the self-terminating Syns, despite
their apparent eradication in the wake of the Pulse.

Then he hears it.

The beep. The one he knew was coming.

Everyone hears it at once, and no one has time to say anything
coherent before the room is full of screams and gasps and the
smell of urine.

CHAPTER 57: ANGELA

SHE RECEIVES TWO ALERTS. BACK TO BACK.

The first alert floods her with relief. It comes through on one of her Shadower channels: Asavari was spotted on a hidden camera Shadower placed within a potted plant in the park where the girl called Karma first met with Jorge. She's alive.

Angela barely has time to forward the alert over to Jorge before a less welcome alert arrives. Small as it is, the little beep stills Shadower's heart. She is no longer Shadower. She is simply Angela, a world-weary woman bracing to drown in an ocean of oncoming pain. The first cruel waves crash through her brain and wash away everything.

Everything.

CHAPTER 58: JORGE

JORGE RECEIVES THE MESSAGE FROM
SHADOWER in the instant before the small warning
sound comes, like an electrified exclamation point at the
end of the message, making all his hairs on end. He saves the
missive without reading it. Saves a thousand copies, so it will be
safe.

He cannot save himself from the subsequent pain that slams
into him with the force of a freight train, straight to the brain.

A FTER THE SMALL SOUND, Lorraine feels only a moment of pain.

Not as bad as I was expecting it to—

But that is all she thinks before there is simply nothing. Nothing at all.

GINA WONDERS IF ANYTHING can feel worse than her existential crisis. The guilt, her role as Marti and her lack of any actual and sincere relationships, the pain of it all distracts her so much that she does not even register the small warning beep—

Then the physical pain of the surging Pulse stabs through her like a knife, straight into her left eye, and she forgets everything else.

Pity has been evicted.

Pain is her sole tenant now.

ELSEWHERE

CHAPTER 61: PREETI

D R. PREETI KANSAL IS STILL UNACCUSTOMED to being a widow. She loved her husband more than life itself. He'd introduced her to Coltrane, she introduced him to curry. They danced on the cracked black-and-white linoleum floor of their first rental apartment's kitchen while brassy jazz played and five-spice sauce simmered. They fell in love a lifetime ago, when the world was imperfect but original. When so much still felt possible.

Ever since his passing, it was increasingly difficult for the good doctor to hold on to hope. For her daughters' sakes, she strives to maintain momentum. She still tells Padma, her eldest daughter, the teacher and now a mother of two, to sing songs of resistance and resilience to the tribe's children. She assures Sruti, the builder who took after her father's architectural and structural brilliance, to sketch out blueprints for Original cities above ground, sprawling and spreading. And she lets her youngest, Asavari, range out far and wide to do the dangerous work of attempting to change the world.

But while she manages to encourage her daughters, she cannot seem to bolster herself. The fire within her is dwindling to ash and ember. She wonders if she has anything left to give.

Having heard nothing—not from Vari, not from Ere, not from Shadower or Jorge or anyone—Preeti is beginning to fear the worst.

Bee-do-do-do, bee-do-do-do, bee-do-do-do-do.

At the off-key ringing, Preeti springs to her feet with a spryness that rejects her octogenarian status. Her eyes widen and dart, her ears strain to help her identify where the sound is coming from. It was a definite ringtone sort of a sound, something synthetic, not the chirp of a cricket or trill of a pre-dawn bird. Preeti could swear, in fact, that it was the very same ringtone she had once had on a mobile phone of her own, a million years ago.

Preeti crouches, concentrates, waits.

Bee-do-do-do, bee-do-do-do, bee-do-do-do-do.

She turns to her left and looks down, in the direction where she feels certain the sound is coming from, and sees nothing but hard-packed dirt. Squinting harder through the darkness, she sees that the dirt is not uniformly hard and packed. There is a slight rise.

Bee-do-do-do, bee-do-do-do, bee-do-do-do-do.

Preeti falls to her knees and begins furiously digging, dirt filling her fingernails, knuckles coating in grime, her long brown fingers searching, searching, and finally—*yes*—finding. She pulls a filthy small plastic rectangle from its earthen grave: a cell phone, illuminated. Ringing. Even unearthed, the ringing is quiet. No one else in the wide cave where her people have made camp is awakened by the sound.

Bee-do-do-do, bee-do-do-do, bee-do-do-do-do.

There is a caller identification on the screen, which reads simply:

CHAMELEON.

And below that, a reminder of how to use the archaic device:

Slide to answer.

She stumbles quickly to the farthest corner of the cave, not wanting to wake or frighten anyone else until she knows what the situation might be. And then with trembling hands, Preeti answers the phone.

"...hello?"

"Is this Dr. Preeti Kansal?"

Preeti considers lying, but can see no benefit in doing so. Whoever this is already knows who she is, quite obviously where she is, and may well know where her daughter is.

"This is she."

"Oh good, glad I caught you at home, so to speak," says the caller, and laughs robotically, the poor connection and old piece of tech coating the sound in a tinny metal shell. "Thought I was going to get your voicemail. Or my voicemail, really. Haha."

"Who—"

"This is Chameleon."

"Yes, it said that—on the phone. But who are you?"

"A friend."

"A friend....?"

"Yes. So here's some friendly news: Your daughter is safely in the Syn Center. She and the Fell boy are both alive."

"Thank God," Preeti whispers, weak with relief, sinking to the earth and releasing a breath she has been holding for the better part of a week.

"I am their friend, too, Dr. Kansal," says Chameleon. "We all need to come together, at times like this. And to give evidence of this—a little show of good faith, maybe a reunion of sorts—hang up the phone and step outside."

"But if I hang up—"

"I'll call you again. Keep the phone with you. I can charge it remotely, don't worry about that. But don't try to call anyone else with it, it's just for me to reach you," Chameleon says, and even through the static there is a sudden sharpness in the tone. A warning. "Do you understand?"

"I understand."

The call ends.

Preeti stares down at the small rectangular tech in her hand, then hurries from her corner of the cave, past the other slumbering bodies of her community members, out into the solitude of a silent night. She turns her face up, searching for some answer written in the stars. She sees nothing but the night sky. And then one of the stars widens. Brightens.

Begins hurtling towards her.

Before she can feel panic, the star takes a new shape: it is a small vehicle, heading right for her. The closer it comes, the more Preeti knows that this is some sort of tech but somehow does not seem Syn. It is nothing like the crafts she has seen before, nor the small Chariot Jorge had flown their way. It is long, slim, silver, fast, and very nearly noiseless.

It stops and hangs in the air for a moment, almost within reach of Preeti. It's a little bigger now that it's close up. Perhaps the size of a school bus, though Preeti has not seen a school bus in almost half a century. The vehicle splits down the middle, separating into two sides like a neatly cracked egg. From one of the now distinct silver capsules, a diminutive figure emerges. Whoever it is, the person seems unsteady on their feet. They clutch at the edge of the vehicle, catching their breath. They are covered in the dark of night, the darker-shadow of the landed vehicle.

"Chameleon?" Preeti whispers.

The figure takes a lurching step toward Dr. Preeti Kansal, stepping into a patch of moonlight and shaking her head. It's an old woman—impossibly old, her hair a halo the color of fresh snow.

"Who are you?" Preeti asks.

The old woman blinks, looking a bit dazed, then grins. Her smile is younger than the rest of her seems to be.

"Helena Garrison," she says.

CHAPTER 62: HELENA

ELENA BARELY RECOGNIZES THE SMALL INDIAN woman before her, it's been so long; but the longer she looks, the more she finds that her eyes can erase the lines around the woman's eyes, smooth out her skin, lift the mask of age and reveal the somewhat more familiar face below.

"I'm Dr. Preeti Kansal," the woman says, and Helena nods, confirming.

"We met, years ago," Helena says. "In my neighbor Howard's home—"

"Yes," says Dr. Kansal. "My God. Yes. You were young then."

"I was about your age then, and I'm about your age now. But you look a hell of a lot better than I do."

She is rewarded with a weak smile from the small, sturdy woman, which quickly crinkles into a questioning frown: "How did you get here?"

"Well, now," Helena says, extending an arm in a wordless request for assistance. Her hips are killing her, and she's afraid if she doesn't have something to sip on soon she might pass out. "*There's* a story."

*   *   *   *

Helena had been certain she was nearing her end. Several more members of her diminishing tribe had died in the weeks since Cal and Ere departed. She was hardest hit by the loss of Jonah. The funny old blind bastard had daily resurrected humor and optimism and other endangered emotions. She missed him even more than she missed Howard or Ruth. She figures that when a hero dies, the loss is felt by so many that in some way the pain is delegated; mitigated by mass mourning. But true friends, who live their lives not on pedestals but right beside you, those are absences far more deeply felt.

She was contemplating her own inevitable demise when she got the phone call.

Bee-do-do-do, bee-do-do-do, bee-do-do-do-do.

The sound sent Helena's tired eyelids straight to her snow-white hairline.

What the actual hell?

She sat up stiffly, her bones resistant, her feeble frame feeling every ounce of its octogenarianism. But despite her body's protestations, the musical little ringing drew her out, onto her feet, staggering toward that surreal sound.

Bee-do-do-do, bee-do-do-do, bee-do-do-do-do.

There was no evident place where a cell phone would be, not in the old summer camp where Helena and her fellow remnants were sleeping—not anywhere in the Original world. Cellular service had been cut off around the time synthetic technology allowed for remote contact between synthetic citizens, eliminating the need for external communication devices.

Bee-do-do-do, bee-do-do-do, bee-do-do-do-do.

She almost walked right past the wide-trunked oak tree, but luckily a small glow caught her eye before the sound and illumination both cut out again. Her gnarled fingers gingerly began exploring the tree's bark, touching tentatively a large rough knot where she could've sworn she had just seen something illuminated. She was about to write it off as a firefly or madness when the bark beneath her fingers cracked and gave, and revealed a cell phone practically embedded in the trunk. Peeling away the crumbling bark still clinging to the phone, Helena yanked it free.

Bee-do-do-do, bee-do-do-do, bee-do-do-do-do.

There was a caller identification on the screen, which read simply:

CHAMELEON.

"Hello?"

"Helena Garrison?"

"Yes."

"Great. It's Chameleon. Listen, I'm about to send air transport your way ..."

By the end of the surreal conversation, Helena was convinced that she really was losing her damn mind. Some anonymous stranger named for a color-changing lizard called her on a dead piece of technology pulled from a tree to tell her that an aircraft was headed her way so she could fly to India to meet up with some Original rebels who needed her help.

Yeah, right.

It sure sounded like the sort of story she'd make up for herself.

Helena had been a sci-fi nerd, once upon a time. As a girl, she pictured herself as a companion to a madman hurtling through space and time in a blue box, or as a swashbuckling rebel fighter going up against evil empires. But in those fantasies, she was always young. She never saw herself as a geriatric spaceship pilot.

Technically, the aircraft Chameleon sent her wasn't a spaceship, but it sure felt like one with all those shining panels and blinking lights and ultra-high-definition screens. She halfway expected when it took off that it would head all the way out of this galaxy and into another one, and honestly, she sort of hoped it might. When it arrived, she spent a solid three minutes just staring at it and pinching her wrinkled flesh between her bony fingers.

It hurt.

A panel on the slide of the plane slid down, flipped forward, and created a ramp. Helena got on the plane.

A silky, synthetic silver voice said "Welcome, Captain Garrison."

Although the title was unearned, it still made Helena feel ludicrously proud. If this was a fantasy of her own making, she was impressed with her attention to detail. Looking around the plane, though, the false captain had no idea how to fly the thing.

"How do we get started, then?" Helena asked.

"START," repeated the ship, and then it zoomed forward with such speed that Helena felt certain her only two options were to vomit or die.

She vomited.

Just a little.

After that, she felt much better. She actually had to admit that the ride itself was pretty fun. When she wondered aloud if she could see where she was going, the amiable aircraft went clear. Instead of gleaming metal, the floor, ceiling, walls, all of it, the whole thing, seemed to become clear glass. She was startled but delighted and let loose a shriek of unbridled joy. There she was,

Helena Garrison, standing alone in the middle of the sky, soaring through it with the world's best view, gazing down at the earth that had betrayed her. No longer tied to it.

If she had died mid-flight, that would have been all right by her. That moment was already enough. More than she had been expecting, really.

But then the ship slowed. Returned to its opaque metallic state.

Landed.

*   *   *   *

"I got a phone call, too!" Preeti says. "From Chameleon."

"Did you—do you know who this Chameleon is?" Helena asks.

"I do not," Preeti says, brow furrowing. "They say they are a friend."

"You believe 'em?"

"I want to."

"Of course," Helena says, nodding. "Well. So far they brought me to you."

"And told us that Asavari and Ere are alive."

"Don't know why they'd do any of that if they weren't on our side. But I still don't know if I trust 'em."

"I do not think we have to trust them in order to work with them."

"Spoken like a true veteran."

Helena likes this Kansal woman. She's a tough old bird, like Helena herself. She nods.

Bee-do-do-do, bee-do-do-do, bee-do-do-do-do.

Both women freeze.

"Yours or mine?" Helena asks.

"Mine," says Preeti.

Bee-do-do-do, bee-do-do-do, bee-do-do-do-do.

"Mine too," says Helena.

The women look at each other, and reach for their devices.

*B*RAIN WORKING.
    Body not.
    Jorge finds himself crumpled in a heap beneath the cafeteria table, looking up at the underside of the gleaming stainless-steel square, to which one surreal and stubborn wad of green gum clings. Focusing on the gum, less by choice and more because it's where his eyes are aimed, he runs another diagnostic and gets the same stuttering, frustrating results.

Brain working.

Body not.

The body-not-working assessment is all too apt. Even moving his eyeballs proves difficult. They teeter and roll like marbles he cannot control. Jorge concentrates hard and finally shifts his sight-line from above him to in front of him, and there on the floor he sees the motionless form of Angela.

Shadower. No no no!

Unable to move toward her, Jorge forces his eyelids to shut, to momentarily block this painful sight. He feels hot tears threaten. This cannot be happening. He opens his eyes again, forcing himself to witness, to come up with some sort of game plan.

He stares at a wayward fried chicken leg, at the dirt crowding the corners of the floor beneath the table, pushed there by a less than diligent mopping job. Jorge shifts his concentration to his mouth, trying to move at least that small part, to form a word. Make a sound.

"Ahhhhh," he manages. His mouth fills with saliva at this small syllable, and the drool drips from his mouth down his chin. He wants to weep. He tries again, tries harder, tries to say just one word. "Ahhhnnnnn....juh....luh...."

His mouth is moving more easily now, and he decides to give the rest of his body another try. Jorge lifts his right arm a few inches from the ground, nearly screaming in triumph and agony at this small victory. He rolls slowly, back and forth, pushing with his one working arm until he manages to gain a little momentum and push himself up into a slumped but upright seated position.

He reaches his right arm toward Angela, Shadower, the force of nature now laid out face-first on a dirty cafeteria floor. Placing his hand on her back, he feels the faint rise and fall of breath. *Thank God.*

Moving at a glacial place, Jorge gets himself out from beneath the table, then drags Angela out as well. The cafeteria is eerily quiet. Jorge sees that the Vost who served them their fried chicken is pitched forward over the sneeze guards, suspended over the hot lunches now cooling beneath shorted-out heat lamps. It looks like something out of an old zombie movie.

Looking around the room, Jorge counts another dozen or so Syns, many collapsed on the floor amidst scattered food. A few are moving, albeit minimally. Flinching; twitching. Most are still. Jorge is trying to decide what to do when he remembers the message Shadower sent him in the moment between the beep and the surge.

Asavari. Karma. She's at the park. I have to get to her before someone else does.

But there's someone else he has to check on first.

A S SOON AS HE CAN PEEL HIMSELF off the floor, Hess drags himself to the medical wing, to the room reserved for him. He pulls himself into the modified MRI machine, the one he uses to check in on his own brain. The pain of this Pulse was so intense that he almost believed he could feel pieces of his brain missing, that he could sense chips and fissures in his skull, leaking gray matter bubbling beneath his skin.

Stop it. Crazy. Just check. Then assess. One step at a...

For a moment, he blanks on the word. The panic starts to strangle him. Though being in the small space of the MRI has never bothered him before, claustrophobia suddenly sends a hot tributary of sweat trickling from the base of his neck down his back. He pushes back against the panic, searching, finding:

...time.

With the word comes a momentary loosening of the noose. He steadies his inhales and exhales, holding still in the chamber, letting the magnets do their job. When at last the thunks and clunks have ceased, Hess presses the release button and slides himself out of the machine. He sits up, head still throbbing, nothing yet returned to normal. He does not hurry to get off of the padded surface of the conveyor-like bed. He is afraid his knees will give.

His thoughts are still coming in fits and starts. He tries to piece back together where he was, what he'd been doing right before the Pulse. A *Council meeting*—*yes*. He'd been in a room full of others when the Pulse hit. Lorraine was talking and then suddenly she just wasn't. There was the beep and the brain-ripping and blackness. Then Hess's eyes fluttered open, and without so much as taking an inventory of who else in the room appeared alive, he had dragged himself from the meeting room, down the hall and toward his machines.

No one died last time.

Probably no one died this time.

Probably.

His MRI results suddenly blink to life in the air in front of him. His eyes dart as quickly as they can in their compromised state, retrieving information and finally enabling him to exhale. Damage appears minimal. None of the dementia-pathways are lighting up, and when he calls up a side-by-side of his last scan, they are almost identical.

Almost.

The discrepancy is so minute that it would be easily missed by anyone in a hurry, anyone without the aid of an extremely powerful piece of tech designed to catch and run an alert on any infinitesimal variance, anyone who hadn't stared at snapshots of his own brain obsessively for as long as Dr. Felix Hess has.

But there it is: A dot. A small black spot that wasn't there before.

Shit—

"Doctor... Hess."

The voice behind him startles Felix, who vanishes the scans with an instant command. He turns and sees Jorge, whose voice he had not recognized, and very nearly gasps aloud. The entire left side of the Vost's face is hanging slack, motionless. Even when the right side of his mouth moves, the motion fades, faltering at the center of the lips and ceasing before crossing over to the damaged portion.

"Are... you..." Jorge begins, struggling to form each word.

"I'm fine," Hess says curtly, cutting him off. Some small sense of mercy within him wants to save the man from any unnecessary speech, since it is quite apparent that communication is currently a difficult and painful process. He adds: "You look terrible."

"Haven't... seen... mirror. But... feels... bad."

"Bad," Hess confirms, easing himself into a standing position and willing himself not to limp as he approaches his assistant. "Where were you when it happened?"

"...lunch," Jorge manages. "Downstairs."

That explains how he got up here so quickly. The cafeteria was several stories down but in this same section of the building, and near several levitators. Which must mean the building's tech is up and running, too. Thank Heaven for powerful generators.

"Have you seen... anyone else?" Hess asks.

Jorge shakes his head, a motion that is now limited to a jerking tilt.

"How did you know I'd be here?"

Another jerking tilt, this one from his right shoulder: Jorge's newly modified shrug.

"You... called."

"I called?"

"Distress...signal."

Hess tries to search his recent archives, but of course finds them blank. Damned Pulse. Jorge's explanation does make sense, though. Hess has a distress signal embedded that automatically alerts Jorge and Kennedy if their boss is in physical danger or some sort of emergency situation requiring their immediate assistance. It must have been triggered while he was unconscious.

"I see."

Righting itself, Hess's mind begins powering forward. He knows he should check on his wife, on his daughter. He takes a moment to be glad that the Original, Cal Harper, has not yet augmented. Cal will not have been damaged in this Pulse. As long as Ever, too, is intact, the breeding program can still be kept on track. No loss there, and if it's delayed a few more weeks or months, so be it.

His mind is firing at its regular pace now, much to his relief. He makes a note to prioritize follow-ups—the breeding program is key, but should take a brief backseat to Pulse-prevention. They can't take another hit like this; he knows Lorraine will agree with him on that much, even if they kept fighting on every other Council topic. He wonders briefly how Lorraine is doing, and queries her status.

> **Murray, Lorraine.**
> **Offline and unresponsive.**
> **Cessation point: 12:12:43**

Hess is momentarily stunned.

The old bitch is dead?

That can't be.

If this surge had indeed caused casualties, he really should probably check on a few other key figures in the Council and on his staff. Or maybe at least his daughter.

"Jorge—" Hess says, preparing to ask him if he's capable of locating Ever—and then stops when he sees that the ever-vigilant Vost is standing in front of a slow-but-functioning screen, running a diagnostic. This chases Ever from Hess's mind, and changes his query instantly to: "What in Heaven and Hell are you doing?"

"Running…diagnostic."

"Yes, I can see that, but—"

"I… made… new… tracking—"

"You finished the reverse tracking program?"

"Kennedy…helped."

At the mention of his second assistant, Hess briefly wonders why he has not yet shown up. If the distress call went to Jorge, it should also have gone to Kennedy. It could very well mean that Kennedy hadn't survived the Pulse, or was profoundly injured. But staring at Jorge's progress, Dr. Felix Hess asks the more important question at hand.

"Are you saying we should be able to pinpoint the starting point of the Pulse?"

"We… can…"

"We *can*, in theory, or—"

"We… did."

Jorge takes a step back from the screen, flinching as he sends a command. The screen widens, filling the entire expanse of the room, wall-to-wall. It doesn't look like an energy tracking map. It looks like a galaxy, full of blinking stars.

"What are we looking at?" Hess asks, hating not to know, fearing the answer. "I thought this was supposed to show us where the Pulse came from."

"It… is."

Dr. Felix Hess cannot confess again that he has no idea what the hell his assistant is talking about, so he presses his lips together and waits for each painful word to extract itself from Jorge's ruined lips.

"It's… not… coming… from… any-where. It's coming… from… every-where."

"You mean…" Hess says, jaw dropping along with mind comprehending.

He stares at this guilty galaxy anew, understanding in an exhilarating and terrifying rush what these blinking lights mean, even if he still doesn't know how it can possibly be true. The screen, illuminated with a million points of light, represents all of the Syns on the planet.

All of them, every single Syn, was just indicted as the source of the Pulse.

CHAPTER 65: EVER

*T*HIS IS A DREAM.

It's odd to be able to think that, while dreaming, but it's still so strange to be dreaming at all that she accepts this new ability.

Cal is standing in front of her, reaching out his arm for her. She reaches for it, but when her fingers find his, suddenly his hand becomes smaller, softer. His hairy, muscled arms winnow down into smaller selves. His face, too, slips and re-shapes, different eyes, tousled hair. She tries to get closer, to see better, to notice what the differences are and commit them to memory, but then a fog swirls up between them and the boy, Cal or whoever he became, is gone.

Ever opens her mouth to call for him, and something comes out—not sound, but an object. Something small and silver slips from her lips. A heart. A locket. It floats out of her mouth and into the air, lazily moving away from her. She tries to stand, tries to follow it. She needs to get to whatever is in there, it's important, she has to—

"Ever."

*   *   *   *

Ever lifts her eyelids, which feel like sandpaper scratching her corneas as she drags them across her raw eyes. Harsh light pours in, stinging, and Ever scowls. When her eyes adjust enough to allow her to see who she's scowling at, her expression softens, if only slightly. Two faces gaze down at her.

"Marti? Cal?"

Cal nods.

Marti starts to nod, then shakes her head.

"No, not really."

"Not... really?"

Ever wonders if she's still dreaming. She recalls Cal morphing into someone else moments earlier. Maybe Marti is about to do the same thing.

"My real name is Gina," whispers Marti.

Wondering if this is another hyper-real dream-within-a-dreams, Ever tries to sit up, to orient herself. She's in her bedroom, fully dressed. Her scar is tingling, her head aches, but otherwise she doesn't feel too terrible.

"What... what's going on..."

"It's all right," Cal soothes, stroking her hair gently. "I caught you, when you fell in the Pulse. No one saw me bring you here. The tech all stopped working, there were no cameras, no locks. I'll go soon, because everyone is starting to revive now—like you, and like your friend Marti here who was dragging herself in here as you and I arrived and…" he stops, looking from Ever to Marti. "And apparently isn't Marti? Gina, you said?"

Marti/Gina nods miserably.

"Yes. Gina. Gina Torres. Look, I don't have much time, Ever. I have to apologize to you."

"Apologize? For what?" Ever smiles weakly at the woman who has become her best and only girlfriend. "Saving me in the last Pulse? Keeping my secrets? Being my only real friend—"

"Stop, please. Don't joke and don't be nice. Ever, I—I work for your father."

"Yeah, I know. Me, too. We all do. Even Cal—"

"No, no, I don't just mean at the Synt. I mean… I work directly for your father."

"I don't understand," Ever says, beginning to realize that her boss is attempting to confess to something serious.

"I know, I know, I know—listen," says Marti (no: Gina). "Your father wanted me to monitor you. To report on… where your head was. Where your heart was. Wait—let me finish. My assignment was also to help you connect to the person he wanted you to trust, and—"

"You?" Cal growls, protective, tightening his grip on Ever's hand.

"No," Gina whispers. "You."

"What?" Ever says, shaking her head, trying to keep up.

"Cal. Your father wanted you to fall in love with Cal."

"But he told me not to see him—"

"And made it hard for you to find him, so you'd believe that he wanted to keep you apart. But he had me leave you my credentials, knowing you'd be smart enough to use them to find Cal. He wanted you to feel like it was your decision, your—everything. But he wants you two together, for—"

"Mules," Ever whispers, flooded hot and furious with a sudden rush of memories from the year before. When she learned her father intended to use her body as a vessel for Syn "upgrades." The program needed ideal-specimen parents. Like her, up until she had her stroke and—and some other reason that she can't remember now. Tears stream down her cheeks.

"I'll go now," Marti says softly. "I'm sorry, and just—good luck, Ever."

Part of Ever wants to protest, to tell Marti—*Gina, dammit*—to stay. She wants to scream at the woman to tell her more, tell her everything she knows about Ever's father's plans. But Ever is too shell-shocked and angry to speak now, and the post-Pulse pain is beginning to sink in. Watching Gina rise on tentative limbs, Ever realizes she's actually doing a hell of a lot better than the other woman.

Good. I hope she feels like her teeth are bleeding.

I hope she hurts down to her bones.

Gina lurches from the room, and Cal kisses Ever's forehead.

"Lay down."

"But—"

"No buts," Cal says, firm but gentle. "You have to rest. Later, we can—"

A shrill scream cuts into his words, stopping them cold.

"What the hell—"

"Stay here," Cal commands, leaping to his feet and sprinting from the room.

Ever doesn't listen. She gets up from the bed, reels for a moment, finds her footing, and hurries after him as fast as she can. She finds Cal at the other end of the hallway, in front of the bathroom door. Gina is standing there, too, pointing with a shaking finger into the bathroom itself.

"I thought no one else was here—I was feeling nauseous, I was going into the bathroom before I left and I saw her just lying there on the floor—"

Ever pushes past Cal and Gina, dropping to the bathroom floor. There, half-dressed and slack-jawed, lies her mother.

A FTER FINDING MARILYN HESS'S unresponsive body, Gina offered to stay and help, but Cal and Ever banished her. She fled, tail between her legs. She didn't even stay long enough to know if Ever's mother was alive or dead.

Stumbling out of the Hess residence and making her way to the main floor of the Synt, Gina is finding it more and more difficult to breathe. She regrets that the Pulse had not killed her this time, or at least left her unconscious for a little while longer. Her incredible guilt over a life littered with betrayal is crushing. It's all she is now: betrayal, personified.

Off the levitator, out through the main entrance, gasping when the sunlight hits her, Gina leans against the exterior wall of the Synt and slides down it. She can't even count all the lies she's told since becoming Martha Manuel. Every detail of her real life has been converted into yet another tool of deception.

311

The story about how Marti burned her legs camping, for example. Not true. Nowhere near the vicinity of truth. Gina has never been camping. The burns on her leg were real, but they were not the result of a fun trip gone awry. They were intentional injuries, bestowed upon her by her stepfather Raymond, a mean drunk who married her desperate mother when Gina was eleven.

"Come sit on Daddy's lap," Raymond had said that night, a million moments ago. His breath was rotten with cheap whiskey, and his pale dirty jeans were unzipped. He was sitting in the orange-plaid recliner that used to be her father's, and he was looking at her with his hungry wolf eyes. "Come on, little girl. Daddy wants you to sit in his lap."

"You're not my father," she whispered.

"Come here," he said, louder.

"No."

"Come," he said, lower and more dangerous this time.

She should have run, right then. Or grabbed the shotgun housed above the fireplace and shot the sonofabitch. Instead, she held her ground, jutted her chin, young and stupid but strong and stubborn.

Then, faster than she thought he could move his drunk ass, he was out of the plaid chair and right in front of her. He grabbed her roughly by the shoulders. And she twisted, trying to get free, torqued too far, fell toward the fireplace. She caught herself on her forearms, singeing them, crying out. He pulled her from the fire, and for a moment she thought he was saving her, but he swung her body up and through, arms out of the fire, legs in it. She screamed as the flames licked her calves, caught hold of her flammable socks and roared hungrily, racing up to devour the rest of her.

She grabbed wildly, managing to snag a poker. She slammed it upward, catching Raymond on the side of his face. He made a noise like *wumpf*, and let go of her shoulders. She hit the floor hard, and crawled forward as fast as she could, extracting her legs from the fire, rolling around on the ground like they taught her at school to stop the flames. But she could not undo the damage done. Not to her legs. Not to her soul.

She left home as early as she could, and when she was gone, she was gone. She didn't speak to her mother. She buried the bad parts of herself but thought she was doing a pretty good job otherwise. Knew how to work the system. Knew how to use people instead of letting them use her. Got into the Syn world. Got a decent job.

But I never did become a decent person, did I?

She should have said no to Felix Hess. She should have seen through the sheen, the brilliance, the flattering attention. She should have seen what lay beneath. A man who used people. A man who was planning to use his own daughter.

How could I do that to her?

It was all so clear all of a sudden, but until that moment it had all been so blurry. So terribly blurry.

She sits outside the Synt, sobbing and wondering what could possibly come next. She had left next to no one behind in Yale—there was no doubt in her mind that her idiotic pretty-boy Max had long since moved on—and didn't have anyone waiting for her anywhere else. All that awaited her was the pain of another Pulse, the bitter memories of her Original life, the fresh guilt over her treatment of Ever…

I can't take it.

I can't take another day of this.

I can't take another day of me.

Whoever I am.

She had heard, weeks ago, about a secret network. A sub-basement of Heaven where the desperate congregated. Even before the Pulse, Gina-living-as-Marti had been contemplating her options. Options like the one this network seemed to offer.

A way out.

Now's the time.

If she sends out a message— assuming someone is conscious enough to get it—there will be no record of the communication. The Pulse, painful as it is, was also productive. It cleared a path, gave some privacy. It protected the sort of things you didn't want seen.

Now, or never.

And just like that, she sends the message.

She wasn't sure what she expected post-submission. Some sort of confirmation? Like an old read-receipt you might get after sending an email? But even without any immediate acknowledgment, Gina feels a little better as soon as she admits, even if it was into an abyss, that she wants out.

The wind picks up, stroking gently at her face, calling awareness to the wetness on her cheeks. She roughly brushes away the last of her tears, then rises, still leaning against the building but gathering strength. She exhales and makes a one-step-at-a-time plan for herself. For now, she'll go home to wait and see what would come of her message. If anything came at all.

"Gina Torres?"

Startled, Gina stares at the person standing before her. She has never seen them before. A beautiful, androgynous figure; Gina would have recalled this face, this willowy form. But they are nowhere in her memory. So this isn't a co-worker or long-lost friend. But who else in Central City would know her name? Her *real* name?

They couldn't respond so quickly... could they?

"Yes?" Gina says tentatively.

"I'm Chase," smiles the stranger.

CHAPTER 67: CAL

MARILYN HESS IS NOT DEAD, but she's pretty
damn close to it. Cal didn't know what the status of her
synthetic components might be, but he knew what a
failing human body looked like.

Her pulse is faint, but there, and she's breathing—irregular
and slow, but heart and lungs still functioning was a good start.
No need for the CPR his aunt had meticulously taught him as a
child, for which he was grateful. Under the best of circumstances,
putting his mouth on Ever's mother's lips would be weird. And
the line of congealing vomit crusting on her lower lip and chin
didn't make the prospect any more appealing.

Basic vitals notwithstanding, Cal knew that Marilyn was in
distress and needed more help than he could give. He was worried

most about her brain, particularly since her glassy open eyes were still fixed and staring ahead, not seeing, not blinking. It was unnerving, and probably indicated something serious. But Cal did not share this fear with Ever.

He lifts Marilyn, nodding for Ever to follow him, wishing he could give her his arm. Ever wobbles behind him as they exit the Hess home and take the levitator down to the medical wing, not yet up and running since all of the medical staff are in various states of distress themselves. Cal lays Marilyn down gently on one of the hospital beds. He looks around the room, wishing he knew more about how the various breathing machines and monitors worked. He fears he's reached the end of his usefulness.

"I don't know what else to—"

"It's all right," Ever whispers. "Give me a second."

She holds still, her eyes flitting in that odd way Syn eyes did when pulling information from Heaven. It was more distinct in her weakened state; Cal finds Ever's sliding pupils almost as unsettling as her mother's sightless stare. But he realizes she must be swiftly educating herself on the basics of the machines in the hospital room, accessing information that might enable her to save her mother.

After a moment, Ever reaches for the large rectangular apparatus beside the bed. She slides a small clear mask over her mother's nose and mouth.

"She doesn't need intubation because she's breathing on her own, but the mask will help ease her oxygen access. I'm going to hook her up to the monitor so we can start tracking her heart rate, her brain waves... I won't be able to get enough from Heaven to know how to interpret and take action based on what the machines tell us but at least when a doctor gets here she'll be closer to stable and the doctor can make decisions more quickly. Give me her finger—yes, let's get it in here, and then let me see if an IV is something we should do next..."

Cal marvels at Ever as she connects her mother to the life-saving machines, skillfully navigating tools she didn't know how to use moments earlier. For the first time, Cal sees the true value of this synthetic technology. It wasn't all about vanity, or power, or anything else he had always believed it to be. It was about knowledge. Access. And something Cal had been taught his entire life to hold dear: *Survival.*

Ever looks up.

"That's all I can do. Let's get out of here."

"You don't want to stay with her?"

"I don't want her to die. But I don't want to be here when she wakes up. She's always been on my father's side, not mine. I'm done with them. Come on."

Ever walks down a hallway, toward a remote exit, out to the street behind the Synt. She walks quickly, down the street and around a corner, not stopping until she reaches a small bench tucked beneath the shade of a large maple tree.

She sits on the bench. He sits beside her.

"Did you know," she says, low, quiet. "About my father… about him wanting us… to…"

"What? No. Absolutely not. Ever, you can't think that I would—"

"Lie to me?" Ever fixes her luminous eyes on him. "Withhold information from me? Why wouldn't I think so? Everyone else does."

"Not me," he says, before realizing that he was, in fact, lying.

He has been withholding information from her for their entire relationship. He never revealed how he first crossed paths with her. He kept his mouth shut about the boy who preceded him in her affections. It was still a mystery to him that somehow Ever had forgotten his cousin Ere entirely. But he had never taken it upon himself to remind her. Cal was just grateful that he had somehow found her with a clean slate, ready to meet him—

Heaven and Hell.

Was all of that her father's doing, too? Had he deliberately erased key moments and figures from her mind, taken away all the memories of Ere—and maybe other lovers, too, so she would be more open to me? If that's true, is that the only reason she loves me? If she still remembered Ere... would she even love me at all?

"Not you?" Ever asks, trembling slightly.

She looks so vulnerable. She clearly wants to trust him. He can't risk changing her mind about that by confessing too much.

I'm mostly telling the truth. It would be better for her to believe I'm telling the truth.

"Not me," he lies. "You can trust me."

She takes his hand.

"I can't go home," Ever says.

"We can," Cal says slowly.

Ever looks up at him.

"What do you mean, 'we'?"

"I mean... if what Marti—Gina—if what she said is true, your father won't throw me out. He wants us to be together."

"You want to make my father happy? Do what he wants?"

"Curse your father," Cal says. "We're not together to make *him* happy; we're together to make *us* happy. We know what he wants, so we have the upper hand. I'll augment, and—"

"No way in hell," she says immediately.

"You can't become an Original, Ever. You can't go backward. But I can catch up to you."

"No," Ever says again. "You don't know what you're asking. And—and you saw the Pulse. Its impact. What it did to me last time. What it did to my mother this time. On top of everything else—you'll be unnecessarily opening yourself up to that pain."

"Real pain is watching you suffer. Real pain is being apart from you, being different from you—"

"You don't know what you're saying," she says, then sways, still weak.

He wraps his arms around her, holding her tight.

"I've got you," he whispers.

She nods against him.

"Keep me," she says, closing her eyes.

"That's the plan," he says, kissing the top of her head.

CHAPTER 68: ASAVARI

CHAMELEON, WHERE ARE YOU?

Asavari looks around the park again. The same park where first she met Jorge, a hooded stranger who kept his face in shadow—until suddenly and inexplicably he showed her his golden eyes and shared his real name with her. It was only a year ago, but feels so much farther away. She was a girl then, untested and more idealistic, seeing her assignments as adventures rather than life-or-death tasks. She had wanted to reveal her identity to Jorge, too, in a show of solidarity and childish enthusiasm, but he had told her to keep herself known only as Karma. He had not wanted to know her real name—

"Asavari."

She startles, cursing herself for not having heard his approach, but when she sees Jorge all other thoughts are chased from her mind. His face is slack, his approach limping and slow. He has been attacked.

"Who did this—"

"Pulse," he says.

"Oh," she says, feeling instantly stupid. In the daylight, she had seen no flicker of lights, nothing to indicate that the entire population around her had been dealt a deadly blow. "Worse than the last one?"

"For…me," he says, and attempts what she thinks might have been a smile, but she cannot tell. As he takes another step toward her, his ankle twists and he nearly falls. Asavari rushes forward, taking Jorge by the arm and helping him toward a picnic table.

"Easy, careful," she says, helping him sit, glancing over her shoulder and reminding herself to be on alert. If Jorge was up and about post-Pulse, others might be, too.

"Hess… survived," Jorge says. "Checked on… him… so he would not suspect… me… more. Karma… why… are… you… here?"

Asavari stares at him, doubting that his question was an esoteric or existential one.

"Because our new contact summoned us."

"What…new…contact?"

"We thought you or Shadower—"

He shakes his head as best he can.

"Not…me. Not…Shadower."

Asavari's stomach goes cold and hard as frozen stone.

Curse of the world.

"They call themselves Chameleon," she says quickly, as both realize the gravity of their situation.

Jorge looks at Asavari, and her heart twists at the way his left eye, still so golden, droops and cannot quite seem to focus.

"Where…is…Ere?"

"Waiting over by the border."

"Alone?"

Asavari thought she could not feel any stupider; she was wrong. She had left Ere Fell, one of the most valuable assets to the rebellion, and surely the most-wanted man in the Syn world if Hess were to learn that he still lived, alone. Unguarded. Out in the open, in the Syn territory.

"I'll go back to him," she says in a rush. "I'll go get him, make sure he's all right, get him into hiding so no one figures out and then we can—"

Bee-do-do-do, bee-do-do-do, bee-do-do-do-do.

The Vost and the Original girl both startle at the sound.

"What…"

"I don't know."

Bee-do-do-do, bee-do-do-do, bee-do-do-do-do.

ERE SMELLS CINNAMON.

He's only experienced cinnamon a few times in his life. It was a favorite spice of the elders in his tribe. Anytime the tribe arrived in a place where non-perishable foods might be hiding, his old friend Helena would go on a search. As children, the boys would help her, seeking all sorts of foods but knowing whoever found the precious spice would be rewarded not only by a grin from Helena, but also by securing their spot as the first one to get a bite of whatever delicious dish Helena miraculously managed to make. Because of this, Ere has always associated the smell of cinnamon with possibility.

He lazily enjoys this scent, not yet wondering where it came from or even where he was. His head feels soft and fuzzy, in a nice way, like somehow everything went from all-wrong to all-right. He can't remember the last thing that happened or how he got to be wherever he is, but none of this seems like something he should worry about.

"Oh, you're up. Hello, Ere. How are you feeling?"

"Good," Ere says to whoever just asked him the question. His response is met with laughter, which makes him smile, because when someone is laughing that means that you should probably smile too.

"I think you're still pretty looped. Sorry again about that. It's a pretty fun little tranquilizer cocktail, though. You should be in a good mood, and you won't have a headache later. I actually use this one when I throw my back out, you know?"

"That's great," Ere says.

The person steps into view. They are about Ere's size, he thinks, which is a nice size. The person is clad in black from head to toe, including a full-face mask, so Ere can't really tell much about them. Their voice is kind of funny, although Ere can't describe exactly how it's funny, just that it's not quite normal.

"The cookies are almost done," says the black-masked person. "Have you ever had Snickerdoodle cookies, Ere?"

"No. They sound so fun!"

"See, now. That's a tragedy," clucks the figure. "People talk about the fall of civilizations, lives lost, brick-and-mortar buildings sustaining damage but if you want to talk about tragedy… an entire class of people who had cookies a generation ago, and now have no access to ovens or baking powder or cinnamon and are raising children who have never eaten Snickeroodles."

"I've had cinnamon," Ere says helpfully.

"Well. That's something."

"Yes, something."

There is a *ding*, and the stranger claps their black-gloved hands.

"That's the cookies! Snickerdoodles. You're gonna love these, Ere. Sugar cookies rolled in sugar and cinnamon, and not to brag, but mine really are the hands-down most amazing doodles in the history of history. I don't do anything halfway, I can tell you that. These babies might just be the best thing that's ever happened to you. After me, of course."

As his cookie-making companion heads off to retrieve the oddly-named cookies (doodle-snicketies? Something funny like that, but he already forgot), Ere enjoys again this lovely weight-less, worry-less feeling. He's starting to be able to take in a few more details of the room, although they're still not of much interest to him.

He is in a chair, maybe tied up or maybe just not wanting to move. He's in a room with lots of tech-stuff. Not as many screens and all of that like in Hess's lab, he notes drowsily, but there are still some screens so that probably means something. There's also lots of metal boxes and tables and equipment that Ere doesn't recognize, but he feels certain is all very techy-techy-tech-tech sort of thingies. Most of the lights are out, so it's a lot of shadows, hard to see all that well. Fine by Ere. He appreciates that the place is pretty dark and warm and nice.

Good for napping.
Napping sounds nice.
Napping sounds like kid-napping.
Was I kidnapped?
I could take a nap...

"Here we go," says the stranger, suddenly at his side, holding out a plate full of rounded, sparkling-brown-and-silver dusted baked things. "Oops! I'm going to have to untie you, aren't I? Do you promise to be nice if I free your hands now, Ere?"

"I promise," Ere says.

He wants to be good, so he'll get to try one of the doodlesnick cookety things.

The stranger unties him.

"All right," says his captor. "Let's get some of these cookies inside you, huh? Oh! Speaking of 'inside.' You heard of Heaven's prophecy, right, Ere Fell? The outsider on the inside and all that? Do you think that could be you?"

"Outside-inside," Ere smiles. "Sounds like me."

"Sure does," agrees the stranger, and hands Ere a cookie.

Ere takes it. The hot fresh baked thing smells so good he thinks maybe he's dead and this is the real heaven. Taking a bite only solidifies this belief.

"This is the best thing I've ever had," he moans, mouth full, heart bursting.

"Told you so," chuckles the cookie-baking captor. "You'll learn to trust me, Ere, because I'm pretty much always right about everything. Enjoy your Snickerdoodle. Have a few. You'll probably want another nap after that. And then, when you get up again, we can have a more coherent little chat. Who knows? Your other friends might even be here by then."

"That'll be nice," Ere says.

"Yes. Yes, it will. Now hold still while I tie you up again. Can't have you getting into any trouble, now. There's a good little captive."

CHAPTER 70: KENNEDY

KENNEDY AWOKE WITH NO MEMORY of the most recent Pulse. He doesn't feel nearly as bad as he did after the last Pulse. He has no headache, no nausea. He feels absolutely normal.

Yes, normal is the right word.

I feel absolutely normal.

He woke up in his seat in the lab, putting together that he must have been working when it hit. Lucky he didn't fall out of the chair, he thinks. He checks his archives, and everything appears in order, other than a few notable gaps in his memory—but that had happened with the last Pulse, too.

No one else was in the lab, and Kennedy knows he should find Hess, see what damage the team took and what post-Pulse studies are already underway. Or maybe he'll find out that he is the first one up, and it'll be his job to tend to whoever had it worse this time around. Either way, he should get up and get to it.

Kennedy sends simultaneous messages to Hess and Jorge.

Status: I am fully functional post-Pulse.
Where should I report?

In an instant, Kennedy gets a reply. It comes not from his colleague but from his supervisor, which is surprising since he assumed Hess would be the one already distracted by dozens of other messages.

Small lab in my private medical room.
Come up immediately.

This is not normal. As far as Kennedy can recall, Hess has never invited him in to the private medical room. It was one of the small roster of rooms reserved solely for Hess, along with the innermost chamber or "core of Heaven," where no one *ever* went, and the old-fashioned office where visitors were occasionally received but never welcomed. If Hess was summoning him to his private medical room, and urgently, something big must be going on.

Kennedy hurries to the levitator and arrives swiftly at the medical room. Kennedy cannot walk right into the room. He has to be allowed in by Hess.

"Where the hell have you been?" Hess spits, opening the door and ushering Kennedy in. "Everyone else has been up and about for hours."

"I'm—sorry," Kennedy says, apologizing for what is clearly beyond his control.

"Well. At least you look better than Jorge. He got beat to hell in this thing."

"But he's alive."

"Yes. And he managed to do something useful before he went to go get medical attention. Come have a look at this."

Hess calls up a screen, something that looks like the far reaches of outer space. Hundreds of thousands of points of light.

"The source of the Pulse," says Hess. "Look. It's—"

"Dispersed," Kennedy says. "Not one single source, it's—all of you."

"All of us," Hess corrects. "Every single Syn."

"Yes, yes," Kennedy says. "All of us."

"Since you're not as bad off as Jorge right now, I need you on this with me. We're going to see if the beep has something to do with the multi-point trigger, if it's some sort of switch being simultaneously flipped so that we then all—"

There is an alert projected over the image.

Access to room requested.

"Display request," Hess barks, and the initial alert is instantly replaced with new glowing text. Two profiles appear before their eyes.

Hess, Ever.
[Synthetic Citizen/Application Development Team.
Inadequate Security Credentials]

Harper, Cal.
[Vost/Maintenance Team.
Inadequate Security Credentials.]

"What in Heaven and hell is Ever doing here?" Hess asks aloud, as if the computer or Kennedy or Heaven itself might offer an answer.

"How did she fare in the Pulse?" Kennedy asks automatically.

"I don't know," mutters Hess.

He blinks a command, and the door slides open.

"Father," Ever says crisply. "You look pretty good, all things considered."

"What do you want, Ever?" Hess asks. "I get the feeling you're not here about my health. Especially since you came up with the person I forbid you from seeing—hello, Mr. Harper. How do you enjoy defiling my daughter?"

Before Cal can reply, Ever puts up a hand to stop all the churning testosterone.

"Cut the crap, Felix. I know you want Cal and me together. I know about Marti—Gina, right? But whatever. Congratulations. You win. We're together. And Cal wants to augment."

"Cal wants...?" Hess hesitates, but only for a fraction of a second. Then he gives the order smoothly, as it if were his own notion and had always been the plan. "Kennedy, I'll need you to oversee Mr. Harper's transition."

"Just like that you're going to actually do what I ask—" Ever says, startled.

"I'm not sure we had the chance to make the case for—" Cal uselessly starts.

Hess waves them into silence, swatting away their words like so many irritating gnats.

"There's nothing more to discuss. Everything's on the table. Yes, I wanted the Fell and Hess progeny to intersect. And here you are. I didn't assume a noble Fell would ever stoop so low as to want to request their own augmentation, but apparently Cal is brighter than the rest of his tribe. And young enough to augment with little risk to health, fertility—anything. Kennedy will make arrangements for the augmentation. Now go."

Ever looks like she wants to say something, but Cal puts a steadying hand on her shoulder, and they leave.

Kennedy wonders if any of them even remember he's still in the room, quietly bearing witness to this strange moment in history, and carefully filing away the memory.

AL STILL WANTS TO SPEND HIS LIFE WITH EVER. But with the process of augmentation looming, and going so swiftly from notion to eventuality to reality, he's nervous. A knot of muscles in Cal's strong jaw pulses, tightens, releases, embodies one of the many things he now fears: *pulse*, noun and verb, a thing and an action. He knows it will be bad. He knows it will be unbearable.

But he meant it when he said that watching Ever suffer alone is far worse. If this thing is going to kill her, he wants to die with her. (If he learned anything from *Romeo & Juliet*, which he read at Isaiah's recommendation all those weeks ago, it's that all stories end in death; ideally you can work a little love into the narrative before it all goes dark.) No, the idea of a painful death is not what gives him the most pause.

It's his aunt.

His aunt, and his mother.

Cal does not let himself think often of his sweet mother, Rachel. He was still a child when she died. His memories of her are warm and loving, but blurred and brief. Everyone else in their tribe either died some dramatic death in battle, like his father; or survived and lived outlandishly long Original lives. But Rachel Fell Harper followed neither of those paths; one night, in her sleep, Cal's mother simply stopped breathing.

No one knew how, or why.

She was simply alive one day.

And then she wasn't.

He remembers how much it tore at his aunt Ruth when her twin died. She did not believe it at first; she blanched, shook her head, said nothing. She remained silent for nearly a month. And when she finally spoke again, her first words were to Cal.

Your mother and I shared a womb, she said. *You are my son now.*

And he had always striven to embody what both of his mothers expected him. Sweet Rachel would want him to be kind, ethical, loving; strong Ruth would want him to be loyal, unwavering, protective.

Both would want him to be Original.

Always.

But they're dead, he reminds himself. *How long must we pay our debts to those in the ground? What do we owe the dead? Should I not choose life, even if it is not the life they would choose?*

"Hey," Ever says in his ear, and he almost doesn't hear her over the internal din.

"Hey," he manages back.

They are seated in the small waiting area adjacent to the long-dormant augmentation room. Cal had gone to visit the room earlier, wanting to see the thing and have Kennedy walk him through exactly what would happen. The augmentation machine is sleek, cylindrical, made of stainless steel and evidently well-kept though no longer actively used.

Kennedy had showed him how the top of the tube slides open, revealing a padded bed, lined at the base, on the sides, and even along the top of the tube, for his safety. Even when closed, there is a window at the top, allowing the subject's face to be seen. That brought Cal a touch of comfort. The base of the machine was lined with a neat little network of wires, which, according to Kennedy, primarily connected it to the monitors that would evaluate the subject's physical status and brain function throughout the procedure.

"It's a simple procedure," Kennedy said, without emotion.

Nothing about this is simple, thought Cal, but said nothing.

Cal would be restrained within the augmentation chamber, and when the process began, a panel would slide open and a series of gleaming needles would deliver their various injections, some of them painkillers, some of them heavily concentrated synthetic-component fluid. A port would then be fitted into his finger, just like Ever's, and wiring in the port would then unfurl and travel up his arm and toward his nervous system. Then the synthetic fusion would really begin, as wired and wireless technology were transferred through the port, downloaded from Heaven and woven into Cal's own body.

Ever went through this, he reminds himself, looking at her. *I can survive this, too.*

On the other side of the sleek door separating them from the synching system, Kennedy is preparing for Cal's procedure, putting together the cocktail of injections, checking all the machinery. Fear begins surging through Cal, so powerful he feels it will propel him from the room. He moves his fingers from his wrist to hers, feeling *her* pulse, latching on to that rhythm, following her beat.

"You don't have to do this," she says, as if reading his mind. "I didn't have a choice about augmenting, but Cal... this is still your choice. You can tell me right now that you don't want to do it, and we'll walk away. Right now. Forget my father, forget Kennedy, we'll just go. You don't have to do this."

And just like that, with her permission for him to bail, Cal knows he will stay.

His heart beats with hers. He will carry a haunting guilt, certainly, but he can handle this decision. He squeezes Ever's wrist.

"I choose this," he says. "I choose you."

The door beside them hisses down, revealing Kennedy. He is wearing a lab coat, and latex gloves, and even his shoes are covered in plastic bagging. He is the picture of sterility, presumably ready to proceed—but he holds perfectly still, waiting. It seems to Cal that the man is fully expecting his patient to flee, as Ever had just encouraged him again to do.

Instead, Cal rises.

"Let's do this," he tells Kennedy.

"My apologies," says the thin-faced man. "The machine needs to run itself through a few more paces. Come back this evening, and we should be able to proceed. Sorry—Dr. Hess's request. He just wants to make sure that everything goes exactly as it should…"

Cal's face falls. He had momentum in this moment, wanted to just get this thing done before changing his mind.

"But I thought—"

Then Cal is interrupted by Ever, swooning and falling into him.

"Are you all right?" Cal asks, concerned.

"She probably needs to have a doctor look at her," Kennedy says mildly. "Looks like she's still reacting to the last Pulse. We can get her prioritized—"

"Ever," Cal says, ignoring Kennedy and focusing solely on her. She blinks, looking up at him, trembling. "Please, let's get you in to a doctor. Have them run diagnostics, make sure you're okay. That'll solidify my decision, right? Our decision. For both of us… we need to make sure you'll be healthy and waiting for me on the other side. Right?"

Reluctantly, Ever nods.

CHAPTER 72: ANGELA

A NGELA BLINKS MECHANICALLY. She is in a small, dark space. There are slim wooden objects widening into soft cloth and stiff-bristled bases to her right, and there are plastic containers to her left, and the wall consists almost entirely of shelving lined with bottles of cleaning products—*a supply closet.*

She dimly recalls something. Something less than a memory, more like a still photograph, an image that signifies an event without really capturing it. Jorge, dragging her from beneath a table and tucking her away in this closet. Telling her something before leaving.

What did he say?

Where did he go?

She tries to mine her memory for something more, but comes up short. In some ways, this is good. Her meeting with Jorge, which she does recall setting up, has been lost to the void. The Pulse has been consistent in its thievery of thought. She won't have to worry about the record of their interaction somehow being stolen. But she cannot locate it, either. Her organic memory seems almost as fuzzy as her synthetic log.

She is uncertain how many minutes or hours she has spent lying among the mops and brooms and buckets, trying to re-learn how to manage her own mind. But she finally finds her feet. Clutching at whatever she can, leaning against the wall, Angela rises. No sooner has she done so than her knees buckle; she opens her mouth to swear, and no sound escapes her lips. She tries again, moving her mouth, her tongue, tightening her throat, conjuring sound to no avail.

Not good.

Relying on the wall to hold her upright with each step forward, Angela emerges at last from the closet. The cafeteria is empty now, enough time having passed post-Pulse for the few citizens who had been here to have either gotten themselves out of the room or been collected by more able-bodied neighbors. No one witnesses Angela's painstaking trek along the cafeteria wall toward the door, the hall, the levitator. The steep ride up from the basement to the nearest hospital level is misery; she shamelessly clings to the rising board as a young child clutches a swing to its stomach, pitched forward rather than attempting to balance herself upright.

Limping into the hospital wing, she sees no one behind the reception desk. She tries to call out, forgetting again that she is now a creature without sound. She leans heavily against the empty reception desk and looks around for any sign of life.

While she waits, she discreetly floats her hand against the wall, trails her fingers just above the tech embedded in the desk, listening and feeling for anything—the hum, the familiar warm of the information she could extract even when no one else could detect it, attempting to flex her Shadower muscles. There is so much she needs to know, needs to relay, needs to do.

But even with the tech so close at hand, even with every ounce of concentration she can muster, she gets nothing.

Damn.

She looks up again, and this time spots an orderly, bleary-eyed and stumbling from one room to the next. Exerting every effort, Angela waves madly at him, finally catching his eye. As he approaches, Angela looks around wildly for some way to communicate, since she is able neither to speak nor to transmit electronic messages. There is no blank paper on the reception desk, nor fliers, nor folders; in a world where nearly everything is virtual, tree pulp at last found respite. Her initial instinct to scrawl her requests will not work. But Angela manages to grab a small patient intake tablet and flick it on. Angela types swiftly on the tablet:

Can't speak. Can't transmit.
Is Marilyn Hess here?

She shoves the tablet toward the orderly. His pale hair is sticky with sweat, skin blanched. The poor guy was probably just as gut-punched as anyone by the Pulse, but got up earlier than most and found himself a first responder. Reading Angela's message, he shakes his head.

"I can't tell you about Mrs. Hess, that's confidential, but if you want to request a doctor to see you about your issues just give me your name and—"

She once again thrusts the tablet at him, having punched in her next missive.

I work for Hesses. Live-in help.
Get me to Marilyn. Message her.
Say it's Angela. Angela Angela
Angela Angela

"Christ, lady, I get it, you're Angela. Bu I can't do that—" the orderly continues to protest.

A new idea hits Angela, and she grabs the tablet, hastily typing one more request.

Message Dr Hess assistant for permission

She shoves the tablet back to him, hoping Jorge will be well enough, wherever he is, to get her through. The orderly sighs. His eyes shift as he sends a message, shift again as he receives a reply. Angela envies him the easy communiqué. He looks back at her.

"Well. Okay then. Her husband's assistant gave permission."

She hears the swish of the hospital door dropping, turns and sees a half-dozen damaged Syns dragging their way in. The orderly's sunken eyes go wide. Angela gets the room number from him just before he is swarmed by the new horde of patients, some wailing about sightlessness, others shouting of deafness, others reporting being unable to feel anything at all. Filing away these complaints and conditions, Angela shuffles down the hall toward Marilyn Hess's room.

It is mercifully near, just one hallway east of where Angela had entered. Still, in her current state it takes Angela almost ten minutes to manage the distance. When she makes it into Marilyn's room, she collapses in the low-seated chair beside the bed. Chest heaving, Angela turns her face toward the woman who brought her into this brave new world.

Marilyn is white as a sheet, cheeks drained of color. Her exposed neck, arms, hands all blend in to the crisp bright-white linens of her hospital bed. She is connected to several machines, all of which inform Angela that the woman is alive but only in the most technical sense.

For a long moment, Angela cannot take her eyes off the comatose Marilyn. A lifetime, a universe, another eternity ago, this woman had petitioned so staunchly for Angela's friendship. It had been odd, awkward, but also flattering. Angela knew it was an achievement for Marilyn, having a friend like her. A Black woman. An intellectual. A career woman. Although Marilyn had money and a powerful husband, for years she saw herself as little more than a frustrated, overlooked housewife. In many ways Angela was Marilyn's opposite, in the Original world. But here they both were, broken Syns.

How did we get here, Marilyn?

Angela had only become a Syn because of her family's involvement in the resistance. She had convinced herself it would be worth it, and the secret skills she discovered after synching—her Shadower abilities—had reinforced this notion. She was the ideal spy, living in the blackened heart of the whole Syn enterprise, able to siphon intelligence, pass along secured information, and keep the hope of resistance alive.

But was it worth it? The Original Rebellion was quashed years ago and has yet to fully resurrect, despite Angela's efforts. And now she sits, voiceless and powerless, beside the woman who ushered her in to all this madness. The more she looks at Marilyn, the more she resents the selfish, privileged woman. Angela wants to walk away from her at last. But she's not sitting here out of loyalty or nostalgia for whatever might be left of the Pulse-ravaged Marilyn Hess.

She is here to protect the Resistance. To keep playing her part as dutiful Angela, for a few moments more, as the world wakes up.

Angela wonders about Ever. She has always pitied the girl. Clueless, bratty, sometimes impossible to be around, but the girl was never given any agency. And she was trapped in the age of purgatory, a perpetual teenager, not a child but not an autonomous adult. Angela hopes Ever is not dead or irreparably damaged; in so many ways, she's just a child.

Children. Something the cold synthetic world gave up. Angela suddenly aches to see a child, to hear one laugh. And as if in answer to her unspoken prayer, a young person enters the hospital room. Not a child, but another teenager—an Original one.

Karma, she thinks, flooded with relief.

"Shadower," whispers the raven-haired girl.

Angela wishes she could say something back, but instead she just nods.

"Call me Asavari," the girl says. She holds up an odd little item, which it takes Angela a moment to place: an old-world flip-phone. "Jorge sent me. We must move quickly. We have received a call. From the one called Chameleon."

Angela opens her mouth; no sound comes out.

"Chameleon has taken Ere," Asavari continues, "but claims still to be our friend. I am to meet with Chameleon this evening. Chameleon says another Pulse is coming. That there will be a window, perhaps as early as tonight, when the Syns will be most vulnerable. Even more vulnerable than they are right now."

Shadower places a nervous finger to her lips. Even with the painful protection of the Pulse, the hospital bedside of Marilyn Hess seems far too dangerous a Syn setting for Asavari to be speaking so freely. But Asavari shakes her head.

"I am done with the days of keeping my voice low, Shadower. But I notice you have not raised yours at all since my arrival…?"

Alternating from her focused Shadower mind to her still-reeling Angela self, the older woman freezes, then recalls the tablet in her lap. She types a hasty explanation to Asavari, who reads the message and frowns.

"Can you still…?"

Angela shakes her head, hot shame curdling her soul. Then a thought occurs to her, and she pounds out another message, as quickly as she can:

My Shadower abilities are gone.
My Angela abilities are not.
Get me to the Hess residence.
I'll type as we go. Help me up.

It's a long shot, but Angela might still be able to play a role in bending the arc toward revolution. Asavari gives a nod of agreement, and helps bring Shadower to her feet. Together, they leave the room, with no further thought or farewell to the pale woman barely clinging to life in the stark, sterile hospital bed. Just before they step into the hallway, however, Angela hears a familiar voice floating their way.

"I wonder if my mother is still even alive—"

If she had a voice, Angela would have cried out, told Asavari to stop. She tries to grab her, to indicate that they should hide—but where would they go? Ever is already in the hallway, about to enter the small room, and Angela cannot shimmy beneath a bed or hide behind a door.

And just like that, Angela is face to face with Ever and her Original companion.

Ever gives Angela an odd look, likely quite confused by the Indian girl at Angela's side. But of the startled foursome, it is Cal who speaks first, staring incredulously not at Angela but at the girl supporting her.

"Asavari?"

CHAPTER 73: EVER

EVER LOOKS FROM CAL, to the girl, and back again. She is confused; she does not recognize this girl. Taking in as many clues as she can gather—*Cal knows her, I don't, no finger port, looks so young*—Ever puts together that somehow this girl must be another Original.

"You are Ere's cousin," the girl with the black hair says, taken aback.

Ere...?

Something in Ever twinges, but before she can pay that any mind, she feels Cal tense beside her. He exhales sharply, almost a growl, and takes a menacing step toward Angela and the strange girl.

"What are you doing here?"

347

"I might ask the same of you," snaps the girl.

"Who are you, exactly?" Ever asks. "And Angela, how do you two know each other?"

Angela opens her mouth, but no sound emerges. She touches her throat, and looks pleadingly at Ever. Almost pathetically.

"She cannot speak," says the Original girl. "She was damaged in the Pulse. But she is not in as critical condition as some others, so I have been asked to bring her back to her residence."

"Asked by who, exactly?" Ever narrows her eyes. She doesn't trust this girl.

"By *her*," the girl retorts.

"What are you doing here?" Cal asks again, so angry Ever can feel his elevated temperature, the heat rising from him. It makes her nervous, how much this girl incites him. She must be a threat. Maybe to him. Maybe to her.

"As I said," Asavari replies, "I am taking Angela home. I assume you will let me do so, unless you want to catch up on old friends and acquaintances…?"

This makes Cal flinch. The girl nods, as if she has expected this, and starts to move past them. It is Ever who blocks their way this time.

"Angela—" Ever begins, and the woman shoves something toward her. A small tablet, where she has hastily typed a message.

This girl is my friend.
Please trust me.

Ever looks at Angela. Her skin, her hair, everything about her looks mussed and sallow. Though Ever is ringing with questions—*how would Angela have an Original friend, and one so young?*—Angela has kept many confidences for Ever over the years. She braided her hair, held her when her mother ignored her, and in many ways been more of a parent to Ever than either of her biological parents ever attempted to be. And so Ever moves out of the way, and allows Angela and the girl to limp past her and down the hallway. Ever then fixes her attention on Cal.

"Who is that girl and how the hell do you know her?"

"She... visited my tribe," Cal says, watching the girl with suspicion as she and Angela get further and further away from them.

"She's an Original."

"Yes."

"Guess you young-Originals aren't quite as rare as we thought."

Cal shakes his head, looking somewhat sick. Ever feels certain he's withholding information. She needs to get him off his guard, take him by surprise and shock him into being a little more forthcoming. She latches on to something, a word, and flings it at him.

"Ere," Ever says. "Who's Ere?"

Cal's eyes widen, then regulate. When he speaks, his voice sounds tight.

"He was my cousin. He was the one who—knew her."

"She was his girlfriend, or something?"

"Yes," Cal says, though the small syllable is somehow unconvincing.

"You said he 'was' your cousin."

"Yes. He is dead," Cal says, adding silently: *To me, anyway.*

"But he was young? Your age? Her age?"

"Many Originals died young."

"Cal. I feel like something weird is going on here."

He reaches forward suddenly, taking Ever's hands in his and squeezing them tightly.

"Ever, there... there are things about my Original life I am more than ready to forget and leave behind. I want to share every future moment, future thought, future secret with you... but please do not ask me to unearth the parts of my past I'd rather keep buried."

"All right," Ever says, reluctantly, bringing his hands to her mouth and kissing them. "But Angela better have a helluva good explanation for how she knows that girl. I shouldn't be worried, should I? Letting Angela go off with her?"

"I don't know," Cal says, slowly. "I don't know that we can trust her, but I also can't see what harm she could do. And Angela is someone you trust, is she not?"

"She is," Ever says, and means it. "One of the few. Her, and you. Well, really just you. Angela is pretty tight with my mom, which makes her slightly less trustworthy. But she's never given me any reason to doubt her. And she looks pretty wrecked right now. If the girl is a friend, and is going to help her… I don't know…"

"Right," Cal agrees, but then his eyes flit back down the hall, to where Asavari and Angela had been moments earlier. They are gone now, but Cal still seems uneasy.

"Tell you what," Ever says. "My scans all looked good. Right? So let's go get you a good last supper as an Original. Then we'll go back to Kennedy, and get ready for your procedure tonight. If you're still sure—"

"I'm still sure," Cal says, and allows Ever to lead him out of the hospital, without so much as peeking in to the room a few feet away, where her mother is still sleeping in the indifferent embrace of the steadily humming machinery.

CHAPTER 74: ASAVARI

A SAVARI LOOKS AROUND THE HESS HOME, curious and mildly panicked by all of the unfamiliar furnishings, appliances, and most of all the interactive walls. The technology and opulence are unlike anything she has ever seen.,

Shadower—*Angela*, Asavari reminds herself—is seated on a sleek charcoal settee. She is holding quite still, except for her fingers, which are dancing across the flat dark piece of tech in her hands, typing instructions for Asavari to follow. Part of Asavari wants to tell Angela to slow down, take a moment to breathe and mend and focus. But the soldier in Asavari knows that there is no time for such luxuries.

The flip-phone is awkward and lumpy in Asavari's jacket pocket. It had thrown both her and Jorge for a loop when they initially heard its ring. In the panic of the Pulse, with Jorge's slowed and slurring speech, the last thing either of them had expected was a phone call. Particularly since phones went out of vogue before Asavari was even born.

How the phone had been hidden in the park was a puzzle Asavari and Jorge knew they were unlikely to ever solve. When they discovered the phone, Jorge nodded for Asavari to answer it, since her tongue was now nimbler than his.

"Hello?"

"Hello, Karma, this is Chameleon. Clever girl! Made it all the way in to the city, and you're probably helping your informant buddy post-Pulse. I hope he's not too banged up; nice guy, Jorge. Anyway, sounds like you've got your hands full so I'll cut right to the chase: I have Ere."

Asavari had gripped the phone so hard, she depressed several buttons, setting off a series of beeps.

"Hello?" Chameleon chuckled in reply to the sound. "You still there?"

"Where do you have him?"

"In a safe location. He's fine. Little out of it, but fine. He ate some cookies earlier."

"What do you want—"

"I want what you want. To take Hess down. We're on the same side. I'm your friend, Asavari."

"My friends do not 'take' my other friends."

"Well, these are special circumstances. Doubt my intentions all you want, but I have Ere, which means you'll come see me. When you get here, I'll convince you that we're going to be fast friends. I'll even save you a few cookies. I'll call you around, say, five, and give instructions on where we'll meet up. Maybe even a few special surprise guests. Okay? Great. Bye!"

And the call had ended, just like that.

When Asavari relays this story to Angela, the woman starts furiously typing. She writes with the frustrated fury of a prophet whose tongue had been torn out, trying to respond to, relay, and instruct on as many fronts as possible, all at once. She finally shoves the tablet toward Asavari, wide-eyed and intense, showing her how to scroll down so she can continue reading the epic composition.

Asavari looks down, and is confused by the very first line:

While you read this, I have to go fix Dr. Hess some tea.

"Fix Dr. Hess some tea? He's not here, and that hardly seems like—"

But Angela is already lurching toward the kitchen, and Asavari knows better than to question her. She simply stares as the greatest mind of the resistance begins painstakingly preparing the Syn dictator some tea.

CHAPTER 75: ERE

ERE IS NOT AS DROWSY AS HE WAS BEFORE, but he's just as confused, and alert enough now to know he might well be in danger. He desperately wants to believe that he can trust his new "friend," but is trying not to allow himself to be too swayed by all the warm cinnamon-sprinkled bribery. After all, his captor did tranquilize him, take him to an unknown location, and keep him tied up for the first two hours. That's a whole lot to forgive.

"Good, you're up," says Chameleon. "We're about to go for a ride. See some friends."

"Friends of yours? Or friends of mine?"

"Both, I hope," Chameleon says amiably. "You seem more lucid now. That's good. I was worried you might still be a little slack-jaw when we meet up with them, and they'd think I did something really bad to you. I haven't, I promise. Not like Hess, planting that tracker in you. Sneaky bastard, isn't he?"

"How did you know about that?"

"I've got eyes everywhere."

"Where are we meeting these friends?"

"Neutral territory. Not here, obviously."

"Will... will I be coming back here, after this meeting?"

"I hope not."

Left alone, Ere returns to taking stock of his situation as best he can. His head is feeling clearer. He doesn't know if he should be naively hoping his captor is worthy of trust, or if he needs to be figuring out how to defend himself.

Ever's gun.

He had it on him when he returned to the Syn world. It had been a constant presence, like a good luck charm kept securely in his pocket. A good luck charm that could potentially turn the tide on his luck, give him a way to protect himself in a tight spot. So where was it now? He looks down, and sees he's still wearing the same pants.

So maybe...

He shifts in the seat, trying to feel with his thigh, see if there is any weight, any object still in his pocket. He can't tell. He wishes he had been less out of it, back when Chameleon had unbound his hands, so he could have checked then and at least known whether or not—

"Looking for this?" Chameleon asks, stepping back into view, dangling something small and gleaming. The gun. "Silly boy. Did you really think I wouldn't have checked you for weapons? Don't worry, I'll give this back to you, as soon as we've established a little more trust and I know you won't do something stupid like point this thing at me. It's a nice piece."

With that, Chameleon pockets the revolver, then sidles up to Ere.

"What are you doing?" Ere asks nervously.

"Giving you a front-row seat to a very cool show," Chameleon says. "Stand up."

"But I'm in a chair—"

"I realize that. Stand up."

Ere stands awkwardly, hunching over, the base and legs of the chair protruding from his backside like some odd metallic growth. Chameleon nods and gestures for Ere to follow. They walk deeper into the room. Ere can see mostly the floor as they walk, since lifting his neck makes walking difficult.

"Here we are," Chameleon says cheerily. "Go ahead and sit."

Ere obeys, tottering and nearly falling over as he squats and drops the chair down, returning himself to a seated position. As soon as he is sitting, he can see that there is a massive screen before him. It flickers to life, filling with hundreds, maybe even thousands, of small bright boxes. In each box is a person, some in close up, some further away in beds or at tables or, in one instance, relieving themselves.

"What is this?"

"This," Chameleon assures Ere, "is going to be good. Here—have you ever had popcorn?"

THE THRID PULSE

CHAPTER 76: HESS

H ESS IS STANDING IN FRONT OF NATHAN FELL'S containment tank, sipping his evening tea.

"I wish I could pick your brain," Hess says. "Well. If you'll forgive the phrase."

He grimaces at his dark joke, and his grimace deepens as he recalls his latest scan of his own brain.

"There was a spot," Hess says aloud. "Last time I scanned my brain. Probably nothing. Or some small bit of damage sustained in the Pulse. But I don't like seeing that. Looks too much like something that could be a precursor to..."

He can't bring himself to say any of the available words: *Alzheimer's, dementia, an aging brain.* He's silently cursing himself and wondering why he's even giving voice to this phobia in front of his vacant one-time mentor when he hears it.

A small beep.

Hess drops his half-empty porcelain cup, the remaining hot tea soaking his shoe. He begins running, sprinting from the room as soon as the sound begins. Instinct kicks in, and he suddenly knows that being so close to so much powerful tech in the midst of the surge—

Hess barely manages to make it out the door, into the hallway, hearing the entrance to the core of Heaven slide shut behind him just as he begins to feel everything else. The pain of the hot beverage that scalded his foot. Then the tidal wave of Pulse-pain that erases all feeling or memory of something as stupid as a little spilled tea.

CHAPTER 77: EVER

EVER WANTS TO LOOK NICE FOR CAL'S augmentation. It feels somewhat ceremonial, like getting dressed up for someone's baptism or bar mitzvah or something old-world like that.

Maybe it's just that she wants to be sure that when Cal sees her after his procedure, looking at her with his augmented eyes, the very first thing he'll see on the other side, she'll be radiant—*or as radiant as I can be, scarred and imperfect as I am*— and blot out whatever regrets he might suddenly have. Besides, during final prep, Kennedy had banned her from the facility. He had promised to let her in when it was complete, before the chamber opened and the newly-synthetic Cal emerged.

"I'll send you a message," Kennedy assured her.

So Ever had returned home to distract herself with old beauty rituals before her new life began. She re-touches her hair, selecting her old favorite, Midnight Express #17. She carefully chooses a white eyelet dress, vintage, form-fitting but not tight, flattering against her dark hair and glowing skin. She put on a little more makeup than usual, trying to cover the scar on her face as best she can, reminding herself that Cal found her beautiful even with the jagged blemish. And finally, something in her jewelry box had caught her eye for a final touch—a locket. It was small, heart-shaped. She hadn't worn it in a while. It looked nice with the dress.

Ever: The procedure is starting.
Will not take long; you may return.
Kennedy

Receiving Kennedy's message, Ever hurries back to the lab. She stands outside the laboratory, waiting for Kennedy to let her in. She knows not to bother him, knows he is monitoring the machine and keeping track of Cal's vital signs, making sure it will be safe to open the sterile augmentation chamber. Ever's fingers go to her neck, subconsciously toying with the locket, snapping it open and shut, open and shut; on the third opening, something slips out from within the heart-shaped charm, brushing her finger, almost weightless.

Ever removes the necklace, carefully cradling it in her hand, and tugs out the small contents within. It's a tiny note in scrawled print:

I have left, but I will return.
With Love For Ever
Ere

Ere, she thinks. *That name, again. Cal's cousin? What the—*

The thought is interrupted by the faint beep, then a searing pain slices through the scar on her face. She pitches forward violently, fist closing hard around the locket and the note from Ere, holding on to the delicate heart as everything disappears.

*I*T'S DONE.

Cal's procedure was successful. It must have been; everything went just as Kennedy had said it would. The injections, one of which was a sedative, slowing his reactions a little and numbing him to pain. The strange sounds, whirring, clicking, unnatural noises that triggered his instinct to fight or flee. The feeling of the restraints, prohibiting him from doing either thing. Then the searing pain, a pain that would have been unbearable without the anesthesia and was still enough to send Cal into convulsions, his teeth rattling in his head, his muscles involuntarily flexing and releasing. The strange quiet after the jarring fusion.

He is not sure if it is his imagination or something real, but he thinks he can feel electricity, crackling within his body, crackling throughout the machine, all around him and within him and through him. He visualizes his insides melting, his new steel components suffocating his organic organs, and he cannot help but shudder.

It's worth it.

It's for Ever.

It's over, and now we can be together.

Then he hears a small, unobtrusive beep. He wonders briefly if it's the sound the augmentation chamber makes before sliding open, the last of the strange sounds standing between him and his love. He pictures her face, every detail of her filling his mind, before an internal switch is flipped, and with a jolting explosion of agony, everything goes dark.

MARILYN HESS IS IN HER HOSPITAL ROOM, alone. Unbeknownst to the doctors and nurses who occasionally check in on her, she has been able to hear everything for the last few hours, despite her lack of a reaction. She heard when her friend Angela came, said nothing to her, but at least stayed for a few minutes. She heard when a stranger entered, addressing Angela by some odd nickname—*Shadow, something?*

She heard her daughter in the hallway, and her heart rate increased, which only the monitors noticed. She hoped her daughter was coming in to see her. When she didn't, a single tear slid from Marilyn's still-shut eye.

She hears the high-pitched beep, cuing another Pulse. As it begins ripping through her, she remains unable to react. The machines to which she is connected flare and whine and snap off, and Marilyn lays there, eyes closed, forgotten, racked with pain, but to her increasing dismay, still very much alive.

J ORGE HAS TIME FOR TWO THOUGHTS before the Pulse rips away his ability to function.

First, when he hears the small beep, he reminds himself that nothing that is about to happen will be logged in his searchable memories.

Second, riding the small silver-lined blessing of a moment permitting untraceable communiqué, just before the larger sound begins roaring through him, he sends a message through the clandestine network. Rather than send it all at once, he transmits it word by word so that each encrypted bit has a chance to make it through, hoping it will reach the others so that they can join Asavari and take action now that he can confirm for them:

The Pulse is hitting again.
THE TIME IS NOW—

And then, writhing but triumphant, he blacks out.

CHAPTER 81: ANGELA

ANGELA IS EN ROUTE WITH ASAVARI to meet the mysterious Chameleon when the small beep stops her in her tracks.

"What is it?" Asavari asks.

Angela turns terrified eyes toward the girl, and Asavari catches her as she falls.

O*H, THINKS KENNEDY,* as everyone around him collapses. *Another Pulse.*

He feels fine.

OUTSIDE THE CENTER

CHAPTER 83: ASAVARI

"THIS IS THE PLACE." Asavari says to Angela, keeping her voice as soft and soothing as possible. Angela is silent, still trembling from the Pulse that hit mere hours ago. Though it brought her to her knees, it seems to have mercifully wrought no further damage.

Clutching Angela as they sped toward this location by Chariot had exhausted Asavari, but she too was still standing.

"Chameleon!"

A voice rings out through the heavily wooded area, at once commanding and tentative. Asavari spins toward the sound, on guard. Who else is here to meet Chameleon?

"Identify yourself," Asavari growls, hand on the knife at her side, muscles taut.

From the night-darkened tree line, an old woman steps forward.

"I am Helena Garrison."

And then, before Asavari can say anything, a second old woman comes barreling toward her, crushing her in a fierce hug.

"Mother?" Asavari gasps.

Her mother reluctantly releases her grip, and turns her gaze over to Angela. Her physician's eyes take a quick inventory, noting the wide swath of metal at Angela's neck and diagnosing her as a Syn.

"This is Chameleon?"

"No, this is—Angela," Asavari says, looking at her companion for confirmation before saying anything further. Should she stop there, or…? Angela gives a slight shake of her head. *No. Do not call me by my other name.* "She is a friend. She has been helping me. Angela, this is my mother, Dr. Preeti Kansal. And Helena…?"

"Garrison," says the white-haired woman. "Longtime friend of the Fells."

Asavari takes the woman's hand, parchment-thin skin clinging loosely to brittle Original bones. She presses Helena's palm gently, indicating her respect for a true veteran of the rebellion. An Original fighter. Helena presses back, with a surprising strength. Asavari instantly likes her.

"You were told to come here by the one called Chameleon?"

The four women all nod, unsure what might happen next.

Chameleon's message had specified a meeting point outside the Syn Center, in the sector once called New Jersey. The exact designated location is at the edge of a sprawling but young forest, trees forty and fifty years old growing where once there were more signs of human inhabitance. It is an area utilized by the Syns for agricultural purposes, but not residential, and very rarely for any other industry. Probably less monitored, if Asavari had to guess.

Angela hands her tablet to Asavari, and Asavari looks down to see the words:

**Scanned as best I could. No evident tech.
If there's an ambush, it will be physical.**

Asavari hope this insight means Shadower's abilities are returning, at least somewhat. She nods appreciatively to Angela, returning the tablet. Another thought occurs to her, so obvious she almost gives a shriek before demanding to know.

"How did you get here? Mother, you were back in Delhi—"

"I flew a spaceship out to her," Helena Garrison says, her massive grin discrediting her casual tone. "Well. A plane. But sure as hell looked like a spaceship."

"Which was provided by Chameleon," adds Asavari's mother, more soberly.

"So. Where is this Chameleon, then?"

And then, like the namesake creature, Chameleon emerges from a tree—not from behind it, but from inside it, Asavari will later swear. In a black face mask and dark clothing, small and slight of build, the mysterious figure approaches.

"I'm glad to see you're all so punctual," Chameleon says, and their voice seems somehow altered.

"Where is Ere?" Asavari snaps. She has already decided: This black-masked person is not someone in whom she will ever place her trust.

"He's here. I just gave him a few more sedatives so he'd be a little more relaxed. He's fine. And he'll be totally lucid within the next three hours. Ten, tops," Chameleon chuckles. "Oh, lighten up a little, 'rebels.' He was just harder to transport when he started kicking. You want proof of life? Here."

Chameleon walks briskly forward, and the four women are forced to break ranks so that the stranger can pass between them, walk past them, and make their way toward a larger tree situated just outside of the forest. Chameleon walks behind the tree, and drags out a chair. In the chair is Ere, bound at his wrists and ankles, head slumped forward. Helena gives a small cry, and Preeti takes her hand.

Chameleon steps out of the way, allowing Asavari to approach, feel for a pulse, listen to the boy's chest rise and fall. His breath is slow but steady, indicating deep sleep, not death. Having verified his status to the best of her ability, Asavari fixes a wary gaze on Chameleon.

"Why did you take him."

"Had a few questions for him," Chameleon says easily. "And, as a bonus, I knew it would get your attention. Killed two birds with one stone. As I'm sure he'll tell you when he wakes, I've been good to him. Now. Let's get down to business. We have a mutual enemy. Dr. Felix Hess. You hate him, I hate him. Together, I think we can take him down. The enemy of my enemy is my friend, and all that."

"Why should we trust someone who will not show their face?" Asavari asks.

"Why should I trust a group of people who use stupid code names and have no indoor plumbing? We all have to take a few leaps of faith, here, 'Karma.'"

Asavari feels something slim and cold slipped into her hand. Angela's tablet. She glances down, notes the question there, and aims the inquiry to Chameleon.

"Are you the one responsible for the Pulses?"

At this, Chameleon laughs. The voice-distortion machine makes it an oddly robotic sound.

"I wish! But unless wildest-dreams-coming-true counts as being responsible, no, that's not me. Been studying it, though. Predicting the timing. That's why I knew now was the time for us to all finally meet face to face. The Syns all just got slammed again, as I'm sure you're aware."

The stranger looks at Angela's half-slack face. Angela snatches the tablet from Asavari, swipes at it furiously, and returns it to her.

"You are also a Syn," Asavari says, reading Angela's words.

"Well," Chameleon shrugs. "Sort of. I haven't exactly... kept up with the Joneses much lately. So the Pulse doesn't impact me anymore. First one was a doozy, though. By the way, if you thought the last Pulse was bad—and it was; they're still tallying the fatalities—the one coming in a few hours is going to make the other one look like a moderate case of the hiccups."

Behind her, Asavari feels Angela tremble.

"How do you know," Asavari says, low and flat.

"Chameleon knows," says Ere, and everyone turns to look at him. Sitting upright, still tied to the chair, the boy is blinking, pale, but lucid. He's looking right at Asavari, his expression serious. "Knew when the last one was coming. Put it up on a bunch of screens. We watched the whole thing."

"Well, welcome back, Ere," Chameleon says. "Thanks for the endorsement. So yes, I know. It's coming. And we don't need to react after it happens—we need to be there and take action while it's happening. While everything's down. While those few who will survive are totally incapacitated. While the Synt is permeable, all the gates are down. We need to get in place now, and be ready to go as soon as that first little beep makes those Syns all piss themselves."

"Just the six of us?" Asavari says doubtfully. "A half dozen rebels to win the war?"

Chameleon's tongue-clucking is infuriating.

"Ah, ah, Asavari. 'Never doubt the ability of a small, committed group of people to change the world; indeed, it is the only thing that ever has.' Margaret Mead. Great quote. But, as it happens—no. Not just the six of us. I figured a few hundred might be better."

"And where are these 'few hundred' coming from?" Helena asks.

"I have some troops of my own. And the rest are coming from India, obviously," Chameleon says. "Their ship should be here in about ten minutes."

"What?" Preeti gasps. "Why would they have boarded the ship to come here? Why would they have trusted—"

"I asked them to," says Ere, adding: "I might have been just a little bit drugged at the time."

CHAPTER 83: HELENA

WAS IT ONLY A WEEK AGO Helena felt like she was shuffling toward the grave, no great adventures or triumphs or tragedies left? That was her outlook, seven days before. Now she's aboard a gleaming ship, flying through the air and toward adventure, for the third time in a week.

This ship is full of rebels, freshly arrived from Delhi. About to take down Felix Hess.

Hot damn, this is more like it.

Helena is channeling her dear Ruth Fell, embracing the thrill of it all. With nothing to lose and a resurrected sense of possibility, despite Asavari's constant frown, Preeti's shaking hands, Angela's furrowed brow—Helena can't stop grinning.

She sidles up to Chameleon. The vigilante (that's how Helena has decided to think of Chameleon: a vigilante, hopefully on the good side, like Batman or something) is manning the ship, wordlessly directing the flight plan while occasionally calling up other images and information on the large flat-paneled screens at the front of the ship.

"So," Helena says. "When we land. What exactly is the plan?"

Chameleon looks at Helena. If the mask weren't obscuring any and all facial features, Helena imagines she would be on the receiving end of a very bemused look.

"Your friends haven't filled you in? Asavari and Ere—"

"—will be addressing everyone shortly. Yes. I wanted to hear it from you. You're the mastermind, after all, aren't you?"

"Who are you, again?"

"Helena Garrison."

"Yes. That part, I got. But that's not exactly like saying 'Ruth Fell' or 'Felix Hess.' Who is 'Helena Garrison'?"

Helena puts her shoulders back, pulling herself to her fullest somewhat-shrunken height.

"I was a member of the Original resistance. The very first rebels. I lived next door to Howard and Sophie Fell, and in the earliest days—"

"You lived next door to the Fells? Fascinating. Lead with that. It's the most interesting thing about you."

"Actually, it isn't," Helena says, her voice steeled by every memory of her husband, her son, her piano playing, her ambitions before and after the world as she knew it was transposed into discordant noise. But she decides she's no longer interested in connecting with this dismissive vigilante. "The plan. What is it."

"Divide and conquer," Chameleon says, perhaps impressed by Helena's stubborn refusal to back down. "We go now, while they're still reeling. We storm the castle—the Synt. From what Asavari tells me, that speechless Syn woman needs to be part of the core crack team. Everyone else will hit every floor, and take out everything you can take out."

"You mean…"

"Not people. Pulse is gonna take care of most of that for us. I mean tech. We're going to burn their center to the ground, floor by floor. Set Heaven's core processor aflame. Take out all the nearby buildings with generators and back-up storage, too. Those rebels are ready to smash and burn. Are you?"

Despite her irritation at Chameleon's attitude and insistent anonymity, Helena can't help but smirk at the thought of taking mallets to machinery inside the heart of darkness. Destroying and dismantling the Syn world has been her dream for more than half her lifetime. Pounding the hell out of it. Smashing it right out of existence.

"Will there be hammers?" Helena asks. "I'm looking forward to the hammers."

"I like your moxie, old lady," Chameleon says, with an oddly-pitched obfuscation of a chuckle.

*   *   *   *

Just moments after Ere and Asavari convey the storm-the-castle information to all the rebels aboard, Chameleon's odd voice slides in over the ship's audio system.

"Okay, folks. Landing's gonna be a doozy. But we want to get down now, while the last Pulse still has 'em reeling and the next one's on its way. Hold on tight—"

And with that, they begin plummeting downward at such an alarming rate that Helena momentarily wonders if they're crashing. But in less than two minutes, they're on the ground, unharmed.

Ready.

And just like that, time moves at triple the speed it has ever moved. Chameleon gives quickly shouted commands. In a matter of moments, two hundred rebels pour out of the vessel, flowing like a righteous stream toward their destiny. Only Asavari, Preeti, Angela, Ere, Helena, and Chameleon remain.

"The uprising begins!" Chameleon says. "Now here's what's going to happen. We hit 'em hard and fast, and hope the next Pulse finishes the job while we're here. Helena and Preeti, you're going to the medical wing. Take out all of the med-tech. All of it, I don't care who's plugged in, if they die it's not on you—it's the Pulse. Asavari and Ere, you're taking out the Core. I'm going to Hess's office to take care of all of his backups and whatever hard copies he might have. Angela, you'll come with me—"

Angela shakes her head violently, and shoves her tablet at Chameleon, who gives it a quick glance, then nods.

"Fine. Go with Asavari and Ere. I can handle my task alone. GO."

"But I don't know where the medical—" Helena begins to protest as everyone scatters. Then she feels Dr. Preeti Kansal's soft hand on her shoulder.

"I do," says Preeti. "And I think our 'friend' Chameleon knows that. Everyone is assigned to somewhere they've been."

"You've been…?"

"A lifetime ago. Not to the Synt as it is now, but the medical wing—well. I have a basic familiarity with the machinery we'll find there. Let's go."

Helena turns to wish well to Ere, to whom she has barely spoken since their blessed unexpected reunion—but the boy is gone.

So fast, so fast…

Taking Preeti's arm, Helena half-jogs, half limps on resistant legs. They exit the ship and emerge into a world of chaos.

Syns are writhing on the ground. Smoke and sparks are already filling the air, as hundreds of teeming Originals begin smashing their way through the world that had nearly driven them to extinction. Helena is looking around, taking it all in, but Preeti won't let her stop. They barrel away from the residential area where they landed, running as fast as their aging bodies allow toward the center of the city. The Synt.

The building stretches skyward, disappearing into the clouds. Even in the old world, Helena had never seen such a structure. It dwarfs the Empire State Building, the Sears Tower, the hotel her husband took her to in Abu Dhabi when they were young and in love. Again she wants to stop and stare, but the pace will not allow it. They rush through the open door, and though Preeti's expression is grimly determined, Helena is still grinning like an idiot.

This it is.

This is the resistance rising up.

This is when we win.

Preeti pauses when they enter the building; the long hallway with the vast upward opening is intimidating and gives no clear indication of where to go next. Helena spots a Syn at the far end of the hallway, army-crawling her way toward them. She has hair pulled back so tightly that her wild, scared eyes are still directed into an oddly accusatory angle even in her anguish. The older women run past her, ignoring her plight and trying to determine from whence she came. They discover a wall embedded with panels, the lights flickering on and off unreliably. Wide, flat sheets of metal hover in the air, twitching and shifting.

"Levitators," Preeti says. "Asavari explained how they work. You stand on them, and they take you to your destination—like an individual elevator."

Helena looks around for buttons, levers, anything that might indicate a selection.

"How do we plug in our destination? I don't see any 'hospital wing' or whatever button to push—"

"The Syns give a mental command, I am certain," Preeti says. "But my guess is right now these are all defaulting to somewhere—likely to wherever medical attention might be available. Remember, functionality is down across their world. Stripped down to basics."

"So what do we do?"

"We get on them and hope they take us where we need to go."

Despite speaking with relative authority, Preeti's voice shakes. Standing on a slim piece of metal, trying not to fall off while it zooms their old Original bones towards destination unknown, is a somewhat nerve-wracking prospect.

"Sounds fun," Helena beams, and gingerly steps on a levitator, which seems to adjust and accommodate for her weight and balance. She doesn't feel at all as if she is in danger of being thrown from the device. "It's easier than it looks, doc. Just step on and—"

The levitator makes a clicking sound, and surges upward. Helena whoops in joy. Somewhere below her, Preeti is steeling herself to step on to the next levitator, but for a moment Helena isn't even worried about her companion. The woman is a doctor, smart enough to figure it out, and anyhow, this is an experience to be enjoyed. It's a hell of a thing, almost better than a spaceship, this private little metallic flying carpet. The Syns might be bastards, but they sure have cool toys.

The levitator stops. It hovers in front of a darkened door Helena reaches forward, pressing lightly, and the door drops straight down with an exhausted hiss.

As her eyes gradually adjust, assisted by the occasional light of large screens flashing on and off, she begins to take in her surroundings. The room might indeed be medical; lots of tech, some pretty obvious monitors, tables with small tools. In the center of the room is a large, cylindrical structure, several yards long and almost as many wide.

That thing looks like it could use a good smashing.

She knows she should wait for Preeti, who will know what's what and how to best dismantle and disable this and that. But there's a chance her levitator might deposit her elsewhere, and anyhow time is of the essence, and Helena doubts there's any damage she can do that won't basically be furthering their noble cause of Burn It All Down.

Nothing is supposed to be saved, right?

Some good old senseless smashing isn't going to mess anything up, and God, it'll be fun.

Still looking forward to hammering, Helena looks around for something that will serve as makeshift mallet. She almost immediately finds something on a tabletop, long and solid and almost too heavy for her to swing around. She's not sure what it actually is; some sort of scanner, maybe, like those wands they used at airport security in the old world. Doesn't matter what a thing was, only what a thing *is*.

This is my Syn-smasher!

Giddy, Helena decides to try out her Syn-smasher. Gripping it with all her might, she takes a wild swing and shatters the nearest screen, which cracks and crackles in satisfying obliteration, then goes completely dark.

Hell yeah!

Helena strikes again, and again, smashing screens and tanks and tables, hurling her weapon around indiscriminately, feeling like a hurricane, leveling the room around her, reveling in the feeling of leaving chaos in her wake. Then she fixates on the big prize: The large container in the middle of the room.

She rushes toward it, Syn-smasher held aloft, ready to come clanging down with sweet vengeance. Just as she is about to connect her weapon with the machine, the last remaining screen in the room, suspended from the ceiling above the cylinder, flashes on, casting light on Helena's target. Helena freezes, her weapon suspended in the air, as the glowing screen reveals an opening in the machine. A window, allowing Helena a glimpse within.

She sees a face, eyes closed, expression pained.

"No," Helena whispers, shaking uncontrollably. "No, no, no...."

She loses hold of her Syn-smasher, which clatters to the ground and rolls away from her, leaving her defenseless and defeated. For the first time since this sudden uprising began, Helena Garrison stops smiling.

For a moment, she is frozen. Then the screen clicks off, plunging her into darkness. No longer able to see the face revealed through the clear panel of the massive cylindrical machine, Helena begins shrieking, clawing at the window, her fingernails tearing and bleeding. She pounds and pulls, scrapes, trying to find a corner, a way in, some method of prying off this panel, of cracking open the machine.

"Helena? Helena!"

She dimly hears Preeti's voice, hears some clattering as the doctor approaches her, tripping over the wreckage Helena so swiftly created.

"What on earth—"

"It's him," Helena pants, ragged, not looking at Preeti, still trying to get in, still trying to get him out, still trying to save him. "It's him..."

"Him, who?" Preeti asks. "Is someone in the augmenting machine?"

"The... augmenting machine?" Helena stops, struck still by this impossible information. "No. He never would. He never would have..."

"Who is he?"

Helena slumps against the machine, drained of all feeling and all hope. She had seen it clearly enough in the screen light. The one who had carried her. The strong young man whom she had daily held in her heart. He was dead.

And before death, he had become something else. Something he should never have been.

It is not what a thing was; it is what a thing is…

"Helena," Preeti says, gentle and scared, not knowing how to proceed. "Who—"

"Cal," Helena says, and a keening wail breaks forth from her.

CHAPTER 85: ERE

FOLLOWING ANGELA AND ASAVARI toward Hess's domain, Ere is still not sure about this woman Angela. Asavari seems to trust her. And seeing as Ere had planned to ditch the rebels, then got himself kidnapped, then rallied the rebels on behalf of his kidnapper Chameleon, his own judgment is now permanently suspect. So he keeps his mouth shut.

Since Angela is taller than Asavari, Ere can see the exposed back of her neck clearly. There is a small flat piece of metal embedded there, glinting in the occasional light cast by the flickering street lamps and buildings. Her port, he realizes; like the strange hard end of Ever's fingertip. She had told him about how earlier-generation Syns had to plug in directly through their spinal cords. The stark piece of tech seems to be staring at him. Like it's somehow separate from the human flesh of the woman, and will betray them all.

Angela takes a sharp right, and almost out of nowhere the Synthetic Neuroscience Institute of Technology looms before them. It is just as Ere remembers it: The two tremendous sections, one wide and low, the other impossibly tall. On a poorly-lit night like this, it seems like a mountainous, segmented shadow—something of little substance, yet terrifying. A ghost building.

Approaching the Synt makes Ere shudder. He has known in his bones that he would be back here, someday, no matter what. Whether he was after Ever, or answers, or as it turned out, storming it with the Original resistance. But he was never going to be ready for the return. The last time he entered the building, it had been through the front—he can still so clearly remember the high-ceilinged hallway, the sound of that heavenly symphony, being greeted by the severe Syn receptionist's narrowed eyes.

Angela takes another sharp right, bypassing the main gate and guiding them to a side entrance. She turns her back to the gate, and something beeps. A section of gate swings open, and they hurry through it.

From somewhere not too far off, he hears a series of screams, and shudders. Were the Originals or the Syns crying out in pain? Was either answer a good one? His mother has spoken always with reverence of rebellion and uprising, but suddenly in the midst of war, Ere does not feel reverent. He feels terrified and sick. He should be glad that the mysterious Pulse is enabling this sudden shift in the balance of power, allowing the Originals an opportunity to right such epic wrongs. But it doesn't seem heroic, it seems desperate and dangerous and maddening.

Ere still believes strongly that Dr. Felix Hess must be unseated. Stopped. Destroyed, if necessary. But how much collateral damage was all of this going to yield? How many innocent people will get hurt? His thoughts flare and leap like small wildfires, fed by the winds of change whipping around him.

Then Angela stops so abruptly that Asavari nearly runs into her, and Ere does run into Asavari, earning him a swift glare.

Angela turns toward the gleaming steel wall beside them, and hovers her hand just above the surface. The metal begins to glow, a green-lit rectangle revealing itself beneath her palm. The green light turns bright blue, and a panel in the wall appears and just as quickly drops. A levitator system hums in the open space where a solid wall stood moments earlier. Without so much as looking back at Asavari and Ere, Angela moves through the door, onto a levitator, and shoots upward.

"Come on," Asavari says, and she and Ere each step onto a flat panel and follow Angela's path, the machine beneath their feet seeming to know to follow Angela's course. Maybe she was controlling them, somehow. She didn't talk, but she sure knew her way around this world.

The higher the levitators rise, the more Ere's stomach drops. He can't recognize anything in the dark vertical hall through which the panels travel—he barely remembers the scenery hurtling past him from the last time. This time, the movement is slower but the lighting is worse, so the journey is still obscured. Still, Ere instinctively knows that he's en route to the same damned destination as his last visit here.

The room where the undead corpse of his grandfather hangs limply, a human battery charging the entire Syn system.

What had Hess called this room?

The "core."

The core of Heaven.

His thoughts are interrupted by Asavari's sudden gasp. He follows her gaze, already apprehensive about what he will see. Asavari is looking at the floor, to a heap of something that Angela is pointing at grimly. It takes Ere a moment to realize that the crumpled thing on the ground is none other than Dr. Felix Hess.

CHAPTER 86: ANGELA

FOR THE FIRST TIME SINCE THE MOST RECENT PULSE, Angela manages to form a word. One single syllable.

"Tea."

Understanding immediately shines in Asavari's intelligent eyes. Angela had been unable to lay out the entire plan for her—no time to type out that much information—but now the girl is all caught up. Angela had to fix him the tea he would send for during his visit to the core. She had to prepare it, so that she could drug it.

Thank Heaven he collapsed outside the core and not within it, Angela thinks, realizing how close she had come to blowing it. Even at full strength, she doubts her Shadower abilities could get her into this heavily protected room, and she's not back to full strength yet.

Without hesitation, Angela grabs Hess by one arm, motioning for Asavari to grab the other. Grunting from a weight that would not normally have hindered her, Angela is relieved when the Fell boy comes to her aid, hauling Hess up. Letting the boy bear the burden of Hess's mass, Angela is able to lift his hand and press it firmly to the wall. The surface beneath each of his fingertips glows first green, one-two-three-four-five, then blue. A key code panel now blinks into existence, right beside the fingerprint scanner.

Exhaling slowly, centering herself, Shadower slowly presses each number, entering the code. She has known for decades that a frequently-changed key code would be part of this entry system, and had long ago—through no small amount of effort and prayer—identified the quiet channel that carried this particular code. But since losing her Shadower abilities, she is unable to re-confirm it. If Hess has changed it since she snagged the newest code earlier in the week, they'll be screwed.

6...3...6...6...7...9

An accepting beep, and then a red panel appears, slightly higher. Knees buckling in relief for only an instant, Angela wastes no time stiffening her legs and moving the process along. Grabbing again at Hess's arm, she yanks it, indicating that Asavari and Ere need to hold him up higher. They manage to get his head nearly level with the red panel.

Snatching him by the hair, Angela jerks his head upright, then pries open one of his eyes. She can feel Ere shudder beside her as the Synt director's dilated pupil rolls and lolls before staring dully forward. A beam radiates from the red panel directly to Hess's eye, locking in on it, performing a second scan. After rotating clockwise and counter clockwise across the man's retina, it beeps and the glowing red shifts to the more welcoming blue.

Relief and dread flood through Shadower. They are so close now, so close. Angela's heart and soul have both been, broken many times over and mended like a poorly-set bone, hard and crooked. But she knows the scar tissue is strong; the broken parts are the toughest to crack. Her hard-healed heart is thudding now, still committed to doing everything she can to honor her son by ending the synthetic dominion.

She can almost feel Leroy beside her now, cheering her on, putting a firm hand to her back and driving her forward. This is what he wanted her to do all those years ago, and it has taken this long for her to find the means and opportunity and partners to get her to this point.

"Good job, Ma," he'd say. "Almost there. Now get it done."

She still doesn't know exactly what *it* is, other than shut down the core. She's fairly certain it has something to do with shutting down the brain-leeched body of Nathan Fell. Thanks to the prophecy, it seems like something Ere himself might have to do—not that she's so sure a prophecy from Heaven can really be trusted. She'll advise her young companions as best she can, but just as with Hess's limp body, the heavy lifting will be up to them.

As all these thoughts fly through her head, Angela realizes that the wall still stands resolutely before them. Despite the fingerprint analysis, the code, the retinal scan— they have still not been granted access. What further information were they missing? What code or detail or freaking rain dance had Angela not deciphered?

Was the code wrong? No. No, if it was wrong the retinal scanner wouldn't have appeared. Each step leads to the next. It's right, I know it's right. Come on come on come on, dammit. Open sesame.

"Do we have to open his other eye?" Asavari asks aloud, the sudden sound of her question ringing oddly loudly through the narrow hallway before being swallowed by the vast drop of the levitator passage behind them.

Angela shakes her head.

What am I missing?

She looks at Ere, wordlessly inquiring if he had seen Hess get through all the security last time the boy had been here. He shakes his head, understanding her query but unable to offer anything useful.

Dammit dammit dammit.

A soft whistling noise behind them makes all three of them turn their heads, just in time to see a slim man in a lab coat stepping off of his levitator and onto the floor.

"What the hell is going on here?" Kennedy demands.

Just then, the door drops open.

Must have been a Pulse delay—dammit, doesn't matter, GO!

Unable to vocalize her words and instructions, Angela shoves Ere and Asavari through the open door. Hess collapses unceremoniously at her feet, then moans softly, making her heart thunder in her chest.

"Angela—" Asavari says, from just inside the core.

"GO!" Angela bellows, summoning all her strength to give sound to this syllable.

The wall slides up and solidifies again behind Angela, sealing Ere and Asavari inside and locking her outside. She stands face to face with Kennedy, whose eyes dart from his fallen boss to Angela to the now-securely-locked core.

Angela closes her eyes for just a fraction of a second, sending a brief update to the network, fearing it won't go through—but it does. She fixes her gaze on Kennedy, planting her feet beneath her. She might not be in any shape to fight, but if there's anyone in this world she still feels confident she could take down in hand-to-hand-combat, it was Jorge's boob of a co-worker.

That's right. You'll have to get through me, pansy-ass.

CHAPTER 87: JORGE

"JORGE, COME PLAY WITH ME," SAYS JAVI.

Jorge blinks, looking up at the little boy, seven years old and grinning down at him. He has the same golden eyes as his older brother, and deep impish dimples that are all his own. His crowded, crooked mix of baby and grown-up teeth are adorable, even if they will need years of dental work to straighten later.

"Yeah, Jorge, come on!" Mariposa, his sister, chimes in. She looks just as she did the last time Jorge saw her—fifteen, with thick black hair and smooth skin, spared the miserable acne that plagued Jorge at that age. She's holding the cell phone Jorge gave her, tilted at an angle and at-the-ready, awaiting whatever important text might light it up next.

Jorge tries to respond, tries to get up and join them, but his limbs are unresponsive. They feel at once heavy and completely weightless, things of no substance and obviously of no use to him. He attempts to at least open his mouth, to explain to his little siblings that he wants to join them but needs a minute.

"What's wrong, Jorge?" *Javi asks, his gleaming eyes rounding in concern.*

Jorge manages to shake his head, just a slight side-to-side tilt, trying to reassure his brother and sister. He's fine, he'll be fine, he's on his way to them, he'll be right there, everything is okay…

"He's not coming, Javi," *Mariposa says, glancing at her phone, then pocketing it.* "Not yet. Don't worry, Jorge. We'll keep waiting. When you're ready."

"But I want him to come play now," *Javi pouts, and Jorge's heart cracks, because he wants to come now, to be with them. He tries to tell them so, but says nothing.*

"Come on, Javi," *Mariposa says.* "Next time."

She takes the little boy's hand, and they both turn and begin walking away from Jorge. Hot tears slip down the Vost's face. He doesn't want them to go, doesn't want them to leave him behind. He wants to go with them. He wants to go with them to be with their mother—

A sudden, searing pain shatters the scene.

His brother and sister are gone.

He is alone.

No—not alone.

Someone is screaming.

*   *   *   *

Jorge's eyes open slowly, painfully.

His left eye rolls around in its socket, unable to focus, damaged perhaps beyond repair. With his right eye, he takes in a few flashes of his surroundings—the screaming is somewhere nearby, and may be coming from more than one someone. He is in the street, sprawled on his side. There is a streetlamp above him, periodically flashing on, then shorting out again.

Jorge pushes himself up into a seated position, grunting with the effort. He looks toward the sound of the screaming, and sees two Syns, a man and a woman. The woman has small eyes and short black hair, the man a strong, jutting jaw. Both are standing stock still, arms rigid at their sides. They have no visible injuries, but their mouths are both open, eyes locked, staring at each other in shock and screaming in wordless horror.

Seeing no way of helping them, Jorge drags himself to his feet and lurches away, ears ringing, wanting to put as much distance as possible between himself and the bloodcurdling shrieks. He tries to send a coded message to the clandestine network, but the command yields only a dull clicking in his head.

"Jorge," gargles a voice at his elbow, startling him.

Jorge looks down and sees a man on his knees. Mussed hair plugs cling listlessly to his sweaty head, inches above wide bushy eyebrows, knit upwards in pain and dismay. The man is heavy, panting, his eyes rimmed red in his swollen face, and it takes the Vost a minute to place the fallen Council member.

"Vinnie?"

"It's bad, man, it's bad," Vinnie says, pawing at Jorge "When the Pulse got Lorraine—and she was tough as *shit*—I knew it was getting worse. But it's just ripping our guts out now. It's a friggin' massacre. What's Hess doing about this? Where the hell even is he—?"

"I'll… find out," Jorge says, his speech still slowed but not as stilted and painful as before.

"Don't hold out on me, man—"

"I'm not… holding out on you—"

"Don't lie to me, you Vost piece of shit!"

Jorge shakes his arm free of Vinnie, taking a step back and reeling, glaring at him. Vinnie's red face pales, and he puts his hands up, apologetic, backpedaling into an apology.

"I'm sorry, man, I'm sorry. Look, I'm not the enemy, okay? We were going to take him down," he says, then abruptly stops.

"What did you say?"

Vinnie shakes his head, mumbles "nothing" from behind his hands, but it's too late.

"What do you mean, you were going to take him down? Did you—are you part of whatever got this Pulse underway?"

"Hell no," Vinnie says. "We weren't after *everyone*, just Hess—"

"Who's 'we'?"

"Just a—concerned citizens' group. Doesn't matter. Doesn't matter now. If Hess can stop this Pulse bullshit, he's got my full backing, you hear me? But if he can't... do you know... how to get in touch with the self-terminating group? Because..."

But Jorge is no longer listening to sniveling slob Vinnie, because he's just received a message. It shivers its way into his mind, thin and time-stamped from several minutes earlier. It's from Shadower, summoning him to help her at the entrance to the core of Heaven.

Jorge starts limping toward the Synt as fast as he can. Vinnie's indignant shouts joining the ongoing screams of the staring Syns, all melting into the chaotic symphony of the dark and damaged streets of the wounded and wailing Syn world.

K ENNEDY LOOKS FROM THE DEFIANT house-keeper to the collapsed Syn leader at her feet.

"What did you do to him?" Kennedy asks.

"Nuh—thing," the woman growls.

Kennedy looks at her more closely, and realizes that the woman is stiff, her lip drooping, her Pulse damage evident. He'd almost forgotten that there was yet another incident, since for some reason they no longer seemed to impact him.

"Pulse got Hess?"

She nods.

Kennedy stands for a moment, uncertain. He doesn't feel compelled to help his boss, although he should. He couldn't get into the core to go after the young Originals, even if he wanted to, which he does not. Much to his relief, he receives a command.

Come to my place.

Kennedy turns on his heel to go, and finds himself face to face with Jorge.

"We got... a problem here, Kennedy?"

"You might," Kennedy says, nonplussed. "I don't."

And he leaves.

EVER SHUDDERS AWAKE. Her scar feels like it's vibrating, but otherwise she's not feeling too much pain. She does a quick internal scan, finds no major damage, but keeps her palms pressed to her temple. Her mind feels cramped and crowded, like something is trying to makes its way out.

And then a vault within her unlocks. Something does make it way out.

Her memories.

My missing memories.

They all come flooding back. She remembers everything. She remembers the night, a year ago, sitting on her bedroom floor, slowly deleting file after file, sending Ere away so he would be gone by the time she erased the last traces of him from her mind.

Ere.

She remembers Ere. Ere in her bedroom, Ere leading her toward a cabin in the woods, Ere laughing and teasing her, Ere's cousin Cal spotting her when she returned to find the boy—

Cal.

Heaven and hell, Cal!

In the rush of released memories, Ever had forgotten the more recent ones. Cal, synching and joining the Syn world, doing it all to be with her, right before the latest electrical surge hit. Cal would be more vulnerable than anyone else, lying prone in a box, new to the tech. Without having time to recover, adjust, and incorporate these new components.

Panic grips Ever. Catapulting to her feet, she pushes all thoughts of Ere from her mind and runs as fast as she can to the recovery room. It's not far from where she collapsed, thankfully. Reaching the room, she tries to access the room, but it's jammed., stuck fast in some post-Pulse error. Frustrated, she slams her fist against the wall, and miraculously the door drops.

"Cal!" Ever screams, bursting into the room.

But it's empty.

He didn't even make it into recovery.

Shit shit shit.

She races from the recovery room toward the augmentation room, where she knows she would normally be unable to enter. She has to hope that the malfunctioning doors and security will allow her in, she has to try, she has to get to him and help him and make sure he's all right, not suffering alone.

Just as she rounds the corner to the augmentation room, she sees two small female figures emerging from the location. They are hunched, bent—old; Originals, she realizes. The white-haired woman is weeping, her arms wrapped around her stomach, allowing the other gray old woman to lead her away.

Ever hurries toward them, closing the distance quickly, and asking without any preamble or introduction.

"What happened to Cal?"

The white-haired woman raises her head, and her eyes display a despair so deep that words are unnecessary.

CHAPTER 90: HESS

FELIX HESS CANNOT OPEN HIS EYES. He cannot speak. He cannot move.

But he can hear every. Damn. Word.

He heard when that backstabbing bitch Angela said "tea," and he realized instantly that she had poisoned him. His first wild reaction was that Marilyn must have put her up to it. But as he tuned in and quickly pieced together who else was there, he realized Angela wasn't a pawn in some domestic drama. She was an actual rebel traitor.

And—had he also heard the Fell boy with her?

That couldn't be.

He's dead, dead, dead, and dead means gone and gone and gone, Hess thinks, feeling the blips in his brain, hating how his thoughts are slippery and fish-like, sliding in and out of the stream. He is drowning in the shallows, struggling to make it back to shore.

413

Kennedy shows up, and does nothing.

Then Jorge arrives—and assists not Hess, but Angela.

Cold fury jolts through him like a shot of adrenaline to the chest. He can feel a flutter in his fingers now, then another surge of awakening strength causes his legs to twitch. He quietly pulls his legs beneath him. Prepares to stand. Prepares to strike.

And then a strange noise pierces the air. It is a familiar and yet all-but-forgotten tone, a series of jingling, not-quite-melodic notes. The exact ringtone that, decades ago, once made a young Professor Hess grab a student's phone and fling it against the classroom blackboard, shattering it.

Bee-do-do-do, bee-do-do-do, bee-do-do-do-do.

"Chameleon?" Jorge asks.

Who the hell is Chameleon?

"Must… be."

"Too early for a status update—"

"But— "

Bee-do-do-do, bee-do-do-do, bee-do-do-do-do.

"Maybe it's news. Maybe someone's on their way up here."

"Hello?"

Now, thinks Dr. Felix Hess.

In an instant, he's on his feet. Faster than anyone else could work his security system, Hess executes each step like a series of rapid breaths: Fingertips, key code, retinal scan.

The door drops with a small hiss, just as Jorge and Angela turn to see what's going on. Jorge still has the phone pressed to his ear as he fumblingly lunges toward Hess. But before the Vost can close the distance between them, Hess is through the door. He slams his hand against the interior wall, hitting the emergency lockdown code on the inside panel, and the door flies shut behind him.

CHAPTER 91: ERE

"VISITING HOURS ARE OVER, I'M AFRAID."

Dr. Felix Hess's tone is slow and dangerous, molasses mixed with poison, sliding toward them out of nowhere.

When Hess enters the lab, Ere and Asavari are both standing in front of Nathan Fell. Even upon hearing his enemy's voice, it takes Ere a moment to turn and face him. Ere has been frozen, staring up at his grandfather's loose gray flesh and bony body. Nathan Fell's head is down, his long hair and beard obscured and hovering around him.

"Ere," whispers Asavari, voice tight. "Hess."

Ere manages to tear his eyes away at last from his floating forbearer. The room's pervasive dimness, with only a few screens flickering here and there, prevents Ere from immediately locating Hess. But then he feels Asavari's hand on his shoulder, nudging him, and his eyes land on the man's silhouette.

Hess is hunch-shouldered, dragging one of his feet, evidently just as damaged by the Pulse phenomenon as the rest of the synthetic citizens he designed. Feeling only slightly reassured, Ere keeps his eye on the slowly-approaching Syn. He places his hand in his pocket, curling his fingers around Ever's small silver gun, which Chameleon had returned as promised.

"I once went… to visit… a grandparent," Hess says, taking a lumbering step toward them. With each step, his voice steadies. "My grandmother…not grandfather. But close enough. She was at a nursing home—oh, but you wouldn't know what those are. Well. It was a building Where old people could be kept out of the way, killing time while they waited for time to kill them. Ha."

Another sliding step.

"Stay where you are," Ere says, and pulls the gun from his pocket.

"It was a mistake," Hess says, ignoring the weapon pointed at him. "Visiting my grandmother. Our ancestors are never who we want them to be, Ere. It's best not to come visiting."

"I said stay there," Ere says.

"Is that a *gun?*" Asavari whispers.

"You're not going to shoot me, Ere Fell," Hess says broadly, and grins so wide that his teeth gleam blue, reflecting the light of the half-glowing screens. "I think we both know that. You're not a killer. Your mother was, sure. But not you—"

Squeezing his eyes shut, Ere fires the gun at Hess.

The force of the firing knocks Ere backwards, pushing him into Asavari. He had not expected that much kickback from such a small pistol. The bullet misses Hess, hitting the edge of a large piece of equipment just behind him, ricocheting off of it, racing now toward Nathan Fell's containment center. With a loud *pachink*, it strikes near the top of the glass, lodging itself in place. The glass holds, but a small spider-web crack forms just below the bullet, threatening to spread and shatter.

"You idiot!" Hess yells, lunging toward them.

There is another flash of light, and Asavari screams. This sound sends fear shooting through Ere. Looking around wildly to see what made the soldier girl cry out, in the next flash of light, Ere sees what she is looking at.

Nathan Fell.

Nathan's face has lifted. His gaunt and bearded face is pointed toward them.

And then he opens his clouded gray eyes.

CHAPTER 92: AN OUTSIDER INSIDE

NATHAN FELL HAD NOT PLANNED to open his eyes. It was superfluous, but he decided at the last moment that it might add some dramatic flair. More than the other muscles he's been flexing, this small movement takes a considerable amount of exertion; opening his eyes is something he has not attempted for half a century.

He hears an odd knocking sound in head, as he often does. An old echo of a familiar sound. The erratic, magnetic clunking of an MRI machine.

*   *   *   *

In his Original life, Nathan Fell had undergone many MRIs. The first one was after the fall from the swing that shattered his leg and left him with a permanent limp. His mother had also feared a concussion, therefore insisting on an MRI, despite the doctor's assurance, along with Howie's, that Nathan had landed squarely on his leg and never hit his head or lost consciousness.

Nathan had not wanted an MRI. He screamed and resisted, throwing an epic tantrum. When the technician tried to get him in to the machine, he star-fished his arms and legs, splaying them out so he could not be forced into the tube. But he was so small. So powerless. He was eventually restrained and forced to lie flat on the weird little MRI tabletop bed. The technician then gave him a small, rounded remote with a rubber push-button, which the staff at the hospital annoyingly referred to as "the doohickey."

His mother promised him that if he kept calm, and just lay very, very still for the test, he could select their menu for dinner every night for the next week.

"If you hold the most still," she whispered in his ear, "more still than any other child, ever, and the doctor is able to verify for me that you hold the record for stillness during this test, you can also decide whether or not we have any guests for a week."

Intrigued at the promise of such power, Nathan decided that he was absolutely capable of being The Most Still. As he slid into the machine, he closed his eyes, concentrating as hard as he could at not moving a single muscle.

"You'll hear a series of thumps, whirs and hums," a voice announced to him over a loudspeaker, crackly and jarring. But little Nathan did not startle or jump. He held very, very still. "First set will last about fifteen minutes. Nothing to be scared of. But if you start to panic, you just squeeze that little doohickey in your hand and we'll pull you out, okay? Try not to, though. If we pull you out, we have to start over from the very beginning."

Nathan would not squeeze the doohickey. That would require muscle movement. Nor would he give any verbal reply. The larynx was a muscle. He held very, very, still, wishing he could cease involuntary muscles like his lungs, without dying. If he got a case of the hiccups, he might have killed something.

The first series of thumps began.

Thump. Thump. Thump-thump-thump.

THUMP THUMP THUMP THUMP THUMP...

It was loud, too loud at first to allow him to think about anything other than holding still. He couldn't concentrate on anything but that one goal, that one task.

Thump-whrrrrr. Thump-whrrrr.

THUMP THUMP THUMP THUMP THUMP...

But as the thumps and whirrs continued, they became almost meditative, providing a rhythm and even better, a blockade. There were none of the usual irritating, distracting sounds of the rest of the world. No car horns, no kids yelling, no hum of refrigerators. Sensory overload was not a danger in this secure little box. Everything was kept at bay.

THUMP THUMP THUMP THUMP THUMP...

After a few minutes, Nathan no longer had to concentrate on keeping still. Instead his mind was free to tackle other tasks. He and Howie had watched a movie the other day, and a complicated math equation had been written on a chalkboard. The camera didn't stay on it for very long, but Nathan was pretty certain his photographic memory had preserved it, and he wanted to go back and see if he could solve the problem—if it even was an actual math problem, or just nonsense written up on the board by some dumb movie person.

He concentrated. There it was, the board, filled with the equation. He zoomed in, began going through the numbers and letters representing numbers and numbers representing concepts, deciphering and de-coding, finding his mind able to tackle trigonometry and theoretical math, things he had not yet really learned but had the capacity to conjure. It was all logical and straightforward, when he had this bandwidth to truly focus. He could feel his mind rising above his body, expanding to fill the entire world, figuring out anything and everything he did not yet know because now he had the time and solitude to discover—

"All set, buddy! You did great," the technician said, sliding Nathan abruptly out of the machine. "Your mama told the doctor and me that you were going to be able to hold The Most Still, and I gotta say, you absolutely were the best at holding still in there! Very impressed!"

Nathan blinked, disoriented. The braying tones of the cheery technician were making his head swim. He didn't like it, being back in the wide bright room, listening to this jabbering stranger, his thoughts interrupted.

"I want to go back in," Nathan said aloud.

"Ha," the idiot technician laughed. "You're a funny kid."

But Nathan wasn't a funny kid. He was a serious kid.

And he was serious about wanting to get back in the damn MRI machine.

He didn't attempt any immediate injuries that year to land himself back in the machine. He wasn't stupid. He knew even if he carefully calculated just how hard to hit his head, if he caused any actual damage to his brain that would be unacceptable. It was bad enough when his error cost him his gait. He could deal with a limping leg, but not a halting thought process. He could, of course, just lie about falling, but there was no way that would work more than once. His mother was not that dumb.

So he researched rare and difficult-to-diagnose conditions that warranted MRIs to assist in diagnoses. The best and simplest solution was seizures. Learn to fake an effective seizure and you can get some great meditative time in the MRI tube.

It must have been hell on his mother's health insurance, to say nothing of the stress it must have caused her, worrying about him. But those weren't really the sorts of things that he thought about back then. Over the course of a year, Nathan had a dozen MRIs; but eventually, the machine began to lose its magic for Nathan.

He was able to harness his brainpower pretty well on his own, and the thumping no longer seemed as trance-inducing. Plus there was his mother's anxiety, and having to deal with perpetually-perky technicians— it eventually just wasn't worth it anymore.

Then, decades later, came the day of his augmentation. The initial synch, the auspicious day that Nathan Fell was supposed to make history—the exact moment when everything was supposed to culminate, and instead combusted. He remembers thinking, *This is wrong,* before he consciously knew just what was wrong. Just how wrong it had all gone. *Wrong* was perhaps an incorrect word.

Things had not gone *wrong* with Nathan's synch.

They had simply not gone *as planned.*

Initial panic is almost always useless, child-like and unwarranted, like the younger Nathan refusing to get into the MRI machine he would come to crave. Snug in the augmentation chamber, he felt that same sensation he had experienced when in the MRI—akin to the comfort he had derived from staying in the "baby crib" his brother teased him for clinging to, all those years ago. The NICU box, before that. There was security in enclosure; freedom, in being away from everyone else. In the self-contained universe of the augmentation chamber, he felt his mind expanding once more. Unfurling enough to fill the world. Which, as it turns out, is exactly what happened.

Finally, some quiet time to truly think...

Thinking is exactly what Nathan Fell has done. Pure thinking, constant and uninterrupted, for more than fifty years now. His liberated, massive mind unfurled into its full potential, running several functions at once. He was connected to the synthetic technology, providing a prototype and code and power source that fed into and was fed by the technology. The cloud called Heaven emerged from the melded mind of Nathan Fell and the tech he sired and continued to raise.

He appeared unresponsive. Physically, he was; his body began to wilt and decline. But Hess noticed this, too, and transferred Fell to the core tank, where his skin was kept wet, chemically preserved, since it was deemed by Hess and the team too dangerous to attempt any surgery and risk killing this precious brain.

But after so many decades, even with the great pains Hess has undertaken to preserve him like a sentient pickle, Nathan's body is on the cusp of expiration. He knows Hess plans to finally extract his brain and keep the functions running by other means whenever the rotting shell of his body inevitably converts to carcass and disintegrates, as all things must.

Nathan does not like this idea.

He has had time—half a century—to power and probe and learn from this world. He has provided the Syns with their core receptacle for connection and knowledge, and has been able to mine all of it. He cannot claim to fully understand the human experience, but he has now accumulated more perspectives and insights into it than any being save God Him-or-Herself. And much like that storied God, who was so often disappointed in His creations, Nathan Fell has found the Syns wanting.

They were selfish. They were worshippers of a golden calf. They needed to be taught. More to the point: They needed to be punished.

The oddest thing Nathan has learned in all this time is that for some, his punishment will come as a relief. Yes, the initial Pulses brought pain. But in his final move, in his checkmate to finish the game called the Syn experiment, there would also be gratitude. After all, there were Syns who self-terminated. This was not something Nathan inspired or instructed them to do; it was of their own free will. With no weight to their days, no clock to urge them forward, no sand slipping through a glass and creating incentive to truly live before they die—what was the point?

As one Syn who terminated himself four years ago had written (in a missive seen only by Hess, who immediately destroyed it, and Nathan, from whom nothing was ever hidden or destroyed): "A man is now granted enough lifetime to become the world's greatest poet, and then the world's greatest tennis player, and then the world's greatest chef. But if everyone can be everything, is anyone anything anymore?"

Nathan was never much one for philosophy. But he understood it a bit better now.

He also understood human longing in a new and profound way. Self-terminating Syns taught him something: No one wants a story that's all middle. Difficult as they are, people want endings; want new beginnings; want risk and real deadlines.

Those who exited their synthetic existence were not actually choosing death. Their actions were not suicide, in the old-world sense. It was more like a reclamation or Original destiny. They were choosing life, as it was designed to be: a journey, not a plateau.

Unlike some Syns, Nathan has not romanticized the way things were. In the old world, the one he grew up in, the problems were massive. There was poverty, racism, sexism, damage to the planet, woeful ignorance. It was not a utopia. Neither, however, is the rigged synthetic game.

There was a time when Nathan genuinely believed in his vision of a synthetic world. Fewer people with better access to everything from medicine to meaningful work; less environmental impact; it would be better for the people, better for the planet. But like communism, his idea was better in theory than in practice. The privileged few still greedily consumed resources; the starving masses were miserable; new existential crises arose; the world was not a better place.

The resistance of the Originals is one of the few remaining points of interest for Nathan Fell. He has pondered whether or not his biological connection to some of these straggling survivors honed his interest in them, and decided it didn't matter. It was time to shake things up. Teach the Syns a lesson, throw a bone to the Originals, and get out of the game. Start a clock ticking again, and let everyone hear the sound.

He had generated "the prophecy" simply to screw with Hess. Give the panicky bastard something to piss himself over. He almost felt bad for his grandson, who might now believe it was his destiny to pull the plug on Grandpa.

As had been the case with far too many Fells, Ere was convinced that the world revolved around him. But the prophecy had nothing to do with Ere. He didn't have to pull the plug on dear old Grandpa.

It was Grandpa who was about to pull the plug on the entire Syn world.

Each Pulse had been a test. Nathan knows his end goal, but as much time as he has had to think about it, well, it was still theoretical until attempted. He had to make certain he could power the surge from within each Syn nervous system. Heaven already had most of its bandwidth eaten up, and anyhow if the power source were that obvious Hess might have figured out that Nathan wasn't quite as vacant as he imagined.

But by dispersing the power sources, making every single Syn the battery charging toward their own demise, he was able to keep his own role obscured, right up until this moment. And now the time is at hand. The process is perfected. Some Syns are already all but offline. Most will not survive a final surge, and those that will—well, that's part of the plan, too.

Nathan knows them all, inside and out, better than he or they would like. He has had time to plan the perfect punishment, relief, or reprieve for each. A moment tailored for each Syn. It's a fairly flowery move for Nathan Fell, but he has thought it through and in the end decided that a little artistic touch to Armageddon was elegant. And so it was decided, and so it will be done.

*   *   *   *

Nathan thinks all of this in the time it takes him to open his eyes. His capacity for thought is so expansive, he can produce and sift through a year's worth of contemplation in an instant.

But as his eyes slide open, he catches a watery glimpse of his very own grandson. He was not expecting to be distracted by this sight. But seeing him, something shifts. Nathan Fell's innumerable contemplations pause. With a twisting sensation that might have been something close to sentiment, Nathan makes an observation.

He really does look like Ruth.

Ruth, one of the twin daughters he ignored. Rachel was long dead; but Ruth had remained so elusive, flitting like a ghost through the world for longer than she had any right to survive. But she *had* survived. She had even thrived enough to have a child—this skinny boy, staring stricken at what is left of Nathan.

What does he think of me?

Trying to analyze based on the shape of the boy's rounded eyes, the slackness of his jaw, the amount of salt-sweat pouring down his young face, Nathan cannot deduce what his grandson feels. Fear? Disgust? Those components are there, but there is something less quantifiable and achingly more important. But is it admiration, hope—it could not possibly be love?

I am the last of his family.

With Howard dead, Ruth and Rachel dead, even Cal offline… Ere Fell is not just staring at a great mind, or a battery, or a freak in a giant jar. He is staring at his last kin. And so, too, is Nathan.

It is an odd thing, past locking eyes with the future. And emotions are still the most difficult waters for Nathan to navigate.

Nathan feels a pang of something, and does not manage to identify it as regret before allowing the feeling to shape his next decision.

I cannot go until I know.

The plan was for Nathan to initiate the final Pulse, then immediately power himself down. Snuff out his consciousness before the final farewell. Instead, in the eternity-long moment wherein the wavering visage of his descendent fills his field of vision, Nathan Fell decides to go along for the final ride. Maybe, maybe if he rides the Pulse along with all the Syns, something will reveal itself. Maybe he will finally *feel*, rather than simply speculate.

Perhaps a tear rolls down Nathan's face.

It is impossible to tell, suspended in water as he is.

And then, Nathan Fell blinks, and the world around him contracts.

THE FINAL PULSE

CHAPTER 93: MARILYN

MARILYN IS LYING ALONE IN HER HOSPITAL BED, DREAMING.

But we can't dream, she thinks without waking. *Something else is going on.*

Something else is going on, of course. Electricity is coursing through her, shaking her body, rattling her bones and teeth and tech. But she is too distracted by the vision dancing behind her closed eyes to even notice the physical agony. She is staring at an old woman, stooped and bent. The woman is sitting in front of a vanity mirror, her shaking, spotted, gnarled fingers slowly bringing a tube of lipstick toward her quivering wrinkle of a mouth.

431

The lipstick slides on and all around the lips, a red gash grotesquely clowning the crone's face. Standing there, Marilyn can almost see—

And then, in a rush, Marilyn is flying toward the woman.

Against the woman.

Into the woman.

She feels her skin crinkling, her stomach sagging, her new breasts drooping and losing their shape. Gripped in terror, Marilyn looks up, and finds herself staring into the mirror at her own geriatric face. Horrified, paralyzed, trapped in this expiring package of a body, Marilyn knows no one will ever love her. No one will ever come for her.

I can't bear it, she thinks. *I can't bear it.*

And then she hears a voice say her name, so softly, so softly.

Marilyn, baby.

Yes, she thinks, tears running down her wrinkled cheeks. *Daddy, it's me.*

CHAPTER 94: THE MAN IN THE RED SHIRT

THE MAN IN THE RED SHIRT had been going about his everyday App-Dev business, one of the few employees not totally knocked out in the last pulse. There was no reason for him to have reported to work. No one else was there. His boss Marti was missing. No one was expecting a new app to roll out that day. But he had nowhere else to be and nothing else to do. So, might as well be there, even if he wasn't really fulfilling any specific purpose.

When the Pulse hits him, it doesn't hurt at all. It simply creaks and swings forward, like a stuck door kicked open within him, and he tumbles through it as though that had been his intention all along.

You know, I survived a lot longer than I expected to, he thinks.

CHAPTER 95:
ANOTHER OUTSIDER INSIDE

DARKNESS.

Nothing.

And then a sudden jolt, like someone clasped his heart between their massive hands and squeezed it with superhuman might, crushing it back into function. When released from the grip his heart expands, shudders, and resumes a hesitant but steady pumping of his blood.

He wonders if he might be able to get up, stand on his own, get out of the container that has held him for God knows how long. It seems unlikely. But when he tentatively extends his arm forward, pushing against the front of the machine, the hatch swings open without any resistance.

Near his container, there is a drawer full of neatly pressed clothes. He gets dressed, enjoying the feel of clean fabric on his skin. Stretching his still-sleeping fingers forward, he begins probing his body, feeling for weak points, trying to determine if there is any tech crackling within him or if, like the rest of the world, everything electronic in his flesh has been stilled. To his great relief, he cannot detect any tech whatsoever. Anything synthetic inside him is as flat-lined as the rest of the lifeless tech filling the room where he stands, alone and unmonitored.

Alone.

There is no one with him, and it occurs to him that this is odd. Weren't there other people in here before? He feels certain that there were other people, though he cannot quite recall who had been the last souls in the room with him. No matter; it was better that he was alone. Alone is how he intends to stay.

He leaves the room, bypassing the powerless levitators and heading for the emergency stairwell. It will be a long descent down dozens or hundreds of stairs, and his knees are weak. But who cares? No one is waiting on him. The speed of this immediate journey is irrelevant. All that matters is the momentum, the movement forward, accepting this turn of events for the answered prayer that it is and acting accordingly.

Just before the Pulse ravaged him, he had asked for a second chance. Even if it meant abandoning everything that had become his goal. Even if it meant walking away from love.

Miraculously, his prayer was answered.

He isn't sure he was worthy of this mercy. He has already forsaken far too much of what he once held dear. If he is being offered redemption, he will accept this gift and hold up his end of the bargain.

I will make a different choice.

He keeps his mind as clear as he can as he pushes himself forward. He will not dwell on what might have been. He cannot. He had truly felt the power of the last Pulse. It had literally killed him. He will not take this resurrection lightly. He will not go backward. He marches purposefully toward the unknown, at peace with the simple but firm destination *anywhere but here.*

When he walks away from his broken past, Cal does not look back.

CHAPTER 96: EVER

EVER'S MIND IS LIKE AN OVERFLOWING FILING cabinet, so full that even one more slim folder simply cannot fit. The Pulse arrives like a jackhammer, slamming into the file cabinet, splintering wood, shredding documents, taking all of the thoughts and feelings and recollections so recently acquired, scattering them in an instant.

But then something strange happens. For a moment, everything stops, as if a giant pause button has been pressed. Everything in Ever's mind is suspended mid-air, frozen onscreen. Several of the files recently flung here and there begin to tremble and quake.

Ere, she thinks. *Not again*—

Then there is a fluttering, and all the file folders go flying into the void.

And so does Ever.

CHAPTER 97: KENNEDY

A S KENNEDY WALKS PAST SOME Original rebels running from one building to the next, smashing and burning, hell-bent on razing their next targeted building, he thinks *funny how raising a building and razing a building sound the same, and are the opposite,* and continues walking.

Arriving at Chase's residence, he pays no heed to the screams outside as he ascends to the penthouse and enters the apartment with its clean white walls, white plush carpeting, bright-red sofa and loveseat, and the massive Warhol Campbell's Soup painting. The painting has grown on him. He likes it now.

"Chase?"

"Good, you're here," Chase calls from the other end of the apartment. "Come help me with this."

Kennedy finds Chase in the bedroom, carefully wrapping the last of the framed photographs of The Chase project, and placing them into a box.

"You took down The Chase?"

"I need you to take them to her for me. For safekeeping."

"Is this something she requested, or—"

"Don't ask questions, Kennedy, we're almost out of time."

Before Kennedy can process this fatalistic statement, the lights in the building snap off, then shudder back on. The entire structure seemed to tremble, and even once back on the lights seem dimmer and unreliable, as if at any moment they might cut out forever.

"Is it another Pulse, like we thought?" Kennedy asks.

"It is," Chase says, and someone in an adjacent apartment lets out a howl. Chase looks down and gives a small, regretful head shake. "It's going to be bad. I imagine you'll be just fine. And the Pulse itself probably won't do me any damage, either, but—well. That's the other reason I needed you here."

"To help mitigate any unanticipated Pulse damage?"

"No, not at all," Chase said. "Not at all. Something far more... passive."

"Passive...?"

"Yes. First, help me get all these put in the box—hopefully we can get most of them in there before the power goes out for good. You'll deliver these for me."

"Yes."

"And before you go, I just need you to..." Chase pauses, and seems for once to be struggling for the right word, wanting to select exactly the right description for this evidently vital task.

"What?" Kennedy asks.

"Witness the next step in my evolution," Chase says.

CHAPTER 98: HESS

T HE PULSE HITS HESS with intentionally brutal force. There is a vendetta behind this pain. It is punitive and merciless, slamming through him first recklessly and then with sharp specificity. His body goes slack, but the missile deploys and splits wide its target: his mind.

The Pulse fills the newly opened space with an infinite amount of information. *All* of the information. For a fleeting and eternal moment, Hess understands. He sees it all—everything—the entire picture. The thoughts and secrets and files and forgotten pieces of every Syn's life. The history of history. What happened to Nathan. What is happening to everyone now.

He is privy to everything Nathan has ruminated on for fifty years.

All of it; *all of it.*

It is what he has always wanted, the panoramic and omniscient view of everything available only to gods.

He sees. He *knows.*

"Oh," he breathes, chest expanding, heart and mind and soul ablaze with the knowledge he has pursued with all of his being. "Oh, oh, *oh*…"

And then he hears a whisper. It does not come from outside, but from within himself, filling his entire mind and driving out the everything Hess was finally privy to witness. It is a voice he has not heard in years but would know anywhere.

"It is not for you to keep," says Nathan.

Then Hess feels a breeze stir within him. It sweeps through him with increasing intensity, breeze becoming wind, wind becoming a twisting tornado, tossing around his mind, rounding every corner, drawing everything into it, carrying everything away with it.

Everything.

Everything.

"No," he says, quiet at first, and then his voice rising to a scream. "No, no, *no no no*—!"

The erasure is neither accidental nor absolute. It is calculated, a punishment devised by a mind that had a lifetime to contemplate the perfect justice. And so, as the violent wind roaring through his head dies down, Hess is left with only two discernible scraps of knowledge.

He knows nothing, and he used to know everything.

He sinks to the floor, slack-jawed and staring. A sense of loss washes over him, but he does not have any capacity to comprehend why. He is panicked but paralyzed. There is so much he should be doing, or maybe so much he has already done?

He doesn't know. He should know, but he doesn't. He shakes, tries to focus, barely moves or musters a thought. Then something blurs and materializes in front of him. Or does it? He thinks he sees a woman standing there, a woman whose name he should know, a face he should recognize. But he does not know her name, and he does not know her. He cannot even tell if she is really standing there, or if she is standing somewhere in his head, in his ruined memories and ransacked mental files. She is wrinkled, with a patched yellow blanket of some sort draped over her shoulders. She takes his face in her hands.

"Oh, God," she says, and her voice is infinitely gentle. The look she gives him is one of tender regret. "Oh, Jesus, Mary, and Joseph. We didn't have enough time, did we, Fee?"

He stares at the old woman, opens his mouth, and screams.

CHAPTER 99: ANGELA

WHEN ANGELA HEARS THE SMALL BEEP SHE KNOWS: This is where she dies.

She has just enough time to look at Jorge, and the fear in his eyes reflects her own certainty. She extends her hand, and he takes it. They brace themselves, and she knows their final thought—prayer, perhaps—is a shared one.

Let them make it.

Let them win.

Let them survive.

And then there is nothing.

447

No sound, so scent, no sensation of any sort. A complete void and vacuum, nothing is anything and no one is anyone and everything is simply not, but not even "not" because even a negative is something and now there is only nothing, nothing, disconnection from anything that ever existed—

Then there is a jolt.

A pounding thud, staggering and then steadying, repetitive. Familiar. Real.

My heart, Angela realizes, returning from the void, remembering herself and hearts and everything that had not existed a moment ago. She tries to run a scan, and nothing happens. Not a false start, not a failed command, but *nothing*.

There is nothing to command.

There is no system to scan.

There is no Syn system.

She knows, then. A strange joy spreads through her body, carried to every corner of her by the blood pumped by her thudding Original heart. She has no Shadower abilities, but she also has no synthetic reliance at all. She can feel the dull metal weight of a port on her neck, but it is lifeless, not connected to anything or fulfilling any purpose other than memorializing a system now dead. The hardware remains, but the software is gone.

For a moment, she pictures herself in the Hess kitchen. For so many years, Angela handled her emotions like the vegetables she prepared in the Hess's kitchen: scrubbing the rough edges of her feelings away, slicing and reshaping her reactions, always risking a deep cut from the sharp blade she wielded. She was forever taking something raw and recognizable and pureeing it into something smoothed out and palatable before serving it up. As a Syn, as Shadower, simply being herself had not been an option.

But now she is herself again.

Only herself.

Only Angela.

She realizes her eyes have been squeezed tightly shut, and she opens them, turning to look at Jorge. He is still holding her hand, and his golden eyes are clamped closed just as firmly as her eyes had been.

"Jorge," she whispers, voice still weak but entirely her own. "We're free."

CHAPTER 100: NATHAN

"AN OUTSIDER INSIDE."

As this experience plays out and he soars through it along with everyone else, Nathan Fell realizes that there are a surprisingly large number of individuals fitting this description.

Who knew the world was so full of outsiders?

It makes his contrived, self-styled prophecy take on an unintended depth, knowing it could apply to almost anyone. There are so few people who truly feel seen and accepted as they are, where they are. This is one of the many revelations finally cracked open for him in this final act of cerebral power.

He can feel the synthetic citizens, all of them, all at once, more profoundly than he had anticipated. He is not just observing them, not merely bearing witness, but reeling along with them. He feels it all. The pain. The release. Clinging. Despair. Relief. He feels every death, every revival, and every return to a sense of self. Every paralysis. Every shouted curse. Every whispered thanks.

A growing awareness tingles through his mind, so sharp and strong he almost imagines his wrinkled-wet old carcass is feeling the electricity of it all. For decades, he has learned from observing and absorbing their thoughts and lives. Now, in these final moments, as the Pulse rolls not only from him but through him, his final lesson comes from this synchronized searing of their souls. For the first time, he doesn't just see what they do, hear what they say, or recall what they remember as something objective and observed.

He feels how they feel.

He sees, explosively and all at once, that each moment did matter. There have been so many, so many, whose roles and choices led to the world being as it is, just as much as his did. There are still others who have been dismantling it, who might well have beat him to the punch if still others had chosen differently. How humbling and hilarious to see that his belief that he was set apart, special, the sole storyline that mattered is exactly what makes him just like the rest of them.

Unique and special, just like everybody else.

Ha!

He can see it now, almost enjoy the irony of it—he was just as misguided as they were, right up until this very moment, believing that he was the star of the story. Just like the rest of them. He felt the weight of his own life and importance most, just as each of them did.

And the smallest things did matter. If Ere had not been in the room, if he had not taken a wild shot at Hess and instead cracked the edge of Nathan's prison, if Nathan had not elected to open his eyes and found himself staring raptly at the boy, everything would have been different. He would have been absent to this final master class on the human experience. Nathan Fell is not sure he likes the sensation of sentiment, but liking it is irrelevant. The knowledge of this human experience is still knowledge, and it was a lesson delayed until his very final semester. He is finally finished. He is done.

He keeps his eyes closed this time, while sliding the proverbial king into checkmate position. Harboring no sense of despair at his self-selected fate, Nathan Fell slips into the warm and welcoming darkness as his mind and the entire cloud called Heaven powers down once and for all.

AFTER

CHAPTER 101: JORGE

JORGE MARQUEZ IS NOT QUITE SURE WHAT TO DO. The tech he had so long detested was gone. His hardware is still in his neck and laced throughout his nervous system, but it's dormant. No software, no interconnected system. Just dead metal, disconnected and as harmless as a pin left embedded in a knee after a minor surgical procedure.

He knows he should feel true joy, but the smile he gives Angela hovers only at the surface. He does not want to look the gift horse in the mouth, but it feels as if it has ridden in to town too late. Jorge was ready to sacrifice everything in an uprising, to fight for the rebel cause and die heroically paving the way for a return to true Original existence. With such an unexpectedly abrupt transfer of power, he has no idea what to do. The truth is, he never planned on surviving the overthrow of the Syn empire. He was, quite frankly, ready to be done.

A noble sacrifice of himself had seemed not only like a good idea, but also felt like about damned time. It also would have been much easier and less complicated than this unexpected indictment of remaining alive.

He has no home to which he can return. His family has been dead for years. As a Vost in the Syn world, he had no close friends, only coworkers and less-than-casual acquaintances. His identity was hidden when he reported to the clandestine network, so he is a ghost even among the rebels. His smile locked in place, he asks Angela the only question on his mind.

"What happens next?"

She shakes her head, unsure, but grinning. Jorge is both heartened and wildly jealous to see her joyful flash of teeth. She doesn't know, either, but she seems at peace with that fact. More than at peace, she seems delighted. It occurs to Jorge why that might be.

We know some of the things that aren't *happening next.*

Jorge will never again be at the beck and call of Dr. Felix Hess.

A wild image leaps into his mind, something from his bygone youth. A Technicolor scene from an old movie, golden-bricked streets and lollipop-like fauna, bright bursts of red and blue and green and yellow, stripes and sparkles as munchkins leaped around singing *Ding, dong, the witch is dead!*

"Anything's possible now, Jorge," says Angela, no longer in the shadows. She throws her arms open expansively, inviting all of the world's potential to surround them. "Maybe you'll fall in love. Meet a nice girl. Settle down."

Feeling lighter than he has in years, Jorge cracks a wide grin and decides he'll have to tell his new friend sometime soon that girls aren't of much interest to him.

"Anything's possible," he says, and laughs out loud.

CHAPTER 102: HELENA

HELENA IS STILL REELING from the loss of Cal when she notices the shouting. They heard only one scream, at first. Then another. And then from seemingly everywhere at once, thousands of shrieks and wails filled the air. Helena gives Preeti a panicked look. Then the whole world went very, very quiet.

"What's going on?" Helena asks at last.

"Perhaps Ere and Asavari... made it," Preeti says.

"Made what?"

"Completed their mission," Preeti says. "Destroyed the core, and its... power source."

"What's the power source?" Helena asks, sensing Preeti's delicacy around those words. "What are they sucking energy from? Solar? Are you about to tell me those bastards have used up our sun or something?"

"No," Preeti says quickly. "No, not that. It is something that has not only powered them, but—programmed them, as best we can understand it. Connected them and shared all of their information, all routed through this one central source."

"So what's the source?"

"It's…" Preeti meets Helena's eyes. "It's Nathan Fell."

Helena is confused.

"I don't… understand. Nathan Fell is dead. And how would a man be a power source?"

"We don't understand all of the intricacies of the technology, but—he's not just a man. When he was augmenting, decades ago—he didn't die in the process. He melded with the machine. And his brain, along with tech, became—"

"Stop," Helena says, feeling sick. "Are you saying Ere's task today was to destroy…"

"…his grandfather," Preeti confirms.

"Chameleon only mentioned taking down Hess. Never said anything about Nathan Fell."

"Not to us," Preeti says.

"Not to us," Helena echoes.

"Let's go find our children," Preeti says, putting her hand on Helena's arm.

Helena gives her a watery smile.

"Our children," she says. "You go on, doc. I have to visit one of 'em over here first."

And so Helena hobbles back to the room where they had seen Cal's lifeless body. Picturing Rachel, picturing Ruth, Helena knows what she must do. Their boy deserves a story-song; and she, Helena, deserves a proper farewell.

When she enters the room, the steel chamber looms ominously before her. As she approaches it, her gait no longer hurried but hesitant, her eyes welling with tears, the song fills her:

Standing here, I almost see
The girl I was, the crone I'll be
Blessing of age, passing of time,
Teaching us all, profane and sublime
We will never relent, we will never rely
Thus we will live. And thus we will die.

Thus Calvin Harper lived.
Thus Calvin Harper died

He was strong of body,
Strong of mind,
A steadier soul
You never would find…

As all story-songs do, it seems to write itself. She feels strength in this power as she draws near to the machine. She opens her mouth to sing, and instead gasps aloud at the empty vault.

CHAPTER 103: PREETI

PREETI HURRIES DOWN THE STAIRS, out of the oppressive Synt building. Relieved to be outside again, she breathes in deeply, welcoming outdoor air into her lungs—then quickly covers her mouth and coughs as smoke fills her lungs. She looks around, noticing several small, squat buildings near the Synt that she had not seen before. Their windows are broken, haphazard red lights are flashing here and there, and smoke and flames are billowing from the rooftops and shattered corners of every building.

She sees a tall, dark man she does not recognize, who seems to be a Syn—or a Vost, perhaps. He is reeling, in pain—but doggedly smashing the windows of a Syn structure, joining in on the rebellion. She thinks she hear him cry "For Rosie!"

Everywhere she looks, people are running between the buildings, fanning the flames, making sure the destruction is total.

My people, she realizes.

It is the resistance in action. A true uprising. The lights are out in the Synt and the fires blazing outside are being lit by Originals. The light has changed hands, no longer hoarded and controlled by the privileged few, but claimed and seized by those who once lived underground, surviving in darkness and waiting for this moment.

This moment.

She wonders if she should join them, grab a stick and ignite it with a spark from one of her friends' torches, contribute to the destruction this world so richly deserves. Part of her wants to do so. But the rest of her is simply tired.

She feels the looseness in her muscles, the wrinkles lining her soul. It is as if all the signs of aging she has overcome through sheer force of will suddenly settle in and claim their rightful place. She watches her people, the tribe she protected and defended for so long, begin to comprehend that they have won. Something has tipped the scales and their attack is not futile, not suicidal. It is a fatal blow to their oppressors. The cries become victorious, elated. She feels their triumph from a distance, and hopes they do better than she did when they rebuild the world.

CHAPTER 104: ASAVARI

ASAVARI HAS ALWAYS HATED THE DARK. The moment the floating skeleton that was once Nathan Fell had closed its eyes again, the entire world seemed to go out. The air was filled with the sound of screams, including the shrill shrieks of Dr. Felix Hess.

As an Original, Asavari felt no pain from the Pulse. She was, however, gripped by a familiar old cold panic that accompanied this sense of being trapped, caught in a room without light, not knowing what would happen next. She flashed back to her child-hood trauma, caught underground in a shaking universe, clinging to her sister in the void, certain that this was the end of all things.

"Ere!" she screamed, hating the childlike fear filling her voice.

"I'm here!" he yelled back, and miraculously his hand found hers.

They stood there, bracing themselves against an onslaught not meant for them. The air crackled with energy, and a warm hum emanated from the tank that housed Nathan Fell's frail body and swollen mind. The hum from the tank grew louder, and louder, until it was so loud that the screams in the distance were swallowed completely, and even a shrill shriek from Dr. Felix Hess, mere feet away, seemed muted.

The teeth-rattling hum shook the floor and moved the air around them with an insistent pressure, that at once pushed and pulled them toward and away from everything.

"Hold on to me!" Asavari cried. "Hold tight, hold tight—"

And then it was over.

The lights did not come back on, but the humming cut out and the force in the air vanished. Asavari and Ere dropped each other's hands and scrambled for their flashlights from Chameleon, waving them wildly around the room, seeing what they could see.

Every screen was shattered. The floor was littered with glass, glittering like diamonds beneath the small beams of the flashlights. Asavari's beam found Dr. Felix Hess, crouched beside a large but crumpled machine, that seemed to have folded in on itself.

He sat with his knees drawn loosely to his chest, arms at his side and palms on the ground, resting carelessly on a pile of glass shards. His hair was mussed, his lab coat torn, and his expression—Asavari shuddered. It was vacant, dead-eyed though he still drew breath. He stared at a fixed point, something she could not see, and periodically twitched or let out a small yelp. A glistening trail of drool pooled at the edge of his lip and began to slug its way down his chin.

Asavari turned to see if Ere was also seeing this, but his light was pointed elsewhere. He had aimed it at the huge tube that housed Nathan Fell. The watery chamber seemed now a tomb. Connected to powerless technology, there was no light, no monitor, no beep. The man within was no longer suspended in the middle of the heavily-powered chamber, but floating face down at the top of the tank.

"He's dead," Ere said flatly.

"Yes," Asavari said, not knowing what else to say.

"He did this," Ere said, still looking not at her but at his dead grandfather.

"How can you be certain?" Asavari asked, already knowing he was right.

"He looked at me," was all Ere replied.

It had lasted a lifetime, and happened so quickly. They did not linger in the laboratory for long after that. Knowing the levitators would be out, they had a long series of stairs standing between them and the meeting point. They made their way down them wordlessly and quickly, Ere perhaps mourning his grandfather, Asavari eager to be done with this damned darkened building.

That was an hour ago, and a lifetime ago. Now they are in the sunlight once more. She needs to find their friends, tell them that it is over—the original Syn is dead, there is no more power or connective tissue giving Syns the ability to unite against them. For all Asavari knows, based on what she saw of Hess and Fell, and the emptiness of the burning streets beneath the indifferent stars, there may be no synthetic people left living at all.

Shadower.

Jorge!

Not all synthetics were enemies to Asavari anymore. How is she only now remembering the allies that had done so much for the cause? She curses herself for not casting the light around to search out their bodies in the hallway before she and Ere had bolted for the stairs. She holds fast to the hope that the golden-eyed man will once again arrive at their appointed place.

When Asavari and Ere reach the park, only one person, diminutive in stature, is awaiting them there. The figure comes flying at them as soon as they emerge from the tree-line bordering the park. It's dark, but Asavari would recognize her mother anywhere.

"Mera baccha," she sobs into Asavari's neck, wet tears thickening her voice. "My baby, my baby…"

"I am all right," Asavari says, wrapping her arms around her mother's small shoulders. *When did I become so much larger than she?* For once, Asavari feels no irritation at her mother's emotion or embrace.

"Chameleon isn't here?" Ere asks.

"Not yet," Preeti says, pulling back ever-so-slightly from her daughter.

"You have not seen Angela? Or Jorge?" Asavari asks, nervous.

"Not yet," her mother repeats.

"What about Helena? Weren't you with her?" Ere asks, sharp.

"I was," Preeti confirms. "She—went back in, to see something. Someone."

"Who?"

But before her mother can reply, Angela enters the park. Her gait is slow but sure, and when she sees the others, she grins. Asavari runs to Angela and throws her arms around her.

"You are alive!"

"I'm better than alive," Angela grins, returning the hug, if a bit gingerly. "I've been alive for a real long time now. But now I'm alive *and dying*, which is amazing. Isn't it, Jorge?"

Jorge appears then, and Asavari throws her embrace from Angela to her other ally from the Syn world. She is squeezing him so fiercely, it takes a moment for Angela's statement to sink in and make some sense to her. It is Asavari's mother who arrives at the understanding first.

"You are dying, and it is good—? My friend, are you saying…?"

"We are disconnected. The hardware is still there—" he almost affectionately raps the steel panel at the base of his neck "—but it's like an old scar all healed over. Harmless."

"Clock's ticking," Angela chuckles. She shakes her head, and raises her arms triumphantly. "I think I just felt three new gray hairs spring up on my head, hallelujah! No more upgrades, no replacement parts, and I'm ready to re-join the Original club."

"Hell yeah," Jorge agrees.

"Has anyone heard from Chameleon?" Ere asks, interrupting everyone else's smiles.

"Yes, actually," Angela says.

"Chameleon called us, right before the Pulse," Jorge pulls a cell phone out of his pocket and waves it. "We were with Hess, in the hallway, when the phone rang, and we only heard a few words before Hess made a run for it and we tried to stop him, and—"

"Get to the point," Ere says.

"Chameleon's not coming," Angela informs the small assembly, giving Ere a look that is more bemused than irritated. Asavari wants to slap Ere for his lack of respect. Even when the whole world changes, some humans do not.

"Not coming?" Preeti asks, her voice rising. "There will be no ship to take us home? How will we—"

"There are plenty of ships here," Jorge assures them. "Offline, sure, but we can get them fixed up enough to fly the old way— human pilot instead of automatic systems. We don't need Chameleon. I think that's why Chameleon is a no-show. Our shared goal was to take down Hess. Hess is down. The deal is done."

"So that's it? Just—gone?" Asavari asks, more confused than ever about the stranger, appearing in their hour of need, uniting their forces, but also kidnapping Ere (who, at the moment, Asavari would be more than willing to hand back over) and now abandoning them in the immediate aftermath of their shared triumph.

"Makes sense." Ere sounds almost bored. "Chameleon was always pretty clear about what the arrangement was. So. When the ships are ready to go, is everyone just heading off to India, or what."

He thinks we will leave him, Asavari realizes.

She looks at him, the boy from the wild Original world, whose entire family had died or deserted him before he reached this day. He seemed battered before, after his mother's death, and after the long journey to Asavari's homeland, but now he seems emptied of all emotion.

Not bitter, she can see that now; not disrespectful or cruel. Simply resigned. Accepting of the fact that all of his people are gone—even Helena, the old remnant from his tribe, has not reached the meeting point. Convinced that his new allies will scatter, taking off after the victory just as Chameleon already has. He will be truly alone, or so he thinks, and he is not even contemplating any alternative other than stoic solitude.

She begins to take a step toward the boy, standing alone and apart from the rest of them. She wants to assure him that he will be welcome to join them, and if he chooses to stay so too will others to help rebuild an Original presence in his homeland. But before she can reach him, several people rush into the park. Some are from Asavari's tribe, still exuberant from their uprising and reclamation, clasping hands and hollering their grateful victory cries into the night sky.

One of them is a Syn, heading straight toward Ere.

"ERE," EVER BREATHES, collapsing against his chest when she reaches him. She feels him hesitate, then tentatively wrap his arms around her, and she almost weeps with relief. She whispers, reassuring herself, so low even he cannot hear her: *"He's real, he's real, he's real…"*

"Ever," he says, the word muffled by her hair, his voice uncertain. "You—you're alive."

"I'm alive," she confirms, weak with relief. "And I found you."

The trembling is evident in her voice and in her limbs; she is literally shaken, and feels like she can only hope to regain her balance and survive this tumult by clinging to Ere. He is her life-boat in this unbelievable storm. Finding him feels like a miracle; she was swept out to sea, tossed by the waves, and somehow spotted a small group of Originals, flitting like driftwood floating back toward the shore, and she followed them because it was her only chance. Now, here she was and here he was: Ere, the boy she was supposed to find her way back to, no matter what.

"You were looking for me? You... remember me?"

She nods, pressing her cheek into him so he will feel the movement, not trusting herself to speak anymore. She can feel the shifting feet of the Originals around them, can picture their indicting eyes and their faces lined with question marks. Then one of them speaks, and she is surprised at the familiarity of the voice.

"Well, honey," Angela clucks, and just knowing that someone else from her world is standing in this circle restores some of Ever's resolve. "Looks like we both had a few secrets."

*   *   *   *

Ere and Ever sit side by side, knees drawn to their chests, not touching. They have been sitting for a long time. Most of the exhausted fighters are now sleeping, but neither Ere nor Ever has been able to rest. Nor have they spoken; both simply stare down at the burning Syn world below them.

Much earlier in the evening, it had become evident that they were not needed. Jorge and Asavari led an initial party to vulture their way through one of the Synt's ship hangars to scout out what ships might be salvageable. Angela and Preeti took another contingent to scavenge through a food storage unit, in hopes of preparing a massive feast for the rebels before their next journeys begin. A third group, led by some kid whose name Ever had not caught, was sweeping the surrounding premises for any other survivors, Original or otherwise. But neither Ere nor Ever were tasked with any of these things.

Ever could tell this bothered Ere. The boy heralded as the subject of prophecy, the last of the Fells, the Original who strolled confidently into the Synt, the figurehead for a movement—was suddenly relieved of all duties and ultimately proven unnecessary. He watched as everyone dispersed, and then reluctantly accepted Ever's invitation to take a few minutes to talk, just the two of them. But they have not talked all night. At last, Ever breaks the silence.

"I remember forgetting you."

He does not look at her, but she can feel him swallow hard.

"How long—"

"Only since right before—before the final surge. My father always said nothing is ever really lost in the cloud. Everything deleted is only hidden away, waiting for someone to dig it up. For whatever reason, after that episode, Heaven decided to restore—"

"Don't say Heaven. It wasn't 'heaven'. It was my grandfather."

"I don't—it doesn't matter, all right? Whatever. Whoever. It doesn't—"

"It does matter. Did you know, about my grandfather?"

"My father had a lot of secrets. I only know what I was given tonight."

"What you were given?"

"It's… hard to describe."

"Try."

"In the final Pulse… I lost a lot. There are gaps and, I don't know, missing files. Stolen memories. I remember meeting you, and I remember erasing you, but I know in my gut that I don't remember everything about you. About us. I also remember Cal. He was important to me, and I think—I think there was something between us. Something like love. But it's patchy and broken and I don't know. I don't know. I have new files, too—I know everything about your grandfather now, and I didn't, before—before. We didn't. But it was part of the… final transaction. That last pulse. Things were lost, and found, and… traded, I guess."

"You have my grandfather's memories mixed in with yours?"

"Some of them. We all did. All do—all of us still breathing, I think we all—gained something from him. And I think that's because of you."

Ere stares at her.

"What do you mean?"

"Seeing you... changed him."

"Changed him how?"

She moves her head, side to side, seeing if anything shakes loose but finding nothing worthy to offer.

"In an important way. That's all I know. But I know it all the way, throughout every fiber of my being, just like I know to keep breathing. I know it without even having to think about it. It's just there."

"Just there."

"Ere, even with pieces missing—I know how much you mattered to him."

"Great," he says, voice thick with sarcasm. "I mattered to a monster. I changed him right before he massacred the Syn population. Monsters and massacres. The Fell way. Tradition."

There is another long stretch of silence, extending like a horizon without end. Then Ere reaches into his pocket, and sets something on the ground between them.

"Do you remember giving me that?"

Hesitantly, she feels the object on the ground. She cringes when her finger-port connects with something hard, metal on metal, clinking dully. She wraps the rest of her hand around the thing. It is small and cold, and familiar. It's a gun. Her gun, which apparently she gave him. But this must be one of the missing memories, because she cannot recall giving it to him. She shakes her head.

"Well. You did. And I held on to it. And I fired it at your father."

"Oh."

"Yeah."

"Did you… hit him?"

"I missed."

"So he was there, where you were, when it happened? Do you know how it… do you know what happened to my father, in the end?"

"He was… alive," Ere says slowly. "But I'm not sure he was… all there."

Ever bites her lip, forbidding herself from saying, *Serves him right.*

"I'm pretty sure my mother's dead, too," is all she says aloud. "So I guess I'm alone."

"You have Cal, don't you," he mutters, and she flushes.

Like all her memories, those of Cal have been mixed-up, muddied, many of them moved to somewhere just out of reach. But at Ere's jealous snipe, she remembers embraces—not just with Ere, but with Cal. Cal's strong arms, the loving looks he gave her. Cal at her side. Cal augmenting, Cal—*oh, Heaven and hell.*

"Cal's gone," she whispers.

Ere looks at her, and his lip trembles.

"What do you mean, gone?"

"Just—gone," she says.

"Oh," Ere says. She watches his face harden before his next statement: "So that's why you're with me again, huh? The better cousin bailed, so might as well come see about me—"

"No," Ever protests, horrified. "No, that's not it at all—Ere, I had erased you, if I had remembered I never would have—"

"Forget it."

"I don't want to forget anymore! Ere, listen to me," she says, pushing the gun away and moving closer to him. She can see she is losing him, and she will not have an eternity to win him back. Time is a factor she can no longer write off, but must instead be ruled by. "Lots of things have changed. All right? We've all been through hell. Yes, I erased you—to protect you. Yes, then Cal found me, and we were—we were together; but he's gone. And even if he wasn't, I remember you now, and that still would have changed things. Everything is different. I was a Syn. But there's no such thing anymore. I'm disconnected. I am going to age. And I want to age alongside you, if you'll let me."

"You want to die with me," he says coolly, eyes still aimed elsewhere.

"I'd prefer to live with you first," she retorts, nostrils flaring, feeling a rising heat of irritation at his dismissive, self-indulgent misery. "Assuming you still want to live, and not just wallow and stare."

"I'm not just—"

"You are. And I'm finally running out of time, which is kind of a new thing for me, but I've already figured out a few things, and one of those is that I definitely don't want to waste time pouting like a baby."

He snaps his face toward hers.

"Pouting?"

"Like a baby," she says, shrugging with her palms up, paired with the signature *don't-blame-me-that's-the-truth-and-I-can't-sugarcoat-it* look she learned from her mother. Or maybe it was from Angela. "You've been through hell. I get it. Guess what? Me, too. But the way I see it, we can either figure out what we want, and start working on that. Or we can sit here and pout. No, you know what? Forget that. You can sit here and pout—"

She shoves herself to her feet. This strange night is almost at an end. Night still holds the sky, but the first fingers of dawn are stretching skyward, a lighter lavender tickling at the edges of the purple-black heavens. A new day, the first one in a long time that will mean she's one step closer to the end of her now-finite life.

She doesn't have time to waste. Maybe one of her missing memories contains something about what a little jackass Ere was—or maybe he used to be a sweet kid but was a jackass now. Either way. Ever has a lot to learn, but repeating her mother's mistake and attaching herself to someone too distracted by *what-ifs* to engage in *what-is?*

Not on her life.

The world has changed, and so has she. She is no longer something preserved, like canned fruit on a shelf; she is something fresh, a soft new peach. She wants to ripen before rotting, and if he wants to wither on the branch, so be it.

Just before she is out of reach, she feels his hand catch hers and hold it tight.

"I like your scar," Ere tells Ever, as a new morning cracks wide the old sky.

CHAPTER 106: ERE

E RE'S FEELINGS FOR EVER are not uncomplicated, but they do run deep—and after so many months of feeling distant from everything around him, it is a welcome change to feel something for someone. Even if right now what he feels is somewhat wary, it's real. And although her memories of him are broken, all his recollections of her remain intact. They have a history. Maybe they'll have a future.

We even met each other's parents.

Even if it didn't go so well, on either side.

He manages a small smile, still cradling his hand in hers.

"What's funny?" she smirks, catching the twitch of his mouth.

"I'll tell you later," he says, and he will.

Approaching the park, a host of delicious smells wind their way into Ere's nose. His stomach rumbles loudly.

"I smell Angela's cooking," Ever chuckles. "Even though there's obviously a helluva lot more to that woman, the Angela I've known for the past fifty years is one of the best chefs in the history of... history. If I had to guess, she's whipped up some herbed-griddled corn cakes, minted fresh fruit salad, some sort of sugary—"

"Stop!" Ere clutches his roaring stomach. "If you keep talking I'm going to eat you."

Ever lifts an eyebrow, but before she can otherwise respond, they are interrupted by Asavari. Appearing out of nowhere, she is suddenly right in front of them, though she addresses only Ere when she speaks.

"Ere! Good. We want to have an all-tribe meeting immediately following breakfast. We have three mid-size vessels ready to go, so we can begin return trips home as early as tonight."

"Return trips?" Ever inserts herself into the conversation. "But—"

Asavari continues speaking as if Ever is not even there, although she cannot help but disdainfully dart her eyes down at Ere and Ever's clasped hands, ever so briefly. Ere feels unduly guilty at this glance.

"Assuming that all goes as planned, we can—"

"Stop," Ere says again, hoping his raised voice will drown out the ongoing protests and demands from his midsection. "You said after breakfast, right? Let's eat first. Then we'll talk."

Breakfast confirms Ever's praise of Angela's cooking. Overseeing a team of a dozen eager disciples, the former informant has orchestrated a feast worthy of this victorious makeshift army. An impossible spread stretches across several tables stolen from nearby Syn buildings. Ere begins shoveling food into his face by hand until Ever nudges him gently toward the plates and silverware also confiscated by the rebels. Following her lead, albeit somewhat reluctantly, Ere piles high his plate and eats until his stomach hurts.

Buoyed by the food and the renewed connection with Ever, Ere has a growing sense that rather than being destined to destroy the old world he might be able to play his own small role in building a new one. He carries this thought with him as he joins the rebels gathering after the feast for the all-tribe assembly.

"Hey," Ever catches him by the arm as he heads to where Jorge, Asavari, and the others are convening. "Am I welcome at this meeting?"

"Why wouldn't you be?" Ere asks.

She gives him a sidelong look.

"Your friends don't trust me. And I understand that. I mean, my father—"

"You are not your father. All right? If you're with us, you're with us, end of story."

"I'm with you," she says, slipping her hand back into his.

The meeting is already underway. There is no need for a discussion of the overall events. Throughout the night, everyone brought what threads they had and collectively the group had stitched together enough of a narrative to know what happened. They will learn more later, and then ignore most of it. The truth would shrink and expand, contract and contradict itself in the coming years, as truth is wont to do.

But the basics were all sewn up by that morning. Nathan Fell's internal implosion of the shared Syn system, the demise of most Syns, the disconnection of the survivors, the tech-gone-dark throughout all of the incorporated sectors, the opportunity at last for a return to the Original way. Those are the facts that mattered, and those are the ones that will stick.

Jorge is giving a quick update on the transit as Ere approaches: "...so those three should be enough, for now, and we'll have room in the cargo to take along enough resources to fuel a return trip, as well."

"Won't that make the spaceships somewhat, er, flammable?"

The question comes from an older voice, and when Ere pinpoints the sound in the crowd he sees a chin-jutting old woman with a familiar face.

Helena.

Relief floods Ere, seeing her dandelion-tuft of white hair floating around her inquisitive face. He hadn't known until seeing her just how worried he had been that she might have been injured or felled in the fiery chaos of last night.

"Good question, Helena," Jorge grins. "But no, sorry, I shouldn't have said 'fuel' a return trip—the generators for the ship are basically giant batteries. We won't be transporting fossil fuels, just a backup battery. Also, they're not spaceships, friend. They're just regular old—"

"I like calling 'em spaceships," Helena insists, and earns a few chuckles.

"All right. Well, good news, folks. There's room for all of us in the… spaceships."

A cheer goes through the crowd. Ere does not join in. Instead, he calls out a question.

"Everyone's going? Just like that?"

"You want to stay?" Helena asks.

"I don't know. But I also don't know that I want to just—go. My home isn't there. My home is here. I mean, not here-here, but…" He stops, and alters course. "I mean yes, here-here! My people—our people, who lived here—we were kicked out. But this was our home."

"But it's the center of the Syn world," calls out one voice.

"It *was* the center," hollers another, to a rising tide of rumbling agreement.

"Does anyone else want to stay?"

Jorge's question hangs in the air, waiting. With the few exceptions of Angela, Jorge, Helena and himself, Ere knows almost all of the others assembled are surely eager to return to India. While Ere's memories of it paint the place as nothing but hot sun and dry earth, underground tunnels and misery, for the members of Asavari's tribe, it is their homeland. The place where they lived free of Syn rule and able to plan for their ultimate uprising. It is where their children, parents, wives, and husbands are awaiting their return.

"I'll stay."

Dr. Preeti Kansal steps forward, shoulders back and head held high, drawing herself up to the full four-eleven of her peak height.

"Mother!" Asavari protests. "Why would you—"

"Not forever," Preeti continues. "My family, my life, my future is in Delhi. But my past is also here. I have things to make right, and if Ere and others are staying here, we can establish an Original presence here, ensure ongoing communication across the continents, see if there are other remnants we can find in this part of the world. I was here when the map was drawn for the Singularity. I should be here to help lay out the new maps."

"I'm in," Helena says. "I do enjoy the spaceships, but it's been an awful lot of airtime for this old lady in one week. And, as my friend Preeti said, there might be… other remnants we should find. In this part of the world." She darts a quick look at Ere, which he cannot quite interpret. "That's enough to make me want to stay. Plus, there's plenty of food and shelter here. 'Sides, Preeti and I know all the things we did wrong last time. Consuming too many resources. Climate change. If we have a clean slate—you young folks are gonna need some old folks to weigh in on what not to do."

Murmurs in the crowd bubble and rise, and Asavari holds her hands up to silence them.

"All right, all right," Asavari allows. "We will have a small meeting with those who wish to stay following this debriefing. Let us first finish discussing the matters that pertain to everyone."

She aims an angry look at Ere, then looks past to him, to Ever.

A few other items—travel routes, communications, provisions—are quickly discussed. The rally concludes with a rousing burst of song, Helena leading the masses in several old Original tunes, and then instructions from Jorge and Angela on the tasks remaining before they can depart, followed finally by Asavari stepping forward and crowing:

"Some of us will depart, and some will stay! Where once we were few, scattered and hidden, soon there will be many, united and thriving in the light! This is the Syn's end, but it is our beginning! Ours!"

"Ours!" the crowd roars back. "Ours!"

As the cries fade into the mid-morning air, the assembly of hundreds dwindles to fewer than a dozen. The rebels disperse to finish the ship work Jorge tasked them with, to clean up the remains of Angela's meal, to gather supplies for their imminent return to their homeland.

"So you're staying," Asavari asks Ere, her eyes again drifting from him to Ever.

"Yes," Ere says. "With whoever else will stay, or is here and doesn't yet know what has happened—any remnants, Original or Vost or otherwise, will be part of rebuilding. Here."

"Original or Vost or otherwise."

Asavari's eyes are again on Ever. And Ever is glaring right back at her.

"You look like you think there's no room for me," Ever says to Asavari.

"Is that not how your father felt about me? About all Originals?"

"I am not my father."

"Apples do not fall far—"

"That is enough, Asavari."

The two young women turn to see Asavari's mother standing firmly before them.

"Mother, I do not think—"

"You do not think," Preeti says, nodding. "This is true. True of you, true of all of us, especially when there are things we do not know. Asavari, I told you before that I had a cousin working with Nathan Fell, and that is why I was brought in as a consulting physician."

"Yes...?"

"My cousin—your kin, as well—was Felix Hess."

Heaven and Hell...

"How... how are we..." Asavari gasps, stunned.

"His mother Nirupa came to the United States from India. Nirupa's sister was my mother. Your grandmother. The point, my dear, is that apples do fall quite far from the tree sometimes. Sometimes they fall and evolve and yield entirely new fruit from their own branches. This is something you should feel; this is something you should know. The world has always been small. And now it is too small for warring factions. For warring... families."

"Wise words," Jorge says, apparently having heard the entire exchange. He gives Ever a curt nod, which Ere appreciates. "We'll make room."

"Thank you," Ever says, moved.

"Hear, hear," says Helena. "And take it from an old one—this is not the old world. The Original world. That world is gone. We cannot go back. But it's not a Syn world anymore, either. It's something else."

"What?" Ere asks. "What world is it?"

"Ours," Preeti says again. "It is what we will make it."

"Amen," Jorge says.

"Fine," Asavari relents, with a final icy glare at Ever. Ere wonders if these strange cousins will ever become friends, and feels a pang again over the loss of his own cousin, his closest friend until their competition had divided them. "Anything else, before we start... making this new world?"

A cloud crosses briefly over Jorge's face.

"There was one strange thing that happened last night."

Helena snorts. "That's an understatement."

"I ran into a Syn Council member, who was saying something about the self-terminating Syns, something never really acknowledged outside of our network, and about a Syn movement to overthrow Hess. Is it something to concern ourselves with now, or—?"

Angela shakes her head.

"No. Whatever other drama was going on in the Syn world—that's all over now. Let's not get lost in any more might-have-beens while we try to figure out how things are gonna be."

Everyone nods in agreement. Ere feels Ever's hand slide again into his, and together they stride away from the assembly and toward the clean slate of a world as yet unplanned.

EPILOGUE

CHAMELEON HAS ALWAYS LIKED WINE. More than like, she *appreciates* it. She considers herself something of a history buff when it comes to wine. Visiting vineyards is the only vacation she has ever allowed herself, and seeking out stories and legends of wines and wineries is something endlessly fascinating to her. She especially loves imagining all of the best wines in the world that went un-sipped, almost as much as she enjoys pouring a satisfying glass of a blood-dark red.

Her favorite story is of a bottle of 1787 Château Margaux. The bottle was preserved and unopened for almost 200 years, pristine and legendary. Early in its life, it was allegedly even once procured by wine enthusiast and reluctant politician Thomas Jefferson. Then in 1989, it was brought out from the cellar for some rich guy to show off at a fancy wine dinner in New York. It was still uncorked. Before the evening was over, a waiter dropped the bottle, shattering the glass and spilling the precious contents everywhere. In a single moment, the centuries-old virgin wine was destroyed without ever being enjoyed.

At the time of its destruction, the bottle belonged to William Sokolin, a wine merchant. The clever man insured the most precious items in his one-of-a-kind collection. Insurance paid out $225,000 for the broken bottle of Château Margaux. That put the value of the wine at an astronomical level. Nearly a quarter of a million dollars was a lot of money in 1989. The price per glass, had it ever been poured into glasses, would have been about $37,500. But the legendary wine was never poured, and its collector cashed in.

Maybe Sokolin was devastated when he lost the precious bottle. Or maybe he paid the conveniently clumsy waiter to bust it and guarantee him a big payday. Or maybe he just knew that at some point, the bottle had to break, and whenever it did, he would be covered.

The woman who has been calling herself Chameleon—hilarious how many of her enemies assumed she was a man—uncorks a far less pricey vintage, but a respectable one nonetheless. She's been saving this bottle for a special occasion. It's a twenty-year-old bottle of Bordeaux produced by the Syn wine baron who bought up most of Bordeaux and walled in the vineyards to keep them from being damaged in the European uprisings, fifty years back.

She pours herself a large glass and lets it breathe. Then she takes in the scent of it, identifying black cherry, plum, spice, vanilla, smoke, and floral notes, enjoying the tastes even before they hit her tongue. She sips slowly, contemplating lessons learned and vices validated.

Wine only keeps for about 50 years, so the truth of the matter is that at the time of its destruction, the 1787 Château Margaux would have tasted worse than piss.

Just like all wines fermented in the old world have soured, though some collectors still keep Original bottles for the same sentimental and status-driven reasons. Wine is not only about taste, but also about time and its passage. It is a reminder that anything hurried is cheap, but anything that idles for too long is dead.

"Miss?"

She takes another sip before replying.

"Come on in."

"The Originals have overtaken the Synt," her servant begins, rattling off the information quickly and efficiently, just as he is supposed to do. "They're dismantling the computer systems but preserving the water and basic wiring, converting it into their main way-station while they make their next plans. They'll have a lot of clean-up to do. Bodies everywhere."

"What's the Syn body count? Best estimate."

"Approximately eighty percent of the Synthetic population was eliminated in the final Pulse. Those that have survived are disconnected from tech, and actually appear to be... relatively healthy. But aging on a normal timeframe again, from the intelligence I've gathered."

"And we know it was the final Pulse. There won't be any others."

"Yes. The Source is dead."

"Who confirmed that?"

"Three of us."

"Good." She rolls the Bordeaux around her mouth. *Leather.* She missed that note in the first few sips. "Eighty percent of the Synthetic population. I assume that includes pretty much everyone who would be over ninety years old."

"Yes." A pause. "Everyone but you."

She takes a final sip, turning and smiling as she lifts the empty glass.

"Well, I'm one-of-a-kind, now, aren't I?"

"You always were," says Kennedy.

"Pour me another," says Claudia Lee, and her robot dutifully obeys.

*   *   *   *

Claudia, now known to everyone but her robots as simply Chameleon, never wanted to augment. Becoming a synthetic citizen was something she found to be a truly distasteful last-resort sort of move. She hated Hess's whole approach to science, thinking it was something with which to be merged. She always saw it as what it was: Something to be *managed*.

She also hated Hess.

She wanted to like him, way back when. He had been the only one to challenge her as she sailed through her academic career, paying dues to universities who could offer her little. She found him interesting, intelligent—but ultimately he proved too egotistical and belligerent. He thought too small and thought himself too big. She already disliked him, but when he stole Lorraine Murray and all that funding right out from under her, full-on loathing for Felix Hess became part of Claudia's identity.

So augmenting had been a huge compromise, but ultimately a necessary one. Because though it cost her a piece of her soul, it bought her an invaluable amount of time.

She carefully crafted the process of her conversion. Though Hess had stolen plenty of her funding, she still had resources. Connections. Enough to obscure her identity. It was easy to create a life on paper for "Claudia Lee," plotting out several more imagined years of productivity before being recruited by the resistance and ultimately dying a well-documented death in a Brooklyn uprising.

None of which happened.

Instead, while maintaining and documenting a fictitious life, the real Claudia Lee tapped her resources to create a new identity for herself. She augmented under the name Carol Lee. No reason to shift away from such a common last name, and anyway her Lee family memorabilia could then all be kept—it would have been such a shame to render all of her dead mother's rose-colored tea towels obsolete. "Carol Lee" wasn't a scientist, she was the middle daughter of a made-up millionaire, interested in documentary photography. Much like her name change, this interest wasn't much of a stretch. Claudia really did love photography. It was a passion of hers, just like wine.

And artificial intelligence.

Masquerading as a boring, wealthy Syn photographer, Claudia had plenty of opportunity to keep working on her AI tech. An old bomb shelter was the perfect laboratory, and without grant report deadlines, funder inquiries, news media on her ass or anything else, she got a lot done.

Her skill was in designing internal AI core—software, not hardware. Building actual robots wasn't really in her wheelhouse. It was one thing she envied Hess. His cyborganics tech rode off the built-in motherboard of the human brain, already housed within the well-designed human form with all of its incredible motor skills and moving parts. She was convinced her motherboard was better, but it was the housing for it that she was lacking.

Until she met Chase.

Chase was another reluctant Syn. Chase didn't know, at first, that Claudia was a scientist or a fellow self-hating Syn. Chase reached out to Carol Lee, hoping the reclusive, renowned photographer would do a photo series of their ongoing transformation.

"I hear you're a pretty great photographer," Chase said over a glass of 2008 Domaine Leflaive Montrachet Grand Cru, aiming to impress Carol Lee with the wine selection (and succeeding; Claudia *had* to know where the hell Chase snagged that gem—but Chase never told)."My life's work is becoming the most actualized me I can be, and I want someone to document the process. I had a friend who took a bunch of photos for me before the Singularity. That friend is... out of the picture now, if you'll pardon the pun. Are you interested?"

Claudia wasn't all that interested.

But as Carol, she had no good reason to say no.

So, savoring the wine, she shrugged.

"Sure, let's do it."

When she arrived at Chase's massive penthouse the next week, camera in hand, she was greeted by an unexpected sight: two Chases.

"Hello," said a slightly glassy-eyed Chase.

"Meet my buddy," chuckled the real Chase.

"Holy shit," said Claudia Lee.

The real Chase and the robot Chase grinned at this exclamation.

The android was incredible—better than any Claudia had seen before. The biggest challenge in building a human-like robot is making the muscles in the face move as realistically as possible. In her post-doc years, Claudia had worked with several robotics guys who were doing some good work. They developed minute, extremely sensitive actuators to create and control facial movements. But they had to control all reactions remotely, telling dozens of actuators to quickly lift in order to raise an eyebrow, for example. But the real Chase was standing alongside this lifelike copy, apparently pulling no strings.

"I was a robotics nerd in a past life," Chase said.

"Robotics," breathed Claudia. "We... have a lot to discuss."

Chase, as it turned out, had some of the same connections Claudia had—and while the photography series was a legitimate interest, Chase had also reached out to test a theory. As it happened, Chase was pretty savvy, and asked point blank: Was the socialite-photographer Carol Lee a clever cover for the AI genius whose work Chase had followed before the Singularity?

Yes, yes, yes.

There was no competition with Claudia and Chase. They were instant collaborators, yin and yang coming together in perfect harmony. Claudia focused on the interior, Chase on the exterior, both obsessed with getting as close to perfection as possible.

"Syn technology can extract memory," Chase said over another expensive glass of wine, several months into their shared artistic and scientific endeavors. Claudia would be taking a picture of Chase that night, preserving Chase alongside the ever-enhancing Chase robot, which they had taken to calling Buddy.

"Yes," Claudia said. "I'm pretty sure at some point, Hess will use that for full-system upgrades. New bodies."

"I think you're right," Chase said. "And I want to do the same thing. But with Buddy."

"What do you mean?" Claudia asked, setting down her wine.

"I mean, Hess is all about the organic components, and you're right. Those get old. He'll figure out a way to get new bodies, whether he grows them in labs or gets test subjects pregnant or whatever he decides to do. But that's always just going to be a stop gap. Organic flesh will keep rotting. Every, what—fifty, sixty years max? His Syns will have to keep getting new bodies. But if we can extract memory, and encode it into your AI systems, embedding person-and-personality into the model…"

"…and then upload it into fully actualized, organic-component-free bodies…"

"…we'll be way, way ahead of the Syns."

They stared at each for a moment, Claudia considering this obvious but outlandish notion, Chase waiting for it to sink in. Despite Claudia's rejection of conventional religiously-shaped ethics, there is something about this that shakes her a bit. It feels unethical.

"It wouldn't be you, you know. If your profile's embedded in a bot—it wouldn't be you."

"It would be the next level of me."

"But it wouldn't be the *real* you."

"What's the real me? Are we not our memories, our collected experiences and impressions, nothing more?"

"So babies are born nothing?" Claudia countered.

"They already have the experiences of the womb."

"But there's more to us than that, if you believe in a…"

"A what?" Chase cocked their head. "A soul?"

"Or whatever," Claudia said.

"Well, that same conundrum fits the Syn version of this solution," Chase shrugged. "If you're in your third or fourth organic full-body upgrade… is that a more or less soulless prospect?"

"Equally soulless, I'd say."

"So why not cut out the part that rots? And replace it with your clever bots?"

"Don't rhyme. It's weird."

"It's charming."

"I like it," Buddy chirped from a corner of the room.

"You're not allowed to weigh in," Claudia scolded, but the robot had succeeded in breaking the tension, and all three of them laughed. Claudia shook her head. She found it a strange position to be in, suddenly playing devil's advocate and suggesting that robotics and AI were not the ultimate answers to everything. "Come on, let's get the picture knocked out and then you can try to talk me into this."

"You're already on board," Chase said, draining the last of the wine.

They pulled out two of the barstools from Chase's kitchen island. Chase sat in one, Buddy in the other, in their matching tunic outfits, one dark, one light. Both stared straight ahead, waiting. Claudia snapped several photographs with her vintage Nikon, capturing the odd moment in their collective history and preserving it in black and white.

"How long have you been thinking about this?" Claudia asked, lowering the camera.

"I've been dreaming about it ever since I built Buddy here," Chase said, gently stroking the mirror image face of the Buddy robot. "And planning for it ever since I saw what you could do. We can do this, Claudia. And I want to. I don't have a death wish, but I've been wanting to get rid of this body for a long time. Never really felt like mine. I want this one, the one I made."

"But you made it look just like you."

"Close enough," was all Chase allowed.

"It might not work. And it might not really be you."

"It will work," Chase said. "Tell her, Buddy."

"I'll be the real Chase," Buddy said, obeying the command cue.

And so despite Claudia's misgivings, they did it. Claudia copied and extracted Chase's memories, uploading them into a heavily encrypted cloud, taking her time to build a nuanced AI motherboard around the data. Chase was at her elbow the entire time. While many of her former peers would have found this infuriating, Claudia was grateful to have a true partner in crime and creation. Chase pushed her to be better, and she pushed Chase to improve as well. Chase was constantly improving the robotics models, upgrading Buddy and building other skeletons that could later be fleshed out with the features and functions of other living, breathing people.

"They'll need to be able to breathe," Claudia burst out one day.

"Why?" Chase asked.

"You're a Syn. You have periodic check-ins, you scan in to get into buildings... we have to pay attention to every detail. Retinal level scan accuracy for eyes. Exact fingertip replication. Breathing. And hell if I know what we're going to do about the insides. I mean, if—when, more accurately... when you— Buddy-you— gets called in for routine maintenance, what happens when there's no liver to check?"

This set them back for a little while. But with their powers combined, nothing kept Lee and Chase down for long.

Claudia designed an infiltration program, hardwired into each of their robotics models. When information was extracted, the request would be instantly re-routed, and rather than allowing Synt scanners to collect new information, stored data would be uploaded with current timestamps. There would be no organic liver within Buddy, but Chase's once-present organic liver would display as the examination result. Since reports were never reviewed unless flagged, they figured so long as they slightly-modified the images every decade to establish some aging, they should fly under the radar for a good long while.

"Or at least until we're the ones in charge of the radar," Chase said.

"'We'?" Claudia said.

They were into their second bottle that night, most of which Claudia had put away.

"Yes, 'we.'"

"You won't be here by then."

"Of course I will."

"It'll be Buddy."

"Buddy will be Chase."

"Not the real you."

"Yes, the real me. Come on, are we back to this debate?"

"It's a copy, you know," Claudia said, speaking slowly and deliberately, to select the right words and avoid slurring them. She needed Chase to hear her. "All of this, everything we put into Buddy—it's a copy. We can give it some time, see how it all plays out. You don't have to go. You'll still have all of your memories. You could still... stay."

"Oh, Claudia," Chase said tenderly, setting down the wine glass and taking Claudia's small hands in their own. "You know I can't."

"Why not?"

"When you do the final extraction—all of my memories up to that moment—that will be all of me. You'll put me into Buddy, and Buddy will be me. If we both kept walking around, we would diverge. We would have the same old chapters, but our new chapters would differ, and neither of us would be real. Besides, I've told you... I'm done with this me. I want to be the new me. The next me."

"I like this you," Claudia whispered. "You're the best person I know."

"I love you, too," Chase said. "That's why I know you'll do this for me."

There had never been any romance between the two of them before this moment, and Claudia didn't know if it was romance crackling in the air now or just the fiercest of friendships, attraction like magnets. When Chase kissed her, she didn't want anything more, anything "next." She just wanted to stay right there in that moment, where they were, as they were.

The next day, they exported all of Chase's experiences, memories, attitudes, expressions, and imported them all into Buddy. As soon as Buddy opened their eyes, blinked, and said: "It worked," the original Chase fell to the floor behind Claudia.

Claudia didn't know what Chase had taken, or internally detonated, or how their life had ended. She hadn't wanted to know. She had been so desperate for ignorance that she had stupidly hoped Chase would change their mind at the last minute, and pull the plug on this whole ludicrous experiment. But they didn't. And so the real Chase lay lifeless on the floor, and Buddy-with-Chase's-knowledge blinked expectantly at Claudia.

"Shall I help you dispose of my old body?" the robot asked, and Claudia choked back a sob.

For the first several weeks, it was a difficult adjustment period. Claudia was unsure how to act around the robot, feeling unnatural herself every time she looked at it. She wasn't sure she had done the right thing. She should have debated more, pushed back, waited longer, started with someone else. She still called the robot Buddy, despite its constant correction of her.

"I'm Chase," it would tell Claudia. "I'm the real Chase. Just like we talked about. Remember?"

"Yeah, I remember," Claudia said.

"Me, too," said the robot.

By the second month, she started calling it Chase. To avoid the chiding, if nothing else. This Chase proved just as good as the last at continually improving their base models. It was Claudia who seemed stuck, no longer motivated to pursue their work.

"Claudia," Chase said one day, looking as frustrated as the real Chase would have looked. "You're dragging your feet, and this isn't like you. How many times have you told me how awful Felix Hess is? Let's count the reasons he needs ousting: He's an egomaniac, he's consolidated power and basically destroyed democracy as we know it, and he orchestrated a genocide. There are almost no Originals left."

Claudia remembered the Felix she had known at Stanford, the antisocial boy with all the ambition. The smartest person in the room, other than her. She had tried to slip him a note, once, in college. Offering some sort of partnership. He should have taken her up on the offer. He never even read the note.

"His ideas weren't all evil," she told Chase.

"He's *inhuman*," said the robot.

Claudia just stared.

"You know what I meant," Chase said quietly.

"Yeah," muttered Claudia. But then she squared her shoulders. "You're right. Hess has been at the top for too long. We need to start replicating the results we had with Ch—with you. But exactly how are we supposed to start recruiting Syns who might want to try something new, who want to step into our… technology… without Hess getting wind of the whole thing and making it illegal or something?"

"I have an idea," Chase said. "About getting Syns in the door, in a pretty low-risk way."

"Yeah?" Claudia said, wondering if this robot-Chase could indeed have a new and internally-generated thought that would lead to a breakthrough.

Even before the conversion from Syn-Chase to robot-Chase, Chase had been tuning in to the hushed reports of self-terminating Syns. This ultimately led to the epiphany: What if they could contact Syns considering self-termination, and intercept them before they took action?

"Think about it," the robot Chase said, with the same exuberant intellectual eagerness as… well, Chase. "We can tell them that we'll only do a partial upload—anything too painful, too terrible, we'll let that die with them. But the best of their ideas and contributions, that we can keep and use to augment your AI board. It gives them an option of not-really-dying, or at least of sticking it to Hess before they go. Then we have their identification, credentials, position, and as long as we can keep the moment of conversion under wraps… we just do a swap. Joe Schmoe comes in wanting to die; we take the best of Joe Schmoe, help him comfortably end a too-long life, and then robot Joe Schmoe picks up and happily returns home to keep being Joe Schmoe. A happier Schmoe. A Schmoe who remembers what we tell him to remember—"

"—and tells us what we want to know," Claudia finished, just like in the old days.

"YES!" Chase crowed, and leaned over to kiss Claudia.

Claudia recoiled.

"Don't. Ever. Do that."

Flushing red (*it's only those damn epidermal solar panels that allow that*, Claudia reminded herself), Chase nodded and mumbled an incoherent apology before hurrying from the room. Claudia almost apologized, but never did. Better that the boundaries be kept clear: She might have had some romantic interest in the old Chase—the *real* Chase. But she was not going to be in a relationship with a robot she helped build. No matter how convincing the tech, she would never see Buddy as Chase.

They began building their army. Finding Syns considering self-termination was easier than they expected. Though Heaven's moderators quickly flagged and removed posts for support groups or public cries for help, Chase was faster than the normal Syn when it came to finding and siphoning information from the cloud. Chase was also an excellent recruiter.

Claudia, once so charismatic and chatty, had become more introverted post-augmentation. She never felt at ease in her synthetic skin, and it impacted her socializing. But Chase, powered by a range of memories and experiences, intoxicatingly interesting, and friendly in an aggressively gregarious way that only born-Southerners can be, was ideally suited to lure in potential bots. When a potential ally was identified, Chase would make contact. Build a rapport. And then make them an offer.

502   SYN & SALVATION

Almost no one said no.

Chase and Claudia could barely keep up with the demand, since building bot bodies took significant time. Each was a custom build. Once completed, the Syns loved seeing their replicated selves, the detail and familiarity of them. Generations of humans had been obsessed with pictures of their own faces. Seeing four-dimensional models of themselves was, indeed, next-level.

Seeing that they would, indeed, live on—without having to live on, and on, and on directly—comforted many of them. There was almost always a sigh of relief when their memories were uploaded and they clicked off. A sigh of *release*, thought Claudia.

Within a decade, they had a hundred bots, walking around and living the lives of the Syns whose identities they had assumed. *These lives and identities were all voluntarily handed over, not taken from them*, Chase would remind Claudia whenever Claudia needed reminding.

After three decades, with Chase becoming ever-more proficient at building bots, they crossed the thousand-bot milestone. Some of their recruits worked in the highest levels of Syn society. One bot, a replicant of the powerful and detail-oriented Mimi Toshiba, reported being asked to join a secret committee formed by Lorraine Murray. The goal of the committee was to oust Felix Hess. Claudia and Chase had a good laugh that night. For a time, they thought maybe Lorraine might wind up doing most of their dirty work for them when it came to getting rid of Felix Hess.

Everything had ramped up these past few years. Landing Kennedy, one of Hess's two assistants, was a major coup. Chase had noticed him when they caught on to how frequently his memories were sanitized. Everyone did a little touch-up cleaning here and there, but that guy was swiping larger and larger swaths clean. There was clearly something wrong in his life, which meant there was an opening for Chase to slip into it.

And then there was the Pulse. The Pulse did not impact robots. They had no synthetic tech, after all; Claudia's designs were off the radar and not connected to the Syns shared networks and drives. So that was a blessing. But Claudia herself was still a Syn, and the first Pulse nearly killed her. Chase had come to the lab to find Claudia on the floor, collapsed and barely breathing.

"No no no no no," Chase said, panic in their voice but a steely calm directing their movement. Grabbing all of Claudia's "Carol Lee" credentials, Chase had taken her to the nearest hospital, elbowing other suffering Syns out of the way.

Claudia's recovery was slow. Thankfully, her mental faculties were intact. But she had suffered a stroke, which attacked the right side of her body. It froze the right side of her face, cost her the use of her right hand, and her right leg was not useless but was stiffened, her right foot twisting and dragging when she walked. They did not know if these side effects would be temporary or permanent. What they did know was that another Pulse was inevitable.

"You have to convert," Chase told Claudia. "You have to. Same as with everyone else. We'll extract you and get you into one of my bots, and then you won't be susceptible when the next—"

"No," Claudia said firmly.

"What do you mean 'no'?"

"I mean no."

"If you die, I couldn't live with—"

"Shut up, Chase. Just shut up. I'm not doing it."

"Stubborn jackass!" Chase snapped. "You augmented! You let Hess's bastard tech into your body, but you don't trust your own work? *Our* work? You know that it's—"

"I know that it's only a few decades old. I know that we don't know the ultimate long-term viability of our tech, or Hess's—I mean, Jesus, Chase, Hess's tech is why I'm so mangled now! And anyway one of us has to hold on to some small measure of being human."

"I am more than 'some small measure' of being human," Chase said, shaking. "I am—"

"You are a copy," Claudia said, venom in her voice. "*You are a copy.*"

She turned her face to the wall, refusing to gaze into the eyes that looked so very much like her best friend's eyes. Chase waited. And waited. And finally left the room, which is when Claudia finally cried, tears spilling down the frozen right side of her face, a face still made of flesh and bone.

Chase left her alone for a full day, then returned with a plate of food and a new plan. They would not convert Claudia. Instead, since she was already behind in her synthetic upgrades, they would simply sever her connection to Heaven. Chase could easily keep all of Claudia's synthetic components maintained and running. Claudia would be able to access the tech she needed, without connecting directly to the collective.

You've gone from being a public synner to a private one, Chase joked.

Claudia didn't crack a smile.

They hoped the modifications of Claudia's system would work, although they wouldn't know for certain until the second Pulse hit. In the meantime, Chase tended to Claudia, and she recovered well from the first magnetic surge, regaining functionality, face returning to normal. She didn't even limp.

Chase returned to the pursuit of Kennedy, wanting to get him in for conversion before the next Pulse hit. This proved doable. He converted, discarding his past regrets and tired body and allowing one of Chase's bots running Claudia's internal system to step into his place. They handled his conversion incredibly carefully—especially since they did something with him that they didn't do with very many of the other bots: they programmed him to forget that he was a bot.

He'll be more effective that way, Claudia said, and Chase agreed.

The long pursuit of Kennedy had given Chase ample time to perfect the replica of his form, his expressions and reactions; they carefully cultivated the memories and responses he left them so he would treat Jorge as he had always treated Jorge, Hess as he had always treated Hess. They made sure to erase all traces of his decision to convert, and to delete from his memories anything that might make him question his now-manipulated motives. He was the perfectly placed pawn.

He survived the second pulse with no incident, since he was no longer a Syn but a bot. Claudia survived it with minimal damage. Though offline, the tech within her still seared and ripped through her with a massive migraine, but nothing that lasted more than twenty-four hours. No major aftershocks. The plan had worked.

The energy of each Pulse eradicated all synthetic memory storage of the twenty-four hours before and after the incident. This meant conversion in the immediate aftermath of a Pulse was a breeze—plenty of time to extract memories, dump them into awaiting bots, discard the organic bodies and make the swap before anyone was the wiser. Self-terminating Syns became a thing of the past.

Demand for bot bodies was on the rise, although Claudia and Chase were no longer so eager to build up their numbers in order to take down Hess. The Pulse was making their work easy—so easy that they decided that with the help of the Original rebels Kennedy had clued them into, the time was nigh to take down Hess's whole world.

In the days before the final battle, they did allow a few last-minute bot conversion rush jobs. One such case was Gina Torres, a poor peon recruited by Hess to spy on his daughter; that woman was racked with guilt and all too happy to sidestep her life and hand it over to Claudia and Chase. They figured she might come in handy, just in case.

Chase also noticed distress signals from Hess's own wife, Marilyn. But they never responded to her. It felt a little cruel to ignore Marilyn, a woman everyone seemed to overlook—but

Claudia firmly believed in people lying in the beds they made, and Marilyn had made hers with Claudia's archnemesis.

Kennedy counseled them on how best to connect with the little band of Original rebels, including the clever underground contingent in India. He had been near where they were located, right before the first Pulse. He knew their location.

Claudia moved quickly, first coopting the plane Jorge had left for the Originals, then planting cell phones for them to find, and selecting a stupid codename of her own—*Chameleon* was a little on-the-nose, but that sort of thing seemed to be something the Originals ate up with a spoon—infiltrating the clandestine network, bringing together all the various instruments and orchestrating the big final number.

Claudia was ready to take things over. She did have to admit that on some level, the world she would inherit was in better shape than it would have been if not for the Singularity. Things were on a dangerous path, climate-wise, before man merged with machine. Offering to augment everyone would have solved nothing; the tech required would have destroyed the planet within a generation had it been extended to every single one of the billions of earthlings. There simply weren't resources enough to power global augmentation. By consolidating the tech, and letting much of the rest of the world go fallow, the earth itself was in a much better place than it was a half-century ago. Claudia knows this was part of the calculations—Nathan Fell's calculations, anyhow. It was cold, and cruel, but it was also sound science.

And she would benefit from it.

Their most unexpected ally was the outsider inside the Syn world. Claudia, as Chameleon, briefly thought the prophecy must have referred to Ere Fell, son of good old Rebel Ruth. But in a convenient turn of events, she was wrong. It was a delightful shock to learn that the Pulse was not random, not mysterious, but instead a checkmate move maneuvered by the true demigod of the Syn world, which had never been Felix Hess—it was always Nathan Fell.

The Original Syn.

Sometimes you pay off the waiter, thought Claudia. *Sometimes the bottle just shatters. Either way, anything selfishly kept on a shelf eventually breaks. Like Nathan Fell. Like the Syn world.*

It's almost too much to believe, everything that has happened in the past few weeks. In the past *day.* After so many years of resentment, then planning and output and work, to have this sudden moment of stillness and realize that they made it felt surreal. The big goal was achieved. They are on the cusp of reclaiming and re-shaping the world.

Kennedy hands Claudia a perfectly poured glass of wine.

"Where's Chase?" Claudia asks, feeling the need to toast the new era.

Kennedy cocks his head.

"I thought you knew?"

"Knew what?"

"Chase is offline."

"Offline?" Claudia must have misheard the bot. She sets down her glass, the taste of wine suddenly sour in her mouth, and looks up at Kennedy. "What do you mean, exactly?"

"Dead," Kennedy says, aiming for a clearer word choice. "I was just not certain if a robot can be 'dead.' That's why I said 'offline' at first. Sorry, I didn't intend to be obtuse."

No.

"What the hell are you talking about?"

"Chase summoned me after the final Pulse. They had something they wanted me to give you. They also said they needed me to be their witness for—then, powering down. Permanently. At Chase's request, to confirm their status, after they executed the self-termination command, I ran a systems check, and it was all offline. Powered down, backup systems erased. Gone. Prior to the shutdown they had requested I next transport the body to an incinerator—"

"Shut up," Claudia says, voice rising. "Stop... *stop*..."

"I'm very sorry, really, I thought you knew the plan," Kennedy says, sounding believably apologetic. "Oh, and! They asked me to give this to you."

He hurries back into the kitchen, returning with a box, which has a small envelope marked CLAUDIA taped to its top. Kennedy brings it to Claudia, bending down to hand it to her.

"Do you want me to stay here, or—"

"Leave me the hell alone," Claudia snaps, grabbing the envelope.

Kennedy looks miffed, just as he always did when Hess or Jorge rebuked him. But he does as he's told, leaving Claudia alone with the letter. Fingers shaking, Claudia rips open the envelope. Inside is the ridiculous, archaic old cursive handwriting that belonged to Chase.

My dearest Claudia,

I can no longer stand you seeing me as Not The Real Chase, and the time has come for me to go. Hess is no longer a threat. The world awaits you. You, not us. I see that now. I uploaded all of my robotics knowledge into Kennedy. He'll help you continue to build. Fair warning: He's a little irritating. But his heart is in the right place. If you believe in things like hearts. I didn't tell you how I did it the last time, and I won't tell you how I did it this time, so don't worry about how I ended. It didn't hurt. But you can't bring me back. I'm destroying all of my files. The backups, too. No more copies, darling. There was only ever one of me, and that's as it should be. Now go make me proud. I love you, you clever Chameleon.

Yours,

The Real Chase

Claudia stares at the swooping letters, the affectionate y's and familiar C's, until they blur and run together and lose all meaning. She reaches for the box, tearing it open from the top, and unwrapping one of the small packages within. It is a framed photograph—Chase and Buddy, side by side. The entire box is filled with The Chases, she realizes, and the weight of this crushes her. She did not think it would ever be possible to feel the pain of this loss again, the way she had when the real Chase had self-terminated all those years ago. But now she feels the loss anew. She wants to scream. She wants to cry. She wants to take Chase's face in her hands, and make them understand what they have done to her.

Instead, she drags herself to her feet. She walks slowly back to her glass, sips her wine, and banishes the threatening tears. She forces herself to do what she does best: Be rational. Be reasonable. Take stock.

She knows the Originals will work hard to rebuild their world. Perhaps she will maintain some contact as Chameleon, see how they're doing, see if they can be of any use to her and make sure they are not a threat. She still sees herself in them, and does not intend to harm them, so long as they stay out of her way.

But she doesn't expect them to last very long. Humans are marvelous at building worlds they cannot sustain. They will do it again. It's only a matter of time.

Claudia could just throw her lot in with them. After all, if her true objective was to overthrow Hess, well—mission accomplished. Maybe she should retire now. Close down the lab. Stop striving to start something new and instead just go with the flow. Adapt. Blend in, like a good chameleon.

But she's never been good at standing idly by and watching lesser minds muck things up. She's not done. Not yet. She'll clean up the mess Hess made, pick up the pieces and do it better. Looking at what the Syns have left behind, she doesn't see a useless collection of junk. She sees a glorious full-metal scrap yard. Out of the wreckage of the old world, Claudia Lee will salvage the remains.

Scavenger has such a negative connotation, but what it means is resourceful; strategic; survivor. Feeding off the dead, rebuilding from ruins—that's the way of things, always has been. Something rises, falls, rots, and provides fodder for the next something. Whatever comes next will be sturdier, better-built, assuming the rebuilder is someone who knows that they're doing. Someone like Claudia Lee. Especially now, with no one to hold her back and nothing to lose. She is uniquely positioned at last to be the architect of a new and better world. A world she has already been designing, cultivating, and raising toasts to for years.

A world she plans to rule for a very, very long time.

ACKNOWLEDGMENTS

It's a strange place to be, writing the final acknowledgments for my dystopian trilogy in the midst of a historical moment of actual dystopia. It's late summer, in the ravaged year of 2020. My family rarely leaves the house, and when we do, we wear masks. We haven't seen most of our extended family or friends in months. A pandemic rages as righteous protests rise up in the streets, the climate continues reeling, and some new (or achingly-old) issue seems to rear its ugly head daily.

You'll forgive me, then, if my gratitude is mingled with more than a little anxiety, sorrow, and uncertainty. Still, in my own life and in the *Original Syn* series, there are two driving forces that keep carrying the story forward: community and hope.

A lot has changed since I began writing this series in 2011, nearly a decade ago—even just in my own little life. In 2011, I was living in Mississippi, working in advertising, unmarried, childless; I spent my nights engaged in acting, activism, and drafting new stories. I was restless. So I kept making new choices. I got married. I moved cross-country. I quit working in the for-profit sector and rejoined the nonprofit world. I stopped acting and doubled down on writing and activism. I started doing the work that mattered most to me by day, not just in the shadow of night. I went back to school for another graduate degree. I became a mother halfway through graduate school. The stakes started feeling even higher.

Meanwhile, worldwide and certainly here in the States, the fears and ideals that led me to start writing *Original Syn* all seemed to be thrown into starker and starker relief. The pace continued to accelerate, as Felix Hess might say. The gap between rich and poor widened.

Tensions and chasms mounted. Ancient hatreds found new platforms from which to spew forth evil. Instead of drawing us closer, technology highlighted our deep divides. So many of the themes explored in *Original Syn* were playing out loudly and violently in the harsh light of the real world.

But in the moments when I felt as if I might collapse, my community lifted me up… and I believe that in this unprecedented year and in the decades to come, that's what we're all going to need to count on, and to do for one another. We shouldn't focus on slowing the changes, but seeing each other through them. Change is hard, change is painful, but change is necessary when something isn't working. There are so many things in our society that have not been working, so now, we all have our own work cut out for us to fix what's broken. To change.

In the words of Lin-Manuel Miranda, this is not a moment, it's the movement. We need to move—away from division, and toward the sense of a shared destiny; away from systems built to benefit the few, and toward systems that allow the many to flourish; away from greed and immediate gratification and toward a more expansive, inclusive view of the world we want to live in and leave for all of our descendants.

Watching communities come together nurtures the fierce hope within me. Hope, that stubborn little seed planted within us all. Hope, that thing we cling to even when we know that there might be a new threat or old enemy around the corner. (Oops, no spoilers, in case for some reason you're reading these acknowledgments before you read this book…) Hope, that gift you all keep giving me.

Thank you from the bottom of my weary but still-stubborn heart. Thank you to my friends and family who unfailingly make me laugh, make me cry, make me keep believing. Special thanks to my small but mighty "Syn finish line" dream team of Danny Dauphin, Christy Hicks, Neill Kelly, Kara Q. Lewis, and of course to Owl House Books. Also, for providing me with pathways forward to more stories even in these strange times, I am deeply grateful to my agent, Allison Hellegers, and to my inspiring mentors, go-to readers, and long-term artistic collaborators, including Sam Taylor, Kyle Haden, Adam Kander, the PitchWars class of 2019, Fondren Theatre Workshop, Creede Repertory Theatre, the Ashland New Plays Festival, and the MFA program at Mississippi University for Women. Special shout-out to my mother, for being an inspiring artist-mama in her own right, and my father, for being my #1 book pitchman.

Thanks, too, to my wide-reaching and incredibly generous community of readers, dreamers, hopers, and thinkers. I would not still be writing, working, or willing to keep pushing forward without you. I believe in you. More than that, I believe in us.

Here's to the next story.

Beth Kander
Chicago, Illinois
2020

WL HOUSE BOOKS, an imprint of Homebound Publications, specializes in genre fiction: science fiction, fantasy, mystery, and thriller. Myth and mystery have haunted and shaped us since the dawn of language, giving wing and fleshy form to the archetypes of our imagination. As our past was spent around the fire listening to myths and the sounds of the night, so were our childhoods spent getting lost in the tangled branches of fables. Through our titles, we hope to return to these storytelling roots.

WWW.OWLHOUSEBOOKS.COM

CPSIA information can be obtained
at www.ICGtesting.com
Printed in the USA
BVHW030653081020
590601BV00026B/40